## KILL SITE

It seemed like déjà vu to homicide detective Christine Keers. Another body dump of a female prostitute in the northeast end of the city, only a mile from last month's murder site. This body was also nude and strangled, and also left at a new Dumpster enclosure in a business complex. An attractive woman in her late twenties, she had been deliberately posed in a lewd position, wedged on her back between an inner and outer wall, knees pushed up and legs splayed open to expose her genitals. Like the previous victim, her arm was pulled out to her side, revealing the needle trackmarks inside her elbow.

The choice of a Dumpster for the victim told Keers one thing about the murderer: To him, these women were just garbage.

**ORDINARY LIVES DESTROYED BY EXTRAORDINARY HORROR.
FACTS MORE DANGEROUS THAN FICTION.
CAPTURE A PINNACLE TRUE CRIME ... IF YOU DARE.**

# THE
# RIVERSIDE
# KILLER

# Christine Keers
# and
# Dennis St. Pierre

**P**

Pinnacle Books
Kensington Publishing Corp.

http://www.pinnaclebooks.com

Some names have been changed to protect the privacy of individuals connected to this story.

PINNACLE BOOKS are published by

Kensington Publishing Corp.
850 Third Avenue
New York, NY 10022

Pinnacle and the P logo Reg. U.S. Pat. & TM Off.

First Printing: November, 1996

Printed in the United States of America

10  9  8  7  6  5  4  3  2  1

For my children, David and Diana, who lived this tragedy with me daily, and helped me survive it.

Most of all, for the children, brothers and sisters, and parents of the women who lost their lives at the hands of this madman. My only hope for all of you is that the suffering will ease with time, and the fond memories of your loved ones will be in your hearts forever, as they will mine.

—Christine Keers
Riverside, California


For Kymiya, Sasha, and Nina; Mom and Dad; Ken Jr. and Rick; dear friends Ali Akbarpour, Drs. Ali and Ferré Afrasiabi, Afshin Roshan and the staff at OCMDI; Mike Seighali and Moe Assarpour; Bill and Phyllis Marchese; the inimitable Mr. Jo Molnar and the gang at *Off Duty Magazine;* and especially for Chris Keers, whose heroic dedication to justice ended a nightmare for many families and saved untold victims from the same fate.

—Dennis St. Pierre
Huntington Beach, California

# Acknowledgments

The authors would like to acknowledge the following people and institutions for their help and friendship during the preparation of this book: Marlowe Churchill, Darrell Santschi, and the helpful staff of the *Riverside Press Enterprise;* John Hall and Cyndy Sullivan of *The Californian;* Larry Gerber, *API;* the Fort Worth Public Library, main branch, research department; Linda-Marie Pipitone, Riverside County RideShare Office; the United States Air Force, Department of Public Relations, Fort Worth; Paul E. Zellerbach, Supervising Deputy District Attorney, and George Hudson, Investigator, Riverside County Office of the District Attorney; attorneys Randolph K. Driggs and Frank S. Peasley; Karen Williams, legal assistant to Frank S. Peasley; Gary DeVinna, Detective, RPD; Mike Hern, Detective, RPD; Richard L. Albee, Lieutenant, RPD, retired; Doug Wilson, Detective, RPD; Don Taulli, Sergeant, RPD; Duane Beckman, Detective, RPD; William P. Barnes, Detective, RPD; Frank Orta, Officer, RPD; criminalists Steve Secofsky and Faye Springer, State of California Department of Justice Crime Lab; Honorable W. Charles Morgan, judge, and County of Riverside Superior Court clerk Tom Wilson and bailiff Rhonda McGee; the former Ann Suff; Ellen Cunradi; and the families of the victims, especially Alice Peters and the families of Cherie Payseur, Eleanor Casares, Darla Ferguson, Carol Miller, Kathleen Puckett, Susan Sternfeld, and Kimberly Lyttle.

# Prologue

Rhonda Jetmore couldn't remember the exact date, only that the attack occurred one night early in the month of January 1989. Her bizarre lapse in memory was one reason the sheriff's deputy placed little stock in Rhonda's report of a maniac's attempted murder of her. Such an event should have been memorable, even to a heroin-addicted street prostitute accustomed to rough tricks.

Local prostitutes had told Riverside Sheriff's Office (RSO) investigators that Rhonda Jetmore was a murder victim's best friend and probably the last person to see her alive. Word had been circulated that any deputies encountering Jetmore on the street were to direct her to call the Lake Elsinore sheriff's station for a telephone interview about the murder. At the end of that phone interview, Rhonda suddenly volunteered a story of a maniac she had fought off a couple of weeks earlier—speculating with typical hooker-paranoia that her assailant might be her friend's murderer.

The deputy conducting the telephone interview dutifully

noted her tale, but dedicated only a scant two paragraphs to it at the end of his two-page report, considering her volunteered information off the subject. For the same man to be involved in both cases would imply a serial killer.

Prostitute murders weren't exactly uncommon, and seldom were without motive. Drug-addicted streetwalkers often "burned" their johns for money, their suppliers for drugs, and their boyfriends (and each other) for both. The small desert resort town of Lake Elsinore was a favorite hangout for biker and drug-dealing crowds, whose reputations were based on reacting violently to any perceived injustices perpetrated upon themselves. One didn't need to contemplate serial killers to find someone angry enough to kill a streetwalker.

Even so, Rhonda's narrative of an alleged attack by a man named Bill was so graphic that the lawman decided to preserve a mention of it at the end of his report, just for the record.

Just in case.

No one at the Sheriff's Office saw any reason to believe the attack was related to the recent prostitute murder. After all, serial killers hadn't stalked the desert since the days of the Old West bandits.

Knowing better, Rhonda Jetmore moved almost immediately to Northern California, hundreds of miles away. She figured she had done her part, had told the authorities what was up.

She figured it was up to the cops to contend with whatever else Bill had in mind.

# Part I
# The Cop

# Chapter One

Cheryl Coker

*November 6, 1990*

An employee rummaging for wood near the new Dumpster enclosure discovered the body of the nude blonde woman. His female coworker hadn't noticed it when she dragged some wooden pallets out by the white cement enclosure earlier, in the far rear corner of the parking lot behind the new industrial complex. The victim was lying on her back just outside the sandy slab, loosely buried under a pile of branches and gardening trash, which overflowed the structure through the open corrugated metal door.

Because it was so new, the enclosure did not yet contain a Dumpster. However, a few days ago someone had illegally dumped a hill of gardening trash inside, filling the structure halfway to the top with vegetation debris. The littering was a dubious convenience since the Riverside city landfill was just a short distance down the street. An employee of the property management company had complained about the mess when he saw it, disgusted at how some people were so willing to take advantage of others.

This morning, a plumber for the property management company noticed that someone had disturbed the pile of vegetation during the night. Originally, the debris was contained completely within the enclosure. Now, someone had pulled part of the refuse out through one of the double doors into a smaller pile on the sandy parking lot. Making a big mess bigger, for some unknown reason.

Directly in front of the enclosure stood the short pile of wooden pallets that the female employee had dragged out earlier and stacked for garbage pickup. She hadn't noticed the body when she checked the enclosure for room to deposit the pallets. Nor did she pay much attention to the footprints crisscrossing the pool of sand in front of the doors. Noting only that the enclosure was already filled with debris, she had simply stacked the pallets in front of the enclosure ... directly on top of the spread of sand pockmarked with the footprints of a man's athletic shoes.

Deciding he needed a brace for some work he was doing, the male employee remembered the pallets and went out to salvage a piece from the trash. While pondering the discarded stack, something in the nearby tangled greenery caught his eye. At first he thought it was a mannequin's foot, half-buried under the branches and debris. Reaching down to inspect it, he was startled when the foot felt soft to his touch. Searching further, he discovered the supine body, nude and dead.

Shocked by his discovery, the man hurried back to the building and returned to the scene with a male coworker, to examine the find more closely. Both were careful not to touch the body or any other possible evidence. They quickly determined the young woman was indeed dead. It appeared her throat had been cut from side to side. And one of her breasts was missing.

After observing the grisly find a few minutes longer, the men hurried back inside to telephone the police.

A City of Riverside patrol officer arrived on the scene minutes after the call and quickly confirmed the discovery. Minutes after he radioed in the confirmation, two Riverside Police Department (RPD) homicide detectives independently responded to the report.

Detective Christine Keers was in a city car, en route to interview a suspect in another case, when she heard the call about the 187 in the business park. Mike Hern assumed as she did that the murder was already being assigned to a case agent, but decided, as Chris had, to make sure the scene was covered in the meantime. Neither detective was looking to take on yet another murder investigation, but both were hard-core cops and not about to drive by a hot scene without stopping to make sure everything was secured until the case agent arrived. Both assumed it would be just a brief detour.

A tall, deliberate man of reflective humor, Detective Mike Hern was a no-nonsense, by-the-book cop. In manner, he seemed more a soft-spoken college professor than a hardened homicide detective, although the care with which he chose his words was veteran bluesuit: a silent scrutiny given all thoughts before their release for general consumption. A pragmatic investigator, Mike was dedicated to his job—and to preventing it from intruding into his private life.

Working homicide had taken its toll on Mike and was placing a strain on his home life. In his nine years' working in or with the homicide division, he had seen enough dead bodies to last a lifetime. He was getting tired of "looking at dead bodies and picking up people in their worst possible condition." Now that he had a new wife, he felt ever greater pressure to transfer out of the depressing homicide division. His bride couldn't cope with his profession. She was afraid every knock on the door would be news that Mike had been killed at work. So she'd pretend he worked at a bank instead, and by doing so, was able to tolerate the situation for the time being—as long as Mike was home at 5 P.M., when normal people got off work.

Both newlyweds were distressed by the long hours and frequent late-night roll-outs required of homicide detectives, which disrupted their efforts to establish their new life together. Both knew they couldn't go on like this much longer. Now in his early forties, Mike felt he had done his share of the gory stuff. He just needed something to give him that little extra push to actually make the change back to a 9-to-5 division.

Chris Keers was an attractive, fortyish woman with a firm chin, set mouth and coolly penetrating eyes. Her image of stern resolve was softened only by loosely falling auburn hair and an occasional wry tug at one corner of her mouth that hinted at an ironic sense of humor. The sense of humor was usually totally suppressed when Chris was performing policework: a thick skin and tough self-confidence necessary for a woman's survival in the fraternity of law enforcement. On the job, her speech and posture were always precise and controlled, leaving no question about her intent. Although she had repeatedly proven she was as proficient as any male detective, Chris felt she had to constantly maintain the tough demeanor if she were to keep the respect she had worked so hard to earn.

Despite open acceptance of women by some colleagues, and an official departmental position that gender discrimination did not exist, Chris was always quietly aware that out of the fifty detectives in the department, she was the only woman. And although she tried to convince herself that the occasional chauvinistic comment was perhaps a misperception on her part, she often couldn't shake the feeling that it wasn't. This made her determined to succeed at everything she did.

A police helicopter was already hovering overhead, taking aerial photographs of the scene, when they arrived. Mike beat Chris to the scene by a few minutes, arriving just after noon on the warm, cloudless day. A strong wind was kicking up from the northeast. Spotting the center of activity, the two detectives immediately joined the other personnel already on the scene in the rear parking lot of the new business park.

They found some technical people by a white Dumpster enclosure, taking photographs and taking measurements, while the reporting patrol officer and another bluesuit conducted an area check for witnesses and other possible evidence.

The Dumpster enclosure was located on a sandy corner of the parking lot at the far rear of the complex, near some crusted railroad tracks. A long sandy rise encircled most of the blacktopped lot, rising directly behind the enclosure and flowing off into rough, rolling desert terrain. A ridge of mountains walled off the run of the desert farther to the east. Beyond the mountains, the high-desert communities of Palm Springs and Rancho Mirage enjoyed smog-free air thanks to that restricting ridge, which halted the flow of coastal smog from Los Angeles; collecting the brown haze just over the City of Riverside.

The detectives learned from a patrol officer that the remote, mostly vacant business complex was a favorite site for hookers to bring their johns, according to a local resident. They were not very surprised, therefore, to hear the victim was a young, nude female, and that a used yellow condom had been found discarded near her feet. Officers reported the victim's clothes were nowhere to be found.

Among those on the scene were a crime-scene sketch artist, a vice detective, and two homicide detectives who had just been assigned as the case agent and co-case agent for the investigation. Chris was friends with Jerry Miller, the vice detail detective, so she spent a minute saying hello to him. He told her he responded to the scene upon hearing the call on the radio, out of a suspicion the victim might be Cheryl Coker, a blonde hooker reported missing three days ago. Cheryl's street friends were afraid she had become a victim of foul play since she had never disappeared before. One of them told Miller that Cheryl's husband had argued violently with his wife just before her disappearance. Miller told Chris the body matched Cheryl's description and appeared to match her photo, so he was fairly sure it was the missing hooker.

Chris took a look. The victim was lying on her back, one arm thrown out, palm up; one arm twisted behind her. Her neck arched backward as if still straining in death against the missing rope that had tightened until it actually cut a deep gash through her throat. The wound was so long and deep that it had deceived the reporting witness into thinking the victim's throat had been slashed by a knife. The neck wound and most of the visible bruises were reddish in color, indicating to Chris that most of the violence was inflicted antemortem: *while the victim was still alive.*

The largest wound was to the right side of the chest. The victim's right breast had been savagely amputated in what appeared to be a half-slashing, half-tearing downward motion. The lack of any significant bleeding on that extensive wound told Chris the amputation was performed postmortem: *after death.* The woman was at least spared that agony, the female detective told herself. She noticed the exposed hand had only one long fingernail, all the others bitten off, indicating the victim was probably a very nervous person. It was a trivial observation, but one that somehow further reminded Chris of the contorted cadaver's humanity.

Homicide detectives strive to view a body as just a

cadaver, or a piece of evidence—a thing, not a person anymore—as a psychological coping mechanism for dealing with violent death on a frequent basis. Yet the images could linger, and sometimes the humanity could not be denied; some element of a victim's appearance or condition sometimes striking a very painful chord in an observer.

Chris and Mike stayed on-scene just long enough to confirm that case agents had indeed been assigned and were present to handle the crime-scene investigation. They found one of those detectives on the sandy plateau just above the Dumpster enclosure, about fifty feet from the body, standing over the victim's severed breast. Apparently, the killer had hurled the breast up the hillside from the lot. Its substantial distance from the parking lot indicated to Chris either a very powerful murderer or someone with one hell of a rage toward women.

Assured that the case was in proper hands, Chris and Mike quickly returned to their cars—removing themselves from the scene before they could also be drawn into it in some capacity; neither eager to add to their already heavy workload.

Chris took a final mental note of the scene before leaving. Sloping sandbanks surrounded the wind-whipped lot on two sides; the desert running away just beyond. Looming close by, snowless mountains formed a craggy skyline against the November sky. A safe, remote spot for a body dump. And a very lonely place to die.

Mike noticed the usually unflappable Chris Keers seemed somewhat disturbed by the crime scene. Whether that was because the victim, for a change, was a woman, or for some other reason, he didn't know. He knew Chris was professional enough not to let it bother her, and it wasn't his place to ask, so he gave it no further thought. He had enough problems of his own to deal with. Besides, to ask such a thing of Chris might imply he was questioning a feminine weakness on her part, and he knew she could be sensitive on that subject. So he ignored it. He knew Chris could deal with anything. She had proven that many times.

He was just thankful it wasn't his case.

### Susan Sternfeld
*December 21, 1990*

It seemed a case of déjà vu for homicide detective Chris Keers. Another body dump of a female prostitute in the northeast end of the city, only about a mile from last month's murder site of Cheryl Coker. This body was also nude and strangled, and also left at a new Dumpster enclosure in a business complex. All of this victim's clothes were also missing from the scene.

Chris had been contacted in the late afternoon by the RPD Crimes Against Persons sergeant and advised she was assigned as the case agent for the homicide. Detective Mark Boyer was to assist her as co-case agent. It was a random assignment, homicide cases and duties being assigned on a rotating basis. It was simply coincidence that Chris and Boyer happened to be at both of the prostitute murder scenes. That coincidence enabled Chris to note some striking similarities between the two cases.

The body of the young brunette was found inside an empty, salmon-colored Dumpster enclosure behind a large industrial complex. The rear driveway and parking-lot area that housed the enclosure served as access for commercial deliveries and pickups. A trucker had spotted the body propped inside the metal enclosure when he arrived that afternoon to make a delivery.

The Dumpster enclosure was located in the far corner of the long lot, surrounded by a metal gate. Behind it ran a seven-foot-high cement wall with a four-foot chain-link fence atop it, separating the property from an orange grove on the other side. Just to the south was a concrete berm about twelve feet high, with railroad tracks running east-west just beyond.

While turning his truck around in the lot to position it for delivery to the warehouse, the driver saw what he thought were legs inside the metal enclosure. He stopped the truck and got out to investigate. Somehow, he immediately knew the nude woman inside was dead. He also knew not to touch or approach the body, and instead went into the warehouse to ask its manager to call the police.

A team of paramedics beat the police to the scene. They confirmed the status of the deceased, an attractive woman in her late twenties who had been deliberately posed in a lewd position: wedged on her back between an inner and outer wall, knees pushed up and legs splayed open to expose her genitals. One of the victim's arms was pulled out to her side, as with Cheryl Coker. That positioning exposed the needle trackmarks inside her elbow, identifying the woman as an intravenous-drug user. As if, Chris Keers speculated, the killer were advertising to the police that the victim was just a junkie-whore and deserving of her fate.

As with Cheryl Coker, the choice of a Dumpster enclosure for the body dump site told Chris one thing about the murderer: He was making a specific message that to him these women—and perhaps all women—were just garbage. And that deeply rankled Chris Keers.

Upon seeing the lewd pose, one of the paramedics had retrieved a white sheet from his vehicle and covered the victim from view. When he arrived, the scene supervisor immediately chastised the paramedic for doing so; that compassionate act possibly contaminated any microscopic trace evidence on the body. In cases like these, the supervisor scolded, it was often the trace evidence—microscopic hairs, fibers, and the like—that won the conviction in court.

The crime scene was taped off and fully secured by police units when Chris arrived. Prior to her arrival, her boss, Investigations Lieutenant Richard Albee, had arrived, and prior to him, an RPD photographer came and took general orientation shots.

Prior to the arrival of all detectives, a local newspaper reporter, Marlowe Churchill, appeared. However, being unable to gain access to the scene, he soon left; too busy with deadlines to spend hours in the cold waiting for investigators to arrive and reach a determination on what details they could safely release to the press. He knew a telephone call from the newsroom later that night would likely yield as much information from the police as would loitering on the perimeter of the scene for an interview.

When Lieutenant Albee arrived, the scene supervisor briefed him on what he had done and directed to be done so far, and then did the same for Chris once she arrived. Unfortunately, there wasn't much to report. No one had seen or heard anything, and an area search hadn't discovered any evidence. The most basic evidence other than the body—the victim's clothing—apparently was taken by the killer to prevent its examination by authorities.

The interior of the enclosure also provided no leads. It was very clean, with no trash or debris of any kind; this enclosure also too new to contain any Dumpster bins.

Chris found the victim in the corner of the disposal area. The woman's head was tilted unnaturally to the left, and a dry blood streak ran from her right ear down toward her right cheek. Both eyes were closed, and dried blood stained the left eyelid. A dark discoloration was clearly visible on the bottom of her feet, left arm, and buttocks area, from postmortem lividity—the settling of blood in the body. A short column of Asian alphabet letters, tattooed in blue-green ink, was visible down the center of the nape of her neck. The toenails were polished red, but the fingers were clean. The only adornment of the hands was a gold band on the left ring finger.

It had been very cold the entire week prior to the discovery; north winds blowing down from the mountains off and on. It was 42 degrees when the girl's liver temperature was taken that afternoon, and its reading of 45 degrees told everyone she had been dead for some time; maybe two days or longer.

The visible injuries on the body were few, indicating lack of a substantial struggle. The victim probably either knew or trusted her attacker, or was too zonked out on drugs to know what was going on.

Two of the injuries appeared to be postmortem—brownish in color rather than red. They were abrasions near the right ankle and right kneecap, probably caused during the awkward dragging and posing of the dead body. A Band-Aid covered a preexisting injury on the right shin.

The area of prime concern to the detectives was the bruising on one side of the neck, which pointed to strangulation as the possible cause of death. Steve Secofsky, a forensic criminalist (scientist specializing in evidence collection and analysis) from the California Department of Justice (DOJ) Laboratory, was assisting on this crime scene. His inspection of the victim's neck discovered injection marks on both sides near the jugular veins, which, in addition to the needle trackmarks on the inner arms, confirmed that this victim, like Cheryl Coker, was an intravenous-drug user.

Since many female addicts are prostitutes, and virtually all street prostitutes are addicts, Chris radioed a request for a vice detective to respond to the scene and view the body, in the hope he could provide identification. In the meantime, Steve Secofsky continued his examination of the body, obtaining multiple print lifts, tape lifts, and vaginal and breast swabs from the victim, so laboratory analyses could later attempt to link suspects to, or exclude them from, this crime.

A solemn man of meticulous dress and manners, Secofsky devoted a perfectionist's attention to details—professional and personal; as unyielding in his presentation of himself as in the scientific results he developed with brutal impartiality.

He agreed with Chris that the woman's body had been deliberately posed in a lewd position. "The sonuvabitch is taunting us," Chris told Steve. She believed the murderer was familiar enough with police procedures to realize the homicide investigators could not touch, cover, or remove the body for hours—not until all the evidence had been noted and taken. They would be forced to stare at the victim in that lewd pose for all that time—forced by the killer to see his posed "message" for hours. The obvious taunting angered Chris. It made her doubly determined to catch this killer.

Obtaining fingerprint lifts from human skin was rarely successful, but Steve attempted it on this victim; trying everything to catch this taunting killer. Attempting to obtain fingerprint lifts often was an act of desperation on the part of the criminalist, when other evidence-gathering appeared unlikely. It only worked if a killer had touched the body *after* its death, since living skin would rapidly absorb the oily prints, and *only if* the touch occurred inside a very short, precise window of time following the death.

The risk in attempting such lifts was that the process often removed the trace evidence from a significant area of the body. For that reason, Secofsky preferred to use the "film" method of attempting print lifts: pressing pieces of exposed 35-mm film against the targeted skin for twenty seconds, and then dusting the film with a special fingerprint powder. That method was fairly reliable and affected the smallest area of skin, thus limiting the loss of trace evidence. The success rate of print lifts, though, was "far below ten percent," according to Secofsky.

Much more successful were the "tape lifts": applying strips of Scotch tape to a victim's skin to try to lift off microscopic particles, fibers, or hairs that might yield evidence linking a suspect to a victim. Secofsky pressed short strips of one-inch tape on key areas of the brunette's body and then peeled them off and preserved them for later laboratory analysis.

All of the scientific procedures employed state-of-the-art technology and expert analysis, and yet all were basically a crapshoot, relying on selective samplings and the chance that one of those samplings was fortunate enough to be taken of a precise spot that still held a tiny remnant of the murderer's contact with the victim. If found, such a remnant was often an undeniable nail in the killer's coffin. However, the "nails" only worked when used in comparison to a known suspect's samples. Without a suspect, the samplings were generally so useless that the DOJ usually wouldn't even bother analyzing them. They would simply be filed away, awaiting the arrest of a suspect for comparison.

Toward that end, Secofsky took many samplings over the course of hours, bagging and logging anything that seemed even remotely likely to render a speck of evidence he could use in court. Chris's immediate attention focused on the victim's identity.

A vice detective arrived, bringing with him several books containing photos of Riverside prostitutes. He compared the photos to the body in the enclosure, and thought the victim possibly resembled a twenty-seven-year-old Riverside prostitute by the name of Susan Sternfeld. Positive identification would have to await fingerprint analysis.

After concluding her work at the crime scene, Chris set out to confirm the victim's identity. She went to the Orange Street station of the Riverside Police Department and obtained a mugshot of Susan Sternfeld. As the mugshot closely resembled the Polaroids taken of the dead body, she proceeded to the Coroner's Office, where the corpse had been taken, to have a deputy roll the victim's prints for comparison to Sternfeld's. With a print card from a prior booking of Sternfeld in hand, Chris took the victim's rolled prints to CAL ID, where positive identification was made. The body was indeed that of Susan Sternfeld, aka Susan Wicken.

Once identification had been made, the legwork began. Although Sternfeld's murder appeared similar to Coker's, and also seemed a probable strangulation, Chris knew coincidences were possible, especially when dealing with the murders of hookers. Most street prostitutes had similar lifestyles and work habits, and were often treated similarly by johns and by sick and violent-prone individuals. Hookers, by their willing availability, were a favorite victim of abuse and violence, and strangulation seemed a preferred method of murder when one of them was killed, making unrelated murders often seem similar.

Despite her suspicions that the two murders might be related, Chris knew coincidence could not be ruled out. Without more evidence to link the two killings, there was little justification to spend time comparing the two. It was more reasonable to pursue the investigations separately and in traditional fashion, looking first for suspects among the victims' family members and known associates—the most likely pool of suspects.

Two days later, on December 23, 1990, the Riverside Police Department received a phone call from a nervous man with an accent who refused to identify himself. He said he wanted to know the identity of the body in the newspaper—the one reportedly discovered behind the commercial complex. He said the unknown victim might be his friend who had been missing for three days. He said the police could tell for sure if it was his friend by checking for a tattoo on the body. His friend had a tattoo of Chinese writing on the back of her neck and her name was Susan Wicken.

The Front Counter promptly transferred the man's call to Chris Keers, the RPD case agent for the investigation. However, the man hung up before Chris came on the line. Later that day, the same man called back, just as nervous as before. This time, he left his phone number. He refused to leave his address because he said he didn't want the police coming out to see him. He said his name was George.

Chris contacted George and persuaded him to agree to come in for an interview on December 26. In the meantime, she and Detective Mark Boyer pursued other leads.

On December 24, 1990, Mark Boyer attended the autopsy of Susan Sternfeld. Besides Boyer and the forensic pathologist, Dr. Robert Ditraglia, also in attendance was a coroner's technician, police photo technician, and a deputy coroner. Chris checked in on the autopsy as it progressed.

The first major procedure was the completion of a sexual-assault kit—basically a collection of body samples such as anal, oral, and vaginal swabs, and head and pubic hairs. Two blood samples were taken from the victim's heart: one, retained by the Coroner's Office for toxicology tests; the other, released to Detective Boyer for blood typing. A bile sample, to be tested for drug intoxication, was also taken and retained by the Coroner's Office.

About three-and-a-half hours after it had begun, the autopsy was completed. Dr. Ditraglia's official conclusion of cause of death was strangulation.

In his protocol report, Dr. Ditraglia noted the following observations that led to his determination of strangulation: a number of abrasions on the skin of the neck; multiple petechial hemorrhages (pinpoint ruptures of tiny blood vessels "indicative of asphyxia") inside both of the lower eyelids; and a number of internal injuries to the muscles, bones and cartilages of the neck that indicated heavy compressive force had been applied. Structures deep inside the neck were crushed and hemorrhaged, which required a large amount of pressure on the part of the assailant.

The method of strangulation was deemed "manual," or performed primarily by the hands, as opposed to strangulation by a ligature or ropelike device, as had occurred in Cheryl Coker's murder. Broken bones and cartilage indicated manual strangulation—the uneven pressure applied by human hands invariably fracturing the fragile skeletal components of the neck; damage that is rarely seen in a ligature strangulation. This discrepancy from Cheryl Coker's murder didn't dissuade Chris from her belief that the two crimes might be related; some killers do vary their routines.

The stomach contents revealed food material that was still identifiable among the gastric contents, which indicated the victim had eaten only minutes before her death.

The toxicology tests afterward showed the presence in the blood of what Dr. Ditraglia termed "recreational levels" of cocaine and morphine, the chemical that heroin is converted into once inside a human body.

Susan Sternfeld died well-fed and "high"—too high evidently to put up much resistance against her attacker. However, her lack of resistance could simply have been because she was taken by surprise, perhaps because she so completely trusted the guy, because she knew him, or because he presented himself to her as someone totally trustworthy—like a clergyman or a cop. Or perhaps because he had somehow physically rendered her unable to resist before the attack, perhaps by talking her into a bondage session so she would be tied up before he became violent.

It was all just speculation at this point, but it gave Chris plenty to think about. Perhaps too much. If the mutilated body of Cheryl Coker had silently struck a nerve in her, the lewd public display of Susan Sternfeld brought Chris's anger to the surface—the dead victim turned into an object of the coarsest ridicule at a time when her dignity was no longer within her control.

"I'm going to get that sonuvabitch," Chris quietly snapped to Secofsky while staring at the humiliated body. *"I'm going to get him."*

On December 26, the nervous caller, George, met with Chris Keers at the Riverside Police Department to discuss what he knew about the last hours of Susan Sternfeld, aka Susan Wicken. George stated he was a friend of Susan's and that they often "slammed heroin" together. He said they had to conceal their activities from Susan's boyfriend, because her boyfriend was determined to keep Susan off the streets and off drugs, and George was considered a bad influence because he was heavily involved in that lifestyle.

George said the last day he saw Susan alive was December 19, 1990. On that morning, he drove to her Moreno Valley residence to give her a ride to Riverside Municipal Court for an appearance she was required to make. He picked up Susan and her baby at approximately 8:45 A.M., he said, and drove them to the city of Rubidoux, where they left the child with Susan's mother while they went to court. At the courthouse, Susan learned her hearing was postponed until December 26. So she and George went to a friend's house and "got high and slammed some dope."

George said Susan then became worried that her boyfriend might return home and find her car still there, and conclude she was out with George again. He drove Susan home, where they decided she should change and go do a quick trick to earn some money for more dope. Susan was to take her car and meet him behind the Bob's Big Boy restaurant on the corner of University and Iowa avenues at about 2:30 P.M.

At about 3 P.M. Susan arrived in downtown Riverside and parked her car behind the restaurant as arranged. George was waiting for her. He gave her a ride in his car to the corner of University and Chicago, by a Bank of America building, so she could work the street by walking down University Avenue toward her parked car. Susan agreed to meet George in about forty minutes, after she had completed the trick.

George drove to a parking lot behind a nearby Denny's to wait out the hour. That was the last he saw of Susan: walking down University in the direction of the Bob's Big Boy. He told Chris that Susan was wearing black acid-washed jeans, a cream-colored sweater, L.A. Gear tennis shoes, and a gray purse. Chris noted the apparel in case they found it still in the killer's possession at the time of his arrest.

George said he waited until 4 P.M. and then began driving up and down University Avenue, looking for Susan. When he didn't find her, he called her mother and asked if she had seen Susan. Not since morning, her mother told him.

Later, after reading a newspaper article about the discovery of a murdered prostitute behind a commercial complex, George feared the worst. So he called the RPD to confirm his fears—and to voice his own suspicions about Susan's possible murderer.

George told Chris that Susan's car was still parked behind the Big Boy, so the homicide detective sent a patrol officer over to verify his report and impound the vehicle if it was indeed there. It was—exactly as described by George; still locked and secure. Chris examined the vehicle at the tow yard but, as she expected, found no evidence inside; the victim apparently was killed before she could return to her car. The discovery of the car did, however, corroborate at least part of George's story.

Chris called Susan's boyfriend and asked him to stop by the police department for an interview the following day.

The boyfriend told Chris he had known Susan Sternfeld for about five years. They met at the Sybil Brand Institute for Women while Susan was incarcerated there with his ex-wife. When his ex-wife failed to earn release, Susan moved in with him. The boyfriend said he tried to help Susan clean up from her drug addiction. She had worked as a prostitute on University Avenue in the past, he admitted, but to his knowledge she had stopped since her release from state prison in October; an incarceration that followed her release from Sybil Brand. Their infant son was born while Susan was in state prison, he said.

When he returned home from work at 5:30 P.M. on the day of her disappearance, the boyfriend found Susan and the baby gone. He found the clothing Susan had been wearing in the morning for her court appearance, and noticed her court papers were on the table, but there was no note indicating where she had gone or when she would return. He noticed that she had done the dishes and tidied up the house before leaving.

Since she wasn't home when he arrived as she was supposed to be, he telephoned her mother and asked if she had seen Susan. Her mother reported Susan had dropped off their baby about 9:30 A.M., but that she hadn't seen her daughter since. That was basically all he knew, he told Chris.

The boyfriend agreed to take a polygraph (lie-detector) test regarding his whereabouts and/or knowledge of Susan's disappearance, and one was tentatively scheduled. The interview was then terminated. Chris released Susan's impounded car to the boyfriend since there was no evidentiary value in the vehicle and he was the legal owner.

Neither of the interviewed parties struck Chris as a likely suspect. So the search would go on.

* * *

Next, Chris went to interview some of the street prostitutes who might have known Susan Sternfeld, to see if they
had any information to provide. She obtained a consensus
from them about Susan's preferences and routine.

Susan did not take her dates to the orange grove areas
at Iowa and Marlborough avenues in the city, as many of
her associates did, but preferred to take her johns to parking lots close to the area of the pickup. Susan was picky
about her dates—she refused to date blacks or Mexicans.

One person Susan wasn't picky about, the girls stated,
was George. He was frequently in her company—that is,
when he wasn't in the company of other prostitutes.
George was an eager chauffeur for the girls—offering them
rides to their connections' houses in exchange for half the
dope the girls bought there. Evidently, George's friendship
for Susan was genuine. He cared enough about her to
make sure her body was identified, and to try to help the
police find her killer.

One of the prostitutes who knew Susan cast aspersions
on her boyfriend's character and antidrug claims, but the
accusations were nothing to implicate him in the murder.

Chris asked the girls if they had recently run across any
kinky, violent, or suspicious johns. Two of the hookers
suggested the same man, so Chris brought him in for an
interview: a john who allegedly took his money back at
knifepoint after receiving sex from the girls. Police records
showed he had been contacted three times regarding sexual assaults on street prostitutes. During the interview, the
man denied the assaults and all knowledge of any murder.
He stated he had never had contact with any prostitutes—
other than when he worked as a minister preaching to
them in the Los Angeles area. Because of his violent reputation, Chris referred his name for monitoring.

Another suspicious john whom the girls reported to

Chris also denied any knowledge of or involvement in the Sternfeld murder. Chris had to schedule the interview to accommodate his lunch break from his job at a local school. His denial of activity with prostitutes rang untrue to Chris, since she had received separate reports of his behavior from different girls working the streets. She asked the subject to take a polygraph test to confirm his denials, but the man's fervor in maintaining his innocence was equaled by his fervor in refusing to take a lie-detector test.

While providing an insight into the people involved in Susan Sternfeld's life, not much of this helped Chris with the case. She still had little more to go on than she did that first afternoon. It became clear she would close out the year with the homicide still open. Chris knew the longer a murder case went unsolved, the more likely it was never to be solved.

# Chapter Two

Although assigned to the Sternfeld case, Chris couldn't help thinking about the Coker murder—another body dump of a nude prostitute at a commercial Dumpster enclosure. She mentioned the similarities to several coworkers in casual conversation at police headquarters, and found a receptive audience in a patrol officer. The bluesuit stunned Chris by reporting he'd heard from a buddy at the Riverside Sheriff's Office that the Sheriff's Office was also working a couple of recent prostitute homicides.

The coincidence factor shot to disturbing proportions for Chris. She immediately approached her lieutenant and advised him that there now appeared to be *four* recent prostitute homicides in the area.

She suggested the lieutenant should assign someone to contact the RSO and compare notes to see if the four cases were related. The lieutenant agreed—and assigned Chris to do it.

"I didn't mean me!" she protested, not eager to add

any extra work to her current heavy caseload. "I just meant that *somebody* should do it to make sure these aren't a series."

The lieutenant shrugged off her protest. "You're it," he told her, ending the discussion.

After leaving the lieutenant, Chris had another thought about the homicides. This time, she decided to approach her sergeant with the suggestion.

She explained her suspicions to Sergeant Mackey of the Crimes Against Persons unit. "You know, we need to dedicate somebody to this," Chris suggested—formally assign one person to work all prostitute murders and make a determination whether a serial killer was at work.

Mackey agreed and said, "Okay. You're it."

"Well, I didn't mean *me!*" Chris protested again. "I just meant, one person needs to handle *all* homicides that occur with these girls so we can find out if we have a serial-murder case."

The sergeant proved as unsympathetic to her protests as had the lieutenant. Chris was given charge of *all* current and future prostitute murders within the RPD's jurisdiction.

Biting the bullet, she plunged ahead with the assignment. Following up on her own advice, Chris first called the Riverside Sheriff's Office to inquire about their prostitute homicides. Her call was returned by RSO Detective Robert Creed of the Lake Elsinore Sheriff's station. He immediately agreed to her request for a meeting to compare similarities and possible leads in the recent murders of prostitutes in their jurisdictions.

On January 7, 1991, Chris met with Detective Creed in Lake Elsinore. A tall, broad-shouldered, cherub-faced detective with intense eyes, Creed informed Chris the Sheriff's Office was currently working on the homicides of *eight* hooker-addicts whose bodies were found in remote areas of Riverside County over the past few years. The latest victim, one Carol Miller, had been dumped nude in a grapefruit orchard on February 8, 1990 . . . less than one mile from Susan Sternfeld's nude body. Sternfeld had been dumped less than one mile from Cheryl Coker's nude body.

The close proximity of the last three victims' "body dumps" caused bells to go off in both detectives' heads, even before they started comparing the specifics of the crimes. Both feared the sleepy inland empire of Riverside County may have given birth to its first serial killer.

Unfortunately, after comparing notes, there still was not enough evidence to definitively draw that conclusion. Some of the many cases seemed, at least to Chris, to be strongly unrelated.

Although both she and Detective Creed suspected a serial killer was at work, their theory fell on unreceptive ears at their agencies. They were allowed to work their cases as they felt best, but the actual contention that a serial killer was responsible was rebuffed by their respective superiors at the RPD and RSO. To acknowledge that a major criminal was at work carried with it the obligation to launch a major law-enforcement effort to catch the perpetrator—which would be a major expense for either agency. When no hard scientific proof was in hand to confirm such a theory, it was far more cost-effective to adopt a wait-and-see attitude than to plunge ahead into six- and seven-figure debt on a detective's hunch. Especially in the absence of any public pressure to do otherwise.

The two homicide detectives remained officially alone in their suspicion that a serial killer had been murdering street prostitutes in Riverside County for at least two years. But they both kept pressing the issue. In her report of January 16, 1991, Chris compared the striking similarities between the Coker and Sternfeld murders and warned her bosses that a serial-type killer may be the perpetrator of both homicides.

She wrote, "In comparing the two cases we have the following similarities:

1. White Females similar in appearance
2. Prostitutes in Riverside area
3. IV drug users
4. Death by strangulation
5. Bodies found nude, no clothing at scene
6. No signs of struggle
7. Bodies dumped in dumpster areas of commercial building complexes, secluded area of the city, less than one (1) mile apart."

Adding that the RSO's latest victim, Carol Miller, had been dumped within a mile of the RPD's two victims, Chris wrote that "[although] at this time we are unable to determine if the Sheriff's Office [Miller] case is related to our cases . . . we are looking at these cases through DOJ for similarities."

That is, she and Detective Creed had requested the criminalists at the DOJ crime lab to compare the trace evidence found among the various crime scenes to see if any scene could be linked to another. If the same type of trace evidence was found on different victims, a serial killer would indeed be indicated. The more rare the type of evidence found, the stronger the likelihood a serial murderer was responsible.

The detectives' request represented a departure for the DOJ lab. Usually, the lab didn't examine trace evidence until a suspect was apprehended and available for comparison. However, it was hoped that, besides yielding proof of a serial killer's existence, comparing the crime scenes' microscopic evidence might identify patterns or common links in the crimes that could guide the detectives in their investigation. It might also help identify which murders were the result of a serial killer and which were not, so unrelated cases could be investigated without confusion.

Creed informed Chris that a previous comparison by DOJ of the first seven RSO cases failed to establish any link between them. Those results had prompted an RSO spokesperson to dub the evidence "extremely slim," and to comment that the strongest link between the victims was their "troubled backgrounds" as drug-addicted prostitutes. Espousing the official line that the existence of a serial killer remained unproven, the spokesperson commented, "The [only] common thread is [the victims'] history. These women moved in crowds where you can run into some pretty lousy characters, and that's one reason I tend not to believe they were all killed by the same person. But we're certainly not ignoring that possibility."

In fact, the RSO had previously explored the possibility of a serial killer targeting the street prostitutes of Riverside County. Investigators from the Sheriff's Office had conferred with State of Washington detectives involved in the infamous Green River serial-murder case, inquiring if the Riverside County cases showed any link to the Green River Killer's forty-nine female homicides. They asked the same thing of San Diego authorities, who were investigating the murders of several dozen women killed between 1985 and 1989 in San Diego County. The results of both discussions: "No connections, no link." There was simply no hard evidence, from inside or outside the county, that a serial killer was responsible for any of the many prostitute murders that had been occurring in Riverside County.

Now Detective Creed was running to the City of Riverside, holding talks with homicide detective Chris Keers on the same subject. Sheriff's authorities held little optimism the new talks would be any more productive than the prior meetings. It seemed murder was simply a hazard of the trade for drug-addicted street prostitutes.

Related or not, the sheer quantity of dead hookers turning up in roadside body dumps had begun to attract the public's attention. A few people were offended that almost all of the homicides were unsolved—some almost three years old. The accusation was publicly made that the RSO wasn't pursuing the murders very strongly because the victims were indigent street prostitutes without political clout or public sympathy.

A spokesperson for the RSO angrily attacked that slur on his department: "That's insulting. These people were human beings, just like you and me. I don't care if they were prostitutes. I don't care what they've done. They didn't deserve what they got. . . . This department will spare no expense to find their killers."

It was strong rhetoric, but with "extremely slim" evidence available from the crime scenes, no witnesses, and sources of information that were dubious at best, there were few solid leads to pursue even if the RSO was as highly motivated as the spokesperson avowed. Except for a handful of RSO investigators such as Detective Creed and his associate Detective John Davis, few sheriff's people held out hope of ever solving most of the prostitute homicides that had accumulated.

Many citizens were able to ignore the murders because the killers weren't targeting people like them. A clerk at a Lake Elsinore office supply store commented, "I'm not real concerned. It's not the kind of people I have anything to do with, so I really haven't given it much thought."

In a statement Chris Keers would come to hear quite often, and eventually express herself, an Elsinore restaurateur summed up a pervasive sentiment: "If it were a bunch of housewives getting killed, or little kids, then everyone would be running around with a gun, like vigilantes. But if it's prostitutes, people figure it's no concern of theirs. [They feel these victims] just don't count."

An Elsinore real estate agent even complained that the growing media attention on the murders might further hurt his slumping business by scaring away buyers. "It's not like we have a Hillside Strangler here," he said. "We have a health nut. He's just cleaning up the town a little."

A local newspaper had recently railed about the blight of prostitution in the city and quoted business owners as demanding a clean sweep of the offensive drug-addicted streetwalkers. Perhaps this killer saw himself as some sort of crime-fighting street-sweeping vigilante, Chris thought. She remembered how he had posed the victims' arms to display the needle trackmarks so the police would know they were junkie-whores. Perhaps he was advertising that he was just cleaning up the streets. More likely, she reasoned, he probably hoped that pointing out the unwholesome status of the victims would make the police less aggressive in hunting him down.

Undaunted by the official lack of interest in her serial-killer theory, Chris Keers felt strongly enough about it that she contacted the DOJ's Bureau of Investigation and requested a psychological profile be drafted of a possible serial-killer suspect. In the meantime, she kept in close touch with Bob Creed, trying to find a link between their respective cases.

The more Chris and Bob Creed studied the cases, the more dedicated they became to solving them. They figured if they could only find proof that a serial killer existed, it would provide the incentive for a major investigative effort by their respective agencies. Both were convinced a major organized effort would lead to the capture of the sadistic killer.

It would take weeks for the DOJ crime lab to complete its comparison of the RPD and RSO trace evidence. Chris held out a strong hope that DOJ criminalist Secofsky would be able to find something to link the cases together. If links could be shown, that would validate the detectives' work to their superiors and justify an all-out effort on the case.

But before that could happen, another event occurred to light a fire under both law-enforcement agencies: The maniac killed again.


## Kathleen Leslie Puckett
*January 19, 1991*

The victim, this time, was a forty-two-year-old Riverside city prostitute named Kathleen Leslie Puckett (aka Milne, aka Carol Kathleen Swenson). The nude body had been left near a major freeway seven miles north of Lake Elsinore, in an illegal dump site off a dirt extension. An embankment shielded the exact site from the view of the freeway and the closest street. Because the body was located in county jurisdiction, the RSO responded to the scene. Because the victim was a female prostitute, Detective Bob Creed was given the case and dispatched to the site.

Although this crime scene didn't appear any better than the previous ones in terms of available evidence, to Bob Creed it was like the straw that broke the camel's back. The sheer number of victims—apparently *thirteen* now— made him absolutely determined to push the serial-killer issue with his superiors.

He was equally determined that this crime scene, and all future prostitute murders, be treated as high-priority investigations. Creed immediately requested a state DOJ forensic criminalist to be called to the scene, to minimize the chance of any evidence being overlooked.

A service agency for law-enforcement departments, the DOJ criminal forensic laboratory responded to crime scenes only at the request of a law-enforcement agency. Because the DOJ experts often took six hours, or longer, to process a scene, many agencies summoned them only for the most problematic cases, or those of great public concern. Bob Creed was determined that the DOJ should be called out to all prostitute murders from this point on.

Soon after the murder, Creed informed Chris Keers of the details of the crime. The body had been found about 4 P.M. that Saturday afternoon; the discovery made by a young couple who had pulled off the freeway to drink a few beers in their pickup truck before returning home. While backing the truck toward the embankment to conceal their drinking, the male driver was startled by his girlfriend suddenly shouting, "There's a dead body next to us!" Not believing her, he looked for himself and saw the nude body of a woman lying in a scattering of trash and debris. The couple immediately drove to the RSO's Lake Elsinore station and reported the discovery, then returned to the site with sheriff's deputies.

The body was lying on its right side, facedown in the trash and litter, sprawled on an old, discarded, faded red robe. The corpse had been deliberately posed, with the legs positioned at a right angle to the torso so the genitals were facing the road. Postmortem lividity and rigor mortis were present, and consistent with the position of the body, so the victim had been alive not long before the posing.

She was tall and slim and looked in her forties, with brown hair and what appeared to be blue eyes, although the autopsy would later attribute the color to a blue-tinted hard contact lens in one eye. Her fingernails bore red polish, and the right ring finger wore a silver metal ring. Old needle trackmarks were obvious on the backs of both of her hands. The hair had been neatly combed prior to death, and was pinned in one spot by a silver metal barrette. The body, although nude, was very clean. There was a bruise on her forehead and some postmortem abrasions on the heels and buttocks, but they seemed most likely to have been caused by the body being dragged through the dirt. There were no signs of life-threatening trauma and no obvious indication of cause of death.

It was left for the autopsy to determine that Kathleen Puckett died from a combination of strangulation and asphyxia—the latter caused by a white sock being stuffed so deeply into her mouth that it occluded her airway. The murder had been a manual strangulation; both superior horns of the thyroid were found broken, which was typical of being strangled by a pair of hands. The information about the sock, Creed told Chris, was to be kept secret, as a key clue, to aid in identifying the correct perpetrator. He also advised Chris he was arranging to have the coroner's records of the autopsy sealed by law.

The autopsy also found numerous petechial or pinpoint surface hemorrhages, indicative of strangulation; an incomplete tattoo of a heart on the right hip; and the absence of many of the victim's teeth, predating the murder. Examination revealed multiple anal tears. The stomach yielded a substantial amount of partially digested food, including obvious pieces of hot dog, which meant Kathleen Puckett, like Cheryl Coker, had eaten shortly before her murder.

Crime-scene investigators found a distinguishable tire track near the body. They made a record of it, although it remained to be seen whether the track bore any connection to the murder. Still, in a case with very little evidence, it provided at least a glimmer of hope.

Creed's background investigation of the victim uncovered that in the past two years Kathleen Puckett had been charged with prostitution, possessing a hypodermic needle, and being under the influence of a controlled substance. Most of those cases had still not been adjudicated and, in some, warrants had been issued for failure to appear. Creed learned that Puckett was a known user of heroin and speed, but toxicology results found no trace of alcohol or drugs in her body. As with Chris's victims,

Puckett was known to work as a prostitute in the notorious University Avenue area, in the downtown district on the east side of the city of Riverside.

Puckett was at her sister's Riverside home the previous afternoon, January 18. When she left, she told her sister she was going to find a ride so she could visit her children in Whittier. She either never found that ride or changed her mind, because she was last seen alive on University Avenue about 10:30 that night. She was not seen again until her body was discovered the next afternoon by the thirsty couple.

As with the other murders, there were very few leads or clues left at the scene. The strongest link between the victims remained their "troubled backgrounds." It was still up to the DOJ lab to find some irrefutable link between the cases.

For Chris Keers, the flagrant discarding of the woman's body in a trash dumpsite was no different than the selection of a Dumpster enclosure for Coker and Sternfeld's bodies. The killer clearly was making the message that these women were just garbage.

The Puckett murder, coming on the heels of Chris Keers's advisories about a serial killer, made it difficult for the RPD not to follow the female homicide detective's lead. The city police department decided to mount a major effort to search for a serial killer. On January 29, 1991, Chris and every detective in the RPD detective bureau began a concentrated sweep of the city. Chris invited sheriff's detectives Creed and Davis to join in the effort.

Because it seemed all of the latest prostitute victims were being picked up on University Avenue, Chris recommended the RPD conduct an intense surveillance of the avenue. She recommended they employ roving stakeouts, in which unmarked cars with plainclothes detectives would cruise the area and observe the prostitution activity, talk to some of the girls, and look for suspicious behavior by the johns. The purpose, Chris stressed, was strictly to observe and look for signs of the killer, not to interfere in the prostitution activity or otherwise make any obvious contacts that might tip the killer to their presence. Other officers, equipped with infrared glasses, would stake out the foothill areas where Coker and Sternfeld's bodies had been dumped.

Chris worked the roving stakeout in a car with RPD homicide detective Mike Hern. They contacted several of the local prostitutes and surveilled vehicles seen soliciting girls for sexual acts. They talked to some of the girls when it was discreet to do so, telling them as before that their purpose was only to solve the homicides.

Chris would tell them, "This is what I'm working; I'm a homicide detective. I'm not working vice and I'm not working drugs. I know you're all loaded and I know you're out here screwing these guys, but what I'm here to do is to try to keep you alive. And I need your help to do that."

After hearing that, most of the girls were very straightforward and honest with Chris. It really surprised the detective, since she had worked vice in the past and was familiar with how much a prostitute could lie when she wanted to.

One girl told of being stopped three weeks before by a white male in an old black truck who showed her a roll of hundred-dollar bills and asked if she "was afraid to die." She was. Despite the flash of cash, the girl refused to date the john, deciding he was too "weird"—aware that other girls from the avenue had recently been murdered. Chris took down the information for follow-up investigation and counseled the girl to be careful. Chris advised all of the girls they spoke with to work in pairs and watch out for each other, and to jot down license numbers whenever one of them saw a girl get in somebody's car. The girls promised to do so, but Chris knew very few actually would; most of the street girls were too intoxicated, fatalistic, or simply lazy to make even such a small effort.

Chris begged the girls to call her at the police department if they saw anything strange or had any funny feelings about a john. The girls also promised to do that, but Chris knew they would be even more unlikely to call the police for a chat—especially if they had to walk around with an official police business card in their purses to remind them of the phone number. For a street person to be caught by her friends carrying a cop's business card could mean big trouble—it could cause them to be suspected of being a police snitch. Chris knew she had to do something about the physical problem of communicating with the girls if she was going to stand a chance of getting any information from them.

For two tense weeks, the roving stakeout operation continued. None of the leads panned out despite intense efforts and earnest intentions on the part of even the prostitutes. When no solid results were produced by the end of that time, the brass decided that the equally intense overtime pay that had accumulated was cause to kill the operation. The RPD's investigation devolved back onto Chris Keers alone.

That decision frustrated and angered Chris. She wondered if the operation would have been shut down had the victims been coeds from the college farther down the avenue instead of common prostitute-junkies.

However, she didn't let the cutback faze her. Instead, she kept hammering at the case on her own, with only Mike Hern lending a hand and sheriff's detectives Creed and Davis providing information and moral support through the informal working relationship she had initiated with the RSO.

Chris felt in her heart they would catch this killer—that he simply *had* to be caught. She wasn't about to give up when they had only just started.

* * *

Chris thought the best chance of catching the serial killer was by concentrating on his latest murders, where the evidence was freshest. Since she had been at the Susan Sternfeld murder scene and was the original case agent for that homicide, Chris decided to focus her efforts on that case. She directed Mike Hern, recently assigned as her co-case agent on the serial case, to take over the Cheryl Coker homicide. Detective Boyer had run into a dead end on the Coker case and was happy to relinquish it. In similar fashion, across the county, RSO detective Creed focused his efforts on the latest case, Kathleen Puckett.

The serial-killer profile Chris had requested from the DOJ arrived. Chris had provided the psychological expert with information on the various RSO and RPD cases she and Creed agreed were probably related.

Among that information were the details on one of the most brutal and bizarre of the prostitute murders: the RSO's 1989 homicide case of Tina Leal, who, at twenty-three, was the youngest victim in the suspected series.

The body of the young Mexican girl seemed the most violently beaten. It was left in the middle of a dirt roadway in the remote, hilly Quail Valley area of the county. Unlike most of the other victims, however, Tina was not left nude. As with the others, her clothes were missing, but she had been re-dressed in men's clothing: blue Gitano jeans; blue, gray and white-striped gym socks; and a blue sleeveless souvenir "muscle shirt" bearing a map of King's Canyon National Park.

Although the armholes in the sleeveless shirt were very large, Tina's arms had been tucked inside the garment as if to confine her movements after death. The motive behind the re-dressing was a mystery to investigators, but they were certain it was intended as some kind of sick joke upon the victim or the authorities.

In the photos Chris examined, the pretty, childlike face of the young woman was heavily bloodied. It had taken a severe battering—bleeding from all facial orifices. It seemed a punitive beating to Chris, since the victim's tiny size (eighty-six pounds) and state of intoxication made it unlikely she was capable of offering substantial resistance to her killer. It had to take an awfully cold bastard, Chris thought, to beat like that on such a baby face.

A dark rope burn on the girl's neck provided visible evidence of her strangulation. Death had resulted from the ligature strangulation and from four precise stab wounds to the center of her chest, two of which penetrated the heart.

The autopsy on Tina Leal revealed her killer had spent more time working with her dead body than with that of any other victim. Before lingering to re-dress her in men's clothes, the murderer had assaulted her corpse with a knife—slicing her clitoris and the left breast by the nipple, and stabbing her vagina.

Following those mutilations, he had inserted a large 95-watt lightbulb far up the dead woman's vagina. It was an amazing feat to accomplish on a small, nonreceptive corpse—requiring delicate, time-consuming maneuvering of the fragile bulb to prevent it from breaking. It would have taken considerable patience and a steady hand; amazing emotional control for a man who had just violently raped and murdered someone. After that, he had fully re-dressed his victim in men's clothes. *Whose?*, Chris wondered. *His own?*

To have lingered so long and so calmly in the middle of a murder scene just to play a couple of jokes on the authorities told Chris much about the psychotic nature of this killer. It told the DOJ psychologist even more.

The murderer's actions upon the body of Tina Leal helped the psychologist draw conclusions about the egotistical nature of the perpetrator—an ego that compelled the man to flaunt his superior intellect through a perverted sense of humor.

In the profile, the psychologist concluded the killer "has a high degree of self-control and a willingness to take the required time [to perform the mutilations]. [The Tina Leal murder] was a methodical, time-consuming, painstaking and precise exercise in postmortem mutilation and the insertion of a foreign object. It was done not only to humiliate and degrade the victim, but also to shock and offend those individuals who would discover the body."

That act, according to the psychologist, indicated cool self-control even immediately following a very violent murder. That control, and the taunting joke he left for the authorities, indicated to the psychologist a killer utterly without fear of capture.

# Chapter Three

Chris quickly solved the problem of how the prostitutes could contact her without fear of being considered a police snitch. She went to a print shop and had a box of personal business cards printed up that displayed only her name and phone numbers. She even went so far as to instruct the printer to emblazon the feminine-colored pastel cards with a rainbow-style spray of flowers, just to make sure no one could mistake them for any type of official stationery. That way, the hookers' street friends, most of whom were drug users, would have no concerns that the girls were secretly informing on their drug-dealing activities.

With the flowered business cards in hand, Chris hit the streets again. She passed out the cards to every street prostitute she could find, advising all of them of the homicides currently being perpetrated against Riverside's hookers, and counseled each of them to be careful and alert. She told them to call her anytime—day or night—whenever they had any concern over a john, regardless of how trivial or even mystical they thought the reason was. She urged them to work in pairs, with one girl jotting down a license number whenever her partner drove off with a john.

Almost immediately, some of the girls began providing Chris with license-plate numbers of suspicious johns, and some even started working in teams but, overall, success was limited. "It was difficult," Chris discovered, "because most of them were too intoxicated to be aware of license-plate numbers, and once one of them got in a car, the other one [simply] went away."

Those who did take Chris's visits to heart would call her at all hours of the day and night, often paging her only to breathlessly race through a description of some kinky guy who wanted them to perform some kinky act, or because a girlfriend had driven off with a john and not immediately returned as expected. Sometimes they'd run up to Chris's rose-colored, unmarked T-bird on the avenue and scream, "I haven't seen so-and-so and she's missing!" Chris would always calm them down and offer reassurances ("Let's give it a few hours"), then follow up on the information provided.

None of the missing girlfriends ever failed to return, however, and unfortunately none of the early leads panned out. But Chris knew that something like this had to be given time. She realized that the streetwalkers were far more likely to spot the killer than the cops were, so she just had to maintain her street contacts and bide her time, waiting for the guy to make a mistake at a time when one of her alerted hookers was watching.

Chris took comfort in knowing she had heightened the awareness and alertness in most of the street prostitutes she encountered, and in knowing that at least some of the girls were being much more careful working the streets these nights. Chris became aware that some of her advice was being taken perhaps too literally by some of the girls she had admonished about working in teams—at least two of them now literally worked together on "dates," offering themselves as a pair for sex, just for safety's sake.

Unwelcome confirmation that the prostitutes were placing their trust in her came to Chris from some of the other officers in the department, who now found occasions to chide and kid Chris about the feminine business cards she had passed out to the street girls. The cops would tell Chris, "Yeah, I just arrested so-and-so and she had this stupid card of yours in her purse!"

Chris let the wisecracks slide. She knew it was critical to stay in close touch with the local street girls, so she kept up her contacts on almost a daily basis, developing a powerful rapport with many of the prostitutes and even some of their families, who were genuinely grateful for her efforts to save their girls. Chris was surprised at how warmly the families welcomed her into their houses—especially considering that most of those households had several members with long-term involvement in drugs and gangs, and a deep antipathy toward the police.

More often than not, the girls' families would boast to the lady detective of their fallen relative's devout new efforts to quit drugs and prostitution; certain that this time, with Chris's inspiration and the specter of the serial killer over their heads, their girls would finally succeed in reforming themselves.

More often than not, upon leaving those houses afterward, the girls in question would confide to Chris that, contrary to their claims to their families, they were in worse shape than ever with their drug addictions, and prostituting as much as ever; the stress of worrying about a serial killer perhaps pushing them even deeper into the comforting escape of heroin. At least two of the allegedly reformed girls even confessed to offering threesomes, taking on tricks in partnership with other prostitutes, performing bisexual acts for added safety and income.

The girls' incriminating candor often touched Chris.

Despite her efforts to maintain a professional distance, Chris found herself developing personal friendships with several of the prostitutes; some of the girls forming an almost instant attachment to the friendly lady cop, who treated them with respect. It was an emotional reaching out on their part, and the dependent, deep trust it conveyed to Chris was hard for even the veteran detective to rebuff or ignore. Sometimes the girls would even call Chris to invite her to lunch at a fast-food restaurant, where they would bend her ear about their problems or nightmares or hunches about the serial killer.

Chris brainstormed with some of them about the modus operandi of the killer, drawing on their experience with johns. She was stumped on how the guy could so easily overpower such a variety of victims, especially knowing that some of those victims were sober at the time of the murder and had violent reputations themselves. She and the girls would discuss different possibilities on how the killer was able to accomplish the murders—such as suddenly grabbing a throat while receiving a blow job, or engaging in sex from behind the girl and suddenly throttling her neck. Because some of the victims bore ligature marks on their wrists and/or ankles, Chris even considered that the killer might be paying his victims for a bondage session so he could tie them up and render them helpless before the murder. She even bounced ideas off her captain's wife, seeking a civilian woman's perspective on the killer.

The scenarios and theories that resulted were many, with any one as good as the others. The only thing that Chris was reasonably sure of was that the killer was not a regular john, because there was never an eyewitness to his pickups, and none of the leads provided by surveillances, the girls' tips, or police records had turned up any likely candidates. If the murderer were a regular john, Chris reasoned the police should have encountered his name by now. Riverside was not the overpopulated metropolis of Los Angeles;

there was only one main drag in the city for prostitutes, and the girls and the johns who frequented it were a fairly small and well-known pool of characters.

Although the victims were usually raped, it seemed the killer only dated a girl when he wanted to kill. It made sense from a criminal standpoint: There would be no witnesses to his presence on the notorious avenue. It told Chris the killer was very smart and very careful about his murders. The fact that he was able to easily overpower sober, street-fighting women told her he was also unbelievably persuasive or sneaky. It made the case incredibly frustrating—and frightening.

The fear came from an unexpected source: one of the wisecracks made by a cop in the department; the macho males' jokes about the dead hookers inevitably leading to a crack about AIDS. Chris was stunned when she suddenly realized she had attended the autopsy of a prostitute without wearing a surgical mask, too intent on the details of the medical investigation to realize that this murder victim was a prime candidate for the disease. Aware that the various autopsy procedures often sent body fluids airborne, Chris immediately had herself tested for HIV, and waited anxiously for her results and those of the screening tests on the dead prostitute. She learned that not only did the autopsied girl not have HIV or AIDS, but none of the thirteen prostitute victims to date had tested positive for any diseases.

It was the only piece of information offering her any relief or hope so far. It also sent her mind speculating on a new theory, wondering if perhaps the killer were seeking revenge upon prostitutes for having contracted AIDS from one of them. A possibility, but again, just another of many.

Chris's co-case agent, Detective Mike Hern, was hard at work running down leads on the Cheryl Coker case. One suspect told Mike he had dated Cheryl Coker twice, receiving oral sex each time. The man said Coker told him the Riverside hookers were nervous about the murders, and that some of them would no longer work south of Chicago Street since two of their murdered associates had worked south of Chicago. Others reported they had switched their activities to daytime, since the killer so far had never picked up a victim before dark.

The first person mentioned as a possible suspect in the Cheryl Coker murder had been her husband Boyd, who ran by the street name of "Cowboy." One of Cheryl's hooker friends had told the police Cheryl had argued with Cowboy on the night of her disappearance. And, the hooker informant had alleged, she had seen Cowboy assault Cheryl in the past. She claimed on that fatal night, Cowboy wanted Cheryl to go out and prostitute herself so he could buy some cocaine, but Cheryl didn't want to. A few days after that row, Cheryl's missing body turned up in the Dumpster enclosure on Iowa Street. The friend, as Mike knew prostitutes were likely to do, had convinced herself Cowboy was guilty and therefore was doing her best to make the rest of the world into believers.

Through his investigation, Mike followed the activities of Cheryl's husband on the night of her disappearance. Cowboy, a small, thin, fortyish man with a history of problems with the law, had bought dope that last night at Seventh Street with forty dollars Cheryl earned from a trick in the orange groves off nearby Iowa Street. According to Cowboy, Cheryl had promised to try for one more date while he was off buying drugs. He never saw her again.

Cowboy admitted Cheryl was a heroin addict and prostitute. He said she would not date black or Mexican men, and she smoked "Full Flavor Filter Kings." Mike figured the last part to be true, since he knew an empty red-and-white package of the cheap cigarettes had been found at Cheryl's murder scene.

According to her hooker friends, Cheryl had been taking her dates to the commercial complex where her body had been found. They claimed Cheryl normally wouldn't take on any new dates, especially with a killer known to be at large. She would only date people she had either been with before or knew through one of her friends. Mike knew such fussiness usually went out the window whenever a prostitute addict needed "to get well." Or, perhaps in this case, to get her husband off her back.

Adding to the hooker friend's fingerpointing at Cowboy was a police report stating that Cowboy's brown Honda was seen in the area of his murdered wife's body dump not long after the murder. It turned out that Cowboy and another prostitute friend had merely gone to the scene looking for any evidence the police might have overlooked, the widowed husband determined to catch his wife's killer.

An interview with Cowboy's investigative cohort found the prostitute friend shaking with fear at the very mention of their joint search—the girl was convinced they had discovered one wall of the Dumpster coated with human blood and streaked with fingermarks, as if someone had been sliding down the surface while being butchered. The girl confided she had been suffering nightmares ever since that discovery—envisioning the horrible, violent death she was sure Cheryl had suffered. The heroin-addicted hooker was surprised to learn that no bloodstains were left on the Dumpster or anywhere else at the scene; Coker's blood loss was minimal since most of her wounds occurred post or perimortem. The gory scenario the hooker had been tormenting herself with was a delusional concoction.

Thanks to Mike's efforts, the information in the Coker file grew as leads were fully pursued and detailed. Most of his expert labors proved of little benefit, simply detailing dead-end leads he had followed up.

That frustration did little to halt Mike's contemplation of a transfer back to the robbery division, where he had originally begun as a detective. There it was possible to work a 9-to-5 shift so his bride could stop dreaming of criminals seeking murderous revenge on her husband, and he could finally escape the ugly images of homicide.

However, Chris had personally asked for his help, so he would provide it as long as he was able.

As long as it didn't become too oppressive.

One lead that looked promising to Chris involved a prostitute named Kelly Hammond, who had been left naked in a parking lot on University Avenue—stabbed and beaten with a hammer, but still alive. That lead also came to nothing; the incident apparently was the result of a rip-off gone bad.

It seemed the usually demure, sweet-faced prostitute had become so heavily addicted to heroin that she had begun cheating her johns and suppliers out of money and drugs; a behavior usually engaged in only by the more violent, hard-core girls due to the risks it entailed. The timid, soft-hearted Hammond had become desperate enough to try such behavior, and evidently someone she had tried to "burn" had punished her for the attempt.

Despite her severe injuries and the strong warnings of her prostitute friends about a serial killer working the streets, Kelly Hammond was back on University Avenue prostituting herself even before she had fully recovered from the hammer attack, risking death from the serial killer *and* the hammer attacker for the price of a fix.

Another promising lead involved a suspect who confessed that he and another man had killed an earlier prostitute victim, Darla Ferguson. However, police expectations came crashing down when the suspect failed a polygraph test and didn't know critical details of the crime, convincing the authorities that his story was a total fabrication.

The break Chris was waiting for didn't come until

March 2, 1991, when state DOJ criminalist Steve Secofsky announced the results of his crime-lab comparison of the evidence from the most recent murder scenes. Secofsky advised Chris he had discovered similarities in carpet fibers and paint chips found on the bodies of Susan Sternfeld and Cheryl Coker, and he had a possible tire match from the Coker scene to Kathy Puckett Milne's murder scene, thereby linking at least three of the cases together.

Chris immediately called her co-case agent Mike Hern and sheriff's detective Bob Creed, then contacted the DOJ in Sacramento to request that a criminal profile be done on the Riverside cases. She advised Creed to do the same for the Sheriff's Office's cases.

The homicide detectives now had scientific confirmation that a serial killer was murdering prostitutes across the county.

Armed with the DOJ report, Bob Creed went to his sergeant and, together with their captain, went to the sheriff himself to press for action. The three told the sheriff they were convinced a serial killer was at work and that he would keep killing.

On March 4, 1991, the sheriff designated Bob Creed and his partner Detective John Davis as an RSO investigative task force in charge of catching the Riverside County prostitute killer. Within days, there were eighteen people working on or with the task force, including Steve Secofsky of the DOJ and, in an unofficial capacity, Detectives Chris Keers and Mike Hern of the City of Riverside Police Department.

The sheriff's formation of a task force both encouraged and discouraged Chris and Mike Hern. On the one hand, they felt a concentrated effort was long overdue. On the other hand, since the victims were now being picked up on University Avenue in the city of Riverside, it made more sense to Chris and Mike that the task force should be based at the scene of the new crimes—at the sheriff's station in the city of Riverside. Instead, it was to be based at the sheriff's station far across the county in Lake Elsinore, where the first victims had disappeared, but which had since been abandoned by the killer. The detectives theorized that the killer had probably changed jobs or residences recently, bringing him to Riverside.

Chris and Mike were exasperated that, except for Creed and Davis, the sheriff's personnel assigned to the homicide task force had no homicide experience—and some were even "light-duty," recovering injured, or office personnel. To Chris and Mike Hern, they didn't seem the most qualified people to work a hard-core homicide investigation.

In Hern's words, "Why [did the RSO select] only two experienced [RSO] homicide detectives to go after this major crime if [the RSO was] really serious about it? Why [did they have us] playing with the bastard child in a small little pissant corner [far from the murderer's current activities]? It just didn't appear that [the RSO] actually felt it would ever be solved."

To Chris and Mike, the sheriff's choice of inexperienced task-force personnel, and the decision to base them in far-off Lake Elsinore, meant only one thing: The RSO didn't believe the killer could be caught. Evidently, the Sheriff's Office believed the Riverside prostitute killer was another Green River killer: a shrewd criminal who would continue uncaught until he eventually disappeared of his own accord—through death, relocation, or prison on an unrelated charge. The authorities were simply putting on a good show for the public until that happened.

It was basically left to Detectives Creed and Davis, as the only veteran homicide detectives on the large task force, and Chris and Mike, as consulting RPD investigators, to seriously pursue the case. They alone knew the real obstacles they were up against with such a devious killer. Their determination to catch him was partly fueled by knowing they were the ones the killer was specifically taunting with his lewd posings of the victims' bodies. For whatever reason, to the four detectives, capturing this killer was more a vendetta than a job.


Creed and Davis pushed the case as hard as they could, seeking help wherever they could find it. "Never having handled a serial killer before, we didn't want to reinvent the wheel," Creed said. So he and Davis conferred with the San Diego Metropolitan Task Force which was investigating over forty murders in San Diego County, and they went to Seattle for advice from the venerable Green River Task Force.

Using information and forms from the other task forces, Creed and Davis put together a database and a "victimology book" that helped draw links between the victims that might not otherwise be apparent. They even tracked down prostitutes in Lake Elsinore, Corona, and Riverside; and added their photographs and personal information to the book, logging in such things as the types of johns the girls would and would not go with, any tattoos they had, and an emergency response card for notifying next of kin if anything should happen to them. By the time they had completed work on the database and victimology book, Creed and Davis had accumulated photos and data on 104 Riverside County prostitutes.

The database steadily grew, with new tips and leads coming in almost daily now that the word was out that a serial killer existed and a task force had been formed. The public seemed satisfied that serious action was being taken and that an arrest would be imminent.

\* \* \*

On March 27, 1991, Steve Secofsky of the DOJ crime lab reported to the task force that, through trace evidence and tire tracks, he had now linked three more prostitute murders to the first three linked cases. The new list linked Darla Ferguson, Tina Leal, Carol Miller, Cheryl Coker, Susan Sternfeld, and Kathy Puckett/Milne. Secofsky continued to work on finding links to the other seven outstanding cases.

Unfortunately, he would have little evidence to work with on at least one such case due to a mistake on the RSO's part. On the same day Secofsky announced the new links, the task force discovered, while itemizing murder evidence for transportation to DOJ for comparison, that a major mistake had occurred in the handling of autopsy samples from one murder victim. Apparently, items of evidence that had been collected from the victim's autopsy in 1989 were never frozen, as required, and had simply been stored at room temperature in the evidence box. Several other items were found to be of compromised value because of improper storage. "Unfortunately," a report on the incident stated, "this particular case is one of the more promising."

At a full task-force meeting on the following day, members listened to a DOJ criminal-profile expert, Mike Prodan, discuss his impressions of the thirteen cases and his advice on establishing a protocol for how best to collect evidence at future body-dump scenes. It was also recommended, and agreed upon, to have detectives from both the RSO and RPD respond to all future body-dump sites, where the agency without jurisdiction at the scene would act only as observers. This was intended to ensure interagency communication and total exchange of case data.

On March 29, 1991, the Associated Press in New York

called the task force, seeking information to possibly link twelve serial murders in New York to the Riverside prostitute killer. Because the New York murders appeared to have occurred almost concurrently to the Riverside homicides, the task force told the reporter there was little likelihood of any link between the two serial cases.

It was decided the task force should implement a special dragnet-style operation, dubbed "Operation Deadmeat," to focus investigative attention on "persons of interest" and their vehicles, now that specific tire tracks had been linked to several murder scenes. All contacts were ordered to be conducted under the guise of a vice investigation, so as not to alert the killer or the press. The operation was scheduled to run for one month, commencing April 2, 1991, with a follow-up administrative review of the results at its conclusion. Additionally, a list of all registered sex offenders for the county was ordered from DOJ for comparison to the task force's list of suspects.

Nearby, March Air Force Base was contacted following information that the base routinely took reconnaissance photos of the county. It was hoped that a review of those photos might yield images of the killer's vehicle at one of the body-dump sites. The Air Force agreed to research photos for the dates in question, and to inquire about availability of any satellite photos of the area for those dates. It seemed a long shot but, with few solid leads in hand, everything was worth a try.

On April 17, 1991, Creed and Davis were required to perform routine firearms qualifications at the Sheriff's Office's shooting range. What seemed like an especially unpromising day took a swift change when a hot lead came in from out of state. A detective from St. Croix, Wisconsin, called to report that a jail inmate was claiming to have information on the Riverside murders, and to know the identity of the killer. The inmate had provided the Wisconsin detective with information on only one of the Riverside murders "as a sample" of what he had to offer on the killings. The guy wanted a deal on his pending cases, the detective reported. The information concerned Carol Miller, whose body had been discovered just prior to Cheryl Coker's. It was information that only the authorities and the killer could know.

The news sent a palpable charge through the sheriff's personnel at the Lake Elsinore headquarters of the task force. Within two days—on April 19, 1991—the task force had already heard enough to decide it had its man. A report from that date states, "At this point in our investigation it appears that arrests in the case are immement [sic]."

The Sheriff's Office failed to notify its sister agency, the Riverside Police Department, that it seemed about to make a big arrest, although task-force members had begun flying to Wisconsin almost immediately following the initial phone call, and had notified the DOJ and county district attorney's office. Three days later, on April 22, the task force called the RPD and advised Chris Keers of the new development.

Determined to make sure the right man was being arrested, Chris hurriedly packed a bag and rushed to the airport. Because family problems prevented him from traveling, Mike Hern did not accompany her. Instead, Detective Doug Wilson of the RPD agreed to make the trip and assist Chris in any way he could.


In Wisconsin, Chris and Doug Wilson immediately conferred about the developments with DOJ criminalist Steve Secofsky and Paul Zellerbach, the Riverside County Supervising deputy district attorney, a lanky, bald, mustached man with intense eyes reflecting a driven personality. As with the RSO task-force personnel, Zellerbach had bought into the news with zeal and jubilation. Chris advised the district attorney that, based on her knowledge of the case and a briefing by the more cautious, scientific Secofsky, she was absolutely convinced this was a wild-goose chase. Zellerbach bet her a bottle of expensive champagne that she was wrong. Chris knew if she were proven wrong that her bottle would be put on permanent display in the district attorney's office for all to see and hear about for years to come.

Without hesitation, she told Zellerbach she'd take the bet.

The Wisconsin informant, Alex, was in custody for a felony weapons charge and was looking at two eight-year enhancements that could be added to his sentence, so he was seeking to make a deal. He said he knew victim Carol Miller by her alias of Carol Hansen, and had learned the details of her murder and the other murders while drinking in a bar with the killer several weeks ago. He claimed two men were committing the murders, but that he only knew the name of one.

The task force considered Alex's facts "extremely specific information regarding the condition of the body, specifics on the cause of death and items left at the scene." Task-force investigators found Alex's information so specific that they believed he was the second man in the murders.

Chris told them they were wrong to believe Alex. She was positive only one man was responsible for the serial killings, not two. She was convinced Alex was lying, but she stood virtually alone in her belief. Only Steve Secofsky seemed willing to share her professional skepticism; the criminalist, as always, preferred to wait for the results of unbiased scientific analysis of the evidence.

Alex implicated Carol Miller's ex-husband as the Riverside prostitute killer and, when pressed for the name of the second man, identified a second suspect. A background check on the second suspect revealed he had ties to Riverside, and even to Carol Miller. The RPD had arrested the man and Carol Miller for burglary in 1988.

The background check on the ex-husband also seemed to support Alex's story. The man was discovered to be a long-haul trucker, and his job would have provided him the opportunities to commit the prostitute murders in Riverside County. Furthermore, he had a history of physically abusing his murdered wife.

Alex announced that a peeled, half-eaten grapefruit had been left in the orchard beside Carol Miller's nude, strangled body. The murderer had coldly lingered to munch on that grapefruit over his victim's freshly killed body. That detail was known only to the killer(s), law enforcement, and the Riverside Coroner's Office—and the Coroner's records on the case had been ordered sealed by a judge, specifically to protect that key evidence from leaking out.

With all that in hand, the task force convinced the St. Croix County District Attorney's Office to obtain a murder warrant for the ex-husband, plus search warrants on various locations associated with him. The paperwork was signed at 4 P.M. on April 24, 1991. The arrest and search warrants were served in a predawn raid the next morning by the St. Croix Sheriff's Department. The ex-husband was arrested at his residence on a no-bail murder warrant, and taken to the sheriff's station for interrogation by the main Riverside task-force personnel. Local officers and some task-force personnel remained at the man's residence and the other search locations, conducting searches and awaiting further guidance from the members interrogating the suspect.

Several hours later, at about 9:30 in the morning, the interrogators directly confronted the ex-husband with the key evidence and demanded to know how, if he were not the killer, he was able to tell his drinking buddy Alex about the grapefruit left by the serial killer at his ex-wife's murder scene. The ex-husband responded that he had simply read the Riverside Coroner's report on the case. He said he called the Coroner's Office, identified himself as Carol Miller's ex-husband, and requested information on her murder. Perhaps unaware of the court order sealing the report, or perhaps believing the order didn't apply to ex-husbands, the coroner's representative who took the man's call obligingly mailed a copy of the report to him in Wisconsin. Later, over drinks in a bar, the ex-husband bared his soul and the details of the case to his friend and former roommate, Alex. Later still, Alex was arrested on a weapons charge. He then decided the ex-husband's trust in him was a means to negotiate a deal with the authorities—by framing the man for his ex-wife's murder.

Unconvinced by the simple explanation, the task-force interrogators asked the ex-husband where this alleged copy of the coroner's report was at that minute. "In a drawer in a cabinet in my kitchen," he answered. A brief phone call to the task-force members on the scene at his residence quickly verified the existence of the coroner's report, exactly where the man said it was. Examination of the report revealed that every specific detail Alex had provided to law enforcement could be found within its pages.

The ex-husband subsequently passed a polygraph test and Alex failed his, confirming what Chris Keers had contended all along: Alex was a jailhouse liar, who was simply trying to con the authorities into reducing his sentence.

Since the only key, unguessable detail in the snitch's report was the mention of the half-eaten grapefruit, Chris asked her task-force associates why they hadn't simply called the Wisconsin authorities to request they ask the suspect where he had obtained that information, before rushing en masse on an expensive out-of-state trip. The task force had no answer.

Chris didn't linger any longer than she had to in Wisconsin. Leaving the rest of the task force behind in St. Croix, she and Doug Wilson rushed back to Riverside on the night of April 27 so Chris could pick up the case before it got any colder.

Incensed at the professional embarrassment caused by the lying jailhouse snitch, District Attorney Zellerbach vented his fury by pushing his Wisconsin counterparts for prosecution of—and a maximum penalty for—Alex for making a fool out of the authorities. The result was that the jailed man, rather than lying his way out of a two-year sentence, found himself awarded an additional ten-year stretch for his deceit upon the Californians. It was a fate Zellerbach deemed well deserved for destroying the time, money, and reputation of the Riverside task force and the Office of the District Attorney.

True to his word, the district attorney honored his bet with Chris Keers and bought her the wagered bottle of champagne. Chris gladly accepted the prize, proud of its symbolic confirmation of her professional expertise. Savoring the irony of the situation, she put the bottle on permanent display on top of her living-room china cabinet.

# Chapter Four

Cherie Payseur

*April 27, 1991*

The night of Chris's return to Riverside marked a horrifying change in the taunting killer's behavior. The serial killer had evidently read a local newspaper article about the task force's trip to Wisconsin following a hot lead, and of their hopes to make an arrest in the case, and decided to react to the news. The day following the article—on the night of Chris's return—the killer claimed another victim. This time, he left the body in a very public place: outside a crowded bowling alley. The busy location ensured the victim would be found immediately, so there would be no mistaking the murder's link to the newspaper article.

This time, all the investigators were in agreement on the key issue: The serial killer had deliberately responded to an article about him in the newspaper. He was showing the world he was smarter than the authorities: while they were off on a wild-goose chase in Wisconsin, he was cleverly stomping around their own front yard, too slick to be caught. It was a grisly taunt: while the cats are away, the mouse will play. Catch me if you can.

Because the murder took place within the city's jurisdiction and appeared to be a prostitute homicide, Chris Keers took charge of the investigation immediately upon her return from Wisconsin. The victim this time was a second-generation prostitute-addict. Small and girlish, with long brown hair, big green eyes, a ready, mischievous smile and a happy, friendly personality, twenty-four-year-old Cherie Michelle Payseur seemed more a sweet pixie than a heroin-addicted street prostitute. Born virtually deaf because her mother had contracted German measles during pregnancy, Cherie wore two hearing aids and communicated largely through sign language.

Her usual haunt was a bus bench by the gigantic Tyler Mall on Tyler Avenue. Uniformed police officers who knew her would occasionally stop and chat with the cheerful hooker, her guileless sense of humor cracking up even the most jaded street cops.

Policemen who didn't know her would sometimes recognize Cherie's purpose as they drove by, and stop to question her. Upon discovering she was deaf, the officers would ask how she communicated and negotiated with her tricks. Cherie was always happy to demonstrate her repertoire of intentionally humorous hand gestures created to make her purpose and prices unmistakable.

"She was sweet and funny as hell," one officer recalled. "She would never lie to us, she would always cooperate fully, and she was always in a happy, friendly mood." To the hard-core girls who plied University Avenue, Cherie Payseur was "that nice little girl who worked on the bus bench by the big mall." She didn't seem to have an enemy in the world. Not until the newspaper article came out and she presented a convenient target for the serial killer.

The body, like most of the others, was strangled and left

without clothing, purse, or identification. She had been placed on her back in an unplanted flower bed alongside the rear wall of the Concourse Family Bowling Center on Arlington Avenue. A drainage spout ran down the wall behind the body, like a giant finger pointing out the corpse to passersby. The ground in the immediate area contained a variety of shoeprints; some from bowlers, some from spectators gawking at the corpse, and some from the killer when he dragged the body over to the wall and positioned it on its back, arms at the side, palms up to expose the needle trackmarks on the inner arms.

The victim's head was turned slightly to the left, almost as if sleeping. This body showed the least amount of violence toward a victim to date. Other than a few scrape marks on her backside and one small bruise, from an external examination Cherie Payseur appeared uninjured. Perhaps the killer had felt sorry for this victim once he discovered she was deaf. More likely, due to the busy location, he knew he couldn't risk the time necessary to mutilate this corpse as he had the others.

Three young bowlers, each around twenty years old, had discovered the body when returning to their cars. Walking around to the rear of the building that clear, calm night, one of them spotted a still white form by the wall and walked over for closer observation "because it looked real weird." Upon discovering it was the nude body of a dead female, the boy ran inside for the manager and excitedly yelled to him in front of everyone. "There's a dead girl, all naked and shit, out back!"

One of the patrons in the bar was a corrections officer from Illinois, visiting California to apply for a job at Chino State Prison. Hearing the excited shouts, he followed a crowd of approximately forty people outside to investigate. Once around back, he identified himself to the crowd and pushed his way to the front to assess the situation. Seeing the poor girl lying dead and exposed to the eyes of the gawking, hovering crowd, he muttered to himself, "This isn't right," and removed his blue denim jacket and draped it over the girl to preserve her dignity from the onlookers. Then he ordered the crowd to back up and not disturb the scene. Standing near him, the Concourse manager quickly ordered an employee to call the police.

The first officer on the scene noticed the victim was very white and cold, with a puffy look to the face and lips, and an odor present as he leaned over the body. He found no sign of a pulse or breathing. Paramedics who responded also found no signs of life. Because the body appeared consistent with the prostitute murders being investigated by Detective Chris Keers, Chris was contacted.

She found the victim lying on her back, face turned away as if embarrassed, both palms up as if imploring mercy from a killer long gone. A single pulsing line of ants trailed down her body from the corners of each eye. From a distance, the ants looked just like thin, dark tracks of tears. They added a very eerie effect.

The similarities at this dump scene to the other murders quickly convinced Chris to summon criminalist Steve Secofsky, also just returned from Wisconsin. The bluesuits securing the scene cleared it of the milling spectators after Secofsky's arrival.

Secofsky had hardly started his work when the automatic sprinklers in the dirt suddenly came on, threatening to wash vital evidence from the body. Unable to immediately find the control box for the sprinklers, everyone on the scene scrambled in a mad rush to contain the water—standing on the various sprinkler heads with their feet to restrict the water's spray.

Because the victim had no property or even jewelry upon her to help in identification, Chris asked the deputy coroner on the scene to take her fingerprints and send them to CAL ID for possible identification. The only identifying mark observed on the body was a heart-and-dagger tattoo on the right buttock.

Despite the loss of evidence caused by the unfortunate timing of the sprinklers, Chris and Steve Secofsky held out hope that this scene might yield some significant clue to the killer's identity. The killer had deviated from his routine with this victim, selecting a busy, populated dump scene, and hadn't lingered to mutilate the corpse. Perhaps he was in such a hurry that he had made some mistakes on this murder and left some identifying evidence behind.

Despite fears that his work might be for nothing because of the sprinklers' wash, Steve Secofsky processed the scene with meticulous care. His painstaking efforts proved too much for one impatient bluesuit who had to stand watch securing the scene until it was cleared. Upon observing the criminalist stop to bag a small feather stuck to the victim's skin by her pubic area, the cop loudly groused, "Oh, Christ—now he's even collecting the feather in the pie!"

That attitude grated on Chris—the attitude that these victims didn't matter because they were only junkie-whores. Although the task force was only days old, and the media hadn't yet come up with a nickname for the killer himself, some of the macho officers at the police department had already come up with a companion moniker: the Dead Whore Task Force. The nickname had seemed mostly macho black humor, without serious prejudice behind it, when Chris first heard it bandied about. But the wider, and faster, its use spread, the more seriously she began to take the hateful, judgmental intent behind it.

Just when things seemed bleakest, Chris saw something that could have ended everyone's misery in a few short minutes. Directly behind the bowling alley stood a public storage facility. Mounted high at the roof's edge, barely visible in the shadows of the night, were video surveillance cameras, focusing down at the grounds below . . . and on the rear wall of the Concourse Family Bowling Alley.

Excited that a videotape of the killer and his vehicle might be spinning on a VCR somewhere in that building, Chris hurriedly tracked down the manager of the storage facility and asked about their taping procedures. The manager quickly deflated the detective's expectations. The cameras were in place only for show, as a crime deterrence; no taping was ever actually conducted.

Even so, Chris took heart from the incident. The killer was indeed getting more careless about his work. Had the cameras been functioning, the authorities might have caught him. Had a bowler exited minutes earlier, he could have spotted the killer in the act.

Clearly, the serial killer was taking more risks and, although his luck was still holding, it had barely held tonight. How many more close calls he could survive if he continued taking such risks, only fate could say. Chris Keers knew fate was not especially sympathetic to grandstanding criminals.

As Chris and Steve Secofsky feared, very little evidence was obtained from the Payseur scene, thanks to the inopportune sprinklers. There were a few partial shoeprints, some unusable tire tracks, a mix of two men's semen in the vaginal cavity, and scant trace evidence from the body: a cat hair was found in the body bag after the corpse was removed at the Coroner's Office.

Both Chris and Secofsky attended the autopsy. The pathologist found so little trauma to the body that he was compelled to list the cause of death as "undetermined." Toxicology results showed Cherie Payseur had been intoxicated with speed and heroin at the time of her death. Needle tracks on her arms confirmed she was an IV-drug user, and the trackmarks on her right arm were new.

Chris and her co-case agent Mike Hern investigated Payseur's background and pursued leads regarding possible suspects from her circle of known associates, but all their efforts led to dead ends, reinforcing the belief that the serial killer, and only the serial killer, murdered Cherie Payseur.

Chris increased her contacts with the prostitutes on the street, becoming more and more concerned for their welfare, and more and more desperate for their help. Surely one of their tips would eventually pay off. She refused to believe it wouldn't.

Her contact caused a steady increase in calls from the street girls. One phoned her at all hours—every time she had a psychic dream about the serial killer. "I think something happened tonight because I got this feeling," or "I feel it's time for him to come and kill somebody again." Although Chris placed little faith in psychic dreams, the calls succeeded in disturbing her.

The mother of one victim called the task force with the name and phone number of a psychic she wanted the task force to use. She was convinced the psychic could lead the authorities to the serial killer.

Bizarre counsel came even from respected experts in the field. Two nationally recognized advisers offered their conclusion that, based on their expert studies, the Riverside prostitute killer was also responsible for the forty-or-so San Diego prostitute murders and, moreover, was the Green River killer himself. The experts claimed the Riverside serial killer had already killed far more local prostitutes than the dozen or so credited to him. Their bodies simply hadn't been discovered yet.

Chris didn't see the connection. The Riverside body dumps were clearly orchestrated to result in quick discovery of the corpses, contrary to the Green River murders, whose victims were hidden so that they often went undiscovered for years. The tie-in seemed so far off base that she felt the experts' conclusion offered more frustration than help.

Added to the frustration were the haunting memories of contacts with the relatives of the victims. The young daughter of one dead prostitute told how, following an article in the newspaper about the murders, her classmates teased her with cruel jokes. They told her that her mother deserved to die because she was a whore, and taunted her by asking how much was her mother's selling price.

Operation Deadmeat, the RSO's month-long dragnet sweep for suspects, finished its run with more leads than when it started, but none were especially promising, and several were dismissed after being more thoroughly investigated.

The task force simply pushed on, exhausting lead after lead; some of the investigators worked the case in their own fashion—all searching for a tip or a piece of evidence to point a finger at the right man.

Unfortunately, most realized that such a break would only come from a mistake the killer made in one of his murders, and so far he hadn't made any they could take advantage of.

They would have to wait for him to strike again.

## Sherry Ann Latham
*July 4, 1991*

The next murder came a little more than two months later with the discovery on the Fourth of July of the body of a prostitute from San Bernardino. The location this time was a desolate area overlooking Interstate 15 in Lake

Elsinore—within eyesight of two of the killer's earlier body dumps. Found by a jogger about 6 A.M. that Thursday morning, the victim had been dead at least one day before her nude, partially decomposed body was spotted in some weeds only about ten feet east of Grape Street, a mere half-mile south of the heavily traveled Railroad Canyon Road. The body's location indicated, as with the others, that the killer intended his handiwork to be quickly discovered.

Sherry Latham, thirty-seven, had a history of prostitution and drug addiction. She had been charged with both types of offenses several times over the last few years, and had two outstanding arrest warrants for drug violations at the time of her death. Within the last few months she had physically deteriorated into a thin, drug-ravaged state. A female friend, who spotted her soliciting on the corner of H Street in San Bernardino, recalled, "She looked real skinny, and had dyed her hair to disguise herself from the police. She didn't look good."

Chris Keers was invited to the scene as an observer, per the mutual arrangement established by the task force. Steve Secofsky of the DOJ was also on the scene: the criminalist was now exclusively assigned to the prostitute murders by the crime lab, at the request of the task force.

Officers at the scene recognized the body despite the dyed hair. Latham was fairly well-known to local law enforcement, due in part to her colorful garb and heavy makeup. She favored bright pink shorts and lots of blue eye shadow, and blush. Her brilliant makeup had earned her the street name of "Rainbow." Officers remembered she liked to hang out near the Circle K Food Store on Main Street in Lake Elsinore. She had recently been living in San Bernardino, and was a familiar face to vice officers in that city, although they hadn't seen her around town for several months.

Friends considered Rainbow "troubled but pleasant,"

and very confident of her abilities to fend for herself. Despite widespread concerns about a serial killer attacking prostitutes in the county, "Sherry always told me not to worry [about her]," the same friend recalled. "[She assured me] that she could take care of herself. When I saw the story [in the newspaper] that she was murdered, I got goose pimples all over."

What scared the friend even more was that in the same article, she saw the faces of three other victims whom she remembered meeting at Latham's San Bernardino home, street prostitutes who often gathered to borrow drugs, money, information or a place to stay. It scared the friend to realize that *four* girls she had seen alive were now the victims of violent murder.

The task force felt a new excitement after this body dump: the victim's boyfriend came forward as a possible witness to the serial killer. The boyfriend claimed Sherry prided herself on being very cautious with her johns, and usually had him watch the vehicles she left in. As an added security measure, he said, she usually took all her clients to the same location to carry out the sexual transaction. However, on the night of her disappearance—two days before the discovery of her body—Sherry was picked up by a john the boyfriend had never seen before, and the guy drove off with Sherry in a direction opposite to the way she usually took her johns. And that, the boyfriend said, was the last time he saw Rainbow alive.

Sherry's boyfriend provided the authorities with a description of the vehicle and partial details on the driver. "With this latest information," a task-force administrator noted, "we are as close as we have ever been." In addition to the descriptions provided by the boyfriend, some physical evidence was found at the body dump. When added to the evidence from the previous scenes, the administrator stated, "We now have two distinctive tire prints, specific fibers, hair, and a suspect and vehicle description. [Plus] there are numerous other items of trace evidence in which their value is not known yet.''

It seemed cause for optimism, although so had the tip from Wisconsin. Whether the john who drove off with Sherry that Tuesday night was, in fact, the serial killer remained to be seen, but with no other leads looking especially promising, the task force seized upon the news and escalated the intensity of the investigation. The sheriff was impressed enough to add three additional investigators to the task force to help out, since many of the original eighteen were part-timers, or had been quietly pulled away as the case dragged on without results. The sheriff's homicide task force was currently functioning with only five RSO investigators and one deputy assigned full-time.

From a medical standpoint, the killer had treated Sherry Latham's body very similarly to Cherie Payseur's. There were no visible signs of trauma present, and cause of death was determined to be "manual or soft strangulation." The coroner's records on this case were also ordered sealed to prevent key details leaking out to the press.

For the next week, the task force conducted surveillances of prostitution activity and prioritized "persons of interest." It also ran an undercover operation with a female decoy, hoping to lure the serial killer into a trap. Chris went out to monitor the john program the night they used the decoy, "to see who the johns were who were trying to pick up these girls." However, for safety's sake, the decoy was told not to enter any john's vehicle but to entice them instead into meeting her at a hotel where backup officers were waiting.

Chris told the decoy team that such a procedure wouldn't work with the serial killer, because she was convinced he never took a girl to a motel, since he might be seen there. She was convinced the serial killer always took his victims to remote, deserted places for the sex act, and killed them there or in his van, where no one could see him. However, because she and Mike Hern were simply working in a cooperative nature with the task force and were not officially assigned to it, she could only make recommendations regarding procedures.

For her part, Chris ignored any johns who agreed to go to a motel room with the female decoy and took down the license-plate numbers of every john who refused the motel rendezvous and drove away. Then she and Mike Hern began the time-consuming process of performing background checks on those men.

The members of the task force were kept equally busy. After Sherry Latham's death, the task force received an average of forty to fifty tips per week about possible serial-killer suspects. An administrator noted, however, that "the majority [of the tips] were from disgruntled women . . . who want to get their ex-husbands and boyfriends in trouble . . . by reporting their violent or peculiar sexual habits." Other tips were from fathers-in-law who were certain their sexually deviant sons-in-law had to be the notorious prostitute murderer.

One tipster identified himself as a "self-taught profiling expert." He believed a caller to a radio talk show was the serial killer because the man, one "Robert from San Bernardino," had said he used to really dislike cats as a child, but now really hates dogs and wants to kill his wife's dog. The tipster said he was certain "Robert" was the serial killer because he fit the tipster's "set, wet, pet syndrome."

Another tipster sent two letters from New Hampshire with his theory on the killer. Although the letters seemed generally intelligent, investigators were a little concerned that each had been written on the back of a McDonald's place mat.

Civilian help notwithstanding, the task force had about two dozen men it deemed serious potential suspects who fit the DOJ's psychological profile and who had the opportunity to commit the murders. Investigation of those subjects continued through background checks and limited surveillance. Another forty or so subjects had been named as suspects by informants and callers, and were awaiting further investigation.

Seeking to expand its search for help, the task force filed data on each murder with the State Department of Justice and with two federal-crime computer networks. The state computer system was set up to analyze the information from multiple cases and pinpoint similarities in them. The national systems were designed to match designated cases to similar homicides reported anywhere else in the country.

In the meantime, Chris maintained her street contacts. She found herself developing an increasingly close friendship with one heroin-addicted prostitute. Eleanor Casares was a gentle-faced Mexican woman in her late thirties, with a soft, honest demeanor and a strong maternal concern for her teenaged children. The strong mothering instinct in Eleanor, and the frankness with which she confided in Chris about everything in her life, drew the female detective into a confidante/counselor type of relationship with Eleanor.

Chris would meet with Eleanor at least twice a week, often for lunch, often exchanging advice—Chris advising Eleanor on how to change her life and cope with her problems, and Eleanor offering ideas about the serial case. As with many of the prostitute-addicts, Eleanor viewed her street activity as the only way she could earn the money necessary "to get well," or obtain her daily fixes of heroin to prevent withdrawal symptoms.

Chris presented a strong outside source for motivating Eleanor to kick the habit. In that regard, she was very similar to Eleanor's mother, but not as pessimistic or judgmental, since Chris hadn't lived a lifetime with Eleanor, as had her mother, who had heard countless broken promises and seen her fail again and again at cleaning up her life. Chris was more like an understanding friend who still had faith in Eleanor's willpower and good intentions—and had great concern for her welfare. Every time they met, Chris stressed to Eleanor that she had to be careful on the streets when she prostituted because she had children who depended on her for love and support, and the serial killer was utterly without mercy.

Like most of the other street girls Chris had met, Eleanor assured Chris she need not worry, that she could take care of herself. For some reason, Chris believed it when Eleanor said it. There was a strong will and inner strength in Eleanor that seemed manifestly capable. Eleanor had no pretenses about her addiction or the prostitution; she always saw them in realistic perspective and she was always able to cope with both. Chris believed this was because Eleanor had an order and routine to her life that was grounded in her family life and her kids. Because of them, she could deal with anything and handle any situation. She wasn't about to let anything or anyone permanently deprive her kids of their mother.

Eleanor's inner strength was a source of comfort for Chris, as well. It often provided reassurance when Chris was feeling especially frustrated or stressed from the lack of progress on the case. Eleanor had enough control of her life that she was able to offer sincere understanding and to brainstorm with Chris about the case. She was one source of reliable emotional relief when Chris was feeling especially down or upset.

The murder of Sherry Latham, seemingly timed so that her body would be discovered on the Fourth of July holiday, had set Chris and the task force wondering if the killer were functioning on the basis of some personal agenda or calendar dates. The task force explored whether he was timing the murders to coincide with famous holidays (perhaps to grab extra attention for himself), or whether he was following the zodiac or lunar calendars. However, no pattern could be found; only occasional coincidences. If

the serial killer was following a calendar, it had to be a
personal one that only he, or those who knew him, were
aware of. In the meantime, that line of investigation
appeared to be just another dead end.

As the weeks dragged on, it also began to seem that the
lead provided by Sherry Latham's boyfriend was not as
solid as first hoped. The fear returned that maybe, like
the Green River killer, this serial killer would never be
caught.

# **Chapter Five**

By July 29, 1991, with the Sherry Latham murder still fresh on everyone's minds and its investigators complaining about the lack of manpower to pursue all the leads that were accumulating, the Riverside County Sheriff's Office decided to seek outside help for its Homicide Task Force. The RSO asked the City of Riverside Police Department to officially assign some investigators to help full-time with the case. Chris and Mike Hern had been working in a cooperative function with the task force, but were still officially independent RPD investigators, and still handling other RPD cases in addition to the prostitute homicides. The RSO wanted full-time help, dedicated exclusively to the case—and operating under the supervision, and at the direction, of its task-force administrators.

The RPD responded to the Sheriff's request by asking Chris and Mike if they would be willing to be assigned full-time to the Sheriff's task force. Chris said she would do whatever it took to catch the killer. Mike, however, strongly objected, because he had worked on task forces before.

"I don't want task-force shit," he bluntly told their RPD boss. "I worked on a task force before, and I don't want that [again]." He was adamant about keeping their relationship with the RSO task force informal, aware of the bitter infighting that often occurred in such interagency efforts.

Explaining his position, Mike said, "A task force has the advantage of being able to easily share information, but it also has the problem of being so large that it gets in its own way. If you have more than one agency involved, you're going to have conflicting policies, conflicting methods, and conflicting attitudes, as well as the normal egos. Everybody that does this line of work *has* to feel that they know what the heck they're doing and that they're good. Otherwise, they're worthless.

"So you get [one] guy, with his experience of doing things one way [based on his agency's method of training], [thrown together] with a guy from a different agency, who learned things a different way, and [so on and so on], and they're all going to be butting heads [about how to do things], and their egos are going to be bumping into each other. You very seldom are going to get a group like that that's just going to meld together, simply because of the nature of the beast. A task force is an unwieldy thing. [Instead of forming an interagency task force, you should] work your [own] areas and work closely together [with the other agencies], but you shouldn't throw it all in one pot because it has a bad tendency of blowing up on itself."

If the RPD was determined to participate on the task force, Mike suggested they send Detective Boyer instead of him, since Boyer was the original case agent on the Cheryl Coker homicide and was also familiar with that serial murder. Mike's boss listened appreciatively to Mike's counsel. But after reflecting on the matter, he decided Mike's wisdom and experience would be more valuable to the task force. Soon after, he called Chris and Mike into his office and curtly told Mike, "You're on the task force, and not Boyer."

However, concessions were made to the two detectives. The RPD told the Sheriff's Office that it would commit two investigators full-time to the task force, with the stipulation that they would work only out of the police department, and that they would not be available for about three weeks, so the two could wrap up their other commitments, and so Mike and his bride could take a planned vacation.

August 1991 rolled around with no major changes in the investigation. A low-profile surveillance conducted in the city of Corona, directly east of Riverside, revealed that many of the johns seen or arrested in the Corona sweep were the same guys who had been seen or arrested in similar task-force john programs conducted in the cities of Riverside and distant Lake Elsinore—as were several of the prostitutes. This revealed to the task force that even the johns liked to wander the circuit of prostitution activity in the county, which helped explain how so many girls were familiar with the same johns and with so many other girls working the trade in other cities.

Thanks in large part to the frequent maternal nagging of Chris Keers, many of those girls were now working in pairs and looking out for each other to some degree. Chris exerted herself day and night, with very few breaks, to see that the girls on the street were at maximum alertness (within their intoxicated capabilities). She knew their alertness was the only thing that could save their lives, or help catch the killer.

The odds were always against a serial killer because his crimes by nature were continuing: the more times he struck, the more occasions there were for him to make a mistake, or to be seen. Chris knew it could all end if just one person at one of those times saw him.

### Kelly Marie Hammond
*August 16, 1991*

The task force got the call on the body in Corona at about 8:30 that Friday morning, Corona police deciding this female homicide might be part of the series the task force was investigating. The entire team was called out to the scene. Chris got a call from Steve Secofsky about the body dump at about 9 A.M. When the task force arrived, the Corona police turned over the entire scene to them for the workup. Chris recognized the victim immediately as one of the University Avenue prostitutes, a twenty-seven-year-old girl named Kelly Marie Hammond. Chris knew the baby-faced, auburn-haired girl had recently survived a hammer attack from an assailant she claimed she couldn't identify, but the girl had gone back to prostituting on the same streets almost immediately, despite her attacker still being at large.

The nude body was located in a gravel alley behind Sampson Avenue, near the corner of Sampson and Delilah. One analyst wondered whether the killer selected the site because of possible Biblical significance in the street name, although Sampson was not the precise spelling of the Biblical hero Samson. It smacked of a possible religious fanatic bent on a streetsweeping crusade.

A cinder-block wall about eight feet high paralleled the alley. A blue neoprene tarp obtained from the Corona forensic technicians had been set up against the wall to tent the nude body, shielding the corpse from the media and winds that might blow away trace evidence. The body had been posed in a kneeling position, head down toward the wall, buttocks raised up and spread open to expose her to the world. The left leg was pushed upward into her chest area, to prop her bottom up, the right leg pulled away to spread her genitals. The right arm was partially concealed under her body, but the left arm had been pulled out and bent at the elbow, hand positioned palm up on her left foot to expose her inner arm to the view of investigators. A tattoo of a rose with a stem and water droplet was visible on the very white skin of her right shoulder.

Steve Secofsky attempted to get fingerprint lifts from the skin using photographic film, but was unsuccessful. There were no obvious marks of violence on the body, so a determination of cause of death would have to wait until the next morning, Saturday, when an autopsy could be scheduled.

Seeing that the investigation was in capable hands, and that there was little she could contribute at the scene, Chris quickly rushed back to University Avenue to see if any of the other prostitutes had observed Kelly Hammond getting into any cars prior to her murder.

At about eleven o'clock that morning, Chris found the girl she was looking for: Kelly Victoria Jewel Whitecloud, a close friend of Kelly Hammond. Whitecloud was a gaunt, abrasive hooker with a short temper and raucous contempt for public propriety, due in part to her heavy addiction to heroin and to her frustration over a wasted life that had held such promise. Born to a wealthy family and provided the best education available, Whitecloud had crashed into a life of drugs, despair and prostitution following the death of her sister in a car accident at age eighteen. Her demeanor had become contentious and abusive. She adopted severely bleached blond hair and heavy, in-your-face makeup as if to flaunt her contempt for the world and herself, determined to punish both for her sister's tragedy.

Nevertheless, she was very friendly with Chris Keers, thanks largely to the previous contacts Chris had made with her, encouraging her to rebuild her life and urging her to be extra careful in her street activities. Whitecloud had developed a strong trust and respect for Chris Keers, whose concern for the girls working the streets was obviously genuine. She always carried one of Chris's flowered personal business cards in her purse, in case she saw any suspicious johns to report to the compassionate lady cop. When Chris asked her now about Kelly Hammond, Whitecloud became almost hysterical in her eagerness to provide help. She talked animatedly about both her and Hammond's experiences on University Avenue last night. As the details spilled out of her, Chris swiftly began to share her excitement.

Late last night, both Whitecloud and Kelly Hammond were trying to pick up johns on University Avenue. They had positioned themselves in front of a large brick commercial property on the corner of a cross street, diagonally across from a McDonald's restaurant. The property was bordered on the two street sides by a row of short stone posts, each topped by a large round stone ball. The girls liked the location because the posts were just the right height to function as stools when they became tired. Hammond was very intoxicated at the time, and barely able to walk. She was also suffering from a very bad cold, which had her coughing deep, racking coughs.

At about ten o'clock, a gray, late-model van pulled up to the curb. Apparently observing the heavily intoxicated, coughing state of Kelly Hammond, the male driver drove by to Whitecloud and called out to her, asking for a "date." He offered Whitecloud twenty dollars for a "straight lay." She agreed and hopped into the passenger seat. The van had a gray interior, two captain's chairs up front separated by a center console, and a swivel captain's chair directly behind the passenger seat. On the console, she noticed a thick black book that looked just like a Bible.

The driver was a chubby man, about forty years old, with light-brown hair, a small mustache, and stubble on his face. He was wearing a distinctive pair of metal-frame glasses that did nothing to counter his nerdy appearance. He appeared to her like somebody's soft old grandfather. He not only looked harmless to Whitecloud, he looked like the type of wimp she could kick the shit out of if she had to. She decided to "burn" this john.

"Buy me some food first," she asked the guy, indicating the McDonald's across the street; wanting to see if he had enough money to be free with it. It wouldn't be worth the risk of robbing the guy if he was broke. The john readily agreed, and drove the van across the street to the McDonald's parking lot.

Inside the restaurant, Whitecloud became nervous and loud, afraid that someone might recognize her from her many visits to the ladies' bathroom, where she would often cook and then shoot up her heroin. She had been kicked out of the place several times for using the bathroom for such purposes.

She turned on her abrasive side, hoping to intimidate anyone inclined to eject her again.

She ordered Chicken McNuggets and a hot-fudge sundae—and was adamant that the nuts for her sundae be put on the bottom of the cup, instead of on top as is customary. Her loud tone made the john visibly nervous, obviously worrying him about all the attention she was attracting. His discomfort didn't bother Whitecloud in the slightest. In fact, when the sundae was presented to her and she saw the nuts were not on the bottom of the cup as specified, she began to berate the counter person in an even louder voice—so loud that the night manager rushed to the front to see what was the problem.

The john became extremely nervous over her boisterous display, but there was little he could do. He had to simply stand in silent mortification while another hot-fudge sundae was prepared for his hooker. The night manager's disdainful look at Whitecloud told her he recognized her from her previous visits, some of which had involved him personally in throwing her out. However, tonight she was in the company of a male friend and was simply paying for an order to go, so he offered no objections and made no comments to her. He remained at the counter, however, to make sure she was served her order as quickly as possible and that she left the premises immediately thereafter.

Once out in the parking lot, walking back to the van, the embarrassed john began to argue with Whitecloud. He told her it wasn't fair to still pay her twenty dollars for the sex since he had just paid four dollars for her food. He told her he would only give her ten dollars now. She told him the price was twenty dollars, and that she could take him to her house for the sex, instead of a back alley or orange grove. He told her, "I don't want to go to your house. I want to do it in my van up by UCR (the University of California at Riverside, down the street)."

When he became adamant about the price, Whitecloud concluded the john had no cash. Furious, she told him she "wasn't doing him for ten dollars." Without any other notice, she flung open the passenger door and hopped out of the van before it had moved more than a few feet in the lot. "Fuck off!" she yelled back at him, and then slammed his door and stalked away back toward her perch on the stone posts. She saw him look at her with an open mouth, obviously startled at her sudden flight from his van. He said nothing back, however, and made no move to stop her.

Instead, he pulled out of the lot and drove back across the street ahead of her, to where Kelly Hammond sat woozily upon one of the round-topped posts. When the van pulled alongside Hammond, she rose to talk to the driver, to see if he wanted a date. From across the street, Whitecloud raised both hands to her mouth and shouted at her friend. "Don't go with him, Kelly! He's just a ten-dollar date!"

Hearing her, Hammond just smiled back and waved at Whitecloud, feeling too good by now from the heroin to care about such things. She opened the passenger door and climbed into the van.

Whitecloud continued working the street until midnight, worrying about Hammond and the weird john. By midnight, when Hammond still hadn't returned, Whitecloud gave up and went home.

The next morning, about nine o'clock, she went to a vacant field at Sixth Street and Park Avenue. Kelly Hammond lived there, in a large cardboard box, with her boyfriend Russell. Whitecloud anxiously asked him about Hammond. Russell said she hadn't come home last night and he had no idea where she might be. Both became concerned for her safety. When Whitecloud saw Chris drive up, looking for her and asking about Hammond, she knew something must have happened to her best friend.

Chris asked Whitecloud if she thought she could identify the john. When Kelly said yes, Chris decided to have the hooker come to the police station and meet with a sketch artist.

But first Chris had to calm down the hysterical hooker and sober her up. She rented a motel room for Kelly Whitecloud, to get her off the streets, then took her to lunch and told her to get some rest and a shower. Tomorrow, she told Whitecloud, they would go together to the police station and assist a police sketch artist in creating a composite drawing of the suspect.

After making the appointment with the artist, Chris went over her notes from her conversation with Kelly Whitecloud. She had enough specifics to create a flier on this john. Knowing Whitecloud fairly well, Chris believed her story. If true, it meant that Kelly Whitecloud had probably seen the face and the vehicle of the Riverside prostitute killer. If those details could be circulated to the appropriate law-enforcement officers—the guys working patrol, who were most likely to encounter the vehicle—there was a good chance the killer could eventually be spotted on one of his drives through the county.

Tomorrow, Chris would take Whitecloud on a tour of the sprawling Auto Center and see if the hooker could recognize the exact model of van she had seen the night before.

Chris went to sleep seeing a light at the end of the long, dark tunnel.


At about ten o'clock the next morning, Chris Keers retrieved Kelly Whitecloud from the motel on University Avenue and took her to various local automobile lots. The only van that Whitecloud thought resembled the suspect's vehicle was a Chevy Astro van.

About two o'clock that afternoon, they kept their appointment with the sketch artist at the RPD station. Whitecloud helped the artist draft what she felt was a fairly accurate composite sketch of the weird john who had picked up Kelly Hammond. Chris invited a task-force detective to sit in on the rendering, and afterward gave the RSO man copies of the sketch.

Later, she contacted the night manager of the McDonald's to see if he could provide any additional information about or description of the suspect, but the manager stated he couldn't even remember the man Whitecloud was with, so focused was he on the loud, complaining hooker.

That night, other members of the task force spent several hours on University Avenue contacting prostitutes and johns, seeking information about Kelly Hammond. Some of the prostitutes weren't terribly receptive to the sheriff's men's sometimes brusque streetside interrogations. One Mexican girl, whose family had a history of bad run-ins with the law, was especially offended by the RSO men's demands for information. She became "belligerent and uncooperative," according to the detective who tried to interrogate her, so he arrested her "to demonstrate the serious intent of our investigation."

Chris was disturbed to hear from some of the street girls that some of the RSO men had been trying to intimidate them into providing information they didn't have. She felt the best way to get the girls to talk was to earn their trust, not their fear.

Kelly Whitecloud trusted Chris so much that she made two startling revelations to the lady detective. First, she told Chris she was several months' pregnant. Chris yelled at her for prostituting while in such a condition. "Get off the streets!" Chris demanded, furious that the girl would endanger her baby and herself by such crazy behavior.

Rather than becoming upset by Chris's anger, Whitecloud took it as a sign that Chris really cared about her and her baby. The second revelation—no less a shocker—was far more poorly timed. While sitting with Chris in the crowded detectives' bay of the RPD, within plain earshot of every macho detective in the room, the ever-loud Kelly Whitecloud revealed to Chris Keers that she loved her so much, she wanted Chris to be her baby's godmother. "Will you be my baby's godmother?" the painted hooker blurted loud and clear, turning heads all around.

The experience was about as embarrassing as possible for a female cop trying to maintain the macho respect of her tough-guy coworkers. However, it was overshadowed by the request itself, which was the ultimate compliment and respect Kelly Whitecloud could offer a friend.

Chris accepted.


Thanks entirely to Kelly Whitecloud's information, Chris was able to immediately create a flier on the suspect and his vehicle, and to attach to the flier a copy of the composite drawing of the man himself.

Printed on RPD letterhead, the bulletin read:

### POLICE BULLETIN
### Date: August 19, 1991

TO:         PATROL DIVISION
FROM:     INVESTIGATIONS
RE:         SUSPECT AND VEHICLE INFORMATION
              ON 187 P.C. PROSTITUTES.

On 08–16–91, Kelly Hammond, A Riverside Prostitute, became the 15th victim in a series of murders. She was last seen 08–15–91, at approximately 2200 hours, getting into a *late model Chevrolet Astro Van, Two-Tone, Medium Blue over Grey.*

*SUSPECT:*     WM 40 5 10 Brown Hair Medium Build
                    Slight Mustache
*WEARING:*     Metal Frame Glasses
                    Plain Long Sleeve Shirt
                    Faded Blue Jeans
                    Orange Construction Boots

*ADDITIONAL INFORMATION:* The suspect vehicle had bucket seats in front separated by a center console. The witness observed a *BIBLE* lying on the console. The rear portion of the van has one swivel type seat directly behind the passenger seat. The interior carpeting was grey/blue fiber.

This is the first time we have had a witness provide us with suspect information and request the assistance of Patrol in stopping vehicles that fit the above description.

Please forward all F.I. Cards or any additional information you may have as to the identity of this vehicle and driver to Detective Keers or Detective Hern.

Your assistance and cooperation will be the factor in solving this case.


With the bulletin quietly circulating among law-enforcement officers, Chris and Mike Hern spent many long nights cruising University Avenue looking for gray vans and men matching the composite. Sometimes they would spot a suspicious john and follow his vehicle in their unmarked car. Other times, they would request a marked Patrol unit to stop the john's auto once it was out of the area, enabling them to question the man away from University Avenue. If he wasn't the killer, the real killer could be watching the avenue.

Frank Orta, a barrel-chested, pleasant-faced RPD motorcycle cop, frequently observed the pair of detectives prowling the avenue in their unmarked car—a "slicktop," in his parlance. Often they were the only other cops he saw out at night on his shift. He respected their dedication to the case, and sympathized with their frustration at being unable to run the killer to ground. Once he heard the detectives request a motor unit to make a stop for them, and he eagerly responded, hoping his help would be of real benefit. It turned out to be just another kinky john: some old man trying to pick up two hookers. The girls had thought him strange enough to turn down his money, so Chris and Mike Hern had decided to check the guy out. Afterward, Orta wished the detectives good luck, then all three went back to their routine.

For Orta, it was his regular shift: two o'clock in the afternoon to midnight. He knew Chris and Mike were on overtime, and he wondered how their families were taking such long stints without them. He would soon be eligible to apply for a detective position, and his wife was hoping he'd go for the promotion and the money it represented. But Orta's professional love had always been motorcycles, and working outdoors with the public. He didn't think he'd be happy spending most of his time in an office. Seeing the long hours and strain Chris and Mike had to endure didn't make him any more eager to change his status. The extra money would be nice, but if you can't enjoy what you do, what was the purpose? He wondered if his wife would be as understanding about the long hours as Mike Hern's wife must be.

Before they even officially joined the RSO's task force, problems began for Chris and Mike. One day an RPD patrolman stopped by Chris's desk and asked for a copy of the Whitecloud flier and composite sketch. Many officers who hadn't already received a copy had also stopped by and personally picked one up, eager to carry the picture in their patrol cars and hunt for the murdering bastard.

This patrolman was more enthusiastic than anyone realized. Because he lived in Lake Elsinore, where so many victims had been picked up or dumped, he wanted to make a special effort to alert everyone in the area to watch for the killer. He took the confidential police bulletin to a local Elsinore print shop and, not knowing the flier was not for public release, had *hundreds* of them photocopied and posted around town. The media was quick to pick up on the patrolman's errant publicity campaign and also published the composite and details from the flier.

The task-force administrators hit the ceiling. They demanded to know why Chris Keers was spreading some of the most secret key clues about the case all over the county. Even the sister of one of the victims called the task force to rail about the release; the woman was afraid that the publication of his face might scare the killer into hiding, so that he might never be caught.

When Chris learned of the mistake, she immediately contacted the task force and advised them that the release was totally unintended and not authorized. Some on the task force believed her; some did not.

The search went on. One suspect was eliminated because he had a vasectomy and could not have left the sperm found on some of the vaginal swabs taken from the victims. Another subject had a preference for tying up prostitutes and then pretending to stab them, but he was eliminated as a suspect after his work schedule confirmed his lack of opportunity to commit some of the murders. A Lake Elsinore prostitute told of one "strange john" who wanted her to dress him up in woman's clothing and "talk dirty to him to the point where it made him mad enough to kill." She had no name or license-plate number on the guy for investigators to follow up, so her report was simply logged for reference. Another suspect, who was identified by prostitutes as a john, denied ever having any contacts with prostitutes. He stated he "wouldn't lower himself to their level." But investigators found a phone bill in his residence with $1,500 in charges for "976" phone sex calls, so they kept him on the active-investigation list.

The work continued, as did the attrition. By August 21, 1991, before Chris and Mike had yet officially joined the task force, a family situation caused another investigator to leave it. The decision was made not to replace that RSO man, because it would be too difficult and time-consuming to bring a new man up to speed on the case. The task force decided to concentrate on the flier and composite, and ran almost daily low-profile surveillance of areas of prostitution activity in Lake Elsinore, Corona, and the City of Riverside. With the suspect's picture in hand, they simply had to be on the street when he came cruising again.

The local newspaper almost helped the task force. Unaware that the serial killer was responding to newspaper articles about him and the case, the paper ran a two-page story in which they quoted several experts in the field of serial murders and criminal profiles. One declared that the killer's mother must be a prostitute. Stunned by that published statement, the task force feared it might provoke a new murder, as had happened following the article about the task force being on a wild-goose chase in Wisconsin. The entire team was sent out to surveil the streets that night.

Fortunately, the killer made no immediate response. The thought struck some of the investigators that perhaps he knew the authorities would be expecting him to react, and was playing it safe and not coming out when he knew they would have the streets blanketed with unmarked surveillance units. Perhaps he would instead wait until they had resumed normal patrols and dropped their guard.

Or perhaps he had simply missed that edition of the paper.

On September 3, 1991, the local newspaper again indirectly helped the task force. Although aware the paper had formed its own investigative task force to research the case, the RSO believed the purpose was only for a series of articles about the victims. It was shocked when a friendly tipster from the newspaper phoned to reveal the major press effort was actually designed to "investigate [the task force] investigation." Specifically, according to the tipster, the newspaper wanted to learn what law enforcement had actually done to resolve the case, how much money the task force had been willing to spend on it, and why the task force hadn't been able to catch the guy.

The Sheriff's Office quickly contacted Riverside County Counsel and asked the county's lawyers to research the statutes and find legal justifications for controlling the release of information to the press. In response, the County Counsel advised the task force of Government Code Section 6254(f), which states that law enforcement can justify withholding any information from the press if it declares such disclosure "would endanger the successful completion of the investigation or related investigations."

As an added precaution to protect against media scrutiny of the task force's performance, arrangements were made with the records supervisor to return all original task-force reports to the task force's office where they could be kept locked up.

About a week later, on September 11, 1991, in direct contradiction of the recent decision not to replace an investigator lost to attrition, the RSO suddenly expanded the task force to nearly triple its current size—increasing it from five to thirteen assigned personnel. Evidently, the time lost in trying to bring eight new people up to speed on the case would be offset by the impressive image of the task force now assembled.

The timing of the sudden ballooning of the task force didn't go unnoticed. Darrell Santschi, a senior editor of the local newspaper, commented, "While I can't prove that it had an impact on the [Sheriff's Office], shortly after we began delving into [the case], they [more than] doubled the size of the [Homicide] Task Force and added a deputy district attorney for the first time to handle the serial-killer investigation."

Ironically, the newspaper articles were not a secret investigation of the homicide task force, but were simply focused on the victims and their families; the tipster was apparently off the mark. However, her phone call did indirectly result in a large expansion of the task force and a greater pressure on it for results, so the incident proved to be beneficial to the case.

## Catherine McDonald
*September 13, 1991*

On September 13, 1991—Friday the thirteenth—time finally told whether the serial killer had read the newspaper article calling his mother a prostitute: the body of another murdered hooker was discovered, nude, spread-eagled, and butchered. The location this time was out in the open, where the victim could be readily seen, directly alongside a road in a barren, hilly area undergoing heavy development.

The body had been savagely mutilated, as if to drive home the point that the killer was displeased by what he had read. The newspaper article had included a statement that the serial killer primarily murdered white victims, "blonde or brunette with a fair complexion," and that he was probably "a white man of similar socioeconomic background, ethnicity and age to his victims."

To publicly prove the authorities wrong again, the serial killer murdered a young black woman.

The task force received the call about one o'clock in the afternoon: a dead female in the Tuscany Hills area, about one and a half miles from where Sherry Latham's body had been dumped. It was an area of mostly ungraded dirt hills, the consistency of which ranged from hard-packed, well-traveled dirt to soft, impressionable soil. The shoulder of the road on which the victim lay spread out was soft enough to yield several good footprints of the killer. The road itself was of such good texture that long stretches of the killer's tire tracks were clearly visible in different locations. Those pieces of evidence made this crime scene the most promising of all those the task force had encountered to date. It resulted in the recovery of "a substantial amount of physical evidence."

The victim, Catherine McDonald, was a prostitute who had recently relocated to Riverside from Los Angeles. She had been in town about four months, and was so new she was unknown to the local vice detectives. As with many of the victims, she had been stabbed repeatedly in the center of the chest, into the heart. As with Tina Leal, she had also been stabbed in the outer pubic area, five times, perimortem. And as with Cheryl Coker, her right breast had been sliced off.

The curiosity this time was that the victim's breast was missing. With Coker, the killer had hurled the amputated breast up a hilltop, evidently venting some rage. McDonald's breast was nowhere to be found. The site of this body dump was more or less open ground, and soft dirt at that. If thrown in any direction, the breast would have been easily found. Furthermore, because the ground was so soft and impressionable, had any animal carted it away, the animal would have left tracks. According to those knowledgeable in such behavior, any such animal would have eaten its fill of the victim before dragging home the breast to eat later. But there were no animal marks on the body, no animal tracks anywhere near the scene, and very little time for any animal to even stumble onto the scene. It seemed very clear that the killer had taken the breast away with him. But why? For what purpose? No one could even venture a guess.

The autopsy concluded McDonald's cause of death was multiple sharp object wounds and compressions of the throat. It also revealed that Catherine McDonald was pregnant at the time of her murder, although the fetus was not considered viable. The extent of injuries was considered evidence that the killer was escalating his violence.

The DOJ psychological expert who drafted the profile of the Riverside prostitute killer for the task force expressed a belief that the murder "is very likely a result of the newspaper article" that mentioned "that serial killers tend to stay within their own race." The task force saw the news as significant "because it confirms that the killer is following the press coverage of his murders." The thought was raised about possibly "leaking" very carefully selected information, designed to incite the killer "to make contact with investigators in the case." However, just what information could be used to achieve that contact, without inciting a murder instead, could not be determined.

# Chapter Six

Friction between Chris and the task force seemed to increase as time went on. There were meetings and memos about "problems with parallel investigations," "lack of communication," and "lack of cooperation" between the two law-enforcement agencies. Both sides seemed to feel the other side was not being forthcoming with its information. Chris was convinced the RSO was not sharing its information with her, or deliberately not doing so in a timely fashion. At first, she saw the lack of cooperation as directed against the RPD for contributing "only" a woman to the task force. Later, she was sure the antagonism had shifted to her personally.

Adding fuel to the petty antagonism, the Sheriff's Office suddenly curtailed all overtime pay for its task-force members. Aware that Chris Keers and Mike Hern were authorized by the RPD to work unlimited overtime on the case, some RSO men began to express financial envy of their city counterparts, which only added to the friction.

Having the salaries of only two detectives to contend

with, the RPD had given Chris and Mike carte blanche to catch the killer; superiors up the entire chain of the police department were placing their trust in Chris's contention that the case was solvable. The RSO, on the other hand, found itself unable to justify the enormous expense of paying overtime to the dozen personnel of the newly expanded task-force ranks—especially for a case its investigators had been unable to solve for five years. That decision seemed further confirmation to Chris that the Sheriff's Office considered the case another unsolvable Green River-type crime.

The result was simmering envy on the part of some RSO people who didn't appreciate their RPD coworkers earning larger paychecks than they did. It certainly did nothing to stem the flow of hostile memos to Lieutenant Albee.

The memos criticized anything about Chris that her detractors could think of, no matter how trivial. Lieutenant Albee of the RPD, Chris's superior and the recipient of those memos, usually consulted with her about them whenever he received one. Usually, he would wind up agreeing with her that there was little substance in most of them—simply personality conflicts. Albee, however, expressed complete faith in Chris and her abilities. Her word was good enough for him, he told her, and counseled her not to take things too seriously.

Albee provided a ready ear for Chris to express her theories and blow off steam. Whenever he spotted Chris across the big RPD detective bay looking tense or acting frustrated, he would shout at her, "Okay, grab your cigarettes and get in here!" Knowing how tense it could get for a smoker in the nonsmoking detective room, Albee allowed Chris to puff away in his office and sound off about whatever was bothering her. Within minutes of railing away about the dead ends or the frustrations encountered on the task force, Chris would be ready to go back and plunge head-on into the case again.

The Sheriff's Office called the RPD on September 17 to again ask that Chris Keers and Mike Hern be officially assigned to the task force. They had been promised to the task force in August, but the assignment hadn't been followed up on.

Although their help would be a definite asset, the physical addition of the two RPD detectives to the expanded task force would further inflate the number of personnel working the publicly scrutinized case, and would give added weight to the appearance of a serious commitment to solving the murders. Since the allegedly dirt-digging newspaper articles had yet to appear, it was a prudent time to add the two promised faces to the team. Hopefully, the image of the task force would be bolstered enough to counter any negative reporting.

Honoring its previous promise, the RPD officially assigned Chris and Mike to the task force three days later, with both scheduled to report to the Lake Elsinore headquarters on September 30.

Because the task force was a creation of the RSO, Chris and Mike fell under the sheriff's local authority once they reported for duty, and were compelled to carry out assignments selected by the task force's administrators. Chris felt some of the assignments given her and Mike were wild-goose chases assigned as punishment for her outspokenness. However, the two RPD detectives dutifully ran down each assigned lead—and then immediately went out to do what they considered the real police work on the case.

Chris felt it difficult to always overlook the chauvinistic comments and cavalier jests about the victims. In the beginning, that had been possible. But now, after meeting so many of the girls and their families and seeing the terror on their faces, such humor fell very flat with her.

Even the administrators would at times be guilty of black

humor toward the case. The sample form designed to demonstrate to the task force's members how to fill out their daily logs was a case in point. In part it read:

### SPECIAL INVESTIGATION TEAM
#### Daily Assignment Log

Investigator(s):   INVESTIGATOR SIMON SAMPLE

*Time    \*\*\*THIS IS A SAMPLE, YOUR LOG MAY VARY SLIGHTLY\*\*\**

0800    This is the time you begin your day.

1000    Did computer work on POI Elmer Example, obtained current address.

1130    Conducted surveillance on Example, observed him pick up six hookers on University Avenue.

1215    Followed POI Example to Orange Grove where he killed all six hookers.

1300    Terminated surveillance on Example, doesn't look like its [sic] related. etc. etc.

Administrators on both agencies tried to keep relations running smoothly between the two law-enforcement departments and among all the members of the task force. However, the physical move to the task force did nothing to solve the personality conflicts between Chris and her detractors. The spectrum of problems and frustrations she continued experiencing with the task force and the case made Chris seriously consider quitting both. However, she felt an enormous obligation to the dead girls, and those still on the street, to stay on and help catch the killer. She knew she could never live with herself if she quit and another girl turned up dead. She realized the responsibility for catching the guy was not on her shoulders alone, but she knew she would always feel it was her fault if she gave up and the maniac killed again.

With the chronic lack of success the task force had experienced, and the frustrating way it seemed to be proceeding, Chris felt more and more convinced that without her to keep pushing them to move in more productive ways, the task force was likely never to make any real headway in the case.


Before leaving for the task force, Chris wrote her captain an interoffice memo to update him on the city's prostitute homicides. She told him, "We have contacted approximately one hundred persons of interest and were able to eliminate two-thirds of these subjects by either samples of their biological fluids or other factors. Other means of clearing some of these subjects has been with the assistance of DOJ through trace evidence. On the three Riverside cases, we have had very few solid leads to follow up on." She suggested alternating the vice detectives' hours in case the killer was aware they only worked the streets from two to ten o'clock in the evening. It was not a very rosy update, but it was accurate, and it reflected the long hours put in by both Chris and Mike. Hours that were taking a heavy toll on Mike's marriage. He didn't know how much longer he could keep up the late-night surveillances with Chris.


The task force was concentrating on the tire tracks obtained at the McDonald body dump. Experts indicated the wheel-base information could possibly be used to identify the killer's make of car. Investigators on the task force contacted car dealers, mechanics and body shops to try to narrow down possible suspect-vehicle types and sizes.

The low-profile surveillances and john programs also continued. One night, following the murder of the black

prostitute, two female decoys were used: one black and
one white. Nineteen johns were arrested in that sweep;
none of them a viable suspect.

The fixed-wing aircraft patrols were also begun, flying
reconnaissance over likely body-dump areas. Information
on suspicious vehicles was radioed to ground units, so they
could make contact with the subjects. It was a good idea
but, unfortunately, the flights proved unproductive for the
investigation. However, they did result in the arrests of
several people on unrelated charges, and in the discovery
of individuals engaging in bizarre activities in remote areas.
One young male was spotted asleep in the bed of a pickup
truck parked in the hills. Ground units found him dressed
in his underwear and chained at the hands and feet. The
man claimed he had chained himself "because he couldn't
afford an alarm clock and didn't want to sleep too long."
Because officers could find no reason to arrest him, he
was simply F.I.ed (his information taken down on a Field
Interrogation card), photographed, and released.

The tips continued pouring in. One hooker who worked
University Avenue told of a john who cut off her hair
against her will while she was giving him oral sex. Investigators tracked the man down and questioned him. He was
F.I.ed and photographed, but that proved the extent of
investigators' interest in him.

A chronic caller kept hounding the task force to pursue
an investigation of a man whom he declared was positively
the serial killer. The tipster wanted the subject imprisoned
for the serial killings and threatened to file charges or go
to the media if the task force refused to follow up on his tip.
Investigators quickly eliminated the subject as a suspect,
finding him guilty only of having stolen the tipster's girlfriend. Unfortunately, the tipster's haranguing calls to law
enforcement continued for weeks thereafter.

Much focus was given to suspects who worked in law
enforcement or the military, under the theory that the

killer was using the color of authority to coerce his victims into his vehicle. Most of the street prostitutes by now had heard of the serial killings and were extra alert and careful. Many would now only "date" johns they knew as previous customers. Being street people, they were presumed to be fairly good judges of creepy characters. Logically, it seemed that a stranger, as the serial killer was presumed to be, should have a difficult time picking up one of those girls. Yet the evidence showed he didn't. Several of his victims were known to be extremely "fussy" or "picky" about their dates, especially in light of the murders—yet they had readily succumbed to him. It seemed the serial killer had to be using some incredibly powerful persuasion to be able to pick up such suspicious victims so easily. The supposition arose that he might work in law enforcement, or at least pretend that he did, as had the Hillside Strangler.

Unfortunately, such suspects also didn't pan out. A police officer, a sheriff's deputy, and an Air Force officer were all thoroughly checked out and eliminated as suspects. The task force was still shooting in the dark.

On October 11, 1991, the DOJ's criminalist Faye Springer called to shed a little light on the serial killer. She reported her study of the trace evidence had detected many foreign hairs on victim McDonald's evidence: light brown to blond. The hairs could have come from anyone who had physical contact with the prostitute before or after her death. It seemed reasonable that the most likely source of those hairs would be the last person to have the most physical contact with her body: the serial killer. Chris's eyewitness, Kelly Whitecloud, had described victim Kelly Hammond's last trick as a brown-haired john; the man Whitecloud had initially thought looked like somebody's harmless grandfather. A small piece of the puzzle now seemed in hand.

Four days later, Springer gave the task force a gray carpet sample, advising them that it resembled some gray fibers she had found on McDonald's evidence. Whitecloud had described a gray interior in the grandfather john's gray van. Springer's revelation seemed a second corroboration of the hooker's story.

Springer's criminalist associate, Steve Secofsky, recommended using DNA testing to screen potential suspects, since the killer's semen had been recovered from several of the victims and was available for comparisons. The tests, unfortunately, cost five hundred dollars each. Secofsky recommended the task force contact other law enforcement and support agencies to see if anyone was offering free testing for cases such as theirs. None were.

Soon after her help with the serial-murder case, Kelly Whitecloud was arrested again and sent to jail. She wrote to Chris from her cell, thanking the caring detective for her friendship and telling her of the nightmares that tormented her. Even in jail, Whitecloud continued seeing the faces of her dead girlfriends in her dreams, accompanied now by the face of the deadly brown-haired john who had killed them. If that weren't bad enough, she was tormenting herself with guilt, wondering why she had survived the serial killer and her friends had not. The last sweet smile and little wave Kelly Hammond gave her before hopping into the gray van seemed frozen before Whitecloud's eyes.

In her letters, she thanked Chris for helping to motivate her to reform herself. "You showed me the value of life," Kelly wrote. She proudly boasted that she was entering a sobriety and rehabilitation program—this time of her own accord—and that she felt finally motivated to succeed in changing her life.

Another street prostitute found cause to thank Detective

Chris Keers. The hooker called Chris to report that a john had stolen her purse; she phoned for a shoulder to cry on rather than expecting any action would be taken on her account. Chris asked her to calm down and tell exactly what happened.

The girl reported that a man in a van drove over to her location on the street and asked if she was dating. She said she was, and hopped in his van. He then drove into a nearby alley, slapped her, grabbed her purse, and physically kicked her out. As he drove off, she took down his license-plate number; having a pen and paper ready, thanks to Chris's earlier counseling about being on the alert for the serial killer.

Chris ran the license-plate number through the police computer system and found the vehicle was registered to a man with an address in a distant trailer park. She was incensed at the arrogant nature of the assault, which indicated the man felt no concern for law enforcement pursuing the victimization of a street prostitute. It was an attitude she knew the serial killer also possessed. She made the long drive out to have a talk with the individual.

At the trailer park, Chris easily spotted a vehicle matching the description given by the hooker. She knocked on the door of that residence and a man responded, opening the door. Behind him, inside the trailer, Chris saw a woman of the man's approximate age.

"Hi," Chris told him. "I see you have a woman standing there, so it's probably not a good time to mention this, but can I talk to you for a minute?" She identified herself to the man and brought him away from the door, out of earshot of the female. Chris told him, "Listen, I don't want to talk about this in front of your wife or whomever, because I don't want to create a problem for you, but I'm not leaving here without the purse you took from the girl."

The man strongly protested his innocence, but Chris quickly cut him off. "Listen," she warned him, "don't bullshit me. Either you give me the purse or we'll go back in your house, I'll get a search warrant, and I'll [execute it in front of your female friend and] get the purse." The facade of innocence instantly dropped. "Okay," the thief said. With that, he hurried to his van, rummaged inside, and came back with the purse in his hands, which he surrendered to Chris.

The trip served two purposes for Chris. First, it enabled her to identify a john who dated prostitutes, so he could be added to the database for the serial-killer case. Second, it enabled her to recover the purse for the distraught hooker.

"She couldn't believe it," Chris recalled. The girl became wildly excited at the sight of Chris walking up to her with the purse held on high, like a trophy. Waving her arms in astonishment, smiling from ear to ear, the hooker kept exploding, "I can't believe you got my purse! I can't believe you got it!" She didn't believe anyone still cared enough about her to do such a thing.

After that incident, with word of mouth being what it is on the street, Chris's reputation was more golden than ever with the prostitutes.

Unfortunately, the sheriff's men weren't enjoying as good a rapport with the streetwalkers. In October, two months after the Kelly Hammond murder, a pair of RSO investigators from the task force pressured a prostitute named Debra for information about that homicide. Debra later told Chris and Mike she caved in to the deputies' pressuring and made up some information about Hammond's murder "just to get them off my back." She told the men she saw Kelly Hammond two hours after Kelly Whitecloud said Hammond disappeared in the gray van with the brown-haired grandfatherly john. She claimed she saw Hammond around midnight get into a dark pickup truck with a thin, long-haired man.

Although Chris told the RSO people the new information was bogus, they refused to believe her. They preferred to believe their hooker informant was more reliable than Chris's hooker informant. They advised the RSO patrol units to keep an eye out for that long-haired thin driver in the dark pickup.

Chris still had the RPD patrol officers carrying her fliers with Whitecloud's composite of the suspect, so the RSO's disbelief was not a total loss to the investigation. But that lack of faith in her was just one more incident that grated on her dignity and made her feel even more of an outcast in the sheriff's task force.


By October 17, 1991, plans were being made for another major low-profile surveillance, to be conducted at night simultaneously in Lake Elsinore and on University Avenue in Riverside during the week of Halloween. One victim had been found on a holiday—the Fourth of July—and such dates might be a consideration for the killer in planning his murders. Murders on a holiday would probably generate greater publicity, and this killer certainly thrived on publicity. Chris and Mike were in charge of organizing the program, tentatively scheduled to run from October 29 through November 1. Chris emphasized that the surveillance was to be strictly a "sit back and watch" operation only, with no contacts made with johns or prostitutes unless something truly unusual or extraordinary was observed. She didn't want any more heavy-handed interventions occurring that might alert the killer and scare him away.

The task force's "Person of Interest" suspect list had grown to 204 names, with only fifty of those people eliminated as suspects so far. By the next week, the numbers had grown to 228 suspects and seventy-one eliminations.

*          *          *

By October 25, 1991, DOJ criminalist Faye Springer had found the same types of hairs on enough of the victims to deduce that they belonged to the serial killer. The types of hairs found enabled her to notify the task force that it could eliminate black males as suspects in the killings.

About that time, the task force entered discussions with the founder/director of a Southern California crime-reporting hot line known as the "WeTip" program. The purpose was to explore what it would take to set up a reward fund for information on the serial killings. Offering rewards for the public's help often smacked of desperation on the part of law enforcement, but the RSO felt such action was merited in this case. The murders had been going on for years without being solved, and the body count was not only embarrassingly high now, but the killer seemed to be striking more often and more violently. The murders were coming about once a month now, which meant the case was in the newspaper headlines almost continuously.

If the killer kept to his monthly routine, they were due for a new body dump any day now.

On Monday and Tuesday that last week in October, the task force concentrated on investigating the POIs (Persons of Interest) on its list of possible suspects. Recovered from the home of one subject were numerous photos and home-video movies of the man engaging in sexual acts with known prostitutes. Two of the girls in his photos and home movies were victims of the serial killer: Cherie Payseur and Kelly Hammond. Aware that serial killers often like to keep "trophies" or remembrances of their victims so they can later engage in sexual fantasies about those murders, the task force decided to view all of the movies taken from the subject's house, to see if any other victims were identifiable in the man's pornographic collection.

It seemed a promising lead, but the task force had learned from experience not to get its hopes up. It often seemed that just when something looked the most promising, it would blow up. As if reading their minds, the killer would strike again, taunting them with another grisly message that they were still on the wrong track, still no closer to catching him than before.

That message came quickly this time, as well. The next day, October 30, 1991—the day before Halloween—the killer left another dead prostitute by a busy roadside, ensuring the task force would immediately receive his latest message.

### Delliah Zamora
*October 30, 1991*

The body was found at 7:15 in the morning by a man on his drive to work. It was left on the shoulder of a road paralleling Highway 60, a major freeway, across the street from a park-and-ride lot where commuters daily congregated to share rides to work, usually to the Los Angeles area. The immediate area was unpopulated and rather desolate, except for the park-and-ride lot. In the early-morning hours, it was likely a driver wouldn't even notice that lot.

Apparently, the serial killer didn't. The victim, a Mexican prostitute and heroin addict, was left fully clothed, in her sleeveless white top and black nylon bicycle shorts. She hadn't been mutilated. Investigators surmised the killer had probably not noticed the park-and-ride lot and had panicked when the commuters suddenly began arriving across the street for their car-pool rendezvous. He apparently lingered only long enough to pull the girl's right arm out to the side and turn it up so the needle marks in her inner arm were exposed to the world. Then he had driven off, abandoning the victim where she lay before anyone across the street noticed his unusual activity.

The task force sent a deputy across the street to the parking lot to take down information on every car in the commuter lot—all the makes, models, colors, license-plate numbers, and the last four numbers of the VINs—so the drivers could be checked against the POI list and questioned about whether they had noticed any vehicles or individuals across the street that morning. It was also decided to set up roadblocks for the next several days to contact people who frequented the area in the morning, and see if any of them had noticed the killer or his vehicle.

Because the desert wind was violently gusting—it had already blown the shell off a truck on the freeway adjacent to the crime scene—it was decided to move the body to the Coroner's Office for processing before the winds destroyed any trace evidence that might be on it. The victim was placed in a white plastic coroner's transport body bag and immediately driven to the Coroner's Office for further investigative work.

Chris and two other task-force investigators walked both sides of the road searching for any physical evidence the killer might have left behind. They found nothing.

By 11 A.M. the crime scene was cleared. By 11:10 the body arrived at the Coroner's Office. An RSO forensic technician immediately took overall and close-up photos of the victim, and rolled fingerprints were taken for identification.

There was postmortem lividity present in the right arm and hand, and a bruising type of trauma visible on the front of the girl's neck, just above the shirt neckline. There were no other signs of significant trauma to the body.

The victim's toes were painted red, but there was no polish on her fingernails. She had a star-shaped earring on her right ear, and two silver turquoise earrings on the left one. The forensic technician collected all of those for evidence. The body was then processed for trace evidence, and a sexual-assault kit was completed by DOJ criminalist Steve Secofsky.

The set of rolled fingerprints was subsequently identified as that of Delliah Wallace, aka Delliah Zamora, a thirty-five-year-old woman from the city of Riverside. Chris knew Zamora from contacts on the street. The victim was a close friend of Eleanor Casares, the prostitute with whom Chris had developed the strongest friendship amongst all of her street contacts. Eleanor took the murder hard, and Chris sympathized with her friend over the loss. Chris knew it would be just as if she were to lose Eleanor to the killer; a tragedy both were sure could never happen because Eleanor was too much like Chris: too smart and strong and self-sufficient to ever be taken in by a dirtbag like the serial killer. That thought never seriously entered either one's mind; its possibility so unthinkable.

The roadblocks proved unproductive; no one remembered seeing anything of the serial killer or his vehicle that early morning. Good news did arrive, however, from a different source—the crime laboratory again making a valuable discovery about the killer. Study of the shoeprints left at the Catherine McDonald crime scene had just been identified as belonging to an inexpensive brand of athletic shoes called ProWings, which were sold exclusively by the Payless Shoes chain.

The search had now narrowed to a brown-haired white male who owned ProWings gym shoes.

While investigators tracked Delliah Zamora's last hours and ran down leads on her homicide, other members of the task force recontacted the WeTip director and notified him that six thousand dollars had been made available for a reward fund. The members pushed the WeTip director to commence publicity on the reward as soon as possible.

Believing the serial killer might be arrogant enough to attend his victims' funerals and gloat under the very noses of the families and law enforcement, some members of the task force borrowed an undercover-surveillance van and went to a wake held for Delliah Zamora, where they secretly videotaped all those who attended. They did the same thing the next day at the funeral, secretly taping a crowd of almost one hundred mourners who came to pay their respects to the family of the slain prostitute.

Although no likely suspects were found by the surveillance, the task force didn't lack any POIs to investigate. Investigators questioned two subjects in the neighboring city of Rubidoux after sheriff's deputies stopped their vehicle and found it contained newspaper articles and photographs of the dead victims. The two subjects were added to the POI pool, although both were homosexual and it was known, through recovered semen, that the serial killer had had sex with most of the victims prior to their deaths.

Keers and Hern weren't lacking suspects, either. Their most promising tip to date came in to Chris shortly after Delliah Zamora's murder. A man called to report a chilling conversation he'd had with a drinking buddy just prior to that murder. The informant and his buddy, a retired law-enforcement officer, were both very drunk in the Bull 'n Mouth, a Riverside bar. During their conversation, the buddy suddenly asked, "Where should I dump the next body?"

"What body?" the informant had asked, not understanding.

"You know, number eighteen—the prostitutes—where should I dump her?" the retired lawman went on.

The informant thought his buddy was kidding, just making a sick joke about the subject of endless newspaper articles. So he played along and responded that the sheriff's local fueling station would be a good place to dump her.

"No," the buddy had reflected, "I think I'll dump her off Highway 60 in Mira Loma."

The informant didn't take the statement seriously until five days later when he heard on the radio that a prostitute had just been found in Mira Loma off Highway 60. He then began to panic that his murderous drinking buddy might remember confessing to him about the crime in advance, and might come back to "get" him. So he called the police with the news.

Chris alerted the rest of the task force, and started to personally focus very close attention on both subjects— the retired buddy and the informant. Mike assisted her at first, but the long hours and late nights had taken their toll on his new marriage, and the disruption just could not be tolerated any longer. Mike Hern asked to transfer off the task force and out of homicide altogether. He wanted to return to the regular business hours of the robbery division.

Mike's request was regretfully accepted. His last day with the task force was that Friday, November 15, 1991. Lieutenant Albee asked Chris if she wanted a replacement partner from the RPD to assist her on the task force, but she declined the offer. She told Albee that, at least for the time being, it would be easier to pursue the case on her own. She cited the same argument the RSO administrators had used earlier: It would be too difficult and time-consuming to try to bring a new guy up to speed on the case at this late date. Chris said she would go it alone for the time being, unless the going got too tough on her.

* * *

Almost immediately, the going got much tougher on Chris from all quarters—and then tougher still. All at a time when she no longer had Mike Hern to consult with and lean on when the pressure started to get to her. However, she knew if she quit, any replacement detective would be hopelessly lost for months, and they could unknowingly miss the only chance to catch the killer if it occurred before they were finally up to speed on the case. If the case were to be solved, it would depend on her being there to recognize that fleeting opportunity when it appeared. Whereas the full responsibility for any failure, she continued to torture herself, would also rest solely on her.

Whenever the case really started to get to her, Chris would think of the dead girls and their families, and the live ones who still depended on her, and she would try to draw determination from their faces. However, more often than not, she suffered further depression and more frustration at those images; beating herself up inside for being no closer to catching the killer than she was a year ago. She felt she was letting everyone down—that each new death was blood on her hands.

Her most promising lead yet—the retired law-enforcement officer who bragged of the Zamora murder before it happened—also quickly came crashing to a dead end; another wild-goose chase. When the informant balked at wearing a wire for a follow-up talk with his drinking buddy, Chris shoved subtlety aside and approached the subject directly. Fortunately, the retired lawman was very cooperative and understanding. He agreed to Chris's request for a sexual-assault kit to be performed on him to obtain samples for comparison to the serial killer's samples, and he agreed to take a polygraph. Chris personally selected the polygraph expert to be sure the results were accurate. Analysis of the tests eliminated the subject as a suspect. Apparently, the informant had been so drunk himself that he either incorrectly heard or remembered his buddy's statements. The buddy had simply said that, based on his law-enforcement experience, he was surprised the killer hadn't been dumping bodies on the sidestreets off Highway 60, since they were exactly the type of site the killer seemed to prefer.

That left Chris back at square one, again feeling hopelessly frustrated with the case, and all alone. Just when she felt things couldn't get worse, it suddenly got a lot lonelier. One of the last people she had come to rely on for friendship and emotional refortification also left her.

This one, however, didn't leave of her own accord, and her loss, when it came, was devastating. It seemed to Chris a message directed specifically at her, as if the guy knew exactly who Chris was, and where she lived, and how to hurt her most.

The serial killer had gotten Eleanor Casares.

# Chapter Seven

Eleanor Casares

*December 23, 1991*

On Monday at about 1:20 P.M., Chris received a telephone call at her residence from the RPD requesting her to respond to the orange groves off Victoria Avenue, just west of Jefferson Street. A grove worker had found a murdered female and, because it seemed a possible prostitute killing, Chris had been assigned as the case agent for the homicide.

The site was just down the street from her house, and Chris rushed out so she could arrive while everything was fresh.

When she reached the scene, just ten minutes later, a news helicopter was already circling overhead. Officer Rich Bradley, the first law-enforcement officer to arrive, quickly briefed Chris on the circumstances known at the time.

An orange-grove worker had been driving a pickup truck on a dirt service road bordering the groves when he noticed something out of the corner of his left eye. The object seemed curious enough that he stopped the truck and backed it up, row by row, until he was alongside it. Located just ten feet from the dirt road, spread-eagled in the middle of row four, a nude female lay on her back with a black coat draped over her face and her right breast missing. Upon determining it was indeed a dead human, the worker immediately backed the pickup truck all the way to the intersection with Victoria Avenue. There, he radioed the news to his company and asked for somebody to call the police.

Officer Bradley arrived almost immediately and was briefed by the worker, who then escorted him in on foot along the extreme edge of the road to avoid disrupting any footprints or tire tracks. Once Bradley had visually confirmed the find, he radioed for investigators to respond to the scene.

Chris had Bradley lead her to the crime scene. They entered the grove one row over from the victim to avoid disturbing any evidence around the body. There seemed to be plenty: lots of shoeprints all around the body and visible tire tracks in the road directly in front of it. The body was a female Hispanic, and her uppermost skin appeared slightly lighter in color than the lower part. There was a stab wound visible in the center of her chest, directly over the heart, and a tattoo of a flower on her upper right thigh. As with Cheryl Coker and Catherine McDonald, the right breast had been roughly sliced off.

Confirming the probability that it was another victim of the serial killer, Chris backed out of the area with the officer and radioed for the task force and DOJ crime-lab criminalist Secofsky to respond to the scene. She had the grove worker's shoe soles and tire tracks photographed, and then sent him on his way.

As she waited for Secofsky to arrive and process the scene, Chris wondered at the killer's choice of a body-dump site this time: only blocks from her home. She wondered if the clever bastard had somehow discovered the identity and residence of the local cop in charge of his case and was now playing another taunting game with the authorities: I can operate virtually on your own doorstep and you are powerless to stop me.

No, Chris told herself, that is just being paranoid. Smart as he was, the serial killer just couldn't be *that* smart.

Steve Secofsky did not arrive until 3:15 P.M. Chris had had two hours to agonize over yet one more death she had been unable to prevent. It seemed to her she was no closer to catching the killer than she ever was. Now she had one more family to notify, one more group of eyes to cry and beg her for justice. And they would not be alone: overhead, the press chopper hovered like an angry hornet; a noisy reminder that the media's critical eyes were also on her—also wondering just what the hell the task force was accomplishing on this case.

Chris ran over possibilities in her mind while she waited for Secofsky. A perimeter search had already found the severed breast, two rows over from the body without any footprints nearby, as though the killer had hurled it over the top of a tree in the row beside the body. As the DOJ profiler said, the killer had one helluva rage toward women.

Chris came up short on the possible identity of the victim. Although light-skinned, the body appeared that of a female Hispanic, but it was overweight and puffy, and Chris knew no one like that. The flower tattoo was no help at all. Chris didn't have the slightest idea who this victim might be; the body did not resemble anyone she knew from University Avenue. She would have to wait for Secofsky to arrive and give the okay before they could remove the black coat and check the face.

Once Secofsky arrived and was briefed on what they knew, Chris and the task-force lieutenant led the criminalist to the body. They walked down a yellow-taped path marked off for access to the crime scene.

Secofsky took tape lifts of the body for trace evidence and attempted fingerprint lifts while a technician photographed the numerous footprints in the soft soil around the victim. Finally, Secofsky announced he was finished with the necessary lifts and that it was safe to remove the jacket from the victim's face.

A contorted purple face, bloodied from the fists of her killer, suddenly stared up at Chris. It was Eleanor Casares.

Chris stepped back at the sight, staggered by a rush of feelings that seemed to leap up into her from the bloating corpse. Eleanor had never seemed fat to her—how could this be her? She felt herself slipping into a state of shock, her emotional braces totally unprepared for this kind of surprise. Her private and professional worlds felt as though they were crashing down around her.

Chris knew she had to hold on, with so many macho cops around, and the media helicopter photographing everything from above. She had to be strong, for herself, for the department. For Eleanor.

Then the paranoia swept through her again, the sinister voice of an unseen face taunting even her waking hours. *Could* the bastard know that Eleanor was her friend? *Was* he giving her a message: I can operate virtually on your own doorstep, *within your own circle of friends,* and you are powerless to stop me.

The location of the dump site and the brutality of the attack seemed to say yes; Eleanor's beating seeming worse to Chris than that of all the others before her.

As quickly as the thoughts came, they went. She knew the killer was just doing his thing, and coincidence had simply played a hand in it. She knew the power of reason could control any illogical fear, just as it could solve this case if given the opportunity.

\* \* \*

At about seven o'clock that evening, Chris went to Eleanor's home and broke the news to her family. Some of Eleanor's relatives had drug or gang problems of their own, and none were fond or even trusting of the police. When Chris informed them of Eleanor's murder, one of Eleanor's brothers angrily vowed to hit the streets and personally hunt down the murderer and kill him on the spot. Although aware of the family's violent history, Chris coolly stepped up to the man and stared him in the eye. "Just give me two weeks," she told him. "I give you my word that if you just give me two weeks, I'll catch the guy."

It was an outrageous thing for a cop to do. No cop ever promised to solve a crime because no one ever knew if any crime could be solved—least of all, within any arbitrary time frame. But Chris was so fired up over the murder that she refused to let herself believe she couldn't solve it, through determination alone if need be.

Her determination was persuasive. The brother backed down. He agreed to give the lady cop her two weeks to solve the case.

Eleanor's family provided Chris with the details of her last hours and the clothing Eleanor was wearing when she last left the house: blue jeans, white L.A. Gear tennis shoes, black sweater, and black jacket. She also carried a black wallet containing her California identification card and one of Chris's flowered business cards.

Eleanor's sister, Adela, reported she had spoken with Eleanor on the phone that morning between 11 and 11:30; Eleanor had called to borrow ten dollars. Eleanor had said she didn't want to go out and work the streets then, but would do so around 7 P.M. and would return the money at that time. Adela told Eleanor she could borrow the money but that she was unable to deliver it to her. Eleanor said she would get a ride to her sister's house to pick it up. She never showed up. Her body was found at 1:20 P.M. by the grove worker.

This meant the police had gotten to the body within two hours of the murder. Therefore, its evidence should be fresher and more complete than at any other scene to date. The serial killer's rising bravado, by choosing a day-time strike, had enabled the authorities to get to the scene probably within minutes of his departure. If he kept up such foolish behavior, it would be only a matter of time before he was caught in the act.

Secofsky indicated he could virtually reconstruct the entire action at this murder scene from all of the fresh evidence left behind. That news gave Chris a feeling the nightmare was turning. She felt she was now looking over the killer's shoulder instead of the other way around.

The autopsy on Eleanor Casares determined cause of death to be manual strangulation and a stab wound to the heart. The pathologist couldn't tell from the wounds whether the killer was right- or left-handed. The body had sustained much blunt-force trauma: abrasions to the mouth, face, neck, and wrists, and contusions on the shoulder, chest, and hip. The pathologist indicated many of these were defensive wounds, which prompted Chris to comment, "So our girls fought."

The local telephone company was contacted to see if it could discover from where Eleanor Casares had made her last phone call to her sister. The phone company said it would need a search warrant before it could attempt the trace, so the task force immediately set to work obtaining one.

Other investigators organized a roadblock in the area of the orange groves to solicit information from motorists who may have observed any unusual activity on the day of the murder. One elderly couple recalled seeing a Hispanic man standing on a rise by the grove as they drove by. They reported the man's stiff-body stance seemed unusual, which, coupled with his failure to look up when they passed by, now convinced them a guilty conscience was responsible for his peculiar behavior. They were certain he must be the serial killer. The officers noted their report but, aware that many people visited the groves to steal oranges and firewood, they saw a simpler explanation for the nervousness in the man's behavior; especially knowing that the DOJ had concluded the serial killer was a brown-haired white male.

Other task-force investigators conducted a follow-up look at the crime scene, and discovered a task-force ID card near the location of the tossed breast. One of the team must have dropped it by accident the day before, during the initial crime-scene investigation. The discovery incited a scolding memo from the task-force administration about carelessness.

About that time, the Air Force finally responded to the task force's request for a check of reconnaissance photos in the area of the killer's previous open-air homicide, Delliah Zamora. It reported negative results on the coordinates submitted.

Some good news was received, however. The task-force member who had succeeded in identifying the shoeprints left at the McDonald crime scene, now reported he had identified the tire tracks from that scene as Yokohama brand tires, series Y371. His work on the "shoeology and tireology" brought the task force one step closer to filling in the puzzle on the serial killer.

The WeTip reward program received an added boost. Although six thousand dollars had been offered for information leading to the arrest/conviction of the serial killer, heralded by one thousand large reward posters and a press release, there had been no increase in callers to the program. Following the helpful urging of the RSO, the City of Lake Elsinore and others contributed to the reward fund, boosting it to eleven thousand dollars, as an added incentive. The Sheriff's Office continued its efforts to boost the incentive even further, publicly soliciting contributions to the reward fund from various other agencies, including the RPD.

Chris continued following up leads on the Eleanor Casares murder. Eleanor's sister told Chris that Eleanor had on several occasions confided she had a feeling who the killer was. She said Eleanor told her she "was working on it." Chris doubted that such undercover work played a part in Eleanor's death. However, the thought that her friend may have been out on the street that fatal morning trying to help her solve the case disturbed Chris. It made Eleanor's death even sadder and more poignant.

As Christmas and then New Year's Day came and went, Chris thought about how the Casares family would celebrate those holidays in the future, knowing how strongly linked the season would be thereafter to Eleanor's murder. As the first week in January 1992 ended, Chris's requested two-week run with the case also drew to an end. Unless something happened to break the investigation wide open within the next twenty-four hours, she would have broken her promise to the Casares family and let them down a second time.

The next day, January 8, 1992, such thoughts were immediately pushed to the back of Chris's mind when she opened her morning newspaper. On the front page of the Metro section was an article about the serial murders that caused Chris to finally explode. Another highly provocative statement had been unwittingly made by the authorities—

a statement Chris was certain would provoke the killer to strike again.

And this time the mistake had come from her own department: from the police chief himself.

Since the Riverside County sheriff had publicly solicited the RPD's help with its serial-killer reward fund, the City of Riverside's chief of police chose to respond in kind, in a public city-council meeting. Chief Linford L. "Sonny" Richardson insisted Riverside should not add to the reward fund because such behavior would be a "desperate" sign that lessens the importance of other homicide investigations. In effect, the chief stated that there was nothing different or superior about the serial killer that merited taking any extraordinary action different from that taken with ordinary murderers.

Chris felt it was a direct slap in the face of the serial killer—a direct insult to his intelligence and criminal achievements. She was certain he would not let the slur go unpunished.

Chris immediately went to her lieutenant, Rick Albee, and alerted him to the grim situation. Placing complete faith in Chris's judgment, Albee went to Captain Cunradi, and the two of them in turn went to the chief. Albee found Chief Richardson sympathetic to the news.

"Whatever anybody says about Sonny Richardson that might be bad," Albee recalled afterward, "the overriding factor . . . was that he would always listen. If you came up with something where he might be wrong, he would change his mind. A lot of people aren't like that. . . . I think he held a lot of credence in Chris, in what she was doing. He knew what I thought of her, and what . . . Sergeant Ron Mackey thought of her. . . . And we had every confidence in our sergeants and detectives feeding us good information. So when she told me that, it was good information and I went to the chief with it. And he went with it."

Chief Richardson called an immediate meeting of the department's top brass, plus Sergeant Mackey and Chris. They listened to what Chris had to say about the case and the likelihood that the killer would strike again very soon because of the newspaper article. She told them the murder of Cherie Payseur had followed the article about the task force being in Wisconsin on a wild-goose chase, and the murder of the black prostitute, Catherine McDonald, had followed the article which stated the killer preferred white victims.

Chris was asked what she thought was going to happen next. She told them the killer would probably come out immediately to claim a new victim and prove the authorities' published statements were again wrong. He would be out cruising University Avenue for prostitute victims in his gray-blue van, wearing his metal-frame glasses, and would now be wearing Converse tennis shoes, according to the DOJ's analysis of the Eleanor Casares crime scene. She said they could catch him if they immediately blanketed the area with low-profile police units carrying her flier and composite drawing of the suspect.

The chief accepted her information and her plan. He ordered a special operation put into effect immediately, involving virtually every member of the Riverside Police Department. Dubbed "Operation Apprehension," the all-out dragnet would be advised by Chris Keers on where to go, what to look for, and what to do. It would run for at least four days and up to two weeks, if necessary.

Chris had only one other request of the "brainstorming session." She revealed the problems she experienced with the sheriff's task force becoming too disruptive during previous low-profile surveillances. She told how they had possibly blown earlier surveillances by making many direct contacts with the prostitutes and johns—right on the

street, where the killer could easily spot them if he were
cruising by at the time. The task-force members had persisted in such behavior despite her warnings that the surveillances had to be strictly "sit back and watch" situations,
and nothing more, if they were to succeed. She warned
that the new operation could be blown if this behavior
were to occur again.

She also was convinced the RSO task force was routinely
withholding information from her and was being uncooperative on the case. She saw no chance of success for the
operation if the Sheriff's Office or the task force was
involved in any way. She bluntly said that she was totally
convinced the only way the serial killer could be caught
was if the police department ran the operation on its own,
without any interference from the task force or the Sheriff's Office.

Too many people at the table were familiar with Chris's
homicide expertise to contest any of her advice. Lieutenant
Albee was ordered to call his counterpart on the RSO task
force and formally request that the Sheriff's Office keep
all of its people out of the city of Riverside while the RPD
ran "Operation Apprehension." To help smooth the
waters, the task force was promised that it would be fully
informed of any arrest or case that resulted from the RPD
operation, and would be invited to participate in any
follow-up investigation if a serial-killer suspect was identified or apprehended.

RSO task-force administrators devoted only a brief mention to the RPD effort in their daily log: "This program
[Operation Apprehension] is to augment the Task Force.
Any information, suspects or homicides of prostitutes will
still be turned over to the Task Force. Investigator Keers
. . . will be temporarily assigned back to RPD to coordinate
their programs."

With the Sheriff's Office barred from the city, Operation
Apprehension went into full swing. The "window of oppor-

tunity" Chris had waited for had finally arrived, and she was ready for it. She had the entire city police department on the streets watching for the gray van Kelly Whitecloud had described—waiting and watching on the one night she was certain the killer would come out to cruise for a victim.

Detectives working the operation communicated with each other either by cellular telephones or by switching to secured frequencies on radios reserved for covert operations; frequencies the public couldn't monitor with civilian scanners.

Any vehicles that were spotted picking up a hooker were followed until they were out of the area, and then were stopped away from the avenue, so the serial killer wouldn't be aware of the police action. The driver would be investigated to see if he resembled the details in the flier or the composite drawing. If he didn't, both parties were immediately released because, in the words of Chief Richardson, "We were not after prostitutes, we were not after johns, we were after a killer." However, the chief joked, officers did do their best to "destroy the mood" of those illegal dates before releasing both parties.

On the other side of town, a police helicopter patrolled the sky around-the-clock above likely body-dump sites, reporting anything suspicious to ground units.

Routine police business had to be maintained, and officers had to continue their routine duties. However, even those still on normal assignments were aware of the large operation underway, and were ready to assist if called upon. They realized that unless called upon, they served best by staying the hell out of the way of the operation experts.

At least, that was the way Officer Bill Barnes understood things. He would give the operation honchos a wide berth to do their thing, unless they said otherwise or fate stepped in to call the hand.

At approximately 11:15 P.M., January 8, 1992, fate stepped in.

Harry C's, a bar on University Avenue near Iowa Street, was running a special night for the young crowd that Wednesday, offering cheap drinks and giveaways from a popular rock radio station. Because the RPD had received numerous complaints in the past about fights and dangerous driving associated with the radio night at the club, patrol officers often gathered to observe the place from across the street. At about 11:15 P.M., Officer Bill Barnes was the only officer putting in such duty, parked in his black-and-white unit in the lot of the Farmhouse Motel across the street. Harry C's had seemed pretty quiet and law-abiding, so other officers had left to look for offenders elsewhere.

Barnes lingered to watch the nightclub, figuring things would get rowdy as the night wore on. He was a good cop and proud of it. He was also proud to have read in the morning newspaper that his chief had been gutsy enough to take a stand on a sensitive issue with the city council. Sonny Richardson, the paper reported, had made a bold statement to the council that the Riverside Police Department did not give money to reward funds to try to "buy" arrests. To Barnes, it seemed the chief was telling the world that the serial killings would be solved with good, hard, old-fashioned policing—not reward funds created out of desperation.

Officer Barnes was working regular patrol shift that night, assigned to the graveyard (10 P.M. to 8 A.M.) shift. He had parked so he would have a clear view of the bar's main entrance and parking lot.

About 11:15, he saw a gray Astro-type van drive by, head-

ing eastbound on University Avenue toward the downtown
area, with a white male behind the wheel. Something about
the vehicle clicked in his mind. He remembered a flier
that Detective Chris Keers had put out back in September,
a be-on-the-lookout type about the serial killer. He was
sure it had mentioned a gray Astro van.

Hey, that's close, he thought. Then he remembered that
Operation Apprehension was in full swing and that the
van was headed straight into the midst of the undercover
surveillance teams that were watching the avenue. He
decided he better not interfere in case the operation officers were already secretly watching or following the vehicle.
The last thing he wanted to do was screw up their surveillance and give the killer a chance to beat the case. He told
himself, The heck with it; I'll just let it go. He couldn't
imagine the vehicle driving into the heart of the dragnet
without getting spotted by all those operation boys; it fit
the flier too closely. And if it was the killer's van, it would
be easy to follow: the passenger side had a huge crater-
sized dent in it.

About two minutes later, the van again passed Barnes,
this time heading westbound. The sudden change in direction indicated a cruising behavior to the nine-year veteran
lawman. Upon the second sighting, the cop's instincts were
too strong to ignore. This is too good to pass up, Barnes
told himself. It's probably not [the serial killer], it's probably just some guy [who's] lost, but . . . I'm going to follow
it, maybe call one of the task-force guys, maybe stop it. At
that point, he was compelled to satisfy his professional
curiosity, regardless of the risk to the investigation.

As soon as he put the patrol car into gear, there was a
loud screeching of tires from across the street at Harry
C's. Barnes snapped his head back to the bar's parking lot
and saw a dark-colored sedan pull out onto University
Avenue right in front of him—barreling so fast it almost
ran down a couple of bar patrons on their way to their

car. The sedan then tore off down the street at a high rate
of speed.

Barnes hesitated, still wanting to check out that suspicious gray van. However, when the group of patrons started
waving at his patrol car and pointing after the fleeing
sedan, Barnes knew he had no choice. He had to pursue
the sedan.

He kicked on the lights and siren, and peeled out after
the drunken speeder, hoping to God he had made the
right choice.

Chris spent Wednesday night virtually without sleep,
hoping for a break in the case. When it didn't come, she
was exhausted; worn out from the stress and from too
many hours without sleep. By Thursday night, she knew
she had to rest. She went home for a fast nap, and prayed
nothing happened while she was gone. Everybody in the
operation knew to call or page her if they saw any vehicle
or subject that fit the description. She hoped they followed
that order, because she would never forgive herself if she
missed her opportunity at the killer for the lack of one
phone call. It was hard for her to rely on others, but she
knew she had to. There had to come a time when you just
had to trust in others' good judgment.

Frank Orta was a veteran motorcycle cop with the RPD
and a lifelong Riverside resident. A barrel-chested, pleasant-
faced man with a broad smile and direct manner, Orta
enjoyed his work and his life. He was in his element on a
motorcycle and being outdoors in the city, and loved both.
There was nothing he liked better than working motorcycle
patrol in Riverside, greeting the public and keeping the
streets safe for everyone's family. He didn't even mind
working the seedy eastside, where the prostitutes and dope

pushers now tarnished the image of University Avenue. He did his part to put those criminals away whenever they broke the law, and he did his part to save their lives, as well, whenever the serial-killer task force investigators would radio for someone to lend them a hand. He'd recently helped Detectives Keers and Hern by stopping a suspicious john for them to interrogate.

It didn't matter the duty; as long as it involved a motorcycle and the outdoors, Frank was happy. He loved being a cop and, like most cops, he loved helping others who enjoyed working hard for their slice of the American dream. He especially admired the homicide detectives, like Chris Keers and Mike Hern, who put in ungodly hours in dogged pursuit of their cases. He only wished he could do more to help them out.

At about 9:45 P.M. on Thursday, January 9, 1992, Orta had just left three RPD friends in the parking lot of the Redlands Federal Bank, across the street from Harry C's bar, and was circling back onto University Avenue after patrolling a park at Thirteenth and Park Streets. As he headed eastbound on University Avenue toward the intersection of Victoria Avenue, he saw a young Hispanic female walk up to a gray van parked in a dirt lot alongside a liquor store. The female approached the driver's window of the van to converse with the white male driver inside.

Orta had seen enough prostitution activity in his law-enforcement career to recognize what was going on. He had also seen the bulletin Chris Keers had circulated about the Riverside prostitute killer. It advised officers to be on the lookout for a gray van and a brown-haired white male with metal-frame glasses. There, across the street from Orta, was a white male with glasses sitting in a gray van talking to a female prostitute. Since the flier had come out, Orta and other officers had stopped and checked what seemed like hundreds of gray vans. He didn't know whether this one would be any different from the others.

He couldn't see the man's face clearly from across the
street, so he couldn't tell yet whether it resembled the
composite he had seen.

He decided to circle the block and "sit up on them,"
to watch and see if the driver picked up the girl or drove
away. However, as he drove past them on his motorcycle,
Orta saw the prostitute turn her head and notice him. She
immediately walked away from the van.

Realizing she had "burned" or spotted him, Orta
decided the van would be worth investigating further. He
drove on to the next light and did a U-turn to bring himself
into the lanes by the liquor store so he could drive up to
the van.

As he headed back, the motorcycle cop saw that the van
had already left the lot and was driving off ahead of him.
It was approaching Park Street, a lighted intersection. The
light was red, and as Orta closed the distance between
them, the driver of the van suddenly turned right onto
Park Street without stopping at the light, evidently in a
hurry to get away from the motorcycle cop. His haste,
however, had just given the patrol officer legal cause to
stop his vehicle.

Orta turned on his red lights and pulled the van over.
It stopped about a block away. The driver was a brown-
haired white male, heavyset, with stubble on his face and
metal-frame glasses that seemed to Orta a perfect match
for those in Detective Keers's flier. The man had a high,
soft voice and was very polite. Orta asked for his license
and registration. The name on the driver's license said
William Lester Suff.

The photo in the license seemed a very close match to
the composite drawing Orta had seen of the suspect. To
Orta, "it was almost like a portrait of the man." The
address on the front of the license listed the driver's city
of residence as Lake Elsinore, where Orta was aware many
prostitute victims had been dumped. That address had

been crossed out, indicating it was a previous residence. When Orta flipped the license over, he saw two other addresses listed: another previous address crossed out, in Rialto, and a current address, in Colton. Orta knew that prostitute victims had been dumped in both cities.

At that point, Orta began to feel butterflies in his stomach. The driver, Suff, was still fumbling around in his glove compartment as if searching for his registration. Watching him, Orta noticed a California Highway Patrol's "CHP" baseball cap on the center console inside. He recalled hearing some theories around the police station that the serial killer might be in law enforcement, or pretending to be. The butterflies intensified.

After a moment more of pretending to search for his registration, Suff turned back to Orta and said, "Well, I don't have my registration with me." Frank simply told him, "Okay." Having worked traffic for many years, he knew that when a driver told you he couldn't find his registration, you knew there was something wrong with it.

The patrolman walked back to his motorcycle and started to run Suff's driver's license and license plate. The information quickly came back: license suspended, and the registration tags on his license plate belonged to a different vehicle. With either offense—suspended license or false evidence of registration—Orta could legally order the vehicle to be towed away. He was determined to do just that, just to ensure that the homicide people got a good chance to look through it for evidence. He decided he would impound the vehicle and put a special flag or notice on it indicating it should be shipped directly to Detective Chris Keers so she could evaluate it and the driver. Orta decided to use the registration offense as the reason for the impounding, since that would require the driver to furnish proof of registration to get the vehicle back, and he knew that could not be accomplished in less than a day. This would give the homicide people at least one full day with the vehicle. He was also going to seize Suff's driver's license, since it was under suspension, so he could show Detective Keers how closely the photo on it matched the composite of the suspect.

A police car drove up with two Operation Apprehension corporals inside: Don Taulli and Duane Beckman. Normally, patrol officers did not radio when they made a traffic stop, unless something was wrong or very unusual, and Orta had radioed about this stop. Taulli and Beckman had decided to stop by and see if the motorcycle cop needed any help.

"Is everything all right?" Beckman asked through the open window of their car.

Upon learning they were working in the big undercover operation, Orta quietly told the two, "Why don't you take a look at this guy?" He then briefly explained the reasons for his request—the gray van, the prostitute contact, the close match to the composite sketch, the three addresses from victim-dump sites, the CHP hat.

When Orta told them he was going to impound the van, they asked, "Well, you have to search the vehicle to do that, right?" Orta told them yes, that it was protocol to inventory the contents of any vehicle being impounded. They offered to perform the inventory search while he finished his paperwork on the citation and the impounding.

The offer to search the van indicated neither officer was taking the stop seriously as a possible serial-killer contact. If they truly considered the driver a suspect, both men had enough experience to know better than to approach the vehicle and possibly contaminate any trace evidence. Also, Detective Chris Keers had issued a strict order to all task-force personnel that she was to be immediately contacted if any gray vans were stopped, and neither officer felt strongly enough about the stop at that point to call her.

Orta asked the two officers if they had a camera in their

car, so they could take photos of the driver and the vehicle for Detective Keers. Beckman said they did.

The patrolman returned to Suff and explained to him that his license had been suspended and his registration was false, and that he was going to impound the van. He asked if Suff would mind if they took some photos of him and his van. Suff said he didn't mind.

Orta had Suff come to the rear of the vehicle and stand for photos which Beckman quickly began to take. Orta started to return to his motorcycle to fill out all the paperwork. Before he could, though, Suff complained that he was cold and asked to be allowed to go retrieve his jacket from the van. Orta told him, "That's all right—I'll get it for you." Although he still wasn't sure if the harmless-looking guy was the killer or not, the patrolman wasn't about to take any chances. He walked back to the van and felt through all the pockets of Suff's jacket, just to make sure there was no weapon inside. He brought the brown coat back and gave it to the cold driver to put on. He then straddled his motorcycle again and went on with his paperwork.

At the van, Corporal Taulli started searching the driver's side of the vehicle. He saw pieces of natural-fiber rope in different locations in the van, which made him curious. On the floor behind the driver's seat, he found a thick black schedule book, which made him more curious— recalling that the flier listed a black Bible in the suspect's van. The schedule book was a dead ringer for a Bible.

Looking under the driver's seat, Taulli spotted a kitchen knife tucked neatly inside the metal track of the driver's seat, positioned so that a dropped hand would naturally fall on the handle. Retrieving the knife, he saw what appeared to be blood on the blade. He quickly tossed that item on the seat, not as concerned with it as he was with the hefty item he saw next to it under the seat: a large

revolver in a holster that appeared to be a Colt Python
.357 magnum.

From his vantage point on the motorcycle, Orta could
see Taulli and the driver's side of the parked van, plus
Beckman and Suff standing off to the right rear corner of
the vehicle, at the curb. There was no way Beckman and
Suff could see Taulli on the other side of the van.

Upon finding the gun, Taulli suddenly jerked upright
and stepped back from the doorway, holding the discovered weapon up at chest height. As soon as Orta saw Taulli
rise with the big magnum in his hand, a jolt of electricity
hit him like a slap. All the biker cop could think of was,
"Man, he wanted to walk back to that van for that!" Orta
was shocked—wondering if the harmless-looking driver
had intended to take on all three cops in a shoot-out.

"Put the handcuffs on him!" Taulli angrily barked from
the driver's doorway. Startled, Beckman began to comply,
wondering what the hell was going on as he did so. Taulli
started striding down the length of the van, heading for
Beckman and Suff. "You know what this is about, don't
you?" he roughly demanded on the way.

Beckman watched Suff's head dip, nodding in dismay—
and then saw his knees suddenly buckle as the shock of
the arrest overwhelmed him. Beckman had to catch the
suspect by the shoulders to keep him from collapsing.

Taulli rounded the corner and held up the revolver for
them to see: "What do you call this?"

Suff's face lit up into a big, relieved smile. "Oh, that's
not real!" he said. "That's just a pellet gun!"

Checking it out, the officers realized he was telling the
truth. But Beckman wondered why the hell Suff had nearly
collapsed at Taulli's statement, when he couldn't see Taulli
or the pellet gun. *Something* had nearly given Suff a heart
attack when Taulli had said, "You know what this is about!"

Beckman went back to the van to help Taulli in the

inventory search, to see what else might be inside that vehicle to cause concern to Mr. Suff. He had to use the front passenger door to look inside because the sliding passenger door was caved in by a large crater-sized dent from an accident and couldn't be easily opened. He soon found a parole identification card in Suff's name, and returned to ask Suff about it. Suff shrugged it off, saying he was "on parole out of Texas, for ten years, for simple assault—for putting a guy in the hospital for three weeks for fucking my then-wife."

The parole card only added to the peculiarities with this traffic stop. Even so—even with all of their suspicions, the three cops knew this could still be a wild-goose chase. They resisted jumping to conclusions and incurring ridicule later on.

However, when Taulli looked again into the van, he saw something that startled him as much as before. There, starting on the driver's inside wall and arcing up across the ceiling, was a dry, red splattered line, like a sudden squirt of blood would make.

He walked back to Orta on the motorcycle, a weird look on his face. "Frank, there's *blood* all over the walls of the van!" he told Orta.

Aware of Taulli's reputation as a jokester, Orta told him, "Come on—bullshit!"

Taulli said, "No—really! I'm serious."

Orta walked back to take a look for himself. What he saw *did* look like blood splots. But then again, he had seen stranger things before and knew better than to jump to conclusions and look foolish in front of his friends; aware of the ribbing he would get over any act of seeming stupidity or hysterics. Then again . . . He looked at Taulli and felt his stomach churning. "I think we better stop what we're doing and get somebody here," Orta said.

\* \* \*

Sergeant Steve "Skip" Blythe responded to the radio request for a supervisor. The three uniformed cops briefed Blythe: Some curious items had been found in the van, both they and the driver had been photographed; the van was going to be impounded for homicide's evaluation; and the driver was going to be ticketed and released. Blythe decided to play it safe and record the stop in more detail. He put out a radio request for a unit with a 35-mm camera to respond to the scene to take better quality photos.

Hearing the call and having one of the desired cameras, Officer Bill Barnes responded to the traffic stop. Barnes took one look at the gray van with the dented side and told Sergeant Blythe he had seen the same vehicle cruising University Avenue just last night by Harry C's, but had been unable to pursue it due to a reckless speeder.

Unsure of exactly what they had, Sergeant Blythe decided he better get an expert decision on the matter before they released the driver. The decision was made to contact Chris Keers and see what she wanted to do about the traffic stop. Blythe used a cellular phone to call Chris at home. Chris asked him what model of tire was in the driver's-side front position. Blythe ordered Taulli to bend down and identify the tire. "It's a Yokohama," he called back.

"Freeze the scene," Chris commanded. "I'm on my way."

The news spread rapidly over the radio and curious police officers began flocking to the scene.

"Gee, this sure is a lot of cops for a traffic stop," Suff commented.

Upon her arrival, Chris was briefed on the situation. The gray 1989 Mitsubishi van was a model that closely resembled the Astro Van Kelly Whitecloud had picked out as closest to the vehicle the suspect had been driving when he picked up Kelly Hammond. Chris took a fast look at the tires on the vehicle, checking for herself which brands were present and at which locations.

She looked inside the van without touching anything. She noted the "blood" splatter that had prompted the phone call to her. All too familiar with homicide scenes and real blood, Chris realized the long splash of red wasn't blood; the color too bright and too red to be real blood. She guessed it to be ketchup or taco sauce or some similar condiment. However, she was happy that mistake had prompted the officers to contact her. There was no doubt in her mind that this vehicle belonged to the serial killer. There were three different brands of tires on this van—the exact same brands, and in the exact same locations on the vehicle, as DOJ had already determined existed on the serial killer's vehicle, based on tire tracks left at the Casares and McDonald murder scenes.

Inside the van, Chris spotted other possible items of evidence consistent with the fiber trace evidence DOJ had identified from the murder scenes. Chris Keers had met more frequently with DOJ crime-lab criminalist Steve Secofsky than had any other investigator on the case. Secofsky had never seen a homicide investigator become so deeply involved in the crime-lab aspect of a case. He felt Chris was more familiar with the trace evidence on the serial murders than anyone outside of the DOJ crime lab itself.

Secofsky had informed Chris that gray, red, white, blue, gold and green fibers had been found on some of the prostitute victims, and that natural rope fibers had been found on some of the victims' wrists and ankles. Inside the van, Chris saw gray carpeting and upholstery; a blue and red nylon sleeping bag with white stuffing poking out; a gold pillow; a multicolored afghan; a green blanket; and assorted pieces of natural-fiber rope scattered here and there. All of the fibers were visually consistent with the DOJ trace evidence left by the killer.

Also in the clutter of the van's interior were a plastic container of Vaseline lotion; a pair of crutches; bottles of prescription drugs; a package of yellow Avon gloves; a washcloth with stains; a black organizer book that resembled a Bible (as Kelly Whitecloud reported observing in the suspect's van); a CHP hat; some Brylcreem hair dressing; a matchbook from a Colton motel; a stuffed brown Garfield doll stuck by all four feet to the rear window; and a variety of large plastic drinking bottles with straws. Chris knew that many street prostitutes carried those bottles when they worked the streets; heroin addiction causing an almost constant thirst. Vice detectives generally considered the bottles to be one of the telltale signs that the woman carrying it was a working prostitute.

Chris ordered a flatbed truck to transfer the van to police storage, so that none of the dirt or other evidence embedded in the tires would be lost during transport. Then she called Steve Secofsky and Lieutenant Rick Albee with the news, and asked the criminalist to respond to the police storage right away to check out the van. Secofsky knew Chris well enough by then to tell from her voice something major was up.

Unfortunately, the supervising deputy district attorney, Paul Zellerbach, wasn't as easily persuaded. He refused to respond to the scene when Chris called him on the cellular phone.

"I think it's the guy!" Chris told Zellerbach, stressing the urgency for his presence.

"Well, has he confessed?" Zellerbach countered.

"No," Chris said. "But we have *so many* things that are consistent." She rattled them off for the sleepy DA.

Unimpressed, and too used to wild-goose chases by now, Zellerbach quickly dismissed her. "Well, just talk to him and see what he says," he told Chris, then hung up.

Chris looked at a few more items of evidence that were consistent with what was known about the serial killer, and then called Zellerbach back and told him in stronger terms that he should respond to the police station and be available during the questioning of the suspect. Again, Zellerbach told her to proceed without him. He told her to call him if she obtained a confession.

Chris phoned the RSO lieutenant in charge of the task force and notified him of the development. He was instantly interested in every detail, readily recognizing the significance of what Chris was reporting. "Where's Zellerbach?" he demanded.

When Chris reported that the sleepy DA didn't want to roll out of bed on another wild-goose chase, the task-force boss said he would personally tell Zellerbach to "get his ass" down to the police station and assist in the investigation. The lieutenant would also notify the entire task force and send investigators to meet Chris at the police station to assist her in the interrogation of the suspect.

Chris approached the increasingly nervous driver and identified herself to him. Looking down at his feet, she noticed he was wearing a pair of Converse tennis shoes.

"Mr. Suff, I'm Detective Keers," she told him. "I'm a homicide detective and I would like to ask you some questions down at the police station."

Operation Apprehension, in effect less than twenty-four hours, had resulted in the capture of the serial killer. The apprehension occurred almost exactly two weeks after Chris Keers promised the Casares family she would catch Eleanor's killer. In response, the struggling family sent Chris a dozen expensive peach roses and a large thank-you card. The gesture meant more to Chris than any accolades or awards could have.

Riverside County warehouse clerk William Lester Suff,

forty-one, was not charged with any murders until five days later. The delay was designed to minimize publicity over the arrest, and not offend or slight the Sheriff's Office or its task force for their lack of involvement in solving the case. Suff was initially charged only with the murders of Eleanor Casares and Catherine McDonald, although he was suspected in the deaths of as many as nineteen victims. Other charges were gradually added as time passed and additional evidence was evaluated. The list ultimately grew to an indictment for thirteen murders and one attempted murder. The latter charge was added when a sheriff's investigator remembered a January 1989 telephone interview with Rhonda Jetmore, who told of surviving an attack in a deserted Lake Elsinore house. Rhonda reported her assailant wore metal-frame glasses and a belt buckle that read "Bill." He had tried to strangle her after handing her a dollar for sex. Rhonda had provided a detailed description of Bill Suff at the time, but her report was simply filed away and forgotten until Suff's January 1992 arrest by the RPD.

Subsequently, Chris Keers repeatedly applied for the eleven-thousand-dollar reward money on behalf of Kelly Whitecloud, the eyewitness who had provided the information for the flier and composite drawing that directly led to Suff's arrest. The RSO task-force administration flatly denied each request. The explanation offered was that only Officer Frank Orta was responsible for the arrest and that peace officers are not eligible for rewards. It was also claimed that Kelly Whitecloud was ineligible because she had phoned Chris Keers with her information instead of calling the actual WeTip hotline number listed on the reward poster. Whatever the excuse, the message was the same: the Sheriff's Office was not about to reward anyone connected with the city police department's arrest of the Riverside prostitute killer.

# Part II:
# The Killer

# Chapter Eight

William Lester Suff was born on August 20, 1950, in Torrance, California, the oldest of five children: four boys and a girl. His parents were married November 26, 1949, in Virginia, and moved to California prior to their first child's birth. Suff's father worked in aerospace but dreamed of being a professional drummer; his mother was a strict, uncompromising housewife. From Torrance, the Suffs traveled to Fresno, where more children were born, and marital problems between the parents came to a head.

In August 1960, Bill Suff's father filed a complaint for divorce against his wife in Fresno County Superior Court. At the time, Suff was ten; his siblings, eight, four, three, and two. In the father's complaint, he accused Suff's mother of "mental cruelty" and "associating with men other than her husband, and not related to her, at the home where the minor children were presently residing." He demanded full custody of the children. Suff's mother denied all claims of infidelity, claiming instead, "It was him that was running around."

The divorce action never proceeded past the original complaint; the two reconciled after a short separation. Almost immediately, the family moved to Riverside County, where they finally put down roots.

The Suff family spent most of their years in the hot, deserty "inland empire" area of Southern California, southeast of the City of Riverside, around the small, sweltering communities of Perris and Lake Elsinore.

Although populated by successful middle-class families, the area also seemed a mecca for the down-and-out; for those in society who had fallen by the wayside financially, morally or functionally. It was a place of minimum expenses and expectations, where families and individuals on subsistence incomes could survive.

It was also a region that attracted a high number of outlaw biker gangs and people deeply involved in illicit drugs and sex of the most inexpensive varieties. It was an area that even one of Suff's strongest defenders described as heavily populated by "piss-poor protoplasm" type of folks, comparable in that person's eyes to a neighboring district where, the local joke went, "not only would they kill [you], they'd eat [you, too]."

The Suff family often teetered between the two sides of the community: the respected, hardworking, churchgoing, family-oriented side, and the scandalous, impoverished, luckless, ne'er-do-well side. Although they appeared to make serious efforts at fitting in with the more positive elements of their community, the Suff's accrued more detractors than supporters. Some of the strongest detractors came from within the family itself. They hurled a spectrum of accusations against one another that helps to explain the cold, often antagonistic nature of the family members toward each other.

The move to Riverside solved none of the problems. Suff's father couldn't put aside his dream of being a drummer. Although he had enjoyed a lucrative job with excellent benefits when they lived in the coastal counties, Suff's father changed careers in Riverside. He became a drummer in small country-western bands, working the smoky little bars of the inland communities. Some said he was abrogating his paternal obligations by switching to such a low-paying job; others said his oppressive wife drove him into his own little world. His newfound happiness, unfortunately, came at a big price for the family. The sudden financial drop in the family's income put a strain on everyone.

The boys usually had to share a bedroom, and the good times with the family seemed increasingly a thing of the past. In Fresno, their mother had been a Cub Scout den mother and their father a Boy Scout troop leader. Suff had earned enough merit badges to cover a sash. He'd also, at his father's inspiration, taken up the trombone and trumpet, which he continued playing after the move as a member of the Lake Elsinore High School band. But things were different in Riverside County. The simmering rancor in the marriage was greatly compounded by the financial strain.

The kids tried to ignore the problems by taking advantage of the new recreational facilities the move provided. When they first came to Lake Elsinore, they played on the sand dunes in the middle of the lake before it was filled with water. Later, when they moved again within the area, they had the Cleveland National Forest for their backyard. One brother remembered Suff leading them all up to a spring in the hill, to a huge rock face they called "soap rock." They would slide down the slick face until they had holes in their pants. Although their mother was quick to criticize, she offered only a scolding for their misdeed. Unfortunately, she offered little affection, as well.

Suff's father finally decided he had had enough of the marriage soon after the family opened a small café near Lake Elsinore as a way of supplementing their income.

One morning at the café in 1967, he told his wife he "was going home to change his clothes [and] that he would be back at three-thirty." He never returned. He simply went home, gathered together his belongings, and left without any message; returning to Flint, Michigan, to stay with his aging parents. Some damned him for it; others expressed amazement he hadn't fled the cold, dysfunctional family years earlier. Suff was sixteen at the time.

"She was involved with another guy, and that's why I left her," Suff's father explained the desertion, years later, from his Michigan mobile home. He eventually remarried, had two girls, divorced, and married again by the time of Suff's arrest for the serial murders.

Suff's mother sued for divorce in Riverside County, and was granted the divorce in February 1968. Her husband's desertion left her with few options. She went on welfare to care for herself and her five kids.

Suff helped to fill the role of parental figure for his younger siblings, following at times in the strict, critical pattern his mother presented. It proved less than successful, earning him no special bonds to his siblings. He was not especially astute at meeting the demands of school, either. Although he performed well in band, Suff's high-school grades were mostly Cs, Ds, and Fs. He did poorly in English and government, and graduated eighty-seventh in a class of 144. His former vice principal remembered him as only a "marginal" student. "The other kids just ignored him," the man remembered. "He was a loner . . . different from the other kids. I don't think he ever had a girlfriend. I don't think he was ever interested in girls." He was, the man admitted, "likable" but "pathetic."

There was no history of violence or misbehavior on Suff's part in high school. Nor was he totally withdrawn. He involved himself in the school band and chess club, and frequently attended the Temple Baptist Church in Perris. His hobbies were painting and music.

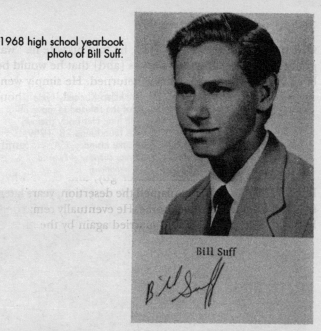

1968 high school yearbook photo of Bill Suff.

Bill Suff

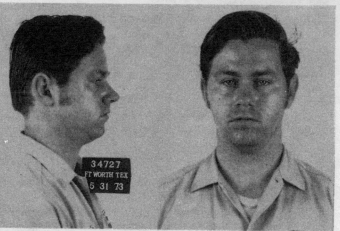

Mug shot of William Lester Suff taken after his arrest for the murder of his baby daughter Dijanet.
(Photo courtesy of Fort Worth, TX, Police Department)

Suff killed Kimberly Lyttle after she refused to move in with him. Her body (below) was found June 28, 1989, in Lake Elsinore, CA. (*Photos courtesy of Riverside Investigations*)

On December 13, 1989, Tina Leal, Suff's youngest victim, was found in Quail Valley, CA. She was dressed in men's clothing with her arms tucked inside a sleeveless shirt. (*Photo courtesy of Riverside Investigations*)

Darla Ferguson was found on January 18, 1990, in Sun City, CA (below). Months earlier, she had met Suff while he was babysitting her neighbor's children. (*Photos courtesy of Riverside Investigations*)

A half-eaten grapefruit was left in the Highgrove, CA, orchard beside Carol Miller's body on February 8, 1990. (*Photo courtesy of Riverside Investigations*)

Footprints in the sand near where Cheryl Coker was found murdered on November 6, 1990, in Riverside, CA, helped tie the crime to Bill Suff. *(Photos courtesy of Riverside Investigations)*

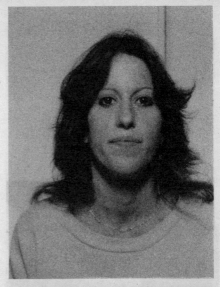

Susan Sternfeld's body was found in a dumpster on December 19, 1990, in Riverside, CA. (*Photo courtesy of Riverside Investigations*)

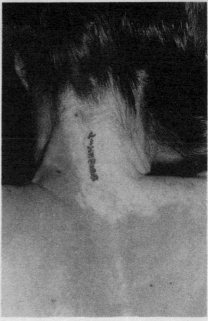

The Chinese tattoo on Susan Sternfeld's neck helped identify her body. (*Photo courtesy of Riverside Investigations*)

Kathleen (Milne) Puckett was found on January 19, 1991, in Lake Elsinore, CA. A tire track near her body helped tie her murder to Bill Suff. (*Photos courtesy of Riverside Investigations*)

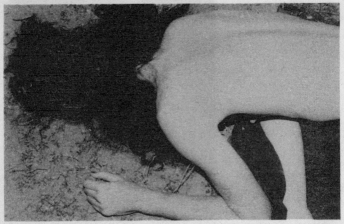

Cherie Payseur was found on April 26, 1991, in Riverside, CA. A bystander draped his coat over her body to protect it from the stares of a crowd of onlookers. (*Photos courtesy of Riverside Investigations*)

A hair recovered from the body bag of victim Cherie Payseur matched those of Bill Suff's cat Callie. (*Photo courtesy of Riverside Investigations*)

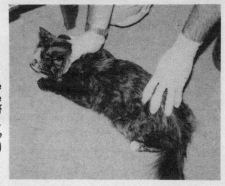

Sherry Latham was found on July 4, 1991, in Lake Elsinor, CA. Her boyfriend was able to provide police with information about the vehicle her suspected killer drove. (*Photos courtesy of Riverside Investigations*)

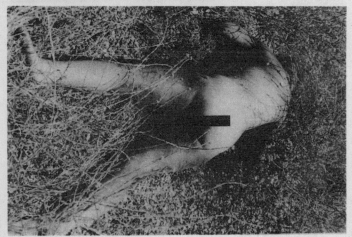

On August 16, 1991, Kelly Hammond's body was found in Corona, CA, carefully posed to display the needle marks on her inner arm. (*Photos courtesy of Riverside Investigations*)

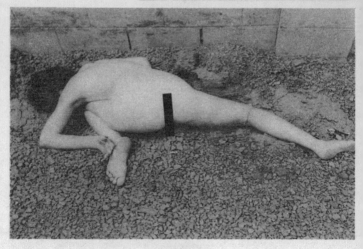

Catherine McDonald was found on September 13, 1991, in Lake Elsinore. She was killed after a newspaper article reported the serial killer primarily murdered white prostitutes. (*Photo courtesy of Riverside Investigations*)

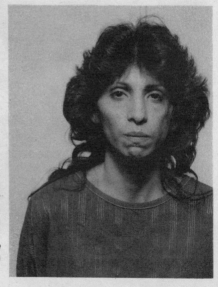

Delliah (Wallace) Zamora was found on October 30, 1991, in Glen Avon, CA. Investigators felt she had been left fully clothed only because the killer chose a location too close to a commuter parking lot. (*Photo courtesy of Riverside Investigations*)

Suff's last victim, Christine Keers's friend Eleanor Casares, was found in an orange grove, a black coat draped over her face, on December 23, 1991, in Riverside, CA. (*Photos courtesy of Riverside Investigations*)

# RIVERSIDE COUNTY
# SERIAL MURDERS . . .
# Our Nation's Nightmare!

Killing without provocation...Destroying a string of human lives!

> The **Missing Link** to a specific case, is often that anonymous call that provides an extra clue, leading to the solution of the puzzle, the arrest of the suspect and the conviction of a murderer

## YOUR HELP IS NEEDED!

IF YOU HAVE INFORMATION ABOUT
ANY MAJOR CRIME, CALL

# WeTIP.
## (800)78-CRIME
**TOLL FREE - NATIONWIDE - 24 HOURS A DAY**

### REWARD
UP TO $11,000

IF YOU HAVE **ANY** KNOWLEDGE OF SOMEONE WHO HAS COMMITTED A MAJOR CRIME, CALL THE WE TIP NATIONAL TOLL FREE HOTLINE. **NOBODY** WILL KNOW WHO YOU ARE...NOT US...NOT EVER!

We Tip, Inc., P.O. Box 1296
Rancho Cucamonga, CA 91729-1296
Business Office (714)987-5005
Fax (714)987-2477

SERIAL MURDER

Poster from WeTip reward program. (*Photo courtesy of Riverside Investigations*)

Bill Suff at the Riverside police headquarters following his routine traffic arrest on January 9, 1992. (*Photo courtesy of Riverside Investigations*)

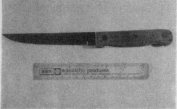

Kitchen knife found inside Suff's gray van. (*Photo courtesy of Riverside Investigations*)

Suff's athletic shoes, whose sole pattern matched footprints left at several homicide scenes. (*Photo courtesy of Riverside Investigations*)

Kelly Whitecloud's eyewitness report to Chris Keers resulted in the capture of serial killer Bill Suff. (*Photo courtesy of Riverside Investigations*)

Suff in court while being tried for murdering thirteen women. (*Photo courtesy of The Californian, Temecula, CA*)

Bill Suff's ex-girlfriend Bonnie testifying at his serial murder trial. (*Photo courtesy of* The Californian, *Temecula, CA*)

Bill Suff's mother during a break in her testimony at his trial. (*Photo courtesy of* The Californian, *Temecula, CA*)

Former Riverside Police Department Detective Christine Keers.

Richard L. Albee, Lieutenant (ret.),
Riverside Police Dept.
(*Photo courtesy of Dennis St. Pierre*)

Frank Orta, Officer,
Riverside Police Dept.
(*Photo courtesy of Dennis St. Pierre*)

Don Taulli, Sergeant,
Riverside Police Dept.
(*Photo courtesy of Dennis St. Pierre*)

Duane Beckman, Detective,
Riverside Police Dept.
(*Photo courtesy of Dennis St. Pierre*)

Riverside County Superior Court Judge W. Charles Morgan. (*Photo courtesy of* The Californian, *Temecula, CA*)

Prosecutor Paul E. Zellerbach. (*Photo courtesy of* The Californian, *Temecula, CA*)

Randolph K. Driggs, one of the two attorneys who represented Bill Suff at his serial murder trial. (*Photo courtesy of* The Californian, *Temecula, CA*)

Attorney Frank S. Peasley, arguing in court on Bill Suff's behalf during his trial. (*Photo courtesy of* The Californian, *Temecula, CA*)

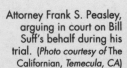

Suff's small stature may have played a role in his meekness in high school. He seemed to grow more aggressive as he grew in size. He weighed a beefy 210 pounds when arrested.

Suff's childhood (as with most of his noncriminal adult life) was not noteworthy, to the point of being virtually unnoticed by most of the people he came in contact with. Many have only vague memories of him, if any at all. A typical reaction was that of Darrell Santschi, a senior editor at the *Riverside Press Enterprise* newspaper.

Following Suff's arrest for the serial murders, the paper was scrambling for any photo of the notorious killer, but surprisingly could find none. Even Suff's nearby high school had no yearbooks available. However, when Darrell Santschi overheard the reporters mention the name of the school and the graduation year, he realized they were discussing his own graduation yearbook: Perris High School, 1968. "Holy shit, I think I have a yearbook at home with this guy in it!" he told them. He did, but he admitted to the reporters that he had no recollections whatsoever of Bill Suff to give them.

Underscoring the nondescript manner of the murderer, Santschi discovered that Bill Suff had signed his name or written a short message in *four* separate places in Santschi's yearbook—at every occurrence of Suff's own photo. This classmate who had signed Santschi's yearbook more than any other student was a totally blank memory for him. There was simply nothing about Bill Suff that stood out in Santschi's, or most people's, mind. He seemed a quiet, ordinary student with few friends, and a personality and behavior that seemed numbingly undistinctive.

At that time, Suff's life seemed fairly unguided, as well. Unsure of what he wanted from life, he took a job as a state forester. As was to become part of his pattern in life, Bill quickly decided he was cut out for better things than his current job, and quickly left that employment.

One better thing seemed to happen to him in 1968, while attending a Rose Bowl game in Pasadena with his school band. Suff noticed a pretty girl in white Levi's sitting on the stands near him. When she stood up, he saw her jeans bore an imprint of the dusty seats. He seized the opportunity and, commenting on her soiled jeans as a means of introduction, he impressed the girl with his sense of humor and got her to agree to a date with him. Her name was Ann. To her, Suff "seemed very nice, good-looking, pleasant; the kind of guy a young girl would want to meet, because he seemed very sincere."

Although she was only fifteen and he was eighteen, they continued to date. Wanting a major change in his life, Bill took two dramatic steps. He enlisted in the Air Force in January 1969, and he asked Ann to marry him. The young girl's parents asked her, "Well, are you sure you want to do this?" She assured them, "We're not going to do this until I graduate from high school."

Bill went to basic training at Lackland Air Force Base in San Antonio, Texas, where he attended drum-and-bugle school. He then put in six months at the Shepherd Air Force Base for medical training. From there, he was assigned to the Carswell Air Force Base in Fort Worth, Texas, where he served as an aide in the pediatrics ward of the base hospital. While at Carswell, he received a disturbing phone call from Ann. She called to tell Suff she had to break off the engagement. She had been date-raped and was pregnant. She told him her religion prevented her from having an abortion, so she felt the only honorable things to do were to give up the baby for adoption and break off the engagement with him, because she "didn't feel it was right to start a marriage like that."

Suff thought about it and called her back. He told Ann he wanted to marry her anyway: "It doesn't matter. The baby will be brought up as mine." Initially reluctant, Ann gave in.

They were married in Suff's Perris home on December 13, 1969. A justice of the peace performed the ceremony, and no photos were taken. Although Suff had promised to raise the baby as his own, he and his family were able to convince the young girl that she would be unable to properly care for the child because of her inexperience and age.

Ann lived with her in-laws while Suff returned to duty in Texas. He promised to bring her to Texas once she had delivered the baby. He promised her he'd find a way to return to California for her.

He did. Suff got emergency leave by telling his commanding officer his new baby had suddenly died.

Upon his return, Ann told Suff she was having second thoughts about giving up the baby for adoption. Despite his promise that "the baby will be raised as mine," Suff scared the sixteen-year-old mother into giving up her child. He told Ann the lie that had gotten him emergency leave from the military. He warned her the Air Force would throw them *both* "in prison" if it discovered the deception. Too young and naive to know better, Ann took her husband at his word.

Suff's solution was to give the baby to his mother to raise as her own. He even pressured Ann into signing adoption papers to that effect soon after they returned to Texas, in April 1970, ensuring that the other man's baby would not share his roof.

In Texas, life was much harder than either Suff or Ann expected. He quickly demonstrated a very jealous, possessive side. At one point, Ann exploded at Suff that she was not his possession, she was a woman. He told her, "No, you're my wife and that's all."

There were allegations on both sides of infidelities. Suff had bragged to Ann on her arrival in Texas that he had had a girlfriend while waiting for her to join him. He described her to Ann and insisted that she cut her hair and dye a blond streak in it just so she would look like that girlfriend. When she refused, he threw Ann across the room.

It got so bad Ann threatened to leave him. She was seventeen and working as a waitress, and they were having another argument over his insane jealousy. Suff often accused her of cheating on him if she came home from work a few minutes late. When she threatened to leave him if he didn't cease his jealous behavior, Suff said that she couldn't survive without him. In anger, Ann yelled that she would survive even if she had to be a prostitute. It was obviously a hollow threat, but he backhanded her across the face for it, knocking her across the kitchen.

Ann left Suff at least twice. The first time, she stayed with a friend who was also in the Air Force. That escape lasted only a week. Suff went to the commanding officer and tried to cause problems for the person Ann was staying with. Ann called her mother for advice; both times she left Bill and was counseled to return to her husband and try to work things out. So she did.

Sexually, Suff was very aggressive and demanding, often asking Ann to let him tie her up. She always refused. She recalled he thought of himself as "God's gift to women," and said any bedroom problems were her fault because she was frigid.

Ann said Suff was so possessive he didn't allow her to go to the grocery store without him, and would call her workplace several times to check on her. When she was almost nine months pregnant with their first child, Ann recalled walking home from a movie with her husband. "Some guys in a car whistled [at me], and [Bill] went absolutely apeshit over it. He started screaming at them, and then screaming at me . . . 'Who are they?' And I said, 'Hell, how do I know?' [And then] he was chasing them down the street [threatening to kill them]. I said, 'Christ oh-mighty, Bill, I'm pregnant. How sexy can I be when I'm almost nine months pregnant?' And he calmed down after that, but it was kind of unnerving.''

The violence wasn't limited to Ann, either. On November 27, 1971, their son, William Lester Suff, Jr., was born. Almost from birth, he seemed to be sporting mysterious bruises. Suff would tell Ann that "Little Billy" had gotten the bruises from "the knob on the cradle." Later, Ann saw firsthand evidence of Suff's violence against the infant. Once, when the boy was teething and acting up, Suff slapped him hard across the face. She yelled at Suff never to do that—only to spank him on the bottom if he needed it. Suff told her that the boy needed to learn to stop crying when he told him to. He was the father and he'd discipline the boy in the manner he saw best.

Another time Ann saw him slap the child, she became so angry she took the baby and went to a neighbor's house. The visit came as no surprise to the neighbor. At least one neighbor had already seen Suff hit the little boy, and the word had spread.

Finally, the beatings became so severe that the Suffs had to take the little boy to the hospital. On March 10, 1972, Little Billy was treated for bruises on his face, abdomen, and back near the spine. Suff claimed the child hurt himself by hitting himself with a rocking crib. The hospital couldn't prove abuse but suspected it. The boy was turned over to Child Welfare as a battered child. However, the case worker in charge of Bill Suff, Jr., could not legally justify keeping him very long, and Little Billy was soon returned to Bill and Ann.

Ann was happy to get her son back, but the episode had no lasting effect on Suff. Ann soon saw further evidence of her husband's temper. One night in their bedroom, their kitten came up the stairs and in the door. It was "meowing and doing little kitten things," she recalled, and Suff suddenly picked up a BB gun and shot the kitten. He claimed he was only aiming to scare it, but his shot hit the animal in the head and killed it. Unable to believe he would intentionally do such a thing, Ann took him at his word that it was an accident. However, his behavior was starting to form a pattern.

Suff's career was forming a pattern, too. Although he enlisted in 1969 for a four-year hitch, he served only fifteen months as an aide in the pediatrics ward of the base hospital at Carswell AFB in Fort Worth. He was discharged more than two years early, in December 1970. Suff testified in a Texas court that he received an honorable discharge, but sources dispute that. Although the records explaining the early discharge remain sealed, one of Suff's brothers admitted it was a dishonorable discharge, and another reliable source indicated the discharge was for psychiatric reasons: an inability to function in a military environment. In other words, Suff didn't like taking orders.

Financial hardship followed the discharge. Both Suffs had to take low-paying jobs. Ann went to work as a waitress and telephone solicitor, while Bill ran through a series of various jobs and unemployment. He wasn't sure what he wanted to do with his life, although he told Ann he thought he'd like to be a cop. Instead, he took menial jobs as a fry cook, delivery-truck driver, ambulance aide, warehouse worker, and parking-lot attendant. Suff got fired from three jobs in a row. He lost the ambulance attendant job after getting into an argument, was fired from the storage warehouse, and was not only fired as a parking-lot attendant, but arrested and convicted of auto theft because of his activities on that job.

John L. Gamboa, Suff's attorney in Fort Worth, commented, "It probably troubled him deeply to be an intelligent, extremely manipulative man obviously not reaching his potential. He felt he was dealt a bad blow in life . . . just one of those people who just didn't seem to fit in." He also noted that Suff had strange mood swings: On one visit, he'd be extremely talkative, the next withdrawn.

Another problem was added to the financial burden already oppressing the Suff family: a new baby was born on July 20, 1973; a little girl named Dijanet (pronounced DEE-zhuh-nay) Jawn Suff, "DeeDee" for short. Soon after her birth, Suff was so troubled by his financial problems that he tried to give the baby away to a neighbor. The neighbor refused.

During August and September of 1973, Ann noticed bruises on Dijanet—more and more bruises, off and on. Suff explained them away, claiming their twenty-one-month-old toddler "Little Billy" had caused them by hugging his baby sister and "loving her too much." When Ann doubted his explanations, he would remind her that he had worked in a pediatric ward in the base hospital at Carswell and knew what he was saying. Only twenty herself at the time, Ann naively trusted her husband's contention; unwilling to believe a father could hurt his own child.

However, when Dijanet began violently throwing up one night, Ann was much harder to contain. She told Suff, "We need to take her to the hospital!" "No," he replied, "babies do this all the time." Again he reminded her he had been a corpsman in the military in the pediatric section. Again she assumed he wouldn't lie about it when it was his own baby's life at risk.

The next morning, September 25, 1973, Ann went to work, leaving her husband home to sulk about his current state of unemployment. Little Billy was asleep in his room when she left and Suff was watching cartoons.

Around noon, Suff called Ann at work. "It's DeeDee. Come home quick."

Ann found Suff upset and crying when she arrived. "Please don't hate me for leaving her," he cried. "Please don't hate the world." After checking on Dijanet, Ann frantically ran outside to find a phone and called for an ambulance.

Suff told the authorities he had been cleaning the living

room that morning and, when he went into the bedroom to check on DeeDee, she was lying facedown on the floor instead of in her bed. He couldn't find any vital signs, so he ran out to a pay phone and called his wife to hurry home.

Suff told Ann a different story. He told her that his work as a corpsman in the Air Force had been a "cover" to conceal his real employment with the CIA. While he had briefly stepped out, the CIA had sneaked into their apartment and murdered Dijanet as a message to stay quiet about something.

Although only a short-term corpsman, Suff proved accurate enough about his diagnosis of his infant daughter, Dijanet. The baby was pronounced DOA (Dead on Arrival) at the hospital.

Following his own "CIA" advice, Suff played it quiet with the authorities, claiming ignorance of the murder. He stated he didn't know who had killed or injured the child, although he indicated his son may have injured the baby while he was out using the pay phone, or that someone may have sneaked in to commit the crime while he was gone. He didn't try to blame his wife, although she was the only other possible suspect, but neither did he try to protect her from suspicion.

Suff's peculiar behavior extended to his own lawyer, John Gamboa, who sought some mitigating facts from Suff's early years to help solicit mercy for his client. Suff was steadfast in his refusal to talk about his parents and siblings, even for a lighter prison sentence, if it came to it. "His family—that was always off-limits for some reason," Gamboa said. He was never able to learn why.

Two-month-old Dijanet Jawn Suff died of a ruptured liver, an organ seated deep inside the body and protected by cushioning tissue. Extreme force is necessary to rupture a liver, the medical experts testified. A force that her twenty-one-month-old brother would not possibly have been able to inflict.

The baby's body was covered with bruises from head to toe. She had injuries and fractures that were two to three weeks old. She had thirteen broken ribs, a broken arm, a palmprint bruise across her face, adult-human bite marks on her forehead and stomach, and a cigarette burn on the bottom of her foot so severe it reached the bone. It appeared, the experts concluded, the baby had been tortured and stomped to death. Ann had to borrow money from her mother to have her buried.

Witnesses—neighbors, visitors, landlords—were called to testify to Bill Suff's violent behavior. He was depicted as lazy and short-tempered, and his apartment as the "filthiest" most had ever seen.

A female neighbor testified that a few days before the murder, Suff told her how he had caught Billy, Jr., taking a candy bar from the dresser. Suff said he "had beat [his young son] to sleep" for the misbehavior. Suff stated he "had to beat him to make him mind." The same neighbor reported she saw Suff's bondsman come to Suff's door on the day of the murder, but Suff didn't answer it although she knew he was home.

Another neighbor, who would often drop by for a chat with the Suffs, was also not allowed to enter their apartment on the morning of the murder; Suff, for once, refusing to chat with her.

The landlady testified she heard Ann arguing with Suff the day before the murder. The outraged young wife was heard telling Suff "he was going to have to go to work or get out." Suff, the landlady said, "was mad at [Ann]" for her threat. She was aware he had turned down work although he was unemployed and able-bodied.

One male neighbor who had allowed the Suffs to move in with him reported he kicked them out after nine days when they wouldn't help in any way.

A female neighbor told the court Suff was a big show-off who had gone around for a while carrying a gun and claiming he was a security guard, when he was not.

Bolstering that report, a male neighbor stated he once saw Bill Suff handcuff a person to a rail and leave him there for several hours. The person reportedly was a male youth who had dared to ride his bicycle on the sidewalk in defiance of Suff's warnings that it was illegal to do so.

Then came the reports of infidelity. Neighbors reported Suff had accused Ann of sleeping with other men, and had stated to different people on different occasions that he did not believe his children were his. Several people testified that they had personally witnessed Suff being violent with his children.

Even Ann admitted under cross-examination that Suff had a temper and had punched holes in their doors and walls. Further, it was shown that the Suffs had been forced to pay repair bills for the battered walls and doors.

Suff denied all responsibility for his baby's death, and tried instead to portray himself as a caring father and a former Air Force corpsman too medically dedicated to even consider inflicting harm on another human.

The prosecutor refused to tolerate any showmanship on Suff's part. When Suff sought sympathy from the jury by claiming he loved his new baby so much he wanted to personally handle her delivery in his own home, the prosecutor pounced.

"You don't have a doctor's license, do you?" the prosecutor inquired.

"No, sir," Suff admitted.

"How in the world do you think you would be qualified to deliver a baby in your own home?"

"I've done it three times before."

"You've done it three times before?"

"Yes."

"Where?"

"In California."

"In private homes?"

"No, sir."

"Where?"

"In back of ambulances on the way to the hospital."

The prosecutor let that issue drop, having no ready proof to contradict Suff, although he suspected they were lies.

Suff testified he received a full honorable discharge from the military, although he served less than half his enlisted hitch. When the prosecutor asked, "How did you get a full honorable discharge without discharging all of your obligations to the Air Force?", Suff replied, "I have no idea." He flatly denied receiving any psychiatric treatment, or having any mental problems, while in the Air Force.

The entire courtroom seemed too offended by the nature of the crime and the helplessness of the victim to tolerate either Suff's or Ann's claims of innocence. The jury took just thirty minutes to convict the couple of murder with malice. The Texas judge called the decision "a fair verdict."

The same day, the Suffs decided not to offer a case in the sentencing phase, hoping they could get a lighter sentence if they threw themselves on the mercy of the court. Their lawyers pleaded with the jury that the young parents had already suffered enough, and asked for leniency. The jury delivered speed, if not leniency. It quickly returned with seventy-year sentences for both Suffs. (Suff also received a sentence of three years on a felony theft charge about the same time.)

Ann visited Bill in prison once or twice a week following Dijanet's death. Women were housed on the opposite end of the building. Each time she visited him, he would say things like, "You are seeing someone, aren't you? I know you: A woman like you needs someone all the time." The accusations eventually drove her to stop her visits.

Twenty months later, in January 1976, Ann's conviction

was reversed by the Texas Court of Criminal Appeals, which stated there was "not a scintilla of evidence" proving her involvement in the child's murder. The grieving mother, the court said, had been convicted simply because of innuendoes "bolstered by moral outrage."

Suff's conviction, however, was upheld. The appeals-court decision stated that the trial record showed an "appalling history of abuse of the dead girl and her brother" by Suff. Suff expressed outrage that Ann should be freed without him. He even complained about that to Ann and her mother.

To Ann, the reversal of her conviction and the upholding of Suff's conviction helped convince her of what she already feared: Bill was indeed guilty of the murder of their baby. She contacted a lawyer and began divorce proceedings even before her release. "I just want a divorce," Ann told Suff. "I just want my maiden name back, I don't want anything from you, I just want out of the marriage."

Suff began a letter-writing campaign to Ann and her mother, trying to win her back. He wrote, "I'm surprised and very deeply hurt. Why, oh why, are you filing for divorce? That's a very wicked thing to do. What's more, it doesn't sound like the devout Jehovah's Witness you profess to be. . . . Well, if that's what you really want, I'll not contest it in any way, shape, or manner. 'Let your conscience be your guide.' " It would have sounded more sincere had the inmate lawyer who conveyed the letter to Ann not also told her of Suff's verbal message: If he couldn't have her, nobody would.

Suff went on in his letter to commiserate about himself:

> I have finally realized the truth in a verse of a sad song I heard once. It applies to me very well. You see, in a way, the D.A., the courts, and the state have been trying to kill me: by removing me from their society, they have effectively ended my existence.

That's the very best way to kill someone: put them where knowledge of them is forgotten. That's when I see that the verse to that song was meant for me. You ask what the verse is? It is this: "You cannot kill that which has never lived. For without love, there can be no life. . . . Without love, the beauty of the world cannot be felt. And there can be no warmth where there is no love."

I've only recently realized how it applies to me. You see, for awhile, I thought I was alive. It wasn't until [you asked for a divorce] that all hopes for life were at last completely denied me! So all I can say to [the D.A. and courts] is that they cannot kill me by locking me up for 70 years, 100 years, or life. You see, I was never really alive to begin with. And how can you kill someone that is not alive? It's a horrible word that can finally show a person that he no longer has even a chance at life. And of course, you know that word very well, don't you! Divorce is the second worst word in the human language. The first is goodbye!

Bon Chance! Et Au Revoir.

William L. Suff, Tenth Floor, "B" Row, Cell Five

In a letter to Ann's mother, Suff tried to cast the blame on Ann and exonerate himself, although the appeals court had just announced opposite findings. Suff did so, hoping to persuade Ann's mother to convince her daughter to return to him. In his letter, Suff claimed he was religious enough to forgive Ann for the murder, and could still love her and care for her despite her crime. What other man could be so forgiving?, he was trying to say.

In the letter, Suff claimed he took two polygraph tests "months apart" and passed both of them—while Ann "refused to take a polygraph test 3 times!" In fact, Suff had failed his, but that didn't stop him from trying to persuade Ann's mother otherwise.

He tried to make the point that even murder was not an issue for a religious person to worry about because "only Jehovah knows who caused the death and can judge the guilty person or forgive that person. All I can do is forgive and ask Jehovah's blessing for those that have done me wrong. I've been praying for Jehovah to bless and forgive [Ann] for any thoughts of divorce she may have in her mind. I've already forgiven her." Perhaps the blood on his hands caused Suff to write so much about the need to forgive murderers.

He went on in the letter to further libel Ann in her mother's eyes, telling of affairs he suspected Ann of having, while writing of his own high moral values that enabled him to forgive her and to refuse offers of extramarital sex that were made to him. Such offers included, according to Suff, wife-swapping, which, he claimed, he refused because "my own beliefs and religion would not allow me to even consider it."

Suff ended with his most direct accusation yet:

> If, and I have to say if because I do not know, if [Ann] is responsible for Dijanet's death, I have to forgive her for that, too. I *know* that I didn't hurt Dijanet and so does Jehovah. I know that this trouble I am experiencing is just a test I'm being put to, and I'm confident that Jehovah will see that I cannot be deterred from my faith for Him. And also that I can only forgive those who do harm to me, just as I have been and will continue to forgive [Ann] for her wrongs. I cannot do otherwise, it's not my place to judge anyone. . . . That's all I can say now. May Jehovah watch over you.

Neither Ann nor her mother answered Bill's letter. Ann went ahead with the divorce, which took effect February 25, 1976. "I lost three children because of Bill," she commented afterward. "He took basically everything from me that I ever wanted."

Little Billy, who had been placed in a foster home on the day of his sister's murder, was diagnosed as mentally retarded, a result of his many beatings. The authorities persuaded both Suffs to relinquish parental rights to him in October 1976, and he was adopted almost immediately. Through the effort and love provided by his new parents, he grew to normal adulthood with virtually no sign of the problems he originally exhibited.

Suff was a model prisoner, although he continued his misrepresentations. He told other inmates he'd been imprisoned for attacking his wife's lover, or similar macho fabrications. None of them ever knew the real reason for his incarceration, and not many paid much attention to him, anyway, just like most people Suff met on the outside.

In prison, Suff played by all the rules since disobedience meant swift punishment. He offered no disruptive behavior, he played in the prison band, and he studied very hard; hard enough to earn a bachelor's degree in Sociology in 1980 from the Steven F. Austin State University in Nacador. This won the attention of his parole board. His family even drove out from California to attend his graduation. Ann's first child, the young girl he had talked his mother into adopting, came with them to see her "brother." Later, when she was older and finally told the true circumstances of her adoption, she developed a hatred for Suff "for murdering her sister, Dijanet."

Suff had entered prison for the murder of his daughter in June of 1974, sentenced to seventy years' incarceration.

He left the prison only nine years and nine months later, paroled because the Texas prison system was overflowing with prisoners and a court ruling mandated lower prison populations. Everyone believed Bill Suff was a good candidate for parole; a low-risk offender.

Suff submitted a residence plan prior to his March 1984 parole date in which he indicated he wanted to move back to California and find a job. Officials in Texas and California investigated and approved the plan. He was released and paroled to Riverside County.

In the interim days, Suff stayed with a couple who performed prison-ministry work. They'd met him in the prison and were impressed by his intelligence and religious zeal. Suff told them he was in prison because a young woman who'd been living with him and his wife died suddenly one day when his wife was at work and he was asleep on the couch. Suff didn't know what happened to her, but he was arrested and sent to prison. Another innocent man. The couple sympathized with him. They allowed him to stay at their residence when he was released, and the husband drove Suff to the airport and put him on a plane for California when it was time. Suff sent them a Christmas card every year except 1991.

California parole officials checked monthly on Suff for the next three years. They met with him at home and at work, and were reassured on each occasion that he was steering clear of crime. Therefore, in 1987, Texas relaxed Bill's parole status, requiring only an annual report to be filed with its parole agency. Suff filed only one such report, but his failure to continue complying with the terms of his parole went unnoticed by Texas officials. It took Suff's arrest for five years of serial murders to alert the Texans to their agency's oversight. One which would have meant an arrest in 1988 for parole violation for Suff.

# Chapter Nine

In March 1984, Bill Suff returned to Riverside County to stay with his mother and her new husband on Hemlock Lane in Sunset City. Suff's mother met the man while struggling to recover after her husband's desertion—having one additional little mouth to feed, thanks to the manipulated adoption of Ann's firstborn child. The family had been thrown into monetary collapse by the desertion of Suff's natural father, and had gone on welfare to survive. Within two years, Suff's mother remarried, and stability temporarily returned.

The stepfather was described by the Suff children and others outside the family as very strict, critical, and demanding; a male counterpart to the tough maternal influence in the household. One of Suff's siblings stated their stepfather treated them as though they were in the Navy. It was said that Suff's mother intensified her critical attitude following her new union; falling in line with the sterner guidelines set by the stepfather. An in-law described her as "not the softest person I've ever known. She was cold . . . very much the matriarch. She set the way things were going to be in her mind and that's the way they were going to be."

For whatever reason, Suff and his stepfather took a quick disliking of each other. But Suff apparently showed the man respect to his face, as had become his pattern with authority figures. One of Suff's brothers, who stated he was never close to Suff, recalled one incident out of what he called a history of arguing and fighting with his brother. After Suff's return to California, during an argument between this brother and their mother and stepfather, Suff suddenly interceded and grabbed his brother by the throat, telling him to watch how he talked to his mother and father.

Ann's adopted daughter also didn't seem to care very much for Suff. Ann said that, from her talks with her daughter, the girl "didn't like Bill at all and argued with him a lot. She said she tried to avoid him as much as possible. And sometimes he would search her out and start to argue with her, and then she would say, 'Get out of my face' and 'Leave me alone.' I don't know why she didn't like him; she never said. She just didn't like the way he acted." Later, after the girl learned her real parentage, her dislike turned to hatred over the murder of her baby sister, Dijanet.

Suff got along fine with his mother, however. He borrowed a sizable amount of money from her upon his return from Texas, telling his mother one of what she would come to call his "whoppers" of lies. He told her he needed the money to pay for a divorce from Ann so he would be legally free of her. Ann had already paid for the divorce herself and been awarded the divorce on February 25, 1976— eight years earlier. The subject came up in a later phone call between Ann and Suff's mother, who, Ann reported, was "rather surprised" to learn she had been defrauded by her own son.

Suff had only one attempted contact with Ann after his return to California. He called her in Texas and left a message with her roommate that he was out of prison and back in California. "He said he knew where I was and if he couldn't have me, no one would," Ann said.

She was terrified by the threat. To her, a man who was capable of beating his own newborn flesh-and-blood to death was capable of anything. She called the Californian authorities and was finally routed to the parole agency in charge of Riverside County. She couldn't understand why no one had notified her that Suff was out of prison, especially since she had complained previously that he had made threats on her life.

"What's going on here?" she demanded to know. The parole agency representative told her Suff was doing fine, that he was doing what he needed to do. She asked, "Well, what is to prevent him from coming to Texas, because the last time I talked to him he threatened me? I'm afraid."

The representative told her, "Don't worry. He can't leave California without our permission."

"Yeah, right," she told the rep. "You can't keep an eye on the man twenty-four hours a day."

Whatever reassurances the representative offered failed. Fortunately, after that, Suff never got in contact with her again, and Ann was able to push him out of her mind again, until the newspaper headlines about his arrest for the serial killings brought it all back.

Suff stayed with his family about four months, acting like a "know-it-all" and "talking a lot." Another change in his behavior was an obsession, for a time, with wearing all-black clothing. One of his brothers learned it was Suff's rebellious answer to the all-white prison uniform he'd been forced to wear for ten years; a silent taunt to the authorities who had tried to control him.

While with his family, Suff went to work for a couple of months at a computer company on Sixth Street doing data entry. He left that job to work for six months as a cook and general cleanup person in a McDonald's on Mission Trail and Railroad Canyon Road in Lake Elsinore.

In July 1984 he met an older woman named Bonnie and fell in love with her. He eventually moved in with her at her Lake Elsinore mobile home, and stayed in a relationship with her for five years. (They split up in the summer of 1989 by mutual decision.) Suff's attraction to the older, more successful woman was perhaps a reaching out for an affectionate mother figure. He was to seek relationships and companionship with married women whenever possible after leaving prison, perhaps seeking in those female heads of the house a maternal link he was missing in his life.

With Bonnie, Suff was never aggressive, abusive, or violent, just as he never was with his mother. He'd never even raise his voice with her. Bonnie recalled that the most aggressive thing he ever did was sometimes hide her watch in one of her shoes when he was angry with her. This was not a man, she believed, who could be violent with anyone.

The two enjoyed their life together. They even took a vacation together, to celebrate life one last time before Bonnie was to undergo a surgery that she feared might be fatal. They went to King's Canyon National Park, where they took photos of each other and Suff bought some souvenir patches and T-shirts; Suff enjoyed having trophies of his more pleasurable accomplishments, although his finances were very limited.

When Suff was alone, he liked to drive in the hills, and sit and stare at the vast open vistas. He prided himself on his knowledge of the winding back roads around Lake Elsinore and the nearby areas, and was always eager to show off his knowledge of shortcuts and scenic routes whenever anyone was willing to go for a drive with him.

Starting a new lifestyle, Suff was suddenly overly helpful to everyone he met. He would always volunteer to help anyone do anything, in part to obtain an audience for his rambling pontifications and self-glorifying tales, and in part to ingratiate himself with people so he could approach them for "gas money" loans that were often never repaid.

He was very helpful with Bonnie, helping to maintain her home and properties, and helping to care for her invalid mother. He even recruited one of his brothers to help him clean up Bonnie's yard one day. The brother later told how, while standing outside looking off toward the nearby Dunes Casino, Suff had suddenly made the statement that he hated prostitutes. The bizarre non sequitur puzzled the brother, the topic totally out of the blue. Suff dropped it quickly, but his strange mention of it stuck in his brother's mind.

Suff's statement was strange considering that he had begun patronizing prostitutes soon after his return to California. He sought out the drug-addicted, alcoholic chain-smokers, despite being adamantly opposed to drugs, alcohol, and even cigarette smoking. He had been a smoker until 1969, and knew the procedure well enough, despite his denials, to have been able to burn a hole through to the bone in the sole of Dijanet's foot.

One prostitute who admitted that Suff was one of her johns in the Lake Elsinore area was able to give the names of two other local prostitutes he was seeing. She said Suff let her use his apartment to shoot up drugs. She said the professedly devout Jehovah's Witness was into bondage and whips. The landlady at a Lake Elsinore apartment Suff was renting once caught a prostitute breaking into his apartment through a rear window. The hooker claimed Suff had told her it was okay to do so. When the landlady confronted him about the incident, he confirmed that the girl had his permission to enter his apartment and retrieve the item she was after.

In November 1984, Suff switched jobs yet again, taking a position as a stock person and computer operator for a

Lake Elsinore company. He was a regular on Elsinore's Main Street by then. He routinely ate in the same restaurants on the brick-fronted promenade, frequented the same Main Street barbershop, and even found short-term work in a video shop and general store on the street. He seemed irresistibly drawn to the notorious cruising strip where haggard prostitutes hustled local johns and the occasional tourist for ten or twenty-dollar sex, blocks away from the huge recreational lake from which the small town derived its name.

One restaurant owner recalled, "He loved burritos, *chile verde* burritos. He [came] quietly and [left] quietly, without making any waves, without talking to anyone." The man's wife agreed Suff was "so quiet, very shy." The barber, on the other hand, found Suff to be a "talker." He said he often came to the shop dressed in a white ambulance-attendant uniform.

Another restaurant Suff patronized was the former Granny's Kitchen, where the owner was known around town as a softhearted touch who often tried to help the prostitutes with a cup of coffee and advice. One of those she counseled was Sherry Latham, whose body would be found lewdly posed near Grape Street on July 4, 1991.

Suff's latest job at the time lasted about five months, until April 1985, when he was offered a position by a mom-and-pop computer store on Main Street in Lake Elsinore. Suff had often dropped by the place to chat endlessly about computers and anything else the couple would sit still to hear. In his social visits, he'd offer computer advice to the husband, and sympathy to the wife about the "blighted" condition of Main Street, which had fallen into decay and become "overrun" with prostitutes and drug abusers.

The couple talked of soliciting support around town for a revitalization campaign to restore grandeur to the buildings, and initiating a campaign to rid the town of the disgusting hookers. Suff helped hang posters and pass out fliers to get the cleanup effort going. He effused support for the morality drive—decrying the blight of prostitution on the area. Suff loved to express his disgust of the prostitutes, and agreed the streets should be rid of them. Whenever he spotted a hooker on the street outside the computer store, he would rail about her offensive presence to whomever was in the area.

Feeling sorry for the poor, kindred soul, the computer couple offered Suff a job as a salesperson. Payment was to be strictly in commissions.

In six months at the computer store, Suff failed to sell a single item. The owners sometimes would give him money out of compassion, or pay him to baby-sit their kids or help around their house. They grew very close to him over a short period of time, and even offered him a room in their house to repay his friendship, since Suff helped the wife so much when the husband was gone on his frequent out-of-town trips.

Bonnie, however, put an end to Suff's move before it began. She made it clear she did not approve of him moving in with the couple; perhaps suspicious of his relationship with the wife who was so often alone. She gave Suff an ultimatum to move in with her or lose her. He meekly complied, and reduced his ties with the computer couple.

In 1985, he bought a blue 1973 Toyota Celica from a friend of Bonnie's, and obtained the personalized license plate "BILSUF," seeking the attention of the world. The plates didn't work, unfortunately; people continued not to notice him.

In June 1986, Suff took another job in downtown Lake Elsinore, working as a part-time clerk at John's Service Center, an appliance store situated directly across the street from some benches that were a favorite gathering spot for hookers seeking johns. Suff's duties were to answer phones, sort mail, and handle sales. The elderly owner recalled him as a "very reliable" person.

However, unknown to the owners, Suff would steal money from the cash register to pay hookers for sex—grabbing whatever amounts he thought he could get away with. When the elderly couple would go to church on Sunday morning, leaving Suff alone in the store, he would bring a hooker into the store itself and have sex with her in the back room—and then pay her from the cash register afterward. Eventually, the theft was discovered, but Suff readily confessed to taking the money and promised to pay it back, so the owner was forgiving. However, he never repaid the money. When he finally quit that store, in April 1989, he was gone for good.

The owner's grandson remembered Suff as a "real nice" guy who "used to buy sodas for all the grandkids." Suff told him he was writing a science-fiction book, and even showed him some pages from it. "It was all about these dogs that went nuts and started killing people," the grandson remembered. "[Suff] talked about how we put dogs on pedestals, call them 'man's best friend' . . . but what would happen if they reverted back to their old wolf instincts?"

Suff broke his pattern with the job at John's Service Center—keeping that job even when a better one came along. Evidently, either its location, directly across from the main congregation of hookers, or the owners' trust in leaving him alone with the cash register, was too powerful an attraction for him to easily walk away from.

In October 1986, Suff got a job with the county as a stock clerk at the county warehouse, filling orders for office supplies and furniture. He lied on his job application to get the job, denying any criminal convictions in his past. Some of Suff's orders were for the Sheriff's Office. Sometimes sheriff's deputies would drive over to pick them up from Suff, sometimes he would drive over to the deputies or other law-enforcement representatives. The RSO's homicide task force, when it was formed several years later, was a major consumer of office supplies, and made frequent trips to the warehouse to pick up materials. When Suff drove the supplies to the task-force headquarters, he sometimes commiserated with the deputies and task force members about the serial murders, and would ask how the case was progressing. He even offered one deputy his theory that the killer was murdering the hookers just to clean up the streets.

Suff loved that job. The work was easy, the pay was good, and there was plenty of opportunity to socialize with the people in the warehouse, or by telephone with his personal friends, so he always had an audience for his tales. He signed up for the employees' bowling league and even helped organize the first chili cook-off at the annual county employees' picnic.

However, he hadn't yet found a relationship he liked. His long-term live-in relationship with Bonnie seemed destined for a breakup in 1987. Suff moved out of Bonnie's place at her request. Shortly thereafter, in June 1987, he had a motorcycle accident that injured his back and gave him a concussion. He was hospitalized for three days at Kaiser Hospital in Fontana. Feeling sorry for him, Bonnie invited him to return to her place so she could tend to him until he recovered sufficiently to go back out on his own. Suff readily accepted.

The motorcycle accident gave Suff a new source for bragging. He told anyone who would listen that he would surely receive $87,000 in insurance money for his injuries. He even borrowed some money from friends on the promise of repaying them with the insurance money when he received it. When it finally came, two years later in a much lower quantity than he had predicted, he quickly spent most of it on himself and failed to repay his friends.

Things seemed to finally be looking up for Bill Suff as January 1988 approached. It seemed he finally had a good

job, a woman who loved him, and money on the way from
an insurance company. Perhaps, with all those things going
for him, he finally started to feel the inner confidence he
so often boasted of possessing in his many exaggerated
tales about himself. In any event, in mid-January 1988, he
decided to take his thrill-seeking, risky sex with prostitutes
one step further. He decided to kill one.

Lisa Lacik was twenty-one years old in January 1988; a
pretty black girl about five feet four inches, 118 pounds,
with light skin and black hair, and a small amount of
cocaine and heroin circulating in her veins. She was a local
prostitute in San Bernardino, and was standing on the
corner of Eighth and H Streets, in front of a convenience
store, the night Bill Suff decided to pick her up.

Connie, a gaunt, sun-beaten, blonde prostitute friend
of Lisa also spotted her working that night. It had been
raining, and was wet and cool, dreary. Connie was also out
looking for a date, accompanied at a distance by her friend
Sam. She had known Lisa for six months, and decided to
say hello as a car pulled up to the curb by the black hooker.
Connie saw it was a light-colored, old model Dodge two-
door with a dangling muffler. She approached Lisa from
behind and tried to peer in at the driver. She couldn't get
close enough to hear their conversation, but she saw that
the driver was a thirtyish, "heavy" man with facial stubble
and unkempt brown hair. He looked dirty, as if he had
been working. Connie thought the "car was similar to the
person: not well-kept." She didn't like the looks of the
john. Her instincts told her the guy was trouble.

Inside the car, Suff probably appeared nervous at the
prospect of the new career he was undertaking—especially
since a second hooker had suddenly appeared and was
eyeballing him intensely. This was San Bernardino—an
hour's drive from home—so it was unlikely anyone in this

location would recognize him. But that second hooker was staring at him as if she could read his mind. So he did something he probably thought would immediately end the girl's hesitation so they could get out of there. He offered her a hundred dollars for sex.

When Lisa turned to Connie and told her what the john had just offered, Connie became doubly nervous. The greasy john sure didn't look like a hundred-dollar trick to her. She thought the john was not the type to spend a hundred dollars even if he had it.

Lisa told the john she'd be right back, wanting Connie's thoughts about this guy who was offering about five times the going rate. She turned and walked into the convenience store, and Connie followed her. Connie told Lisa she shouldn't go with the john because she had a real bad feeling about him. Lisa said, "Don't worry. I can handle it." It was a hundred bucks, after all. She told Connie she'd be right back, and that she was just going to her regular place, the Palm Hotel.

Both girls walked out of the store and back to the Dodge. Connie stood at the curb and watched Lisa get into the dirty car and drive off with the "yucky" guy. The blonde hooker tried to get the license plate as it disappeared, but she could only remember three numbers: "776," or "778." She wasn't sure about the last digit because she wasn't wearing her glasses. But it looked like a "6" or an "8."

Lisa Lacik's body was found by hikers in the San Bernardino mountains on January 18, 1988. She had been dead for two to five days. The passage of time made it impossible to determine if she had been raped or strangled, but she had clearly been stabbed by a serrated steak knife-type weapon that caused fatal wounds. The single visible stab wound was in the abdomen just above the navel, but the blade had been redirected (punched repeatedly) into the same hole at least three to four times, as though in a struggle. The inferior vena cava had been cut in at least two places, as had another major vein. Lastly, before leaving, her killer had cut off her right breast after she was dead.

On April 22, 1988, at 5:55 P.M., a sheriff's deputy stopped Bill Suff in an unincorporated area of Lake Elsinore and wrote him a traffic citation for driving while wearing a radio headset. Suff signed the ticket "Bill Lee Suff" instead of "William Lester Suff," his legal name, as if attempting to hide his identity. But the license check came back to him, anyway: William Lester Suff of Orchard Street, Lake Elsinore.

The vehicle he was driving was a green 1975 Dodge Duster, a two-door model, bearing Arizona license-plate number "DPT 770"; Connie's eyes mistaking the "0" for a "6" or "8."

There was no law-enforcement bulletin about the vehicle, so Suff was simply ticketed and sent on his way.

He knew then that he had bested the authorities and gotten away with murder.

Suff attempted to duplicate his success in early January 1989. This time he was even bolder, obviously enjoying the theatrics of his criminal life. He drove down Main Street in the city of Lake Elsinore, where he was widely known by then, and picked up a hooker from one of the main prostitute hangouts: the benches across from John's Service Center. He used Bonnie's white station wagon, aware that it was well-known in town since Bonnie was now a local real estate agent and often cruised the area in the vehicle.

The girl this time was a wiry young woman with yellow-blonde hair. Her name was Rhonda Jetmore. Suff offered her twenty dollars for straight sex, the going rate; evidently learning from the Lisa Lacik incident that extraordinary offers only invited hesitation and suspicion. The girl readily agreed and hopped in his car.

Jetmore told Suff there was a vacant house down the street they could use for the sex act, where no one would disturb them. He agreed and quickly drove her there.

Once inside the house, Jetmore used a flashlight to lead Suff to a bedroom at the front of the place. She then sat on a bed and turned to face him, holding out her hand for payment in advance.

The dark, spooky setting evidently inspired Suff to another display of theatrics. He handed her a one-dollar bill. It took the hooker a minute to focus on the bill in the dark. When she realized she'd been cheated, she looked up to complain at the insult, and Suff lunged on top of her, strangling her with both hands, just like a monster springing out of the night.

Unfortunately for Suff, Jetmore was sober and strong. She fought him off and fled the house. Outside, she encountered two friends driving by and sicced them on Suff, the drama of the night taking a sudden unexpected turn. One of her friends took a couple of shots at him as Suff ran to the light-colored station wagon and sped away, but none of the bullets hit him or the car. And no one gave chase.

Although he had failed in the murder, Suff had succeeded in escaping. When no cops came knocking on his door the next day, he figured he'd gotten away with it again.


Suff lived for months in Lake Elsinore at several locations, sometimes with his family. He often touted himself as a police officer or security guard, and claimed to be involved in neighborhood-watch programs and other efforts to keep the communities safe for decent people.

At the Morro Apartment complex in Lakeland Village, some of the residents referred to Suff as a self-appointed baby-sitter and guardian to women and children. One man said, "I felt relieved that he was looking out for my wife and kids. He would warn me about all the bad people in town, about the drugs and the thieves and worse."

A young mother recalled, "He was always offering to baby-sit [and] was really careful and good with them. My oldest girl would crawl to him the minute he came in— and she called him 'Unkie Bill.' It struck me as odd that a single man would do that. But he told me his baby had died and I just assumed he meant by crib death or that it was stillborn."

With his insurance money, Suff purchased a new 1989 Mitsubishi van, silver-gray with gray interior. He ordered vanity plates for this vehicle, too: "BILSUF1." He was happy to offer rides in his new van to anyone who consented to accompany him—especially married women. The young mother whose daughter used "Unkie Bill" for a baby-sitter often drove with him in his new van through the desolate hills surrounding Lake Elsinore. She later stated Suff knew the back roads extremely well, and she remembered helping him clean his van on several occasions. "He was cleaning it every day almost," she recalled.

Another female neighbor later remembered riding with Suff in his van through the back hills of Lake Elsinore. She recalled the van at the time was outfitted with a Rebel flag on a pole and contained police paraphernalia such as handcuffs and batons. "He really knew the back roads," she said.

For two months, Suff and his family also baby-sat the children of neighbor Darla Ferguson, a friendly young mother who was also a drug-addicted prostitute. She evidently struck a special chord in Suff, but not for long. Months later, he would add her as one of his victims.

\* \* \*

In June of 1989 Suff and Bonnie finally split up for good, and he went back on the singles circuit. His first effort was to attempt to deepen his relationship with a local prostitute he had been "dating." He told her he wanted to move in with her. The woman, a youthful-looking redhead named Kimberly Lyttle, turned him down. She already had a boyfriend.

Suff's response showed her a side of him she hadn't seen before. He raped and strangled her, leaving the body lying facedown in the dirt in a desolate area, covered with a blue bath-sized towel. To be rejected by a girlfriend was one thing, but he evidently was not about to tolerate rejection by a prostitute.

Before he left, he re-dressed the body in one of his Western-style shirts. Suff had progressed from his all-black period to a Western style of dress, which he often accented with sleeveless "muscle" or "body" shirts. He also pulled back the shirt from one of her arms to reveal the abscesses and needle tracks on her skin, exposing to the world that she was a heroin addict.

He read in the paper that her body was discovered on June 28, 1989, just one day after her twenty-eighth birthday.

From his turndown by Kim Lyttle, Suff rebounded into another attempted relationship, hoping for better luck with a nonprostitute. However, this woman found him to be a "Mr. Goody Two-shoes"—a nerdy guy who spoke of marriage and meeting his mother after only two dates. He wasn't aggressive enough for her.

After her, Suff pursued another woman, named JoAnne, for nearly three months before finally realizing it was a lost cause. JoAnne had been given "Weekender" duty by the court, which was a work-release detail in place of a fine or jail sentence. Because part of Suff's duties at the County Yards warehouse were to supervise the Weekenders' work, he was able to take advantage of the opportunity to get to know her. He even offered to drive her home after work, although it was a forty-five-minute ride. The rides became a daily routine with them.

During one of their drives, Bill sought Joanne's attention by playing on her sympathy. He claimed that he divorced his wife because he'd caught her in bed with another woman. Furthermore, he said his next love, Bonnie, had thrown him out on his ear and kept some of his stuff. JoAnne later recalled, "He said all he has been is hurt by women."

Later, when she had served her time, JoAnne went to work at a convenience store called Circle K, working the graveyard shift. Without invitation, Suff started showing up during her shift. He helped her stock beer and told everyone he was a security guard for the place, and even put up posters to that effect. Often having more success persuading mothers than their daughters, Suff made an effort to meet frequently with JoAnne's mother so he could plead his case with her, hoping she would help influence JoAnne to go out with him.

The mother, however, was all too aware that JoAnne had no romantic feelings for Suff, so she often changed the subject instead. She'd tearfully tell him about her oldest daughter, a prostitute who had been murdered by an unidentified killer whom some authorities suspected might be a serial killer of such women. If so, her daughter was probably his first victim, the investigators told her. The grieving mother's tears and anger didn't seem to affect Suff. He'd just listen politely to the sad tale, and then try to change the subject back to JoAnne whenever possible. To the family, he seemed just a nice, lonely guy.

JoAnne, however, grew increasingly disturbed by her persistent suitor. She'd often ask her mother how to get rid of him without hurting his feelings. "How do I tell him he doesn't turn me on?" she asked. To her, Suff was short and fat and a little weird. She even told him she had a boyfriend. Suff responded by bragging that he was going to receive an insurance settlement so big it would enable him to take better care of her than any boyfriend could. In the meantime, though, he borrowed fifty dollars from her. When he finally left for good, her fifty dollars went with him.

Three women filled the brief interim in Suff's life before another love interest materialized. Unfortunately, they were each his murder victims.

The first was Christina "Tina" Leal, a pretty, baby-faced Mexican girl from Perris. She was tiny and weighed only about eighty pounds. She looked more like a child than a twenty-three-year-old woman and mother of four. Only the tattoo of her gangbanger boyfriend, "Sadboy," and the needle tracks on her inner arms indicated she might be more than the innocent child she appeared.

Suff savaged her body more than any of his victims before or thereafter. He pounded her face with his fists, almost sliced off her left nipple, slashed her clitoris, and both stabbed and strangled her to death, using repeated stabs to the heart and a ligature around the throat. After the murder, he delighted in playing with the body. He lingered to insert an oversized lightbulb far up her vagina, then re-dressed her in his own clothes, including one of his souvenir body shirts from King's Canyon National Park.

His work upon her took a much longer time than did that on any other victim, suggesting he had a rage and an ego to satisfy following so much personal rejection in his life. He was clearly determined to show the world he was smarter than the authorities and was free to taunt them and women in general however he saw fit.

The next month, January 1990, Suff took his revenge on Darla Ferguson for whatever offense she had committed against him, either while he had been baby-sitting her children on Morro Way, or perhaps when approaching her later on for a relationship. Whatever the motivation, he killed her January 17 or 18, strangling her with his hands or some soft, broad material. He evidently had to restrain her first, because there were ligature marks found around her wrists, possibly from handcuffs. When he was done with her, he pulled a large plastic trash bag over her head down to her waist, as if to emphasize his opinion of her as a piece of garbage. He dumped her body less than a mile from where he'd left Kimberly Lyttle's body, leaving the message that the crimes were connected and a master criminal was at work.

Early the next month, February 1990, Suff killed Carol Miller and dumped her body in some orange groves on the outskirts of the City of Riverside. He stabbed her repeatedly in the chest: close, careful blows of near-perpendicular alignment, indicating precise control of the blade, designed to ensure each punching stab found its mark. They did: straight into the heart.

Afterward, he stuffed a shirt into the victim's mouth and coolly stood over her body munching on a grapefruit, admiring his work. When he was done, he tossed the half-eaten grapefruit by her body, to taunt the authorities with his utter lack of concern over fleeing the scene.

After the Carol Miller murder, Suff returned once to visit JoAnne and her family, to show off his shiny Mitsubishi van. He told them he planned to drive it by Bonnie's house and make the ex-girlfriend crazy with envy over it. "I'm going to go to that bitch's house and blow the horn and let her eat her heart out!" he told them. The anger in his voice surprised the family. They had never seen that side of him.

JoAnne's family felt better later when they heard Suff

had finally switched his sights to a new romantic target. They heard that Suff, by then forty, had started dating the teenager who replaced JoAnne at the Circle K. They hoped the new girl would occupy his romantic attention for a while at least.

She did. Suff married the eighteen-year-old in March 1990, after dating her for one month.

# Chapter Ten

Bill Suff first met his new wife in February 1990 when Cheryl started working at the Lake Elsinore Circle K. Cheryl had just moved out of her family's Rialto house and was living with the convenience store's manager, Judy, who suggested she apply for a job at the Circle K. She did, and almost immediately met Suff, who had become a daily fixture in the place by then.

Although JoAnne no longer worked at the store, Suff had continued dropping by almost daily, willing to settle for long talks with Judy if no better offerings were in sight. Romantic possibilities with the friendly manager were out of the question, though, because the woman was overweight, and Suff, with his self-deluded image as a ladies' man, would never consider being seen dating such a woman. However, Judy was always happy to listen to his tall tales and lectures about everything that was wrong with the world, so he kept coming by to visit his eager audience of one. When Cheryl started working at the Circle K, Judy introduced Suff to her, happy to have the teenager meet such a smart, helpful, and moral man.

An extremely naive young girl, considered by many acquaintances as "slow," Cheryl was swept off her feet by the garrulous older man. They started dating almost immediately, and she soon moved in with him.

At the time, Suff was living in an apartment on Chestnut Street in Lake Elsinore, across from a bar. He had invited a young teenage girl named Kristina to move in with him after her brother kicked her out of their house for getting pregnant at such a young age. Suff offered her a roof over her head and some friendly advice about what a brutal world it was for a young girl alone. He frequently cited the harsh life of prostitutes as an example. Kristina remembered Suff was always talking about prostitutes. He'd tell her they wore too much makeup and were just sluts. And that he hated them. As a religious man, he considered it immoral for them to flaunt their bodies as they did.

Nevertheless, that didn't stop Suff from arranging his own nude encounter with Kristina. One day while she showered, he quietly lurked in the bathroom waiting for her to finish. When she finally stepped from her shower, he was standing there to meet the young pregnant girl— a Polaroid instant camera in hand. Suff snapped three fast photographs of the startled girl before fleeing the bathroom.

Kristina immediately took the nude photos, tore them up, and threw them away. She said he acted as though he considered the incident a joke. If it was a ploy to win her heart, it didn't succeed. Kristina reported she never slept with Suff, and even invited her boyfriend to move in with them.

Once, Kristina recalled, Suff gave her a pair of woman's used jeans while she lived at his place. However, the waist was too big and the legs were too long, so she didn't keep them.

Kristina and her boyfriend lived with Suff for four to six weeks. While they were there, Cheryl moved in, too. Suff even married Cheryl while they were there; a quickie ceremony in Las Vegas on March 17, 1990. Kristina and her boyfriend moved out about a week later, but not before witnessing the newlyweds' less-than-blissful honeymoon. One day, they heard Suff arguing violently with Cheryl in the bedroom, and when she emerged, Cheryl had a red mark on her face. She told the teenagers he had slapped her a couple of times.

Shortly thereafter, the apartment manager visited Suff with a curt message to move. Suff told the teenagers the manager had discovered Kristina and her boyfriend were staying there without paying rent, and was threatening to evict him if they didn't leave. The kids understood and packed their bags, ready to believe they were to blame, as he claimed. In fact, the manager had simply given Suff his final eviction notice for Suff's own persistent nonpayment of rent.

Almost immediately after Kristina and her boyfriend moved out, so did the Suffs—evicted by the manager. The newlyweds, married little more than a week, moved in with Cheryl's parents on Eucalyptus Street in nearby Rialto. Cheryl's mother thought Suff seemed all right to her, although he was "very temperamental" and easily became upset if anyone tried to interrupt him while he was watching TV or using his computer. What she couldn't understand, however, was why a forty-year-old man would marry an eighteen-year-old girl.

When Cheryl's parents first met Suff, he promised they wouldn't marry until Cheryl finished high school, and he boasted that he would provide a big wedding for their daughter. However, Suff broke both promises and eloped with Cheryl to Las Vegas a few months before her graduation. Now the big spender was forced to move in with them because of nonpayment of rent.

Suff was always broke while he lived with Cheryl's parents—and always borrowing money from them: "For gas."

(Later, when a baby came along, Bill would tell the grand-parents he needed cash to buy the newborn "milk and diapers.")

Suff and Cheryl stayed with her parents for about seven months, long enough for his true personality to manifest itself. Suff quickly became "very domineering" toward Cheryl, trying to control the young woman to the point that she started letting him speak for her.

The parents often heard Suff tell his bride she was too fat and "never did anything right." Both noticed he seemed to go out a lot at night and be gone until early in the morning. Suff explained his late-night disappearances by claiming he was visiting friends in Lake Elsinore, or performing work for his county job, teaching earthquake-preparedness classes to county employees at distant locations. Even Cheryl, as undemanding as she was, began to finally question his nightly activities. He'd tell her the same excuses, and that seemed to satisfy her curiosity, as well.

Ultimately, Suff's arrogance got to a point where nobody in the household was able to stand him, so Cheryl's father finally told the young couple they had to move out. In November 1990, they moved to the Vineyards apartment complex on Beechwood Street in the same city, Rialto. The forced move evidently didn't sit well with Suff; this second eviction—from in-laws, no less—came as a slap to his ego.

For whatever reason, on or around November 4, 1990, Suff again asserted his ego to the world. He murdered prostitute Cheryl Coker. He picked her up from University Avenue and murdered her shortly after she ate a fast-food meal, which he probably had provided. He then tossed her nude, mutilated body under a pile of vegetation debris in an empty Dumpster enclosure on the outskirts of the City of Riverside. It was the first of his crimes to occur within the jurisdiction of the City of Riverside, and the first, therefore, to involve the Riverside Police Department. This added another law-enforcement agency on his tracks.

The blonde hooker was killed by strangulation and stab wounds to the heart. Suff used a ligature to strangle the woman, and pulled it so tightly around her neck that it sliced a long gash in her throat, causing the worker who discovered the body to assume a knife had caused the wound. The deed indicated great strength on Suff's part, and a rage against his victim. Coker had fought the attack. She left scratch marks in her throat where she dug her nailless fingers into her neck trying to release the pressure from the ligature.

Afterward, Suff sliced off the victim's right breast and hurled it over fifty feet up a dirt hillside—so far away that it caused at least one homicide investigator to comment on the incredible rage the killer must have felt at the time.

Suff's rage got the better of him at this murder, and he unthinkingly dropped a vital clue to his identity at the scene. By the nude victim's feet, he left a used yellow condom with his semen in it. There was blood in his semen, which explained his use of a condom at this murder scene—the only time a condom was used in his entire series of murders. Suff's physician had advised him that he had contracted a venereal disease and would experience pain during sex unless he used a condom while his sores healed. Antibiotics, he was told, would clear up the problem within a few weeks.

Suff's stepfather died soon after, throwing the family again into financial chaos. The funeral physically demonstrated the lack of closeness in the Suff family, everyone taking separate cars to the ceremony at Salton Sea where Suff's mother and stepfather had moved. The stepfather had loved to fish in the vast desert lake by their property.

Suff's mother cast his ashes over the water as a final resting place for him.

Although most of the grown children lingered after the service "just to be with Mom for a while," Suff chose not to. Before he left, he informed his family that Cheryl was pregnant.

As soon as his sores healed, Suff was after another victim. In mid-December 1990 he picked up Susan Sternfeld and, as with his previous victim, left her nude body in an empty Dumpster enclosure on the outskirts of the City of Riverside, only about a mile from where he had left Coker and Carol Miller.

Suff exposed the needlemarks in the victim's arm and posed the body in a lewd position as an insult to her, and a taunt to the authorities who would come to investigate the crime. He wanted the police to know he had utter contempt for his victim and for their efforts to catch him. The repetition of a trash enclosure as the dump site for his victim made it clear such locations were deliberate choices, designed to broadcast his opinion of the drug-abusing prostitutes.

The next month, January 1991, Suff struck again, making it three victims in three months just as he had the previous year. This time, the victim of his rape and murder was Kathleen Puckett, a thin, brown-haired prostitute from the City of Riverside. He forced a white sock down her throat and then strangled her with his bare hands, her death resulting from a combination of both efforts. Again treating his victim like a piece of garbage, Suff discarded the body in an open trash site north of the I-15 freeway.

As with many of his other victims, Suff lingered to pose

Puckett lewdly so her genitals and needle-tracked arm would be exposed to those who would come later.

Whether for reasons of ego, or simply due to his scofflaw nature, Suff continued to take risks with the law, seemingly determined to add to the risks he was already taking. He refused to pay any of the traffic tickets he incurred, or to go to court for required appearances regarding the possible suspension of his license. He allowed his driver's license to be suspended on October 6, 1988, for driving without proof of insurance—and then again on June 23, 1990, for the same reason and for an unpaid ticket. It was suspended a third time on December 19, 1990, for failure to appear in court. On January 30, 1991, he was ticketed for driving without current registration.

Any one of those minor offenses could cause law-enforcement attention to be brought onto him and, in the cases of a suspended license and invalid registration, could result in his van being impounded by the police. The van in which he bound, raped and murdered most of his victims. It was a risk a cautious man wouldn't take.

But getting caught evidently was something Suff never considered possible.

Around the apartments, Suff developed reputations as both a surly show-off and a nerdy nuisance. To some residents (usually the adults), he was an overly helpful nerd who was always dropping by uninvited to ramble on about whatever was on his mind. He seemed meek and nerdy to them, and very intrusive. One man dubbed him, "The neighbor from hell."

To others (mostly juveniles or those obviously less empowered than he), Suff acted loud and aggressive—swaggering around with a bullet on his keychain, often wearing surplus unlabeled sheriff's uniforms from the county warehouse, pretending to be a security guard or law-enforcement officer. Teenagers at the apartments reported Suff claimed to be a highway patrolman, and he showed them the monogrammed baseball cap in his van as "proof." He also threatened to write $500 citations to any kids he caught trying to use the adults-only pool.

Suff's first wife Ann explained the dichotomy: "Bill could be very quiet and very wussy, wimpy. He could also be very strong and domineering, depending on what he thought was needed at the moment." He basically acted however he thought would serve him best with the people he was with.

Suff found that pretending to be in law enforcement impressed many people, so he played that role whenever he thought he could get away with it. One neighbor noticed Suff kept a uniform, badge, handcuffs, and a baton in his home. Suff told her he was a security guard and used that equipment for his job.

Suff told a neighbor who actually was a security guard that he had been a cop in Dallas/Fort Worth. He liked to talk to the man about firearms and police weapons, and had stories to tell from his Texas "cop" days. He told of one case he supposedly investigated that ended with the suspect successfully pleading temporary insanity for killing his wife and her lover. Suff advised the neighbor that, based on his Texas law-enforcement experience, a husband who finds a man in bed with his wife can "blow both of them away" and get away with it "nine times out of ten."

He told another friend that he met Cheryl while stopping a holdup at a convenience store. Suff claimed he captured the robber and held him for the police.

He also liked to brag that his wife had been a virgin when he met her. He was proud that she had saved herself for him, and yet he brazenly flirted with many of the women who lived or worked in the apartments—sometimes when

Cheryl was at his side. One friend said Suff "was a real flirt . . . Complete strangers, he'd hit on them." He liked to whistle and make joking comments, such as "Ohhh, baby!" when he passed women in the apartments. Cheryl seemed to endure silently, not taking her husband too seriously about many things.

Suff, on the other hand, treated Cheryl very seriously, determined to keep a tight rein on this wife. She was not allowed to wear makeup or use profanity, and had to defer to him on most matters or be severely chastised. He also restricted the clothes she was allowed to wear. One day he ordered her to remove a red sweater she had on because the color supposedly reminded him of all the blood he witnessed when he worked in the pediatric ward at Carswell.

Suff and Cheryl's social life consisted largely of visiting the neighbors or watching television. He liked to listen to country music or watch the TV show *Star Trek: The Next Generation*. He also liked to read the Star Trek books; apparently a more devout Trekkie than he was a Jehovah's Witness.

Sometimes Cheryl would accompany Suff on drives. She learned that he liked to get gasoline at the station by the Concourse bowling alley, where he bowled in a league with his coworkers. He also loved to fill up on University Avenue, in the seedy downtown district.

On two separate occasions when she was in the van with Suff on University Avenue, he pointed out female pedestrians he claimed were hookers. "See her, she's a hooker," he told her, like a guide pointing out the sights. The women didn't look unusual to Cheryl so she asked how he knew. He said, "You can tell by the way they look." Cheryl looked again but the women still didn't look out of the ordinary to her. She figured he must know more than she did. Another time, in Lake Elsinore, Suff began pointing out the hookers to Cheryl as they slowly drove down Main Street. She was amazed at how he could pick them out so easily.

At work, Suff was also known as a somewhat laughable character, although his eagerness to help his coworkers and willingness to volunteer for special projects earned him their respect and friendship. Almost everyone at the warehouse liked Suff. This was probably because Suff actually liked being there, and so was inclined to be friendly. His job was not demanding for a man of his abilities, and allowed him to spin his tales pretty much at will. It was, in short, a place where he could be lazy and sociable and be paid for it. So he was very happy there, and he made sure everybody stayed happy with him.

A female coworker considered him "almost too helpful sometimes . . . a really nice nerd." They worked on computers in the same upstairs office for a time, when Suff was on light-duty assignment following his motorcycle accident. Suff loved to talk to her. Sometimes they'd talk about computers, sometimes about her marital problems, sometimes about his writing. Once, he brought in a science-fiction story he had written. Set in a future beset by epidemic mutations, it was the story of a father and son who are attacked by an animal while visiting a zoo. One of the son's arms gets bitten off, but the father tells the son not to worry, because luckily they have three arms and can afford to lose one. It appeared from the printout that Suff had written the story on a home computer.

Although both he and the coworker were married, Suff attempted to establish a romantic relationship with her, again following his pattern of pursuing married women. However, she gave him little opportunity. She told Suff she was transferring to another county location. He took advantage of the occasion to ask her out to dinner, claiming it was a farewell gesture. Over dinner at Denny's, he poured out his heart about his own bad marital experiences, again soliciting sympathy for the pain that women had put him through. He claimed he lost custody of his beloved son because of his first wife, Ann. And Cheryl wouldn't clean the house and played her music too loud. He asked the coworker to make them both happy by leaving her unhappy marriage for him—promising he would treat her better than her husband. The coworker politely rejected his advances by telling him she was trying to work things out with her husband.

Suff's other efforts at work were more appreciated. His bosses happily noted that he was always eager to volunteer for any special assignment. For example, he volunteered to pick up the marshal's work-program assignees on Mondays and drive them to the county warehouse. By doing so, he had an opportunity to look them all over before anyone else from the warehouse did, so he could try to talk the cute ones into working under his supervision. This was how he met JoAnne and, although that hadn't worked out, he knew the work-release people assigned to the warehouse often included prostitutes, so such duty remained an attraction for him.

One Weekender he met found special cause to remember Suff. Joan Payseur was flattered when Suff approached her in the gathering area in the county building where she and the other inmates were awaiting a ride to the warehouse. After surveying the crowd, Suff asked if she'd like to work with him in his area when they got to the warehouse. The woman thought the gesture was very friendly, so she said yes. She found him very friendly to work with—a "happy-go-lucky" man. Not at all like someone who would soon murder her deaf daughter and dump her nude body outside a bowling alley.

Another noble volunteer effort on Suff's part involved the county "Rideshare" program, which tried to induce county employees to carpool to work. Suff solicited coworkers to ride to work with him in his van, and even contacted the Rideshare Office offering to take on additional passengers. The Rideshare folks were so impressed by his enthusiasm for the program that they sent a photographer out to take a photo of Suff and his van for the next edition of their newsletter. Accompanying the photo of Suff standing alongside his new van, smiling proudly, was the following text:

> Bill Suff, from the purchasing department, drives his van to work everyday. He asked the Rideshare Office to find some passengers for his van. He commutes from Rialto to the purchasing department on Washington Street, making one stop in Downtown Riverside on the way in. The Rideshare Office found some interested employees, but Bill still has a few seats open. Anyone interested?

A close look at that Rideshare photo shows Suff wearing a pair of ProWings athletic shoes—the same brand that had left its unique prints at several of the serial-murder scenes. Suff's carpooling van was the van that had been used in the most recent serial murders.

The photo of Suff smilingly inviting the public into his murder van, accompanied by the solicitation, "Anyone interested?", struck some after his arrest as bizarre. To others, it seemed eerily reminiscent of the old *Twilight Zone* episode in which a smiling stewardess cheerfully invited passengers on board a plane that was destined to crash; her perky exhortation, "Room for one more!", ironically urging travelers on to their deaths.

Suff also volunteered to set up two displays showcasing earthquake-preparedness brochures and kits. The displays had to be set up at two different county locations, and the work had to be accomplished during normal business hours. Suff was happy to volunteer. It gave him the chance to leave work and drive to other sites, where his time couldn't be closely monitored.

He was also happy for another reason. Although only two daytime trips were required, and no classes or presentations were involved, his wife and her family had no way of knowing that. By simply showing his relatives some of the brochures, Suff was able to create a plausible excuse for his frequent late-night disappearances—claiming he had to go conduct classes on earthquake preparedness for distant county employees.

In yet another act of volunteerism, Suff was happy to help out the county by buying some of the used or surplus county products that frequently accumulated. He took special interest in old sheriff's uniforms, although they had the official patches removed from them. He even wore some of those pants to work at times.

Perhaps Suff's most celebrated act of volunteerism at work involved the annual county employees' picnic. He volunteered to organize a chili cook-off competition in 1989, and it became an annual event. Suff won the competition in 1989 and again in 1991. He was so popular for his success at the picnic that some Riverside County supervisors and other high-level officials were proud to have their photos taken with him at those gatherings.

Most people at work were proud to know Suff, and liked him well. Some kidded him about having such a young wife, but he seemed to take the ribbing in stride, which was unusual for him. Perhaps it was because he himself was notorious at work for his sexual jokes and stories. Most people didn't object to Suff's bawdy behavior, since it seemed entirely in jest, although one female coworker admitted she felt uncomfortable around him because of his risqué language and the open sexual discussions he often had with other female employees in her presence.

Negative comments about Suff from coworkers and superiors were generally qualified or played down. The most common complaint appeared to be that he spent a lot of time "bullshitting": talking to anyone about any subject, and making many personal phone calls to friends while at work. Someone often had to keep track of him to keep him on the job.

And Suff used more sick leave than any other employee. He often used every sick day he had coming each year. "Allergies" were Suff's stand-by excuse for many of his sick days.

When it came to his actual work performance, Suff was viewed as hyperactive and easily distracted. It was said he suffered from a short-attention span. But on the plus side, the qualification would always come, Suff was outgoing and always eager to help.

Although Suff often claimed he had a bad back as a result of his motorcycle accident and could do no lifting (establishing an alibi if ever accused of carrying around dead bodies), his bosses never noticed him having any trouble lifting supplies or furniture. His job description even required the ability to lift up to sixty-five pounds. To his bosses' recollection, Suff was always able to perform such labors, except for the brief recovery periods following his two traffic accidents, at which times he worked in a light-duty capacity upstairs in the office.

The most negative comment came from a coworker who said Suff sometimes borrowed money from coworkers and didn't always return it. However, the qualification came, it was usually only two to ten dollars each time and always for gas. At least, that was what Suff told them, and they saw no reason to doubt him.

So Suff seemed pretty happy at work in the warehouse. Yet, he couldn't resist playing his ego games there, even when he knew law-enforcement personnel sometimes moved unannounced through the building. Perhaps he played those games because of that; always eager to prove he was superior to those trying to capture him.

From the very first murder, Suff adopted the modus operandi of taking all of the victim's clothes and possessions with him. Law-enforcement experts assumed it was an effort to prevent those articles from being checked for incriminating fingerprints or trace evidence; a smart move by the killer. However, instead of throwing the items into garbage receptacles or otherwise disposing of them so they would never be seen again, Suff took them home and gave them away as gifts to friends and relatives. He'd wash the clothing in his laundry room so it smelled clean to the recipients. Sometimes, when Cheryl would spot the clothes in their apartment, he would explain their presence by claiming he found them, or was given them by a coworker, or that somebody must have put them in his dryer or laundry basket by mistake. The naive young girl proved gullible enough to believe any story her husband made up.

Some of the items, such as jewelry and small purses, Suff kept around him as souvenirs until he found someone suitable to give them to, or had acquired new souvenirs to replace them with. He'd even keep the victims' identification cards and papers in the purses, perhaps because that added so much to the risk he was taking.

Deliberately compounding that risk, Suff kept most of the jewelry and purses in cardboard boxes on the shelves behind his workstation in the warehouse—items that incriminated him in multiple murders, if not the entire series of prostitute killings. Anyone could discover these items if they simply thought to look in the boxes.

But no one did. No one thought to wonder what was in those boxes behind Suff's work area. Or, if they spotted any of the purses sticking out of those boxes, no one thought to question why there were women's purses in an all-male warehouse. The female employees only worked in the upstairs offices, not on the ground floor where Suff worked and the inventory was maintained.

Suff must have delighted in the many times law-enforcement personnel came to his station to use his phone or ask his help pulling supplies—all the time standing over the shelves and boxes containing enough evidence to solve the biggest case in the county. He must have fought a smile as he talked with those lawmen—some of them from the task force itself—as they complained about the impossible case they were pursuing and how difficult it was to find evidence against the killer. Suff would offer them sympathy and suggestions, and wish them good luck.

Then he would lean back with newspapers during his breaks and at lunchtime and thoroughly search for any mention of his deeds or himself, enjoying his notoriety and law enforcement's utter humiliation at his hands.

On April 26, 1991, he read an article about the entire task force having gone to Wisconsin and about to make a major arrest in the serial-murder case. Suff couldn't pass up the opportunity to taunt the task force in a way that was sure to make the headlines—showing the world how stupid the lawmen were and how unstoppable his criminal genius was.

He decided to claim a new victim to prove the task force was pursuing the wrong man and that he was still operating at will in the area. He decided to leave the victim this time in a very busy, public place, to ensure her immediate discovery so he would make the next edition of the paper. He decided to leave her at the Concourse bowling alley he used to frequent in league games with his county coworkers. His past ties to the location would be one more personal joke upon the task force, a deliberate clue only he could understand; just one more reason for him to celebrate his genius over them.

The victim he picked that night was a deaf, petite prostitute named Cherie Payseur. Suff probably had no way of knowing she was the daughter of Joan Payseur, the Weekender he had selected to work under his supervision over a year earlier.

After raping the young girl, he strangled her in a gentle fashion that left no mark on her body. So little evidence of violence was visible that the pathologist officially listed the cause of death as "undetermined."

Perhaps Suff gave her such a gentle, "soft smother"-type of death because he somehow felt sorry for the deaf girl. Perhaps her death was gentle only because that method was the quietest—something necessary if she was killed in the van near the busy bowling alley, a populated area where a quiet death was more prudent. He didn't linger to mutilate this victim, fleeing quickly before he could be discovered by anyone leaving the crowded establishment. He simply left her nude, on her back, with one arm turned up to expose the trackmarks on her skin. It seemed the change to a more public crime scene caused him to act more quickly and discreetly than usual.

In any event, Cherie Payseur was just as dead, and the task force was humiliated as desired. However, his new deed—responding to a newspaper article about himself—provided one more bit of information about Suff for the authorities to ponder.

# Chapter Eleven

While Bill Suff's stepfather lived, there was a semblance of financial security for his mother and the young children residing with them. When he died, the suffering began anew. Suff told Cheryl that his mother complained about everything after that, and especially about not having enough money because she was on Social Security. His mother even asked him to loan her five thousand dollars.

In response, Suff withdrew two thousand dollars from his credit union and gave it to his mother with great fanfare. He told her that although he couldn't afford to give her the full five thousand, she could have the two thousand to make up for everything she had done for him and to repay her for her help while he was in Texas. His mother was very touched. She felt her eldest son had finally matured.

Months later, Suff asked his impoverished mother for the money back—telling her at that time it was actually only a loan.

*  *  *

Suff went two full months without killing after murdering Cherie Payseur on April 26, 1991. He had spent minimal time with that victim, simply dumping her nude body at the rear of a bowling alley. Law-enforcement experts conjectured the serial killer may have become "spooked" by the frequent vehicular and pedestrian traffic at the location, and abruptly fled when he heard or saw someone he feared might discover him. The close call may have thrown a good scare into him—enough to keep him inactive for a time. Just before the Fourth of July, 1991, he struck again. His selection of a holiday caused some investigators to wonder if that timing were deliberate, a part of some pattern on the killer's part. No pattern was ever established by the authorities for when or why Suff chose to kill.

The victim was Sherry Latham, a prostitute from distant San Bernardino; Suff had perhaps gone out of the area for a victim to play it extra safe. He dumped her in a desolate area in Lake Elsinore that overlooked the I-15 freeway, within eyesight of two of his earlier body dumps (Kimberly Lyttle and Darla Ferguson). He strangled Latham with his hands and, as with Payseur, didn't otherwise mutilate her corpse.

Called Rainbow by her street friends because of the bright, colorful makeup she favored, thirty-seven-year-old Latham was known to hang out near the Circle K Food Store when she used to prostitute herself on Main Street in Lake Elsinore. It's likely Suff met her while he was hanging around the Circle K trying to make time with the clerk JoAnne. In the store, he'd often speak of his disgust of the prostitutes who hung around the place, drinking sodas or coffee at the tables outside. He would sometimes volunteer to go out and shoo them away. However, none of the store personnel usually accompanied him outside to hear the actual conversations he conducted with the hookers, so it is not known whether he was actually harsh with them or simply arranging dates.

Despite having wasted away to a physical shell of the person she used to be, Sherry Latham wasn't ready to leave this world, or her children. She fought back violently against Suff's attack—scratching his face and arms before finally being overpowered.

The Suffs spent the Fourth of July with their apartment manager, with whom they had become very friendly, and visited her again the following night. The woman recalled that on the second evening, Suff was suddenly sporting fresh scratches on his face and arms.

Suff told most people he sustained the injuries while breaking up a fight between two men and a woman at Kaiser Hospital during one of his visits to get some medication for either his allergies or bad back, depending on which version he told. According to Suff's story, the men were arguing and, when he stepped in to calm them down, one of them pushed him. Suff pushed the man back—unintentionally knocking the guy down by the strength of his push. This, he said, infuriated the man's wife, who then jumped on Suff's back and scratched his face and arm with her fingernails, causing the very visible injuries. He claimed the hospital security guards came running out to their location (which was either the parking lot or the emergency room, depending on which version he told), and thanked and praised Suff for breaking up the fight.

Most saw no reason to question the explanations. Everyone considered Suff such a harmless "nerd" that even those who doubted the notorious "bullshitter" read nothing sinister into his actions or injuries.

That same month, July 1991, two events changed the Suff household. First, two of Cheryl's friends moved into the apartment with them and, second, Cheryl delivered her baby, a girl they named Bridgette Ann Suff, on July 26, 1991.

Cheryl had taken a job with a mail-order company in Perris in August 1990, and there met a young woman named Terry, who quickly befriended her. They worked together until November 1990, when Cheryl quit. Before she left, Suff sold one of their three cars, a brown Ford Pinto Cheryl's father had given them early in their marriage to help them with their financial difficulties. He sold it in November 1990 to a security guard at the mail-order company. That left the Suffs with two cars: the blue 1973 Toyota Celica, license-plate number "BILSUF," and the new 1989 gray Mitsubishi van, license-plate number "BILSUF1." That same month, November 1990, they moved into the Rialto apartment after Cheryl's father booted them from his Rialto house.

In May 1991, Suff sold the blue Celica to Cheryl's brother, leaving the Suffs with just the gray van. The next month, Terry told Cheryl her boyfriend Jeremy had lost his job, so they were considering moving to New Mexico to live with Terry's mother. Hearing of their plight, Cheryl invited the friends to move in with her and Bill instead. She told Terry it would actually be a favor to her, Cheryl, since she was a first-time mother and very nervous about everything. Terry could help her prepare for the coming baby, Cheryl said, and help care for it after it came. That sounded fine to Terry and Jeremy.

In addition to baby-sitting duties, it was agreed the couple would pay the phone bill and give the Suffs one-hundred-fifty dollars a month for the rental of one of the bedrooms in the two-bedroom apartment. Terry and Jeremy moved in with the Suffs in July 1991.

On July 26, 1991, Bridgette Ann Suff was born. Called "Brie-Ann" by her parents, she suffered frequent diaper rashes and often cried through the night. Sometimes Suff would get so frustrated at the baby's nightly crying he would carry the crib out of their bedroom and into the living room, where he would leave the wailing infant until the morning. Although Terry and Jeremy never saw Suff hit the little girl, they noticed that he was "very rough" with her, and that she often had bruises on her face.

Then twenty years old, Cheryl was little help for the baby's distress. According to her tenants, she "didn't seem to know what to do." The crying persisted, and Suff's patience grew increasingly short.

On August 15, 1991, Suff evidently decided to take out his frustration in familiar fashion. He cruised University Avenue in his gray Mitsubishi van looking for a new prostitute victim. Spotting two hookers across the street from the McDonald's, he pulled up to the skinny blonde, selecting her over the baby-faced brunette who was weaving on her feet as though she had taken too much heroin, which she had—a lethal dose was coursing through her veins. She was also coughing from pneumonia, contracted from living in a cardboard box on a vacant lot down the street. The blonde immediately agreed to straight sex for twenty bucks and hopped in the passenger seat of the messy van.

The hooker, Kelly Whitecloud, quickly looked around the van, trying to gauge the john's finances by the property he carried in his vehicle—sizing him up to see if he appeared worth robbing. He seemed a harmless, grandfatherly type to her; someone vulnerable enough to "burn" if she thought it worth the risk. She noted a swivel-style captain's chair directly behind the passenger seat, a CHP cap on the center console, and a thick black book that looked like a Bible. There was nothing of obvious value. She asked him to buy her some food at McDonald's before they proceeded, speaking in the hyper, aggressive, machine-gun clip she was noted for by her associates on the street. He agreed.

At the McDonald's, where she had been thrown out several times for shooting up heroin in the bathroom, Kelly came on even stronger, trying to intimidate the employees into tolerating her presence. She caused enough of a fuss over a mistake in her order, that the manager had to be summoned to deal with her very vocal displeasure.

The unforeseen spectacle made Suff nervous and angry because it brought much attention onto him and the hooker. He made sure they left immediately after she received her order. Outside, he decided to take some revenge on the bitchy blonde and began arguing with her over the price for sex, as a way of insulting her by seeing how cheaply she would sell herself. He told her that because he bought her the food, he should only pay her ten dollars for the sex. Notorious for "not taking shit" from anyone, Kelly abruptly jumped from his parked van in the McDonald's lot and told him to "fuck off!"

Suff gawked at her in surprise, not expecting that outcome. He hesitated for a moment, staring at her as she backed off and turned to walk away; perhaps wondering whether to risk chasing her and dragging her back into the van since she had seen his face. He let her go instead, and immediately drove back across the street to the baby-faced hooker, Kelly Hammond.

The intoxicated, coughing brunette staggered over to his passenger window and quickly agreed to sex with Suff for money. Across the street, heading toward them, Kelly Whitecloud shouted a warning to her friend: "Don't go with him, Kelly! He's just a ten-dollar trick!"

Hammond smiled drunkenly back at Whitecloud and waved to her, as if to say, "That's okay." Then she climbed into Suff's gray van and drove away with him into the night.

Suff left her naked body in neighboring Colton, lewdly propped against an alley wall, her face shoved into the dirt, her rear end upraised to the world.

Suff's violence against strangers wasn't sufficient to satisfy his rage and frustration. Roommates Terry and Jeremy

were witnesses on several occasions to his physical treatment of Cheryl. The Suffs fought often, and when they
did, "Bill got real physical. He used to grab [Cheryl] by the
arm and bruise her." The walls and doors of the apartment
suffered from Suff's tantrums, and once he even punched
out a car window to vent his anger at Cheryl.

One time, Terry told Cheryl she should ignore Bill's
prohibition and show him how pretty she looked in
makeup. She gave Cheryl a light makeover. When Suff
came home and saw Cheryl's face, he exploded that she
looked like a "prostitute," and he ordered her into the
bathroom to wash it off.

As for Suff himself, Jeremy recalled he was often gone
at night until very late, and "always making excuses about
why he was late."

On September 9, 1991, Terry and Cheryl began evening
classes in an airline trade school in distant Ontario, California. Often Suff would drop them off at school and pick
them up afterward.

Once, Suff left the newborn baby Bridgette home alone
when he made the long drive to pick up the girls. Jeremy
recalled, "All Cheryl had to say about it was, 'Don't ever
do it again.'"

Suff offered no explanation for the blatant child neglect.
Perhaps he simply didn't want a baby with him during the
special side trip he had planned for that night.

Another newspaper article about the serial murders had
struck a nerve with Suff. In the article, experts claimed the
serial killer most likely was a white male because his victims
were mostly white females, and serial killers tend to strike
within their own race.

On the night of September 12, 1991, Suff returned to
University Avenue to pick up black prostitute Catherine
McDonald. He dumped her body alongside a back road

in a new development area in the dirt hills by Lake Elsinore, where grading workers would find her the next day, Friday the thirteenth.

His violence against Catherine McDonald was worse than on most of his previous victims, leading investigators to fear the serial killer was escalating both the frequency and the violence of his attacks. He stabbed McDonald repeatedly, in the chest and in the pubic area, and sliced off her right breast, as he had sometimes done to other victims. Then he posed her body in a lewd position, spread-eagled on her back.

However, Suff deviated from his routine on this victim by taking the severed breast with him. Before, he'd always hurled the item as far as he could throw it, making it a game for the investigators to find it. Investigators didn't know what he was planning to do with the missing breast, but they felt certain the taunting killer had read the newspaper article and responded to it in a way intended to humiliate them personally; lethally demonstrating that the quoted experts were dead wrong about him.

The very next day—Saturday, September 14, 1991—was the annual picnic for county employees. As usual, it was attended by all varieties of county officials and employees, including law-enforcement officers from the Riverside County Sheriff's Office; some of whom now served on the new, highly touted sheriff's homicide task force assigned to catch the serial killer.

Also as usual, county employee Bill Suff was in charge of the chili cook-off competition. He even entered the contest himself, ladling out his special homemade chili to anyone willing to take a taste. He likely passed out bowls to some of his deputy friends, and perhaps even to some of the homicide task-force members he'd chatted with on their visits to the warehouse.

Two of those task-force members had been in the warehouse the day before to pick up some supplies for their headquarters. They used Suff's phone to call in after being paged. Task-force administrators ordered them to drop everything and immediately respond to one of the dirt hills in Lake Elsinore, where grading workers had just found a new body.

Suff probably stood right beside the two investigators at the time, leaning on his counter, directly over the cardboard boxes full of dead prostitutes' jewelry and purses, offering the men sympathy again for being run ragged by the impossible case. After hanging up, the investigators told Suff to hold their order for later, then rushed out to the serial killer's latest homicide scene.

At the picnic that Saturday, Suff refused to reveal what his secret ingredients were, but his chili won first prize. Later, after his arrest, two of the top people involved in the serial case expressed conviction that one of Bill Suff's secret chili ingredients that day was the black prostitute's missing breast; probably Suff's most gruesome joke upon the authorities who were trying to capture him.

Suff's frustration with baby Bridgette's crying continued to manifest itself in violence against the infant. In late October, the baby suddenly grew fussier by the day. When Cheryl would ask if they should take Bridgette to the doctor, Suff would reassure her that the baby was fine. One morning while Suff was at work, the baby woke up screaming uncontrollably. Cheryl called him at work to come home and drive them to the hospital. At first, Suff tried to talk her out of it, but for once Cheryl was insistent. She threatened to take a taxi if he wouldn't bring the van home.

At the Kaiser hospital, Suff quickly told the doctor he was sure Bridgette was only suffering from a serious cold or the flu. The symptoms seemed at first glance consistent with a simple ear infection, so the doctor drew some blood for tests to confirm it, and then sent the Suffs home with a prescription.

Later that day, October 25, 1991, the lab-test results came back as seriously abnormal—and the doctor called Cheryl and told her she must bring the baby back that afternoon. Again Cheryl called Suff to come home and pick up her and the baby. Again he reluctantly did so.

This time, doctors at the hospital ran the baby through intense testing. Their conclusion was that Bridgette Ann Suff was suffering from such severe child abuse that she probably would have died if not hospitalized and treated that very day. Even so, doctors were surprised she survived.

She had severe brain damage, blood clots in her brain, bleeding inside her eye, bruises on her head, four broken ribs, and a broken left leg. The diagnosis was "shaken-baby syndrome"; unquestionably, injuries sustained from deliberate child abuse. The prognosis was possible permanent retardation.

The Rialto police investigated immediately and questioned all four adult occupants of the apartment. During that first round of questioning, everyone denied abusing the baby and denied seeing anyone else in the apartment perform any rough acts with the child. However, Suff qualified his denial. He worked the day shift and was not home to see what went on when he was absent. "I'm not saying that [Cheryl] has never shaken the baby, but I have never seen her do it."

The other residents of the apartment began pointing fingers as well in subsequent police interrogations. Suff used the opportunity between interviews to plant some suspicious seeds in Cheryl's mind so that, on her next interview, she told the investigator she had talked to her husband about the matter and he had since revealed to her that he didn't feel comfortable with Jeremy around the baby.

In her next interview, Terry admitted she had seen Suff lose his temper with Cheryl and the baby. She said on one occasion, he had held the baby at eye level and yelled, "Bridgette! Bridgette!" into her face as he shook her in frustration.

In his follow-up interview, Suff claimed he had waited forty-one years to finally find someone who could give him a baby, and that he loved his baby and wouldn't harm it in any way. He further claimed that after he left the Air Force he became an LVN (licensed vocational nurse) and worked in the pediatrics section of a medical facility. Suff agreed to take a polygraph on the matter. It yielded "inconclusive" results as to his truthfulness.

Ultimately, Suff blamed their tenant friends for the abuse, and Terry and Jeremy blamed Suff. Rialto police couldn't figure out who to believe, so they ended their investigation without filing charges against anyone.

Suff ordered Terry and Jeremy to vacate the apartment, insisting to Cheryl they were to blame for Bridgette's abuse. Amidst "a lot of hard feelings," Terry and Jeremy prepared to move out of the Suffs' apartment, frustrated that they couldn't convince Cheryl that Suff was the guilty party. They planned to live with Jeremy's parents in Beaumont.

Suff and Cheryl were planning to leave the Rialto apartment soon, too, around Thanksgiving. They told everyone it was because they didn't get along with the apartment manager, not that she was evicting them for nonpayment of rent.

Following a stay at two different hospitals, Bridgette Ann Suff was temporarily placed in the custody of Cheryl's parents, in their new home in Paso Robles in Northern California. The child was eventually placed for adoption; her final prognosis unknown.

Although under investigation for child abuse by the

Rialto Police Department and the county Child Protective Services, Suff didn't hesitate to kill again.

On or about October 29, 1991, just five days after Bridgette entered the hospital and two days before the eviction took effect, Suff picked up Riverside prostitute Delliah Zamora from University Avenue and raped and murdered her. He left her body, still clothed, alongside a small road paralleling a freeway.

It appeared to investigators the serial killer had panicked and fled when he suddenly realized he had picked a dump site directly across from a park-and-ride parking lot. They surmised he had been spooked by the sudden arrival of several early-morning carpoolers at the rendezvous point directly across from his van and the body. He hadn't stripped or mutilated the body, but had simply stolen her purse and some of her jewelry.

Cheryl dropped the airline class when Bridgette went into the hospital, the new mother wanting to spend her time visiting her ill baby.

During one of those visits, while sitting with Suff in the van in the hospital parking lot, Cheryl noticed a blue denim handbag in the van. She asked him whose it was. He quickly said he had gotten it for her, claiming his boss gave it to him because his wife didn't need it anymore.

Upon casual examination, Cheryl saw it still contained a woman's wallet, black pocket phone book, makeup, and personal papers. She absently flipped through the items, but didn't pay attention to the name on the driver's license [Delliah Zamora]; noticing only that the writing in the phone book appeared to be a woman's. She also didn't notice that the papers were police citations for prostitution and drug charges. Cheryl was apparently distracted by concern for her seriously ill baby.

By then, it had become routine for Suff to present her

with gifts of women's used clothing and jewelry, and she no longer gave such things much notice. Most of it she didn't like or couldn't wear, being a large, stocky girl; but some of the jewelry seemed nice, and she occasionally would keep it. That night, in the parking lot, she wasn't interested in anything but her baby.

She probably didn't even ask her husband about the new scratch marks on his face. However, Terry and Jeremy were still living with them, although in the process of moving out, and Terry questioned Suff about the marks. He told her he'd cut a corner too sharply at work and scraped his face on a wooden pallet.

When Suff next saw a member of his family, he told them his baby was in the hospital with blood clots in the brain. He offered no information indicating the problem was a result of violence. However, when his mother heard of the hospitalization, she remembered Dijanet, and it seemed to her too disturbingly like déjà vu.

The Suffs moved to a sprawling complex of garden apartments in Colton on November 23, 1991. Suff wrote on the lease application for the Meadow Lane Villas that the reason for leaving their previous apartment was "Gang Activity, Nightly Gunfire, Mismanagement of Apartments."

The Suffs' marital problems persisted and worsened, even before the move was finished. They had a big fight while packing their boxes. Suff didn't like the way Cheryl was doing it. The argument ended with his slapping her very hard in the face. She told him that was it: she wanted a divorce. And she called her brother to give her a ride to their parents' distant home in Paso Robles.

Even at the time they reached Paso Robles, Cheryl's face was still red enough for her father to notice the slap mark.

Suff spent Thanksgiving 1991 with the female apartment manager, Rebecca, and her boyfriend, intruding himself into their holiday celebration. But he also took the time to write a letter to Cheryl's parents explaining his side of the story, which presented him as a loyal, hardworking guy, and Cheryl as a lazy, filthy, unappreciative wife. He begged his in-laws in the letter to help save the marriage and prevent Cheryl from filing for divorce. After allowing time for the letter to arrive and be read, he called Cheryl at her parents' house and asked her to come back to him. The parents counseled their daughter to try to work out her problems with her husband, so Cheryl went back to Suff the first week in December.

Soon after moving into the Meadow Lane apartments, Suff tried to ingratiate himself and Cheryl with their neighbors by giving gifts of used clothing and jewelry he'd taken from his victims. He may have earnestly given the gifts as a sign of his friendship, but it's equally likely he simply viewed such deeds as a joke on the recipients that only he was smart enough to appreciate.

At the new apartments, Suff was his old helpful and intrusive self, often inviting himself and Cheryl into people's residences for endless chats about a variety of subjects, many of which prominently featured himself. He even used his van to help one couple of friends move from Lake Elsinore to the Colton villas.

On one of those drives ferrying the friends' possessions, the boyfriend involved was sitting in the front passenger seat of the van next to Suff, and happened to drop his hand alongside the seat. His fingers fell onto the wooden grip of a knife that Suff had tucked under the seat. The young man lifted the instrument a little, just enough to see what it was. Verifying it was a straight-bladed knife, he replaced it and thought no more about it; not even commenting on it to Suff because its presence seemed so trivial.

Suff also continued his habit in the new location of wearing security guard-type clothing around the apartments, and pretending to be in law enforcement. He displayed his alter-ego aggressive side as he had before, but again only to those less empowered than he. One neighbor said, "He used to walk around here acting like a cop. He looked at everybody like he hated everybody."

Another recalled how Suff said "he was going to clean up Meadow Lane. And he always wanted to talk about guns, police-type guns. He said if he had to, he'd take drastic measures. He'd walk around the apartments reporting cars in handicapped spots, breaking up fights among kids, and reporting people who were climbing in the hills behind the complex."

Cheryl took an evening-shift job at a nearby fast-food restaurant soon after they moved in. She worked from 4 P.M. to at least 1:30 A.M. Because of her work hours, she often slept until noon or later, leaving Suff unmonitored in the mornings whenever he was off work.

In Colton, the Suffs continued their practice of keeping cats. They had three by then: a calico, a white cat, and a kitten. Once, when Cheryl asked Suff why the cargo area of their van suddenly smelled so bad, he told her it was because one of the cats had crapped in it.

On December 4, 1991, the day Cheryl moved back in with him, Suff had a traffic accident in his van in front of the Riverside Kaiser parking lot on Magnolia Street as he arrived to pick up Cheryl, who was already there for a doctor's appointment regarding Bridgette. While trying to pass a skip loader, he turned too soon and was rammed by the giant construction vehicle. A crater-sized dent caved in much of the passenger side of the Mitsubishi and knocked out the brake lights on the same side.

Later, Suff's security-guard neighbor commented about the illegality of driving the van without functional brake lights. Suff reminded the man of his claim of being a deputy sheriff for the county. As such, Suff said, he didn't fear being pulled over by one of his buddies. The security guard then threw several names at Suff, asking if any of those deputies were among Suff's buddies, since they were also his friends. Suff said he didn't know any of them. The neighbor thought that strange since most of those named had been with the Sheriff's Office for fifteen years.

One report on the accident indicated Suff appeared to be at fault since he was passing illegally on the wrong side of the road. Also, he was operating his vehicle without a current driver's license, registration, or insurance, and, according to witnesses, he appeared to be speeding. Suff told the traffic officer, and other inquiring officials at the scene, that he was not injured.

A security representative from Kaiser hurried out at the time and started taking photographs of the vehicles and the drivers, for liability purposes. The photograph of Bill Suff showed him standing on the sidewalk near his van, a pair of ProWings athletic shoes on his feet.

Never one to miss an opportunity even in a bad situation, Suff informed his bosses at the warehouse of the accident and requested light-duty once more, claiming the collision had reinjured his back. Happy to oblige the always-eager employee, Suff's bosses sent him back upstairs to work on a computer in the office.

Suff proved his back was still in excellent shape less than three weeks later on December 23, 1991. He murdered another University Avenue prostitute and carried her body from his van to the dirt nearby for posing and mutilation.

Suff did not know this victim was a good friend of one of the lead investigators on the task force hunting him.

The death of Eleanor Casares would severely affect RPD detective Christine Keers. It would reinvigorate her dedication to catch the serial killer—escalating that dedication to the point of obsession.

Suff posed the Mexican woman's body spread-eagled, on her back, in the soft dirt of an orange grove. He killed her by both strangulation and stab wounds to the heart. He pulled one of her arms out to the side to reveal the needle tracks, as he usually did, and cut off her right breast and hurled it away. He took all of her clothes, except for the black coat she'd been wearing, which he threw over her face. This victim had put up a strong fight. She had gouged scratches in his chest and on one side of his face deep enough that he would have to find new excuses to explain them away to his wife and friends.

What marked this crime as unusual in his series is that he performed it in broad daylight, probably shortly before noon, and he left abundant shoe and tire imprints in the soft dirt of the orchard. Because it was a daytime kill, the body was discovered almost immediately, and the authorities were able to arrive on the scene soon enough to preserve a large quantity of the trace evidence and shoe and tire prints.

It was the most abundant crime scene to date in terms of evidence. It was so clearly detailed that the criminalist could virtually retrace the killer's every step and action. It gave the task force hope that, were a suspect to be finally identified, the evidence at this scene alone would send him to the gas chamber.

# **Chapter Twelve**

When Cheryl Suff woke up on the day Eleanor Casares was murdered, it was between 12:45 and 1 P.M. She had worked the late shift the night before, while Suff had the whole week off from his county job because of the holidays. When she awoke, Suff was already home from his butchery in the orange groves, and he was sporting fresh scratches on his face and chest. Cheryl asked her husband how he got the marks. Suff told her one of their cats had scratched him. Gullible to the end, Cheryl readily accepted his explanation.

The next day, Suff popped into the apartment manager's office to visit with the girls who worked there. The assistant manager, a young woman named Kristin, was alone at the time, and she noticed the scratches on his face. There were three healing, scabbing marks too thick to have been inflicted by a cat. She doubted Cheryl was responsible for the wounds, because the shy young wife kept her fingernails bitten off. Kristin didn't ask Suff what had happened to him. She wasn't eager to endure another of his long stories.

To any who did ask, Suff told the story of the fight at Kaiser Hospital he had supposedly broken up, claiming again that a combative man's wife had jumped on his back and attacked him while he trounced her husband. One resident recalled Suff really seemed proud to tell that story—sometimes volunteering to tell it to those who declined to inquire about his battle wounds. In the new version, a small child was also involved; Suff interceding in the child's defense in a scenario strangely similar to a scene in the John Wayne movie *Big Jake*. To those who recalled he had told that story before, Suff claimed he was talking about a subsequent incident. As proof, he claimed one of the hospital security guards had even commented after the second altercation that it seemed every time Mr. Suff came to the hospital, he was breaking up a fight.

Following his pattern, Suff washed his latest victim's stolen clothes and then wandered his apartment complex seeking recipients for them. He first asked Cheryl if she wanted the jeans and black sweater, but she declined because the offering was again too small to fit her.

Suff offered the clothes to a neighbor who seemed the appropriate size. He claimed they were Cheryl's but that she couldn't wear them anymore. The neighbor didn't want either piece of used clothing. Her cousin, who was visiting, said she liked the jeans, so Suff gave them to her. The sweater was finally accepted by the friendly apartment manager, Rebecca. She accepted it because it appeared new to her. She was correct. The sweater had been an early Christmas gift to Eleanor Casares from her mother.

Suff had also received an early Christmas present from Cheryl. Tired of the two pairs of old ProWings athletic shoes Suff had worn ragged from perpetual use, Cheryl had presented her husband with a pair of new, black Converse tennis shoes two weeks prior to Eleanor's murder. Suff loved the gift and immediately started wearing the shoes, although he kept the old pairs of ProWings.

Because the Converse soles were brand-new, their deep, sharp treads left perfect footprints in the soft dirt of the orange grove all around Eleanor Casares's body—starting at the exact spot Suff exited his van, progressing to the rear doors where he lifted her body out, and proceeding over to the shady alley between two rows of orange trees, where he dragged her body and then butchered and posed it.

The DOJ criminalist Steve Secofsky could even tell from the tire tracks in the dirt that the serial killer had backed his vehicle in to unload the body. He was also able to determine from those crisp tracks that the killer's vehicle now was sporting two new Uniroyal tires on the passenger front and rear positions. They were an early Christmas present to Suff from himself. He had put so many miles on the van cruising the county for victims and dump sites that he had worn out the treads on three of the original Yokohama tires in only a year. From his examination of the tire tracks at the Casares scene, Secofsky identified the two new Uniroyals and confirmed that the driver's-side front tire was still a Yokohama model, as previously identified from the tracks left at the Catherine McDonald scene. His research, however, still hadn't identified the manufacturer of the third brand of tire, located on the rear of the driver's side.

The next day was Christmas 1991. The apartment manager, Rebecca, held a small party that night in her apartment. It consisted mostly of some of her resident friends, including the Suffs. Someone proposed the group watch a movie, so the TV was tuned to a pay-per-view channel. Those gathered watched as a commercial came on, advertising *Silence of the Lambs,* a movie about a brutal serial killer of women. When Suff saw the commercial, which contained no clips or footage from the film to indicate what action was depicted in the movie, he suddenly blurted, "That girl was stupid for getting in the van."

The comment seemed bizarre to some people, but was dismissed as simply typical of the pontificating Suff they knew; a guy always eager to provide a running commentary on anything that went on, or was mentioned, around him.

No one seemed interested in watching the movie, so that plan was dropped and the conversation changed to lighter subjects.

About two weeks later, on January 8, 1992, Suff woke to a morning newspaper that reported the police chief of the City of Riverside had publicly refused to contribute to the county sheriff's reward fund for the capture of the serial killer. The chief did not consider the serial killer to be any different or smarter than any other killer, and thus did not consider him deserving of any special efforts such as a reward fund. The chief had made his speech at a meeting of the Riverside City Council, just to urge the council to follow his lead and also officially snub the reward fund.

That very night, Bill went searching for another victim. An RPD patrolman who was parked across from a trouble-some nightclub spotted his dented gray van as it cruised up and down University Avenue. Although the vehicle appeared to match a police flier on the serial killer, Officer William Barnes had to forego investigation of the van when a dangerous speeder nearly ran over some pedestrians directly in front of him.

Barnes saw no problem in ignoring the van, since it was headed directly into an area containing a high concentration of plainclothes surveillance teams who were out that night solely to search for gray vans. Homicide detective

Chris Keers had persuaded the top brass in the RPD to launch an all-out dragnet for the serial killer starting that night, based on her conviction that the suspect would surface to retaliate against the chief's published comments. Keers had distributed a police bulletin to all detectives and patrol personnel, describing in detail the suspect and his gray van, as reported to her by Kelly Whitecloud, the only prostitute known to have escaped from the killer. Every cop knew what to "key in on" in their search. Barnes was certain the detectives in the Operation Apprehension task force, up ahead, would key in on the dented gray van as soon as they saw it, just as he had.

However, no one stopped the van that night. Most likely Suff turned down a side street and left University Avenue before entering the surveillance zone, abandoning his quest for the night.

The next evening, January 9, 1992, Suff stopped by the apartment manager's office around 5:15 to tell Rebecca how Bridgette's court case was progressing. The apartment leasing agent was also in the office. She listened as Suff quickly switched to a happier subject. He claimed that he and a brother were going to get rich by opening a new dance club in downtown Riverside. It would be so successful it would take business away from the other two clubs in the area. He was going to go there tonight and help with the construction.

Neither Suff nor his brother had any ownership in the club. His brother only worked for one of the owners, and Suff dropped by occasionally to spend a few minutes bullshitting with him.

Suff drove to the club later that night, sometime between 8 and 10 P.M., to visit his brother. He found a second brother there, as well, and talked with them for about forty-five minutes. He told his youngest brother the authorities had "found another body" by his house, but he didn't specify whether it was a male or female body, so the brother wasn't quite sure what Suff was talking about. Suff then told them he had to get to Kaiser in Riverside by ten o'clock to pick up some allergy medicine before the place closed. He was allergic to the weather, he told them, and drove off.

However, Suff didn't head for Kaiser hospital. He went south instead, cruising slowly down University Avenue through the chilly January night—still looking for a victim to deliver to the insulting chief of police.

Spotting a Mexican hooker in blue jeans and a heavy sweatshirt leaving a liquor store, Suff pulled into the store's side parking lot and quickly did a fast U-turn to bring the van close to the girl, facing the street as she walked by.

The sudden maneuvering of the big gray vehicle in the dirt lot didn't go unnoticed by the prostitute, a thirtyish woman named Roberta. Johns and cops often made dramatic stops to impress or intimidate a hooker. Looking at the heavyset white male driver, she got "bad vibes" about him, taking him for a cop. When he waved her over to the van, she suspected it even more because cops often waved people over to them, the action more dignified and commanding than raising their voices to shout for attention. If he was a vice cop and going to arrest her, she would be very upset because she wasn't even working tonight; she was actually on her way home.

Once she reached the van, Suff asked her if she was dating. She told him no, not tonight. Even so, she later admitted, "He could have persuaded me to go with him, I'm sure. Depends how much he offered."

They never got the chance to discuss money. Officer Frank Orta, a uniformed RPD motorcycle cop, was riding by on the opposite side of the avenue and happened to spot their activity out of the corner of his eye. Roberta saw him watching them. She immediately turned and walked rapidly away.

Orta had fixed his look on them for two reasons. The sight of a gray van contacting a prostitute had tweaked his curiosity, since he knew from Detective Keers's flier that it was a suspect vehicle linked to the serial murders of prostitutes. But the pair had also tweaked his indignation by conducting their transaction on the main avenue itself, in view of all traffic, instead of on a discreet side street as the hookers usually did. Such flagrant contempt for the law offended Orta and made him instantly determined to stop the two and check them out—arresting them if he could, throwing a scare into them if he couldn't, just so they wouldn't be brave enough to be so flagrant next time.

The thought that the john might actually be the serial killer wasn't a strong feeling on Orta's part. Hundreds of gray vans had already been stopped and investigated and their drivers found to be harmless. But, as with most good cops, all the possibilities kicked around in the back of his mind, a vital habit that preserved officer safety on the street. Orta viewed the likelihood of being the one cop to catch the infamous killer as the same likelihood of winning the lottery—it simply wasn't reasonable to expect.

Like the panicked hooker, Suff quickly fled the location. He drove off in the opposite direction from which the prostitute had fled, probably believing—or hoping—the motorcycle cop would chase after her instead of him if he had to pick between the two.

A red light was ahead of the van. In his rearview mirror, Suff watched the motorcycle make a U-turn to bring it into the eastbound lanes with his van. When it neared the liquor store, the motorcycle didn't slow down, obviously not interested in the fleeing woman. It was steadily approaching the gray Mitsubishi from behind.

Panicking that the red light would give the cop time to

reach him, Suff made a right turn at the intersection without stopping at the light. This provided the patrolman with the legal excuse he was seeking to stop the van.

Officer Orta rolled around the corner after Suff, activating his red lights. Suff obediently stopped about one block away.

When he walked up to Suff's open window, Orta saw a face with metal-frame glasses that seemed a close match to the composite drawing Detective Keers had circulated. His curiosity got stronger when he examined Suff's driver's license: The three addresses listed on it were three of the primary cities in which the serial killer had dumped his victims.

Orta asked Suff to wait while he checked his license through the computer. Back at his motorcycle, he decided to radio-in the traffic stop, which brought Officers Duane Beckman and Don Taulli to the scene.

Because Suff's driver's license was suspended and his vehicle had no valid registration, Orta decided to impound the suspicious van. During the impound inventory search of the vehicle, the officers discovered what appeared to be evidence, and called their supervisor, Sergeant Skip Blythe, to the scene to evaluate what they had found.

Blythe used a cellular phone to call Chris Keers at home and ask her opinion on what they had found. She had only one thing to tell him: bend down and see what brand of tire was on the driver's side front position of the van. It was a Yokohama.

Keers said, "Freeze the scene—I'm on my way."

That brief sentence sent the police radio bands abuzz. By the time Chris arrived at the traffic stop, other officers were dropping by just to see what the ruckus was all about.

"This is a lot of cops for a traffic stop," Suff weakly commented. Patrolman William Barnes noted that the caved-in van was the same vehicle he had been unable to pursue the night before.

Within minutes of her arrival and brief visual examination of the van, Chris Keers ordered Suff to be taken to RPD headquarters for interrogation and called DOJ criminalist Steve Secofsky to respond to the impound warehouse and verify what she already knew: They had found the serial killer.

Suff agreed to be interviewed by the police. He'd already been repeatedly interviewed by the Rialto police only weeks before regarding the abuse of his baby, Bridgette, and he'd sailed through that ordeal. Hell, he had even beat their lie-detector test, controlling his bodily responses well enough for the results to be labeled "inconclusive."

Now the cops had a woman in charge of interrogating him. Of all the people Suff had deceived in his life, he'd always had the easiest time with women. They seemed to trust him more readily, perhaps because he looked so harmless and ineffectual. He probably was thinking at the time that he'd be able to talk his way out of anything with the woman detective. Hell, he had managed to talk the most cautious hookers into his death van with very little trouble—at a time when fear of the serial killer was highest. He was confident he could handle Chris Keers.

Chris hoped he would be cocky enough with her to keep talking and eventually confess, but she was taking no chances. She'd have another investigator in the room with her, ready to jump in and take over any time she tired or needed help. She had been without sleep for almost two days, nervously watching every hour go by since Operation Apprehension began, aware that the chief had only authorized four days for the all-out effort to catch the killer.

As soon as the DOJ criminalist, Steve Secofsky, confirmed her findings in the van, Chris had called the sheriff's lieutenant in charge of the RSO task force and informed him of the promising traffic stop. He had alerted the entire RSO task force and sent RSO homicide investigator John Davis to the RPD to assist Chris in the interrogation. Davis would be her backup in the interrogation room.

The questioning started out casually, with Chris primarily asking background questions. Suff lied frequently, starting with one of the very first questions: his full legal name. He replied: "Bill Lee Suff," instead of his true name, William Lester Suff. He specifically insisted his first name wasn't "William," just "Bill." He usually told those he met that his name was just Bill, not William. Within his own family, however, everyone usually referred to him as "William," both as a child and adult. Outside his family, Suff chose to project a different name and decidedly different persona.

He told Chris the hooker by the liquor store had approached him without his permission and propositioned him, which he had flatly turned down. He stated he never used prostitutes, never dated prostitutes, never solicited prostitutes. "I've got no reason to," he said. "I've got a happy home life with my wife." Chris asked if he would be willing to give the police samples of his saliva, blood, and hair. He agreed and she left the room to call for a technician to take samples before Suff changed his mind. Then she returned to resume the interrogation.

In response to Chris's questions, Suff said he'd been a medical corpsman in the Air Force in Texas, working in the pediatric ward of a hospital, "taking care of babies, uh, newborns up to sixteen-year-olds; hand out medication, cleaning them up, take temperatures, things like that." Not exactly the type of training that would have qualified him to deliver his own baby, as he'd told the Texas jury he originally planned to do because of his love of babies and his considerable medical experience.

He said he furthered his education while in Texas by earning a bachelor of arts degree in sociology and social work from the Stephen F. Austin State University. He didn't reveal he earned the degree while serving ten years of a seventy-year prison sentence for murdering Dijanet.

Suff explained the Texas parole card the police found in his van by stating he had served "a week and a half" in Texas for beating up a man he'd caught having an affair with his first wife, Ann. "I found out that he was going to bed with my wife," Suff claimed, "and I went to push him and tell him to stay away from her. And he swung and hit me, and then I hit him back, broke a couple ribs, broke his arm and I think I broke his jaw."

"You didn't know your strength," Chris commented, playing along. She later reported, "When I found out [his time served was actually ten years, and that his Texas parole] was for *murder*, I [was shocked]. And when I found out it was for the murder of *his child,* I'd like to have died. To think that he could sit in there with such a cold attitude of, 'Well, yeah, I was in jail once for, God, let me think, what was it?' I mean it was amazing afterwards. I thought if I'd had all that information in advance, I probably could have approached him in a different way."

Suff claimed that his ex-wife was often unfaithful to him, and that was why he finally divorced her. After Ann, Suff said he had a long relationship with a girlfriend named Bonnie, whom he met on his return to California. He said, at Bonnie's inspiration, he had joined the First Southern Baptist Church in Lake Elsinore. He was a member of the choir there, and the puppeteer at the children's Bible School. As Chris listened, she realized he was steadily building a portrait of himself as a kind, caring, religious person who loved children, medicine, and his fellow man.

If Chris had any shred of doubt left that Suff was the serial killer, it disappeared the instant he crossed his legs and one of his chubby black tennis shoes came into her view. The label on the shoe read Converse—the brand that had left so many footprints around Eleanor Casares's body.

During the long, frequently interrupted interrogation, Chris kept prodding and coaxing, scolding and arguing, trying to draw out a confession. At one point, she suggested to Suff, "[Did] you think you [were] doing a service to the community by cleaning up these sluts out there on the boulevard?"

Suff replied, "Murder is wrong."

When Chris asked him to explain the bloody kitchen knife found in his van, he answered that he kept it in the van for slicing the fat off of ham "and other stuff" he'd buy at the grocery store. He claimed the blood on the blade was his; he had accidentally sliced his finger "a couple of months ago."

When Chris returned to discussing Suff's background, he said he had two children by a previous marriage "but they're not mine."

During breaks in the interrogation, Suff was allowed to take naps, eat, or otherwise relax himself, while the other task-force investigators hurriedly briefed Chris on details they had learned from their hasty interviews of Suff's neighbors, or their searches of his apartment. Suff had readily agreed to let the authorities search his apartment, asking only that his wife, Cheryl, should be there at the time. He probably wanted Cheryl on site to report to him exactly what the police seemed most interested in. However, that ploy backfired, because Cheryl invited two of his brothers to come over and assist her during the ordeal, and all three Suffs wound up helping the police search out evidence against Suff from his residence.

Chris took advantage of one of the longer breaks to have Cheryl Suff brought to the station, so she could personally interview Suff's wife and tap her for clues to get him to confess. During her interview, Cheryl told of Suff's fondness for giving gifts of used women's clothing and jewelry. Her recollections of some of the items recently given out, and to whom, sent task-force members racing to the recipients to retrieve all of that damning evidence. When Chris then asked Suff about his used gifts, he claimed he had obtained most of them "from yard sales and, uh, swap meets."

By then, a fax of Suff's Texas criminal record had arrived, showing he had lied when he told Chris he had never been in prison for a serious crime. He had told her he worked for the prison industry as an employee. Chris confronted him with his lie, which he readily admitted, and then told him, "We're not here because we want to entertain you, and we're not here for you to entertain us. We're here because we have some hard, solid evidence. Do you understand that?" She demanded he cease his lies and tell them the truth. She told him she was going to stop him every time he told them a lie, because she wanted to help him tell the truth.

Chris told Suff they knew he had been at the orange groves because they had found his tire tracks there. He then admitted he had lied, but he insisted he had only driven there to pick some oranges. Chris told him there was something in those groves besides oranges when he was there, and he knew what it was. What was it, she asked.

"There was a dead body there," he admitted, but he claimed he didn't know who put it there.

With Chris's persistent questioning, Suff admitted he saw the body and walked around it. Chris had him close his eyes and describe his activities, step by step, that day, to make it easier for him to finally say the words: It was he who killed Eleanor Casares.

To make it clear that Suff was still talking willingly and freely, RSO investigator Davis interrupted and reminded him, "Couple minutes ago you said you wanted a lawyer. Now, [do] you want to talk to us about this?" Moments before, Suff had said, "I better get a lawyer now. I better get a lawyer 'cause you think I did it and I didn't." Davis had countered by saying, "I'm giving you the opportunity to talk to me. Do you want to do that?" Suff had responded, "Yes, I do, I do." Davis now tried to get Suff to verbally repeat that opinion, again for the record—that he didn't feel he needed a lawyer and that he wanted to continue talking—because it seemed Chris had Suff on the verge of confessing.

Instead, the mention of a lawyer seemed to make Suff nervous again. "I think I need a lawyer over here," he said.

"Did you want to talk to us?" Davis repeated.

"I want to try to clear this up," Suff said. "I want to make sure you end up knowing I didn't kill her. I took the clothes because they were lying nearby her and that's it."

Chris jumped back in: "Do you want to talk to me, Bill? I want to make this perfectly clear to you, okay?"

"I know."

"You know yourself that you don't have to talk to us, you know that, don't you?" Chris said.

"I know."

"Do you want to tell us the truth, Bill?"

"Yes . . . to clear up this stuff."

Suff repeated that he went to the groves to get some oranges, then found the body, took the clothes, and went home.

"What did you do with the clothing when you got it home?" Chris asked.

Suff said he washed it "because I was washing a bunch of dark clothes and I just grabbed it, too."

Chris asked about the bloody knife that was discovered in his van. Each time Suff insisted he simply found it on the ground by the body, Chris would ask for the truth.

Finally, Suff admitted, "The knife was sticking out of her chest . . . in the middle of her chest."

"And what did you do?" Chris asked.

"I pulled it out."

Chris urged him to tell more about how the knife got in Eleanor's chest in the first place, but Suff always hesitated over saying the actual words.

Seeing that she appeared stalled on that murder case, Davis jumped in, sternly telling Suff the authorities also had his tire tracks and footprints at other murder scenes. He pushed Suff to tell about those other cases, as well. Suff repeatedly professed complete ignorance of any other dead bodies.

Chris took over again and told Suff, "We are not going to let you sit there and lie to us."

Unable to explain his presence at additional murder scenes, Suff evidently felt cornered. He abruptly dropped all his efforts and said, "We can't talk anymore, then. Because you think I'm lying and I'm not. I want a lawyer."

By law, the interrogation would have to be halted. The job of nailing William Lester Suff then devolved onto the Riverside County district attorney. With the monumental help of law-enforcement investigators and government crime labs, supervising deputy district attorney Paul Zellerbach would assemble a mountain of evidence against Bill Suff over the next three years that the case awaited trial.

On January 11, 1992, two days after he was taken into police custody for questioning, Suff placed three phone calls to the office of his apartment manager, unable to contact Cheryl because they had no phone in their apartment. Rebecca wasn't in, so Suff spoke with the assistant manager, Kristin.

Unaware that the task force had contacted many people in the villas, and that word had already spread that he had been arrested for the serial murders, Suff told Kristin he was in jail because of some unpaid tickets and an outstanding traffic warrant. She apparently displayed a disturbing lack of reaction to his news, because Suff immediately amended his story to say he had also been accused of being the serial killer.

Suff told Kristin his tire tracks and shoeprints apparently matched those at the murder scenes, but that there were thousands of the same shoes and tires out there in the world. He claimed the Riverside officers who arrested him even told him he was the third person they had accused so far. He was sure they would be releasing him soon.

He asked Kristin to visit him in jail, but she refused. He wanted to know what she and Rebecca had told the police. Kristin said she could not tell him.

On his third call, Suff asked Kristin to leave a note for Cheryl. He wanted her to come and visit him in jail.

And not to believe what the police were saying.


On January 14, 1992, DOJ criminalist Steve Secofsky notified Chris Keers that several items of trace evidence collected from Bill Suff's body and van matched evidence collected at the McDonald and Casares homicide scenes. That morning, Chris visited Suff at the jail to personally inform him he was under arrest for the murders of Catherine McDonald and Eleanor Casares.

As time progressed and the DOJ crime lab completed additional comparisons, more cases were added to the list of Suff's homicides. When the murder trial finally began, in late March 1995, William Lester Suff faced thirteen counts of first-degree murder and one count of attempted murder for the attack on Rhonda Jetmore.

Following Suff's arrest for the serial murders, his mother was so angry at Suff and so determined to disassociate herself from her embarrassing son that she preferred to

talk to the prosecutors rather than her son's defense lawyers. She even made the comment to prosecutors on two
separate occasions, months apart, that if Suff were indeed
guilty of the serial murders, the State "should hang him!"

She wrote a letter to Suff in which she bluntly notified
him that she didn't consider herself at all blameworthy for
how he'd turned out in life. She told him she raised her
kids as best she could and had given them all good morals.
(However, of the three other Suff brothers, one had a
history of drug crimes; the second had a long prison record
for robbery; and the third had repeated arrests for sexual
assaults, including child molesting.) Continuing her lec-
ture on blame, Suff's mother wrote that he should look
inside himself for the answer to why he became the way
he is. She told him, "Stop and think about all the kids
with the last name of Suff and what they have gone through
and will go through [because of you]."

His brothers were equally eager to distance themselves
after his arrest. Two of them were at his apartment when
members of the task force arrived to search the premises
for evidence. Both declared they hardly saw their brother
and knew little about him. One called him "strange and
different" and "secluded." Both helped the investigators
search Suff's home for evidence against their brother, and
even found important items for the task force to use in its
case. They stressed that Suff had never involved them in,
nor told them anything about, any prostitute murders.
They actually barely knew him, they insisted.

Later, when the panic subsided, some of the family
began to contact Suff and offer him words of encouragement. Others, however, continued to distance themselves
from him. At least two in his immediate family attempted
to capitalize on his notoriety by trying to sell Suff's story
to tabloid TV shows and book publishers, one of them
reportedly doing so with Suff's help and guidance.

Given the lifelong lack of closeness and frankness among

the Suff family members, it is unlikely the formative events that helped mold Bill Suff into a serial killer will ever be known for certain, if indeed that is where the foundation of his perversion lies.

All that is known for certain, and what is most critical in understanding the man, is his behavior in manhood. It is a recurring pattern of deceit, frustration, manipulation, and violence that—whatever its genesis—resulted in the brutal deaths of over a dozen women.

# Part III
# The Court

# Chapter Thirteen

Nineteen drug-addicted prostitutes were murdered in western Riverside County, California, between 1986 and 1991. William Lester Suff was brought to trial for thirteen of those homicides; the authorities unable to find sufficient evidence to charge him with the other six. The murder of San Bernardino County prostitute Lisa Lacik was also tied to Bill Suff, but charges could not be filed in that case because it occurred outside Riverside County's jurisdiction.

According to the District Attorney's Office, some evidence in the six uncharged cases had been lost due to preservation problems and the passage of time. Also, in some of the earliest homicides, trace evidence hadn't been collected because the authorities did not initially suspect a serial killer was at work, and did not process the crime scenes in a manner likely to link those scenes to other homicides.

Regarding the uncharged murders, several of the experts who worked on the serial case ultimately concluded

244    *Christine Keers and Dennis St. Pierre*

that at least two of those six crimes were probably not committed by Bill Suff. Whether he committed any of the other four uncharged murders—or additional murders outside the county, as some suspected—remained a subject of debate in law-enforcement circles. The county's prosecutor for the case, supervising deputy district attorney Paul E. Zellerbach opined that justice would be served even if Bill Suff were not convicted of the uncharged slayings. He acknowledged, however, that such a resolution probably would not satisfy the families of those victims.

In general, the relatives of those six homicide victims chose to believe that Bill Suff was the perpetrator in their cases. Suff was known to have had ties to some of the victims or their families. A few frustrated relatives seized upon that as proof of his guilt, driven by grief to resolve the issue in their mind if not in reality. Suff's arrest made him an easy target for those seeking assurances their relative was being avenged—her death, therefore, not for nothing, her killer finally caught and punished, even if not specifically for her death.

To some of the victims' relatives, even that was not enough. One grieving mother stated, "Even if he gets the chair for [the thirteen cases], and not for these other [six] girls, I can't go to my grave in peace."

Another of those victims' mothers agreed, but said she didn't want Bill Suff to get the death penalty. "I want him to sit right there in that damn cell 'til he rots," she said. "Who does he think he is that he can say, 'Your time to die, your time to die'?"

The father of one victim spoke of more immediate revenge. "I would personally delight in executing that bum," he said.

Although there was considerable media attention when the trial finally started in late March 1995, the attention lasted only about one week. It wouldn't return until the verdicts were issued in July.

There were two possible explanations for the lack of media interest. The O.J. Simpson double-murder trial was in full swing in Los Angeles and commanding extraordinary media attention, to the exclusion of other news stories. And there was a strong prejudice against, and therefore lack of concern about, the victims in the Riverside case, whom some viewed as little better than their killer. During the beginning of the murder spree, some local citizens even felt the serial killer was doing the community a service by ridding it of human "trash." Some investigators, such as RPD detective Chris Keers and the district attorney assigned to the homicide task force, felt the investigation was initially given short shrift by law-enforcement administrators because of the unpopular status of the victims.

The participating DA—prosecutor Zellerbach—recalled called "it was difficult to marshal resources and get commitments from our respective agencies to devote to this case" because the victims were drug-addicted street prostitutes. Zellerbach stated he had "often said that if the victims had been housewives instead of hookers, everyone would have been bending over backward [to help solve the case]."

Defense attorneys tried to use the victims' backgrounds to influence jurors' consideration of their client's blameworthiness. They officially protested in court when prosecutor Zellerbach asked permission to show the jury a poster board showing photos of all the victims. The protest was raised because the family pictures depicted the women as normal mothers, daughters, and sisters. The defense insisted the board should instead consist of police-booking photos of the women: grimly unflattering portraits with police-booking cards held against the subjects' chests. The defense called those photos more characteristic of the victims. Concerned with the effect the photos might have on jurors' sympathies, the defense attorneys urged the court to prefer the scowling, sneering mug shots for the poster board, which was to be left in prominent display for much of the trial. The judge flatly denied the defense request.

Because he had been working with the task force for almost a year and was so well-versed in the case, Paul E. Zellerbach decided to handle Bill Suff's prosecution all by himself. Some counseled him that the mountain of evidence and paperwork would be easier to manage if divided among several prosecutors. However, Zellerbach stated he thought it would be easier to keep the massive, fourteen-victim case organized, coherent, and properly linked together if it was kept within one man's constant focus.

Zellerbach clearly did not approach the case as though he considered it an easy win. Often he was both visibly and verbally agonizing over the task of proving the murders were linked together and committed by the same man. As the trial dragged on, he seemed increasingly obsessed with obtaining convictions on all counts so that none of the victims' family members would be left worrying that their relative's killer was a different man—someone still at large and unpunished for his crimes. He clearly wanted the victims' families to feel closure, relief, and satisfaction at the end of the legal ordeal. And he clearly wanted to make the point to the public that the victims were human beings and real women with regular families, and not inconsequential objects or pieces of trash.

Faced with the enormous task before him, Paul Zellerbach was disorganized at the beginning of the trial, and was repeatedly admonished by the judge for being unable to find key documents or photographs, for showing up late to court, and for forgetting to ask questions of his witnesses (two of whom had to remind Zellerbach after leaving the stand to ask the questions). One of the defense attorneys commented, "It was a little funny. Here's a guy, pushing, pushing—you know: 'No continuance! Let's get this trial on!' [And then] he wasn't ready for it."

However, the same attorney admitted Zellerbach "got better as it went along" and "really hit his speed on the DNA [testimony]." He said Zellerbach's closing argument in the penalty phase was a "highlight of the trial."

Zellerbach's initial difficulties were understandable. A very dedicated and intense man, he was consumed with the case and with ensuring that the serial killer he had been hunting would not go free. He drove himself at a harried, unforgiving pace to be sure nothing was overlooked or left out of his presentation. Unfortunately, that harried pace took its toll on his control of the case in the beginning of the trial, but it was a short-lived stumble, from which he quickly and fully recovered.

The trial was divided into two parts: a guilt phase, to determine guilt or innocence; and a penalty phase, which would occur to determine an appropriate penalty if the defendant were found guilty in the guilt phase. A conviction on even one count of first-degree murder with special circumstances would present jurors with a choice of either the death penalty or life in prison without possibility of parole for Bill Suff.

At the onset, the prosecution saw its hardest task in proving that Bill Suff was a *serial* killer—responsible for all the murders. Without being able to prove that link between the cases, the defendant might be convicted of only one or two of the crimes—those with the highest independent amounts of evidence. By being able to show that some pieces of evidence from one scene were linked to another scene, convictions would also be possible in the weaker cases that lacked enough evidence on their own to obtain independent convictions.

The strength of the prosecution's case lay in the crime labs' conclusions about all of the evidence that had been recovered: trace evidence (fibers and head/pubic hairs), tire tracks and shoeprints, and DNA testing of semen found in several victims and of blood found on the knife in Bill's van. In addition, the prosecution would present several pieces of victims' property that had been recovered from Bill Suff's current or recent possession, plus the testimonies of Rhonda Jetmore (who had survived an attempted murder by Suff) and Kelly Whitecloud (who had fled his van and witnessed Suff pick up victim Kelly Hammond on the night of her murder). Other prosecution evidence to be presented consisted mostly of witnesses who would testify that Suff had possessed the opportunities to commit the murders, or had spoken hatefully of prostitutes in the past.

The defense's main objective would be to persuade the jury that the crimes were *not* linked together, and that, at most, their client was guilty of only one or two murders; a total much less likely to result in a death sentence and much easier to deal with on appeals. However, the defense suffered greatly from a lack of alibi witnesses. The defense strategy was limited to attacking the credibility of each prosecution witness and the evidence (its collection and handling, and the true rarity or significance of the laboratory findings).

Beyond that, the defense team would attempt to present Bill Suff as an "average, common man" who "was a victim of circumstance"—just a guy who was caught in the wrong place at the wrong time.

The judge made several important rulings on the case early on. He overruled defense objections and allowed the admission of DNA testimony in the trial. This was to the prosecution's advantage, although the DNA testimony was generally considered superfluous because there was so much other evidence accumulated among the various murders. Zellerbach himself called the DNA testimony not crucial and "just one more nail in Mr. Suff's coffin." Even defense counsel Randolph K. Driggs dubbed it, "just icing on the cake."

However, three other decisions did appear very important, and all were to the benefit of the defense. Judge W. Charles Morgan, a veteran of several murder and sex-offense trials, ruled that the prosecution could not introduce any evidence about Bill Suff's Texas murder conviction in the guilt phase of the trial because it was too inflammatory and prejudicial—too likely to prejudice the jury against Suff, were they to learn he had beaten to death his own two-month old daughter years earlier. The defense was convinced Suff would stand little chance if the jury were to learn about Dijanet. The judge said such evidence could be presented in the penalty phase, as an example of Suff's character and likelihood of reform.

Along the same lines, the judge refused to allow Zellerbach to mention that the defendant suffered from a venereal disease at the time he murdered Cheryl Coker, as proven by laboratory tests on the used yellow condom found near the victim's feet and by interviews with Suff's physician. This was also considered to be too inflammatory.

The judge also refused to allow an FBI expert to testify about serial-killer profiles, which distressed prosecutor Zellerbach. But Zellerbach found greatest distress in the judge's decision regarding the police interrogation of Bill Suff. The judge ruled that none of Suff's most incriminating admissions could be presented in court because they occurred after Suff had requested an attorney: "I better get a lawyer now," Suff had said, "'cause you think I did it and I didn't." It didn't matter that Suff had quickly changed his mind and stated he wanted to keep talking. ("Yes, I do, I do . . . I want to try to clear this up. I want to make sure you end up knowing I didn't kill her.") The judge was persuaded by the defense that Suff had expressed a sincere desire for a lawyer and had continued talking only because he felt intimidated by his interrogators, Chris Keers and John Davis. The jury would not be allowed to hear that Suff had admitted pulling the knife from the center of Eleanor Casares's chest and taking it, and her clothes, after "finding" her body in the orchard while there "to pick oranges."

The importance of appearances wasn't lost on Bill Suff. Although whenever he was being transported to or from the courtroom, he was bound in chains that encircled his body, binding his handcuffed hands to his waist, Suff asked the court that the jury not be allowed to see him like that when he was in the courtroom, so as not to prejudice their judgment of him. Further, he wanted the judge to permit him to also stand, out of respect, whenever the jury entered or exited the courtroom, just as everyone else present did.

The judge said that to do so raised security concerns. He wondered if Suff would give his word that he would not attempt to escape if he were to allow his requests. Suff assured Judge Morgan, "I am not prone to make any escape attempt. I can promise I will not make any escape attempt. . . . No matter what way it comes out, I am going to see it through."

Morgan therefore granted Suff's requests, although he said that whenever only one deputy was present, he must remain seated.

Suff gave equal concern to his wardrobe, frequently complaining that it was wrinkled or not nice enough. He also asked his attorneys to be sure the jury saw him wearing a different shirt every day, and asked one of them to loan him some ties so he could wear a different tie every day, as well.

There wasn't much, however, that he could do about his jailhouse pallor. Three years of incarceration while awaiting trial had faded Bill's skin to a sickly, chalky white—as white as his dress shirt. Although he was overweight and beefy before his arrest, he appeared soft and paunchy at the trial. His slicked-back brown hair was now silver-white from the stress of custody and awaiting judgment. He looked even more like somebody's harmless grandfather, as Kelly Whitecloud had described him. One reporter claimed he saw a faint resemblance to W.C. Fields in Suff's "puffy, pug-nosed profile."

Prosecutor Zellerbach scoffed at any idea that Suff was not enjoying his incarceration and his fame, saying that Suff seemed to really be enjoying the limelight. He reminded any doubters that Suff had served ten years in prison in Texas and another three awaiting trial, "so he's more at home in prison than out."

Suff did seem to be acting like his old, "overly helpful" self. Once, after a female deputy finished securing one of the three padlocks that bound the chains around his waist, Suff told her she hadn't actually locked it, and he reached back to help her with it, offering her advice on how to do it better next time. Sometimes he even helped the deputy chain himself up.

Another example of such "helpfulness" was witnessed by prosecutor Zellerbach at the security elevator off the courtroom. It was used to transport Suff from the third-floor courtroom to the basement, for his underground trip back to the jail across the square. Due to the nature of his crimes, a protocol had been established for additional guards to meet Suff and his deputy at the bottom when the doors opened. One day the deputy escorting Suff was a new person who, although aware of the protocol, was unfamiliar with the procedure. The deputy hesitated at the elevator door, unsure how to call down and alert the guards that Bill Suff was on his way. Observing the deputy's hesitancy, Suff suddenly pushed forward and reached for the intercom buttons, saying, "Here, I know how to do it." And he did. Stunned that the deputy had allowed the helpful prisoner to take charge, Zellerbach loudly commented, "Why don't you just give him a key to his cell and let him lock himself in?"

It was known that Suff was so at ease in his jail environment he was even writing a cookbook during the trial, and often happily discussed it with those around him in the courtroom. He supposedly claimed he had a great recipe for chicken cacciatore, although one person who examined his recipes called them decidedly banal.

Because it was a death-penalty case, Suff was entitled to have two attorneys representing him. His defense team consisted of Randolph "Randy" K. Driggs, a sophisticated, erudite man who favored far-flung references and professorial persuasion. Driggs had been a Riverside deputy district attorney for seven years before turning to private practice. He had worked with Zellerbach while in the DA's office, and even mentioned this to the jury, saying he had enjoyed a good, friendly relationship with Paul Zellerbach back then. (Zellerbach, apparently seeking to dispute anything the defense said, subsequently told the jury he never considered the two of them actual friends.) Driggs's role in the defense was to handle the scientific evidence part of the trial.

Cocounsel was Frank S. Peasley, a criminal-defense specialist appointed to represent Suff following the removal of his first attorney. The court decided a conflict of interest existed in the Public Defender's Office representing Bill Suff, since the office had also represented many of the murder victims and potential witnesses. A barrel-chested, white-bearded, heavy-browed man, Peasley was to handle the nonscientific part of the defense.

Part of the defense strategy was for the two attorneys to play good cop/bad cop, with the friendly, smaller Driggs as the good cop and the more stern, imposing Peasley as the bad cop.

The judge for the trial, W. Charles Morgan, always maintained very tight control of the courtroom and the pace of the trial. Bearing a striking resemblance to Wyatt Earp's older brother Virgil—who actually served as a city marshal in the neighboring city of Colton—Judge "Chip" Morgan seemed determined to run the trial with no-nonsense, Old West efficiency. Under his tight reins, the two-part, fourteen-count murder trial was completed in only five months.

The jury was composed of six men, six women and eight alternates, ranging in age from thirty-two to sixty-two. All were white except for one Hispanic woman, and all were married, except for one twenty-eight-year-old divorced woman. They were selected from a final jury pool of 239, of whom only seven had indicated opposition to the death penalty (Riverside County residents being somewhat notorious for their conservative beliefs). The defense strategy in selecting jurors was to target those people who viewed themselves as leaders. The hope was that such people would be independent thinkers and therefore not easily swayed by emotional appeals or mob sentiment. Toward that end, the defense counsel appeared successful in their selection efforts.

The courtroom was fairly small but, enjoying only local media attention, was often half-empty. The seats were filled almost entirely by victims' relatives (usually numbering less than a dozen), two or three print journalists, and one book author. Television monitors had been installed in all areas, so that everyone within the room was in view of at least one monitor at all times.

That innovation allowed everyone to see almost every item of evidence in clear, graphic detail—including the gruesome photographs of the murder scenes and related autopsies. Although Zellerbach warned the victims' families about the photographs in advance—"I can't express to you strongly enough that some of these photographs are pretty bad"—some relatives bolted in tears at the first sight of them. Those who remained often gasped and cried quietly while a bailiff dispensed tissues.

In general, the relatives who attended the trial had not come to hear the details of the case as much as they had come to be a physical presence in the courtroom, showing support for the prosecutor and his case on behalf of their loved ones. Some even spoke specifically of being there "to make sure [Bill Suff] is convicted."

The trial itself was often tedious, laborious, and very technical. It seemed a torture for many to sit through, especially during the scientific evidence and DNA discussions, which seemed to many endlessly repetitious. Both sides expressed concern that jurors might be getting lost or bored to inattention by the subject matter. But there seemed no other, easier way to accomplish the task at hand. So the jury's indulgence simply had to be begged . . . often.

The opening statement of prosecutor Paul Zellerbach seemed to some "disjointed" at first, as he railed from one topic to another, but it rapidly came together. His main theme was that Bill Suff had taken advantage of "the weak and the helpless"—murdering unfortunate, drug-addicted women when they were in an especially vulnerable position. He told the jury the victims had turned to prostitution to support their drug habits, and that Suff had strangled all of them, and also stabbed and mutilated some. He promised to present an array of evidence and expert witnesses through the trial that would prove Suff's guilt in each and every case, leaving no doubt in the jury's minds that Suff was a serial murderer of thirteen women, and the attempted murderer of a fourteenth. He stated he had subpoenaed 491 potential witnesses for the trial.

Zellerbach's opening statement briefly presented each of the thirteen murders and the attempted murder. Sometimes he employed the video projector to display victim photos on the monitors, which sent some victims' relatives fleeing the room in tears. Afterwards, one victim's sister said the experience made her feel "sad, like going to the funeral all over again." It gave Joan Payseur, mother of victim Cherie Payseur, hope for closure. She noted that after waiting three years for the trial to start, "When this trial is over, I can put Cherie to rest."

Zellerbach told the dramatic story of Rhonda Jetmore, who fought off Suff's attack in the dark, deserted Lake Elsinore house. Before he attacked, Suff handed her a one-dollar bill as payment for sex instead of the agreed-upon twenty, sadistically delighting in insulting his victim before killing her. He told Jetmore his name was Bob, Zellerbach said, although the big brass belt buckle on his waist said Bill. In a dramatic display, Zellerbach then showed a photo of Bill Suff standing by his girlfriend Bonnie's white Toyota station wagon—and then zoomed in closely on Suff's belt buckle in the photo: a big brass belt buckle with the name Bill on it.

After the dramatic display, Joan Payseur stated that Suff was also wearing that brass buckle when she worked with him as a Weekender at the county warehouse, about a year before he murdered her daughter Cherie.

Zellerbach discussed the arrest of Bill Suff, and how the gray Mitsubishi van was rich in evidence incriminating Suff in the murders, including a steak knife containing blood that matched that of his last victim, Eleanor Casares. "All the implements of Mr. Suff's trade were in the back of his van that night [he was arrested]," Zellerbach told the jury. "The knife, the rope, the sleeping bag."

Bill Suff appeared extremely interested in the proceedings. He took copious notes on a yellow legal pad before him, occasionally whispering to his attorneys, rarely looking up except when a photo was displayed on the monitor before him. When the photo was of a victim's body, he often would only glance at it and then look down stonefaced, as if afraid to show any emotion for fear the jury would construe it as a sign of guilt.

Zellerbach concluded his opening statement by assuring the jury, "As the evidence during the next several months will prove to you beyond a reasonable doubt, the person responsible for the murder of these thirteen women sits before you this morning. That person is obviously William Lester Suff."

Frank Peasley promised in the opening statement for the defense that the defense would show many of the problems with the prosecution's theories and evidence, and would persuade the jury that Bill Suff simply could not have committed the crimes in question but is simply a common man caught up by coincidence.

Peasley didn't promise a parade of witnesses from the defense, but rather that "much of what you will hear from the defense will be from cross-examination of prosecution witnesses." He said how many witnesses the defense calls would depend on how the prosecution's case unfolded.

He admitted to the jury that Suff "did employ prostitutes," but claimed "he treated them with respect and was good to them," implying that therefore any trace evidence linking Suff to the dead prostitutes must have been transferred during harmless prior contacts.

Keep an open mind, Peasley urged the jury, and don't be swayed by emotions when presented with disturbing evidence of brutal murders. "Do the right thing and hold the prosecution to its burden [of proof]," he urged, "and find insufficient evidence to convict Mr. Suff."

# Chapter Fourteen

First to testify in the trial was former prostitute Rhonda Jetmore, who had relocated to Northern California following Bill Suff's attack in the vacant Lake Elsinore house in January 1989. With the help and encouragement of her mother, Jetmore had managed to quit her heroin habit and reform her life. The stress of the effort, though, caused her to gain over a hundred pounds.

"That is the man who attacked me," Jetmore calmly stated on the stand, her eyes on Suff. "I'll never forget that face." She said she "had the opportunity to look at his face . . . the expression on his face" when he was lying on top of her, both hands around her throat. She said she managed to escape by knocking off Suff's metal-frame glasses, after which she watched him flee in a light-colored station wagon loaded with boxes of what had earlier appeared to her to be real estate papers.

Prosecutor Paul Zellerbach informed the jury that Bonnie, Suff's girlfriend at the time, was then working as a part-time real estate agent.

Defense attorney Randolph K. Driggs recalled his client was livid at Jetmore's testimony. "I remember," Driggs said, "when Rhonda Jetmore came and testified, she was as big as a house." Bill, he said, told him in a highly irate tone, "I didn't do that [attempted murder] because I *hate* fat women!"

"And then it came out in testimony," Driggs went on, "that she was a hundred pounds lighter at that time. But he was so concerned with that." Suff didn't want anyone to think he couldn't attract pretty women. He was so concerned over that impression, that Driggs finally had to tell him, "Bill, how the hell are we going to get [it said] on the stand that you hate fat women? What, are you going to get up there [yourself and risk your case over that one issue]?"

On cross-examination, defense attorney Frank S. Peasley tried to attack Jetmore's credibility by pointing out that in a follow-up interview she had stated the attack occurred at a different time of night. And, Peasley said, Jetmore claimed that her attacker had worn a red windbreaker, whereas "Mr. Suff hated red clothing—he didn't even like his wife to wear red clothing."

It was unknown what impact that latter statement had on the jury, but it certainly wasn't lost on the victims' relatives in attendance. On important days thereafter— such as the rendering of the verdicts and the sentence— many of the victims' female relatives showed up in court dressed in bright red outfits, in a silent but very visible display of contempt for their loved ones' murderer.


The prosecution's case followed an essentially chronological order in presenting the murders, depending in part on the availability of witnesses. The projection system and monitors were frequently used to display photographs of crime scenes and victims. Bill Suff kept his head down much of the time, scribbling constantly on his yellow legal pad. He seemed to avoid looking at the television monitor whenever a victim's body was displayed, as if to avoid showing any reaction that jurors might hold against him. But he seemed to examine his monitor closely whenever an overview, or long shot, of a murder scene appeared, as if curious if the site looked the way he remembered it.

The murder of Kimberly E. Lyttle, twenty-eight, was next. A construction worker described the discovery of her body, covered by a towel in some bushes, near Lake Elsinore on June 28, 1989. At first, he didn't believe it was a human body. The blue Western-style shirt found on her body did not belong to the victim, one of her friends then testified. Zellerbach said Suff had put the shirt on Lyttle after strangling her.

Sheriff's investigators and evidence technicians testified about their careful handling of the crime scene and its evidence, which had included tire tracks and shoeprints.

The discovery, six months later, of twenty-three-year-old Christina "Tina" C. Leal's body was covered next. A sightseeing couple found her on December 13, 1989, and at first thought she was a mannequin because her arms were not visible, having been tucked inside the large sleeveless muscle shirt with the King's Canyon imprint. Zellerbach told jurors he would provide proof later that that shirt belonged to Bill Suff.

Third in line chronologically was Darla Ferguson, twenty-three, whose nude body was found January 18, 1990, in one of the canyons in Lake Elsinore. A mother and her son who were driving the back road looking for firewood made the discovery after the boy told his mother he had spotted some legs in the bushes they just passed. Not believing the insistent child, the mother had backed their vehicle to the site just to prove him wrong. She found the nude victim, half-covered by a green plastic trash bag pulled over her head.

Fourth was Carol Miller, thirty-four, on February 8, 1990. She was found by orchard workers, a black cloth over her head, a half-eaten grapefruit sadistically tossed by her body. Several tire tracks were also found by both Miller's and Ferguson's bodies—tracks consistent with the tires on Bill Suff's gray Mitsubishi van at that time. And, Zellerbach said, shoeprints near those bodies were consistent with athletic shoes that investigators had recovered from Bill Suff's residence.

Cheryl Coker's husband, Boyd "Cowboy" Coker, testified to his wife's last hours, spent in prostitution trying to earn money for cocaine for the two of them. He said he hadn't contacted the police after her disappearance because he had a long criminal record for burglary and drugs. He was devastated to learn days later of her violent death at the hands of an unknown john.

Zellerbach reported that the DOJ crime lab recovered fibers from Cheryl Coker's body that were consistent with fibers found in Bill Suff's van. Similarly, shoe imprints found in the dirt under the wooden pallets stacked outside the Dumpster were consistent with the tread pattern of one of Bill Suff's pairs of ProWings athletic shoes. Moreover, the semen in a used yellow condom by the body was consistent with Suff's DNA. Zellerbach promised to go into detail on the scientific evidence later in the trial.

As with Cowboy Coker, Susan Sternfeld's friend George told how he had awaited Susan's return on University Avenue while she was prostituting herself, but she had never returned. Sternfeld, twenty-seven, was found nude and lewdly posed in an empty Dumpster enclosure near the edge of town two days later, December 21, 1990.

Suff's ex-girlfriend Bonnie testified that she bought a white Toyota Tercel station wagon in late 1984 or early 1985, and that she worked for a real estate company. She said she was with Suff from about 1985 to 1989. He'd told her he had been a medic in the Air Force.

Bonnie said she usually went to bed between 8 and 10 P.M., long before Bill, so she wouldn't have known if he ever took her car and went out at night while she was sleeping. Bill liked to wear plaid, lumberjack-type shirts while he was with her, Bonnie said, but favored Western-style clothes after they split up. She also had personally seen his large brass belt buckle with his name, Bill, in raised brass letters.

According to Bonnie, Bill was "very big" on putting his name on things. She said he was good at leather work, which he learned in prison in Texas. At first, he had told Bonnie he was an employee at the prison, but later was forced by his parole officer to tell her the truth: He had served time in prison in Texas for the death of his daughter. Suff assured Bonnie, however, he was innocent and his wife or a neighbor who visited in the middle of the night had committed the murder.

In July 1987, Bonnie said they had a fight and she kicked him out of her mobile home in Lake Elsinore. She learned he spent the next two to three weeks living in a basement room at John's Service Center, where he worked part-time in Lake Elsinore. Then he moved to the Morro Court Apartments on Grand Avenue in Lake Elsinore.

She said he had a motorcycle accident soon after he left her, and had trouble making it up to his second-floor apartment with a broken leg and arm, and severe head injuries. Bonnie said no one wanted to take care of him, so she let Bill temporarily move back in with her while he recuperated. That lasted about four months, until May or June 1989.

Bonnie said Bill received his insurance settlement for the motorcycle accident within six months of moving out from her place. She said he got thirty thousand dollars (far less than the eighty-seven thousand dollars he bragged he would get). Using that money, he paid cash for a new 1989 Mitsubishi van.

As for the charges against him, Bonnie said the crimes were certainly inconsistent with the Bill Suff she had known. She said such accusations made her question her sanity. Bill was never violent to her, she said. In fact, she said, the police "almost mocked me" when she told them how nonviolent he actually was. "The person I knew was extremely kind to help with my elderly grandmother," she said. "When nobody else was there, he was there. He was helpful in the church. He was helpful to me. He took care of me when I was sick. . . . He wasn't mean. I mean, he loved little animals. And . . . I thought he loved children. He never hit me. He never swore at me. . . . Whenever he would get mad, I couldn't find my watch and I'd walk around, 'Where is my watch? Where is my watch?' And my watch would end up in a shoe or something like that."

Bonnie said that, on the surface, the most unfavorable thing she could think of about Bill Suff was that he was a mediocre bowler.

She did, though, help the prosecution by providing one intimate detail about Suff's clothing size. Defense attorney Peasley had contended that the King's Canyon T-shirt left on victim Tina Leal could not be Suff's because it was a size medium and Suff wore an extra-large. Bonnie said that while Bill lived with her, he wore size medium shirts. And, while he lived with her, they took two vacations. One of them, she said, was to King's Canyon.

Riverside County Sheriff's Office investigator Bob Creed testified that after the next victim, Kathleen Puckett, forty-two, was found in an open trash site on January 19, 1991, "the homicide task force was created shortly afterwards"; the authorities then strongly suspecting a serial killer was at work.

On April 27, 1991, the nude body of Cherie Payseur, twenty-four, was found in a parking-lot planter behind the

Concourse Family Bowling Center in a residential area of town. During that crime-scene investigation, the center's automatic water sprinklers came on and threatened the integrity of the crime scene. Investigators had to run around, hopping onto the sprinkler heads to try to control their spray to prevent microscopic trace evidence from being washed off the victim's body. It was not a very successful endeavor, DOJ crime-lab criminalist Steve Secofsky reported to the court. Her body yielded the least amount of evidence of any in the series: a cat hair, some semen, and a partial footprint.

Although the cat hair was consistent with that found on Suff's cat Callie, the defense argued that animal hairs are far less unique than human hairs, and therefore too common for one to reasonably conclude that the hair came from Suff's cat. Furthermore, although the DNA of the semen found in the victim was consistent with Suff's DNA, another man's semen was also present, and the defense argued that definitive conclusions were not possible in the case of multiple semen donors, since there was an overlap of results.

In the case of the partial footprint found near the body, the tread pattern belonged to a ProWings athletic shoe, but because a cigarette butt had been found on top of that print, the defense argued the print may have been left there long before the murder. There had been a large crowd of spectators from the bowling alley mobbing the scene until the police arrived, and any one of them could have flicked a cigarette butt into the footprint, but the defense had succeeded in planting another seed of doubt about the case.

Similarly, the case of the next victim, Sherry Latham, thirty-seven, appeared weak in evidence. Hers was the only body from which no semen had been recovered, due to the decomposing nature of the corpse. Before the trial began, the defense had tried to have both Payseur and

Latham's cases dropped from the roster, claiming there was insufficient evidence to link them to the series. The defense attorneys claimed that any convictions in those two cases would be due to a "spillover effect" from the other stronger cases. Judge Morgan had denied their request to drop those two charges against Bill Suff.

Testifying next, about victim Kelly Hammond, twenty-seven, was Kelly Victoria Jewel Whitecloud, the former Riverside prostitute and drug addict who had provided the eyewitness testimony about Bill Suff and his van that resulted in his capture. Whitecloud seemed an emotional wreck on the stand, constantly breaking down into tears at the memories of the night of August 15, 1991, when she tried to warn her friend Kelly Hammond not to get into Bill Suff's gray van.

Kelly told how she got into Suff's van and agreed to straight sex for twenty dollars. She testified she needed the money "to get well," a street euphemism for injecting heroin to fight withdrawal symptoms. She said she asked Suff to feed her first, because she was almost six months pregnant then. He agreed and took her to the McDonald's across the street. She made a fuss in the restaurant when they put the nuts on top of the sundae she had ordered instead of the way she had requested.

She said she and Suff started arguing as soon as they got outside and returned to the van. She wanted to take him to her room for the sex and he insisted on going to the orange groves. "Everything just changed—and the look on his face just changed—and I got scared," Kelly said. Then Suff told her he should only have to pay ten dollars because he had bought her dinner. She told him she wanted to get out, but the van was moving down the street and he refused to stop. She opened the door and held it open with her leg and jumped out by a convenience store—falling flat on her pregnant stomach. As she rose, she saw the gray van drive on to Kelly Hammond and stop to pick her up.

Whitecloud said she yelled to her best friend, "Don't go! It's only ten dollars! It's not worth it!" She said Hammond looked back at her and smiled and said she'd be back. "I waited, but she never came back!" Whitecloud broke down again, sobbing uncontrollably. The judge had to call a ten-minute break to give Kelly Whitecloud time to compose herself. In his only obvious reaction in the trial to date, Bill Suff turned and glared furiously at Kelly Whitecloud on her entire walk out of the courtroom.

After the break, Kelly told how she had described the murderous john to RPD detective Chris Keers, and how Chris had then taken her around to various car lots to try to find a vehicle that looked like the john's gray van. A day or two later, Kelly said she went with Chris to the RPD headquarters to meet with a sketch artist and help create a composite drawing of the grandfatherly suspect in the gray van. She said on January 23, 1992, Chris Keers had contacted her again, in distant Contra Costa County Jail, to show her two different photographic lineups of six male faces that "may or may not contain suspects." One lineup contained the photos of men wearing glasses; one without. Kelly immediately picked out Bill Suff's photograph from each lineup.

The defense tried to imply that Kelly Whitecloud's heroin habit made her an unreliable witness, since heroin tends to dull one's perceptions. Kelly replied that she experienced "reverse" reactions to heroin when she used to use it. "It doesn't make me nod ... it wakes me up."

However, the heroin use, and the nightmares that attended it, often did affect drug addicts' memories, and Kelly's was a case in point. Her immediate report of the incident to Chris Keers hours after it occurred was that she had simply stepped out of the van while it was still parked in the McDonald's lot. However, during the passage of four years of nightmares about the incident, Kelly had convinced herself it was a more horrifying escape—a leap out of a moving van and a violent fall on her pregnant belly; the very telling of which caused her to break down uncontrollably.

Perhaps that is why Bill Suff glared so venomously at her during her walk out of the courtroom—furious at her self-deluded embellishment about the nonexistent fall. One of his attorneys, Randy Driggs, noted that Suff seemed peculiar that way, obsessed with numbers and the myopic view rather than the big picture. To Driggs, "Bill is some-one that, if he did ten of these [murders] and they con-victed him of twelve, he would be incensed because they convicted him of two he didn't do."

According to Driggs, Suff's frequent note-taking also reflected an unusual concern with dates and numbers, which to the defense attorney appeared to be a family trait. He recalled that when two of Suff's relatives were in his office discussing Suff's case and how best to save his life, they repeatedly became mired in arguments over the insig-nificant dates of the incidents being discussed. "They'd say, 'What year was that?' 'Oh, that was 1964.' 'No, it wasn't! It was 1965!' They were so concerned with numbers, they could never see the big picture," Driggs observed.

"And Bill," he went on, "I think there's no big picture [view] there [either]. There's just a very small, honed-on view of things." Driggs recalled once, during the presenta-tion of the Susan Sternfeld murder scene, when a photo-graph of the Dumpster containing her body also revealed a tall wall nearby, Suff was obsessed with knowing exactly how tall that wall was, and even insisted to his lawyers that they ask the witness on the stand that question. Neither defense attorney saw any relevance whatsoever in the request, but they did as requested, and found the number so Suff could write it on his legal pad. Driggs commented that Suff's scribblings were "probably better notes than the transcript" due to his obsessiveness with recording minutia.

"I think the little issues are viewed under a microscope [by Bill]," Driggs concluded. "And he viewed the trial with the same basic demeanor throughout, within a spectrum of no more than ten percent variance."

Testimony about the murder of Kelly Hammond caused one other problem for the defense team. They felt the evidence linking Suff to that homicide was weak—except for the police citation found in the glove compartment of his van; a ticket that had been issued to Kelly Hammond for drug and prostitution offenses within days of her murder.

According to Driggs, Suff insisted his attorneys allege that the citation had been planted in the glove compartment by the police. According to Driggs, "Frank [Peasley] didn't particularly want to say it was planted. You know, [he phrased it that] 'Mr. Suff wants me to say that—.' And, boom, Zellerbach then said Suff was trying to get away with testifying without having to be cross-examined. And what Frank was trying to do was say this argument needs to be made and I'm trying not to offend you by saying it. And that's a very difficult position to be in."

Catherine McDonald, thirty, was the next murder victim discussed. On September 13, 1991, a construction worker driving in the new development area by Lake Elsinore had at first thought the black woman's mutilated body was a tree root or log. He realized after passing it and reflecting a moment, that it must have been a human body. The man used his cellular telephone to dial 911, but the location of the crime scene in the middle of the vast dirt hills blocked the telephone signal. He backed his pickup to the first access road, and tried again, and then was connected to the California Highway Patrol.

Investigators testified that they arrived and found the victim with her right breast removed and body mutilated, including a slashed throat. The autopsy discovered that McDonald was pregnant at the time of her murder, carrying a boy of approximately twelve to thirteen weeks. The young age of the baby precluded the District Attorney's Office from filing separate murder charges.

The next victim, discovered on October 30, 1991, was Delliah "Dell" Zamora, aka Wallace, thirty-five, a woman from a large Hispanic family. Her death sent upheavals through the family and led one teenage niece to contemplate suicide as her only escape from her continuous grief.

Zamora's body could not be processed for evidence at the crime scene due to extraordinarily high winds—the notorious Santa Anas. She was transported to the Coroner's Office for processing. As with the other victims, she had been raped and strangled to death. However, unlike the others, she had not been stripped or mutilated, her killer evidently abandoning her body when early-morning commuters suddenly began arriving at a park-and-ride carpooling lot across from the site.

Chris Keers testified about the murder of the last victim, Eleanor Casares, thirty-nine, found on December 23, 1991, lying spread-eagled in a dirt alley between two rows of orange trees. There was much incriminating evidence discovered at that crime scene, Chris testified, including footprints, tire tracks, and fiber evidence. Chris told of her efforts to alert and protect the street prostitutes. She stated that she had personally known Eleanor, and in a softer, sadder voice admitted, "I had become quite friendly with her."

\*     \*     \*

Autopsy testimony followed, again case by case. A recurring pattern of strangulation, stabbing, and mutilation was established. The stabs were all essentially the same: very controlled, straight-on punching blows aimed directly at the heart. They usually deviated from an absolutely perpendicular angle by less than five degrees, indicating incredible control and calm on the part of the killer. Photographs of the autopsied women and their dissected body parts were shown on the monitors in the courtroom, again causing severe distress to the victims' relatives in attendance.

Occasionally, some of those relatives were called to testify regarding the last time they saw their relative alive, establishing a time frame for the occurrence of the murder, and establishing the humanity of the victim in the eyes of the jury.

A toxicologist testified next as to the presence of drugs and alcohol in the bodies of the victims. Drugs (primarily heroin and/or cocaine) were found in the bodies of ten of the thirteen women. Only Kathleen Puckett, Catherine McDonald, and Eleanor Casares had no detectable levels of drugs or alcohol in their systems at the times of their deaths. Kelly Hammond had a lethal level of morphine (a metabolite of heroin) in her blood at the time of her murder.

The prostitute whom Bill Suff was seen contacting in the liquor-store parking lot the night of his traffic stop was also called to testify. She repeated the occurrences of that night, and then told of being brought to the police station to be interviewed by Detective Chris Keers about her contact with Bill Suff. She said Chris led her to a room and asked her to look inside and see if she recognized anyone. The prostitute said she recognized the man seated at the table as the john who had solicited her. She later learned his name was Bill Suff. She was asked to indicate if she saw the same person seated in the courtroom. She identified the defendant, William Lester Suff, as that man.

RPD officer Frank Orta was called to the stand to report the occurrences of the night of the traffic stop as he observed them. Officers Don Taulli and Duane Beckman followed Orta to the stand, basically reiterating his testimony from their own perspectives.

Chris Keers was called next, and described items of evidence she observed inside Bill Suff's van that helped reinforce her conclusion that he was a strong suspect for the serial murders. She mentioned the DOJ crime lab reported finding a variety of trace fibers at the crime scenes: gray carpet fibers, and nylon and polyester fibers in the colors of green, gold, red, white, and blue.

In Suff's van, Chris said she saw a green blanket, gold pillow, and red-and-blue sleeping bag with white stuffing erupting through the fabric. The carpeting on the floor of the van, and the fabric on the walls and seats of the van, were gray. There were also pieces of rope throughout the van—all of it natural-fiber rope, just like the fibers DOJ reported recovering from the crime scenes. Moreover, Chris stated the officers showed her a kitchen knife they had recovered from under the driver's seat in the van, and it matched the dimensions of the murder weapon, as reported to her by pathologists. She then telephoned DOJ criminalist Steve Secofsky and asked him to verify her findings.

At the police station, Chris asked Bill Suff if he would agree to provide samples of his hairs, etc., for comparison purposes, and he agreed. Chris said she saw human scratch marks on one side of Bill's face and, when he removed his shirt for the technician to obtain exemplar samples of his chest hairs, Chris saw more scratch marks on his chest.

Chris reported she was able to identify the hooker Suff

had solicited from Orta's description of her clothing, having talked with enough of the prostitutes to know their wardrobes by heart. With Chris's help, officers were able to return to the field and quickly find the woman who had eluded their initial search. They brought her back to the station to be interviewed by Chris, and to identify the man who had solicited her.

The defense was only able to weakly attack the testimony of the police officers. Regarding one of the officers' comments about finding a CHP hat in Bill Suff's van, attorney Driggs asked if it was illegal to own a CHP hat, making the point with the jury that Suff had committed no crime there.

Even RPD officer William P. Barnes was called to the stand, to tell of the night before the traffic stop, when he spotted the caved-in gray van cruising University Avenue while he was parked across from a troublesome nightclub. Barnes stated that he responded to the traffic stop upon hearing the radio request for a 35-mm camera and, once there, informed the other officers that he had wanted to stop the van the night before because he had also realized it closely resembled the suspect vehicle in Chris Keers's flier.

After court, Barnes was philosophical about his missed chance at glory. He said, "My initial regret was that it wasn't me who actually stopped him that night [because then] all the accolades could have come to me. But I'd rather have that regret than the regret that I didn't stop him and he killed somebody else [because I let him get away]. That would have been a real bitter pill to swallow."

The investigation following the traffic stop was next. Investigators testified about finding victims' clothing and jewelry in the possession of Suff's friends and neighbors, and then the gift recipients testified about Suff giving them those gifts. RSO investigator Bob Creed testified that Pro-Wings athletic shoes had been found at the messy Suff apartment, as had a road map with two handwritten dots on the body-dump sites of Delliah Zamora and Kelly Hammond. When asked in cross-examination by Driggs how he had come to discover the map in Suff's apartment, Creed replied, "I kept stepping over the map—that's what drew me to it."

RPD detective Mike Hern testified that he found in Suff's apartment two of the unusual, oversized GE Miser 95-watt lightbulbs: one in a free-standing lamp in the living room, the other in the hall closet. Lightbulbs just like the one that had been found inserted far up Tina Leal's vagina. He also said he found a pair of metal handcuffs in a box in the cluttered living room, and several body and Western-style shirts exactly like those that had been placed on victims Tina Leal and Kimberly Lyttle.

Suff's bosses and coworkers testified next about his job performance at the county warehouse and how his work schedule afforded him the opportunities to commit the murders. Some of the Weekender work-release people testified how the boxes of purses were finally discovered on the shelves at his workstation.

One Weekender had needed a box for the pens he had pulled from inventory to fill an order—a box about the size of one of those on Suff's shelves. When he checked the small brown box to see if it was empty, he discovered a woman's purse inside it. The purse was open and had a string hanging out of it.

Investigating further, he found the string attached to a tampon. In the purse were a couple of tampons, two blue Trojan condoms, a smaller brown leather purse, a piece of paper with phone numbers on it and, in the side pocket, several folded police citations. Reading the word "prostitution" on one of the citations, the curious Weekender called some of his coworker buddies over to check out his discovery.

"Wow! She's a prostitute!" one of them gawked. They saw the name on the violations was Delliah Zamora.

The work-release men laughed over the tickets, finding it funny that the female owner of the purse had been cited for such scandalous things as prostitution and possession of a syringe. They threw the embarrassing contents back and forth to each other like kids playing hot potato, or, as the witness put it, "guys just being guys."

When they saw their supervisor coming, however, they panicked and threw the purse back under the counter. One of them didn't get a chance to return the citations to it. He told the supervisor he had to go to the bathroom, and then flushed them down the toilet instead.

A few days later, following Bill Suff's arrest, task-force members came to the warehouse to search Suff's area for evidence and found the purse. Learning the significance of the purse, the Weekender voluntarily told the investigators of the flushed tickets. Later, shown photocopies of Delliah Zamora's citations, he was able to pick out those he had flushed by remembering unusual details about them, such as the strange middle name the woman had: NMN, which actually was a police acronym for "No Middle Name."

Suff's apartment manager, Rebecca, was called to testify about the comment he made at her Christmas party, that a serial killer's victim in the *Silence of the Lambs* movie "was stupid to get in the van." Rebecca also told about the time in October 1991 when Suff mentioned to her she better be careful because the Riverside prostitute killer had just left another victim by Railroad Canyon Road. When she asked how he knew that, Suff claimed he heard it on his police scanner. Rebecca said she later heard about the murder on the TV news that night.

Relatives of the victims were paraded in to testify that the many recovered pieces of clothing and jewelry did indeed belong to their murdered loved one. Many of them, of both sexes and all ages, broke down weeping at the sight of the simple items, tearfully recalling that the last time they saw the victim alive, she had been wearing the cited article of evidence.

Kaiser hospital security personnel testified that, contrary to his contentions, Bill Suff was never involved in any fights or altercations at their facility. He had broken up no fights, rescued no women or children, and had no vengeful wives or girlfriends jump on his back and scratch his face for subduing their men. The witnesses stated that Kaiser enforces a strict reporting procedure regarding any incidents at the facility, and that any such encounters as Bill Suff had described would definitely have been documented and would surely have been remembered by their personnel. The witnesses testified that no reports existed of any such occurrences and that no personnel knew of any such incidents.

Neighbors and associates of Bill Suff were brought in to testify about his hatred of prostitutes. One woman told of an occurrence on August 19, 1989—her daughter's fourteenth birthday. She said she threw her daughter a slumber party as a present, and the girls all put on makeup and dressed up as Barbie dolls. Because her daughter liked their overly friendly neighbor so much, the girl was allowed to take her friends next door to ask Suff to judge who was the prettiest. Suff looked them over and told the girls that the one with no makeup was the prettiest—"more lady-looking," he called it—and the rest of them looked like "goddamned prostitutes."

The young pregnant girl Kristina, who had stayed with Suff after her brother kicked her out, testified that Suff often spoke of hating prostitutes. She said he told her "they needed to be killed" because "they were sluts." She said he told her that "just about every night." The defense suggested Suff was speaking only in hyperbole.

One of Suff's brothers testified about the time he helped Suff clean up Bonnie's yard and Suff suddenly stated that he hated prostitutes—blurting it out for no reason.

Cheryl was called to testify about Suff's many claims of performing earthquake-preparedness classes late at night, which his bosses had already testified never existed. Cheryl produced a calendar in which she had noted Suff told her he would be gone that night doing one such class in a distant location. The notation was "Earthquake show— Temecula." The date was April 26, 1991, the day Cherie Payseur was murdered. Cheryl said sometimes she wrote the notes after the event occurred, just to memorialize the event or remind her when it had happened.

A lengthy series of testimony from California Department of Justice Crime Lab criminalists Steve Secofsky and Faye Springer followed. It regarded the evidence recovered at the murder scenes in comparison to the evidence recovered from Bill Suff and his van and apartment. The criminalists provided detailed, technical analysis of tire track and shoeprint comparisons; blood type comparisons; head, pubic, and cat hair comparisons; and rope and fiber comparisons. Most of the comparisons were presented on poster boards so the jury could visually see the similarities and consistencies between Bill Suff's shoes, tires, hairs, and fibers and those found at the murder scenes.

The defense was unable to counter or significantly attack the criminalists' presentation, which was probably the most powerful and persuasive evidence in the trial. It seemed impossible to deny the visual similarities of the side-by-side comparisons displayed in full color on the oversized poster boards.

The defense was able to mount a better effort against the DNA evidence, since it was a technical, unfamiliar subject more suitable to challenge and obfuscation. It amounted to a battle of scientists throwing numbers and scientific terminology at each other, with the truth sometimes lost in the confusing process. An expert from the FBI laboratory provided testimony for the prosecution, discussing the semen found in all but one of the thirteen victims, and the blood found on the knife in Suff's van. Dr. Harold Deadman identified the blood as consistent with that of Eleanor Casares, and the semen as either consistent or "not inconsistent" with Bill Suff. His statistical probabilities of finding anyone else with the same characteristics ranged from one in several thousand to one in two billion.

The defense countered, in the presentation of their case, by bringing in experts who claimed DNA tests are unreliable due to contamination and handling problems, and fallacious calculations. According to one defense DNA expert, the true range of rarity in the Bill Suff evidence was in the hundreds or thousands instead of the millions and billions, as the prosecution claimed. Zellerbach disputed the defense experts, arguing they were not qualified to render expert decisions. However, he stated he would still be happy to accept the lower statistics offered by the defense, since he asserted they still showed a high enough rarity to strongly point to Bill Suff's guilt.

Chris Keers then returned to the stand to discuss her

interrogation of Bill Suff, after which the prosecution rested its case.

The defense case commenced with the testimony of a DNA expert who disputed the FBI scientist's testimony. The defense team then introduced witnesses who claimed to have seen other suspicious people in the area of some of the murders, including at least one other suspicious john who had picked up one of the victims around the last time she was seen alive. Such testimony, however, often seemed vague, and more opinion than substance.

One defense witness was a prostitute who stated she had frequently "dated" Suff and never felt threatened or in danger around him. She told how Suff would steal cash out of his boss's cash register at John's Service Center to pay for her sexual services, which she provided on the premises while the elderly owners were at church.

Suff's attorneys tried to exploit the victims' criminal backgrounds as a defense against the death penalty aspect of the case—proposing that, were Suff actually responsible for any of the homicides, those killings must have occurred during unplanned acts of violence rather than as premeditated murders that qualified him for the death penalty. The defense contention was that any such deaths must have come about when the drug-addicted prostitutes attempted to rob or cheat Suff, and the resulting argument simply got out of control—Suff simply lost control of himself in a street fight with the violent criminal women. That is, they claimed, *if* he killed any of the victims, *which*, they claimed, he *didn't*.

Prosecutor Zellerbach responded with the following: "It is amazing how inconsistent the defense can be. Mr. Peasley says, 'Mr. Suff did not commit any of these crimes—none! But if you think he did, it's a spur-of-the-moment rip-off, second-degree murder—thirteen times!'

"Ever buy a used car? If you're buying, I'm selling. Mr. Peasley wants you to compromise. But there's no way in God's green earth that you can have a spur-of-the-moment rip-off killing *thirteen times* over three years."

The defense called to the stand a hostile witness: the prostitute Debra who had lied to RSO task-force investigators when pressured for information on Kelly Hammond's murder. The woman told Chris Keers and Mike Hern she made up the story to get rid of the sheriff's men who were "hassling" her. Unfortunately, some task-force members seized upon Debra's story and ignored Kelly Whitecloud's report, focusing the search on the vehicle Debra described. This not only helped to prevent the task force's capture of the real serial killer, but now in trial, was being used by defense attorneys to try to set him free.

Being a cousin of victim Eleanor Casares, Debra was obviously determined not to hurt the case against Eleanor's killer by repeating the fabrication she'd told the RSO men. The defense needed her story to negate Kelly Whitecloud's eyewitness testimony. They wanted Debra to tell the jury she saw a man in an oversized blue pickup truck drive off with Kelly Hammond almost two hours after Kelly Whitecloud saw her disappear forever into Suff's gray van.

On the stand, Debra stubbornly denied all knowledge of anything, including talking to any law-enforcement officers, and even being a prostitute. She adamantly refused to admit anything except her name; obviously willing to go to jail for contempt rather than help her cousin's killer.

The defense tried to solve the problem by calling to the stand one of the RSO investigators who conducted the 1991 street interview of Debra. He was asked, "Is it not true that she told you that . . . ?", repeating each question originally put to the uncooperative cousin, thereby allowing the investigator to tell Debra's story to the jury in her place. However, it seemed abundantly clear that, from her stonewalling behavior, even Debra disbelieved her own story.

It also seemed abundantly clear, after the defense rested its case, exactly where the truth lay in the case of the *People vs. William Lester Suff.*

# Chapter Fifteen

The jury returned from deliberations in exactly one week, on July 19, 1995, being deadlocked for much of that time on one count: the murder of Cherie Payseur. Of the other counts, there was little doubt or hesitation about Bill Suff's guilt. One lone juror adamantly held out that there was not enough evidence on the Payseur case for her to conclude beyond a reasonable doubt that Bill Suff had committed that crime. It was said several of the other jurors often shouted at the woman in outrage for not recognizing what they called the obvious, but she remained true to her civic ideals and would not be swayed. Because a guilty verdict required a unanimous vote, a mistrial was declared in the case of Cherie Payseur.

Of the other twelve homicides, Bill Suff was found guilty of first-degree murder in every case. He was also found guilty of the attempted murder of Rhonda Jetmore.

In the courtroom, the spectator section erupted in gasps, and tears, and sobs of appreciation. At the defense table, Suff appeared in shock, stunned that somebody had finally disbelieved his excuses. He wiped his eyes again and again, until it was apparent he was silently crying at the shock of the verdicts. A female deputy standing nearby roughly tugged two tissues from a box and then strode over and, somewhat contemptuously, tossed them on the table directly in front of Suff.

Suff's tears outraged many of the victims' relatives in attendance. Some were incensed that he dared to feel sorry only for himself—having displayed no emotions throughout the trial for any of the victims or their families. Others believed the tears were purely theatrical, designed to solicit sympathy before the penalty phase commenced, which would determine whether he was to receive the death penalty for his crimes, or life without the possibility of parole.

When asked outside the courtroom about Suff's tears, prosecutor Paul E. Zellerbach coldly remarked, "I think I'd cry, too, if I was looking at the gas chamber. [And] I'd hand him a tissue, too, on his way to the gas chamber—it's the least I could do."

When the jury filed out of the courtroom after rendering their verdicts, Suff did not rise; the only time in the trial he failed to do so. Whether he was too overcome by shock or too angry over the verdicts, Suff offered the jury no show of respect that day.

Suff's stunned reaction at the verdicts surprised some people since the trial seemed to many an obvious lost cause for the defense. Randolph K. Driggs commented afterward on Suff's apparent surprise at being found guilty: "His idea was, 'How can they convict me if no one has seen me in any of these [crime] locations?'" Suff was apparently shocked that he could be convicted without an eyewitness to the murders.

In the hall outside the courtroom, the victims' relatives wept happily and consoled each other over their losses. Detective Chris Keers hugged Alice Peters, grandmother of victim Cherie Payseur, comforting her on the mistrial declared in her granddaughter's case. "He did it," Chris told Alice. "We know he did it. And that's all that matters." Cherie's killer would be just as dead after his execution, even if Cherie's name wasn't on the piece of paper they read at the gas chamber.

Suff's two attorneys had to pass through a crowd on their way to the elevators. The venomous looks the two men received for representing Bill Suff prompted Randy Driggs to whisper to cocounsel Frank Peasley, "Ever feel like you were a leper?"

The hallway also was filled with television-news camera crews; the media finally returning for the rendering of the verdicts. Although Judge Morgan had ordered no interviews be conducted in the courthouse, almost a dozen camera crews rushed with their blinding lights from one relative to another, seeking the families' reactions for the day's broadcasts. One crew abandoned the sister of victim Catherine McDonald in midsentence when a shout went up, "He's crying over there!" Half of the crews rushed to join the floodlights blinding Kim Lyttle's father as he sobbingly reported his life had been destroyed by the loss of his daughter.

The print-media reports generally tended to be very accurate about the proceedings and interviews of the participants. The televised broadcasts were sometimes incredibly inaccurate. Both sides in the case took offense at one particular TV-news broadcast, which reported the victims were all "ten-dollar" hookers and had been raped after they were dead—an allegation never even suggested by either side.

Through his attorneys, Bill Suff tried to express his personal feelings for the suffering of the families of the victims. Randolph Driggs recalled, "[Bill] wanted me to express some sentiments to the news media, especially to Mr. Lyttle [since Bill had dated his daughter]. He was very, very sorry for the deaths of anybody, but he wasn't responsible for them."

As to reflections on the trial, defense attorney Driggs commented he believed the defense was "very, very prepared" and "played well as individual lawyers," but that "the prosecutor comes in on the wings of a god." He said, "You can't draw any conclusions about cases like this [because] they're easy cases—like shooting ducks in a barrel, [although] I didn't think it was so much a slam-dunk [case]." Driggs said he "was disappointed it was only eleven to one for guilty [verdicts], but it just tells you the difficulty in defending these cases. They were very, very strong cases. I mean, there were perfect tire tracks at [the] Casares and McDonald scenes, right there [by the bodies]. And all you could say was, 'Well . . . it doesn't tell you who killed the person and dumped the body there.'"

As for whether it would have helped to put Suff on the stand, Driggs reported it didn't really become a consideration until the penalty phase, after Suff had been found guilty of twelve murders and one attempted murder. Then, Driggs said, Suff did express a desire to testify: "[Bill's] sentiments were, 'It can't get any worse, so why don't I testify?' My view was, it was going to be a very, very unpleasant experience—like nailing a nail into your hand . . . and I could not see any benefit to it. What could you say to change somebody's mind? Bill had never said anything specific to me, like, 'Yes, I did this,' so what could he say?— 'No, I didn't do it'? [In that case he would have just been] fodder for Paul Zellerbach.

"Who knows how he would have reacted? If he'd admitted it and cried, that would have been wonderful. But we didn't have any feeling that Bill would ever admit it and cry. So without that, just saying, 'I didn't do it,' wouldn't do anything. And the victims who had breasts removed,

and the lightbulb [incident], there's just no way [he could
have mitigated such repugnant deeds with tears]. . . . Crying wouldn't have done any good there. Some of them
were a little gruesome.''

Public reaction from Suff's family was practically nonexistent. Most of his relatives wanted to disassociate themselves from him.

However, Suff's natural father, who deserted the family
when Suff was sixteen, did grant one brief interview on
the subject to a newspaper reporter. In the interview, he
seemed intent on disavowing any blameworthiness on his
part, much as Suff's mother had in her letter to her son.
Suff's father implied that if blame were to be assigned, it
probably should fall upon the shoulders of the Texas
prison system for granting Suff an early release from his
seventy-year sentence for the murder of baby Dijanet. ''I
think they made a big mistake there,'' he stated.

The penalty phase consisted primarily of efforts by both
sides to examine Bill Suff's character and deeds, and
thereby show jurors why he did or did not deserve to be
given the death penalty, as measured against a set of legal
guidelines. Jurors were asked to evaluate Suff's character
and past behavior as indicators of whether he was capable
of reform or deserving of a second chance at life. This
persuasion was generally attempted through the presentation of past examples of Suff's behavior, and through the
testimony of those who had known him or been affected
by his deeds.

In the penalty phase, relatives of the victims were allowed
to testify and state how the murder of their loved one had
affected their lives and the lives of their families. Some of
the more gruesome and repugnant details that were not
allowed to be presented in the guilt phase, for fear of
inflaming jurors' opinions against the defendant, were

allowed to be entered into evidence in the penalty phase. Such details were deemed to be illustrative of Suff's true character and therefore valid indicators of his possible future behavior, chance for reform, and merit for mercy.

Some of the victims' relatives let their feelings be known even before they took the stand. The brother of one victim revealed he searched the streets after the murder of his sister, personally hunting for her killer. He said he was glad he never found Suff because he believed he would have killed him had he done so, and then would have gotten in trouble for it, leaving his family to suffer anew.

During that conversation, a law-enforcement officer informed the brother it would probably take ten to fifteen years for Suff to reach the gas chamber if he did, in fact, receive the death penalty. The officer consoled the man by telling him if it were up to him, they'd be building the scaffold outside the courtroom right now. The brother replied that if it were up to him, they could save the wood and just turn Suff over to him.

The surrogate mother of one victim composed poetry about the killer and his victims as a means of coping with her loss and the anger brought on by the case. Her poems were often inspired by the slightest demonstration of emotion from Bill Suff, whose very being was offensive to her.

Prosecutor Zellerbach began his case in the penalty phase by telling jurors of the mid-January 1988 murder of Lisa Lacik. Her homicide also appeared to have been committed by Bill Suff, Zellerbach revealed, but, since that murder occurred in another county, it was beyond his jurisdiction to include it with those he had presented in the guilt phase. He wanted the jury to know that Bill had been killing prostitutes at least a year before he started his spree in Riverside County, with the murder of Kimberly Lyttle in June 1989.

The parade of victims' relatives then began. Lyttle's father was first, telling how when he'd heard Kim had died, he assumed it was a drug overdose. A widower since 1969, Lyttle said Kim's murder hit him very hard. "I can't keep the memory of it out of my mind," he sobbed, breaking down.

After composing himself, he told how he insisted on viewing his daughter's body although it was a closed-casket funeral. He said he was advised against it, since she had undergone a full forensic autopsy, which was a fairly thorough dissection. He told them to open the casket anyway. Inside, he said, he saw a plastic bag containing his daughter's body. Lyttle said he didn't have the heart to open it, so instead he simply felt her "arms and legs and where her head would be," and then had them close the casket.

A bailiff provided tissues to Mr. Lyttle during his testimony—and to many of the jurors, as well.

The surrogate mother of Darla Ferguson testified about trying to help Darla kick the drug habit. She lamented that the rehabilitation programs were usually too full to accept any new people. She told how RSO investigator Bob Creed came to her house to break the news to her. On the table near them at the time was an open newspaper with a headline about the discovery of a new serial victim. "Tell me that's not her," she asked Creed before he had a chance to divulge the purpose of his visit. He said, "I'm sorry to say it is."

She told how she broke the news to Darla's daughter, whom she was now raising. She told the girl her mother had been killed by a bad man. Since then, the girl had been afraid the bad man would come and kill her, too. The six-year-old had gone to counseling for two years to learn to deal with her fear and anger.

Kathleen Puckett's sister told how everyone in the family

tried to help Kathy quit drugs, but the solace Kathy found in heroin was simply too powerful for her to resist. The sister said Kathy described the sedative effects of heroin as "being able to take away any hurt." The last time she saw her sister alive, Kathy was leaving to go watch her daughters play sports. She never made it there.

Susan Sternfeld's sister told how Susan always sent birthday and Christmas cards to all her nieces and nephews, and had been involved in Bible study in prison. She said Susan even visited prisons to lead Bible readings. She loved to have fresh flowers in the house, even if she had to get them from her lawn. Although Susan often tried to get help to stop drugs, by the time a treatment facility would have an opening, she would be in jail again. They either never had an opening or a bed, or the family didn't have the enrollment money at the time space was available.

After she was murdered, Susan's younger brother visited her grave daily and even did his homework there. He told the sister he never wanted to have kids because he never wanted to lose anyone again. The younger children in the family were unable to watch violent television shows after the murder, and became cold and untrusting of strangers. The sister said she was distressed because Susan had suffered so much in her life, and then so much in her dying, too.

Delliah Zamora's mother told the court her family no longer celebrated Halloween because Dell's body was discovered the day before Halloween. She said her daughter's small children frequently wrote love-you notes to their dead mother and left them in an urn on her grave. When the two sheriff's investigators told her of the murder, she had refused to believe it. "No—I just saw her two days ago!" she told them. So they showed her a photo of the body. Mrs. Zamora said she couldn't even cry when she saw it.

She said she first saw Delliah's body nine days later, at

the funeral, and that the corpse, except for the face, was all wrapped up like "a mummy in a museum." She said, "They couldn't even close her eyes or her mouth, [and] they had so much makeup on her."

She said she last saw Dell when she and her husband were driving on University Avenue and they spotted her walking alone by a convenience store. They didn't make contact with their daughter or linger on the scene because they thought she would think they were spying on her. They feared they had already nagged her too much about watching out for the serial killer. "Oh, well, she's all right, so let's go," Dell's father had said, so they continued on to the restaurant they had set out for.

One of Delliah Zamora's brothers testified his seven-year-old son told him, "Aunt Dell is just resting in her grave because she's real tired, but if you pray real hard every day, she'll come alive." So the boy had been praying every day for over three years. Instead of writing about her summer vacation as the other kids did, his eleven-year-old daughter wrote a ten-page paper for her class about her aunt—from birth to death. The brother testified that since Dell's death, his thoughts had focused on killing her murderer.

Carol Miller's sister testified that their sister Kathy had been murdered in December 1973, and that the loss had sent Carol into depression and drugs. Carol "copped out of life and went into drugs" after that, the sister said, because she couldn't deal with it. Now Carol herself had been murdered.

Catherine McDonald's sixteen-year-old daughter stated that she and her two younger brothers and a sister watched their mother leave one night "for the store" and never come back. She said the kids all went to school the next day, assuming their mother would be back when they returned. She wasn't, and they had no key to get into the apartment, so they had to borrow one from the manager to get inside. Between 7 and 8 P.M., the police came by and told them their mother was in the hospital and they would take them to her. However, when the investigators got them to the curb outside, they told the kids their mother was actually dead. The kids were then taken to the police station, and later driven to their grandmother's house in distant Los Angeles.

The sister of Catherine McDonald, who also lived in Riverside, testified that Catherine had moved from Watts with her kids to start a new lifestyle in a safer city, near her sister. She said, "I don't understand why she was killed that way," because she was so sweet and generous. She said she thought if her sister ever died, it would be from an overdose. She said the family joked at the mortuary because one of Catherine's breasts looked smaller than the other. They were told that flesh flattens after death. They had read in the newspaper that a breast had been cut off of some of the serial victims, but she said she somehow visualized that to mean only the nipple had been taken. She said she was shocked to see the prosecution photo in the guilt phase that revealed the entire right breast was missing from the body.

The sister said she became concerned for Catherine's safety after a prostitute's body was discovered behind the Concourse Bowling Alley, which she lived nearby. She warned Catherine to be careful. Catherine replied, "He only kills white girls, and I'm not a prostitute, anyway." The sister said she told Catherine, "Okay, just don't be his first black victim." She said they both laughed at that.

Kelly Hammond's brother revealed their mother has never been told Kelly was dead because the mother had a bad heart and trouble breathing. Whenever their mother asks about Kelly, she is told Kelly is in Riverside and is all right. He said Kelly often took care of their invalid mother. He said their father refused to have a funeral for her

("Leave it like it is") to prevent the media from confronting her kids.

Eleanor Casares's nineteen-year-old daughter said she was unable to deal with the murder and saw her mother's face in many of the cars that pass by on the street. "I keep wanting to kill myself because I can't take it anymore," she cried.

After the parade of victims' relatives, Zellerbach dropped a prosecution's bombshell: the murder of little Dijanet Suff in 1973. Over the course of at least three weeks, twenty-three-year-old Bill Suff had beaten to death his own two-month-old daughter. The ruptured liver, the broken bones, the human bite marks, the cigarette burn on the sole of the foot, the countless bruises that covered the little body from head to toe—all were described. But no rendition could have prepared the jury for the photograph of the dead, battered baby that Zellerbach then displayed on the monitors before them. A wave of gasps exploded from the jury. The bailiff tugged tissues out of her box machine-gun style and walked the length of the jury box, passing them out to men and women alike. Looks of revulsion and hard stares of pure hatred blazed at Bill Suff from the jurors. If he had no forewarning of their verdicts in the first phase of the trial, Suff surely could not have misinterpreted their intent at that moment. The moment Dijanet's photo appeared on the screen, he ceased to be a human being to many of the jurors and descended instead to the level of "monster."

Zellerbach discussed the Texas murder case: seventy years meted out, ten years actually served. However, the jury didn't seem to pay close attention for several minutes, many apparently in a numb state. Many of them stared fixedly at Suff the rest of that day—and for the rest of the trial—as if trying to imagine him committing that crime

upon his own baby. Or perhaps simply out of loathing for him.

Suff evidently did comprehend the significance of the jurors' reactions. For only the second time in the trial, he didn't rise as the jury left the room for a scheduled break, sending the jury a message of his own.

Sensing the incredible damage of that evidence, the defense team tried to imply that, because she was also originally arrested for Dijanet's murder (although later released on appeal), Bill's ex-wife Ann may have actually committed the crime. During the break, the judge sharply censured the defense team for trying to attack the Texas verdict, calling such attempts "superfluous baloney."

Bombshell number two immediately followed, with Zellerbach telling the jury the story of little Bridgette, Suff's three-month-old child from his second wife, Cheryl. Baby Bridgette also suffered weeks of abuse, the "Shaken-Baby Syndrome," which also left her with multiple broken bones and severe brain damage. Suff's ex-wife Cheryl appeared and testified about the ordeal Bridgette went through.

At the grand-jury hearing in July 1992, assistant apartment manager Kristin had also testified to Suff's rough treatment of Bridgette. She stated, "He didn't like the baby to cry. . . . Anytime the baby would put the fingers in the mouth, you know, he'd take the baby's hands out of the mouth. I think Bridgette was only like two months at the time. And I just—he made some comments about, you know, he didn't like the baby crying. And he put rubbing alcohol on the baby's hands to make her stop crying. And I—I just looked at him like he was nuts, you know. I mean that, my initial feeling was how could you put rubbing alcohol on a baby's fingers? I asked him that—'Are you trying to kill your baby?' "

But Kristin did have nice things to say about Suff. She

said, "He was very friendly. People really—you know, they didn't have any problems with him. He was just—I use the term 'overly friendly.' He liked to go out of his way to do things for people. He really liked to make people feel like they were safe if he was there. He wore kind-of-like a security uniform [tan clothes]. He used to wear a hat that was like a highway patrolman hat. He used to say that he would make patrol at night, to walk around, see how the security guards were doing. So he just, tried to be like everybody's friend. He would sometimes offer to watch people's kids."

Zellerbach provided medical experts to testify at length about the injuries to Bridgette Suff and how she had suffered at the hands of her own father. After reminding the jury of the lightbulb sadistically placed in Tina Leal's vagina, and the four-month-old fetus that died with Catherine McDonald, Zellerbach rested his case for the prosecution.

In his opening statement, defense attorney Randolph K. Driggs stated, "I want to talk about Bill Suff as a human being—the side you haven't seen before." The parade of defense character witnesses then began.

A childhood friend of Suff's stated Suff became the father figure in his family after his natural father deserted them. He said Suff was always respectful of adults and authority, always courteous and outgoing, and always willing to help anyone. He said he never saw Suff have problems with anyone or lash out in anger at anyone.

Next was a female former Weekender who testified that Bill Suff gave her rides to work every day when she was on the work-release program at the warehouse, and he was always nice to her and never threatening.

The third witness was a married woman who was befriended by Suff when she worked at the Circle K. She said he was never threatening, and even her kids liked him. On cross-examination, Zellerbach brought out that Suff kept inviting her to go to the mountains or desert with him to take pictures, but that she never did. She admitted under Zellerbach's prodding, her husband liked neither Suff nor his relationship with his wife. The married woman admitted Suff liked to give her used jewelry and that she had no idea where it came from.

The son of the computer couple who employed Suff in Lake Elsinore testified about how Suff used to baby-sit for the family, and how Suff took him to the doctor when he fell on the monkey bars and broke his right arm. He said he never felt threatened by Bill Suff.

The boy's mother testified next. She told how she and her husband first met Suff, as a browsing customer, and how he came to work for them. She said Suff was involved with his girlfriend Bonnie then, and that she didn't care for Bonnie. She said Suff was so moral he wouldn't stay in the same room when they were drinking. She said he helped in their campaign to revitalize the downtown district, and even played an Old West outlaw during "Frontier Days." She testified Suff couldn't stand to hold a gun, and actually gave his gun to her after dropping it—telling her, "I can't stand guns." She said Suff was easily walked on, or taken advantage of, because of his caring so much for people. He became more withdrawn as Bonnie became more jealous of his relationship with them. Suff eventually left them because of Bonnie.

She said Suff's parole officer told them Suff was in prison in Texas for murder, but neither she nor her husband held it against Suff because they felt, "He had served his time." She said she was led to believe it was his ex-wife he had killed. She said neither she nor her husband believes Bill killed the women he is convicted of murdering.

Her husband, the owner of the computer store, next testified on Suff's behalf. He stated he met Suff on his return from one of his out-of-town business trips to Los

Angeles. He hired him on a commission basis but gave him money "to keep him going" because he never made a sale. He said Suff was like a nanny in their household. He called him a "fanatically straight" person who eschewed drugs, alcohol, cigarettes, and anything illegal "because he was scared to death of going back to jail. . . . He would not touch anything illegal with a ten-foot pole."

The man's voice took on extra emphasis when he stated that Suff never made a pass at his wife, or did anything mean to their kids. In earlier testimony, he had told of Suff's taking their son to the emergency room for "some medical thing" because he wasn't available, being very busy and out of town a lot then. Suff tended to his family and helped his wife with the business in his absence, he'd said. Suff's generous attention to them ultimately provoked jealousy from his girlfriend Bonnie.

Judy, the overweight manager at the Circle K, testified to Suff's friendship and helpfulness and love of his baby, Bridgette. She said he had an occasional beer but never swore. However, when Zellerbach asked her if she was aware Suff dated prostitutes, she stated it was out of character for the Bill Suff she knew. Zellerbach then told her of Suff's conviction for his baby's murder in Texas, and asked if that news changed her opinion. "Only the good Lord and King Solomon can tell me" if Bill committed the murders of the prostitutes, she replied.

The elderly owners of John's Service Center then testified to Suff's good character: always punctual, clean, neat; a good employee. Under Zellerbach's cross-examination, it was admitted Suff stole $343 from the cash register and promised to repay it but never did, even after he received a large settlement from a motorcycle accident. Zellerbach asked the couple if they were aware Suff used that money to pay prostitutes for sex in their store while they were at church. They seemed stunned by the news, and said, "It's difficult to believe," just like the murder convictions, "but the evidence says he did commit the murders."

Suff's bosses from the warehouse testified that he was a popular employee and liked to volunteer for things, like the chili cook-off contest at the annual county employees' picnic.

A correctional consultant testified that, based on Suff's Texas prison record and the consultant's study of the grand-jury transcript in this case, Suff appeared to him a good security risk if given life without parole (LWOP) instead of death. He doubted Suff would be a threat to any women, such as nurses, who might come into contact with him in prison. After the trial, defense attorney Driggs echoed that sentiment, stating, "Bill is really, basically, your ultimate coward. I mean, that's the way I'd portray him—[a danger to] just children and these vulnerable prostitutes. To think that he would attack a nurse in the jail or prison—are you crazy? They'd beat the living shit out of him. So there's no way."

Outside of court, even Zellerbach agreed Bill Suff was "definitely not confrontational. When you confront him, he whines and whimpers." However, in court, Zellerbach made the point that it's not whether Suff would pose a threat or not in prison if given LWOP, it was a matter of whether he deserved LWOP or death. Zellerbach pointed out, Suff had been on his best behavior in the Texas prison because he knew that doing so would earn him an early release. He would have no such motivation with a sentence of life without the possibility of parole. Again raising the issue of merit, Zellerbach pointed out that life in prison isn't always unpleasant, especially with marriage and conjugal visits. Again, he asked, does Bill Suff merit such treatment, or does he merit death?

* * *

Of Suff's family members, only his mother testified for him in the penalty phase. Most of his siblings flatly refused, and one slammed the door in the face of Suff's attorneys when they came soliciting help. One brother agreed to take the stand, but withdrew his offer when he learned a book author would be in attendance during his testimony. The brother was himself coauthoring a book, and stated he did not want to hurt his book's sales by giving free information from the stand to a competitor. He withdrew his offer to testify and help save his brother from the gas chamber.

Tall, heavyset, heavy-lidded, with a large, veined nose and beehive hairdo, Suff's mother was a physically intimidating person, even though her testimony was soft-spoken and at times lifeless. She told of her husband's total desertion of the family—never writing or sending money. She said Bill took a job with the forestry department to help out financially. She told of Bill's marriage and move to Texas, and how she and Bill's stepfather went to Fort Worth when Bill was arrested for Dijanet's murder.

She said she didn't learn of Bridgette's injuries until after Bill's arrest for the serial murders. Reading about Bridgette's abuse in the newspaper "ran cold chills" up her back after what happened to Dijanet in Texas. She said she stood up for her son against the charges regarding Dijanet, but would not do so in the case of Bridgette because now she wasn't sure [Bill was innocent].

She said she never saw him lose his temper, even with his siblings. However, she said he was more withdrawn upon his return from Texas and refused to talk about his life there. She said he was never abused or molested by anyone.

She said investigators showed her a lot of evidence against her son. Zellerbach asked her about a conversation she had with Suff in jail, in which she asked him about some of that evidence and his excuse to the police that he was only in the orchard by Eleanor Casares's body to pick oranges. She asked him why he went there to pick oranges when he hates oranges. He told her he was getting them for his wife, Cheryl.

The defense tried to recover from that statement by asking Suff's mother whether he also disliked grapefruit (since Carol Miller's killer had eaten half of one and dropped the remainder beside her body). "To be honest, he didn't like either one of them," she responded. She said this is all like a bad dream for her—"one I won't wake up from." But, she said, "I still love all of my kids no matter what they've done."

Zellerbach presented the information that she had twice told the prosecution team that if her son were found guilty, they should "hang him." Defense counsel Driggs stated she told him she made the statements out of frustration.


Suff's ex-girlfriend Bonnie returned to the stand with more recollections of Suff—good and bad. She told how he helped care for her grandmother, and once even helped fight a fire that endangered a property, "and never asked for a penny." However, she said Suff did steal nine hundred dollars from her grandmother's caretaking account. When confronted by Bonnie about the theft, he admitted taking the money but told her he felt the woman owed it to him for all the work he did for her. Bonnie negotiated a lesser repayment for him, and repaid the balance herself. She asked him to move out, and when he did, he took with him the jewelry he'd given her through the years, photographs, and other items.

Bonnie said the Bill she knew was basically a good person who loved animals and was "extremely caring, attentive, went over and above expectations in working," and was never abusive to her or anyone else. "The person I knew is not the person who is on trial," she said. She said that before the trial, she was pro-death penalty because she never had to deal with the issue personally. She stated she now chooses not to kill anybody when there's an alternative.

Prosecutor Zellerbach jumped on that statement, railing that Suff also had the choice to kill or not. "And *he* chose to kill—again and again and again and again and again!"

In his closing argument, Zellerbach emotionally demanded of the jury, "If Bill Suff is not an appropriate candidate for the death penalty, then who is? If someone who murdered fifteen people [the thirteen he was tried for, plus San Bernardino County prostitute Lisa Lacik and his daughter, Dijanet] is not a candidate for the death penalty, who is? If not, how many more would he have to kill to deserve it? He has killed more people than almost anyone in this country. He is a *serial killer,* and he spent ten years in prison for the murder of his two-month-old daughter—*his flesh and blood!* Who deserves death more than Mr. Suff?

". . . These people who testified for the defense don't know Suff as well as you do. You know the dark side. They only know one side. You know the real Bill Suff. They insult you when they say they don't believe he's guilty when they are shown the photos of his crimes.

"Our whole world is too full of excuses . . . bogus excuses. It's time for people to be held accountable for what they do. Hold Mr. Suff accountable and responsible for the crimes he committed. There's no excuse in the world that can mitigate the things he has done for the past twenty-two years. He was given the benefit of the doubt then and got an early parole, but he doesn't deserve it now. The aggravating factors completely dominate and outweigh the factors in mitigation.

"The death penalty is meaningless if it does not apply

to Suff. Then it applies to no one. He has *earned* the right to sit on Death Row.

". . . We all want to die with dignity when our day comes. No pain, say our last goodbyes, die with dignity. All you have to do is look at those crime-scene photos to know that in no way, shape, or form did these women die with dignity.

"Mr. Suff is a monster [with a] feeding frenzy. It got to a point where he was almost killing one victim a month when he was arrested. He was terrorizing the entire county—not just the prostitutes—by doing that for years.

"[Those] women did what they did to support their drug habits, because they felt they had no choice. They were 'willing to please.' That's the nature of their business. *He* knew that and he took advantage of them when they were the most vulnerable.

"But he didn't stop at killing them. He re-dressed the first two; afterwards left [the next victims] nude; cut off breasts; posed them; left them in places to be found to shock our consciences. He *enjoyed* that. He *fed* off that. And would still be doing it if the 'fortuitous' events of January 9, 1992, didn't occur.

"Think about what these women had to go through. Suffocating women takes several minutes and is a horrible death. He's stabbing them, inserting a lightbulb into a vagina. Did these women die with dignity?

"[He displayed] sadistic behavior all his life. [It's] too late now for mercy and rehabilitation. The time for that was 1974 [when he was arrested for his first murder, that of Dijanet Suff].

"Think about how these crime scene photos affected the family members. He took away [the victims'] opportunity to say goodbye—and their hopes and dreams. They wanted to kick the habit, wanted a normal life, wanted families and kids. Maybe they would have made it, maybe not. But it wasn't Suff's decision to take that [chance] away from them.

". . . It is a rare occasion when we come face-to-face with true evil, and [when we do] we must destroy it. Mr. Suff is truly evil and no longer a member of the human race. He has no heart, no soul, and, by God, he has no conscience.

"Our society protects two groups of people: women and children. Our society sees them as most precious—the 'sinking boat' policy. Maybe I'm being chauvinistic, but I want to protect the women and children." At that, Zellerbach dropped his head and appeared to be crying. Then he angrily raised the photo of the battered body of little Dijanet Suff: "Does he deserve sympathy? Mercy? He is *truly evil!*

"I am confident you will do the right thing. You are in effect the conscience of our community. We don't like to believe someone deserves to die, but sometimes someone earns that right and deserves to die.

"Prison obviously didn't affect him at all, when he spent ten years in prison in Texas. It's a walk in the park for him.

"I speak for the victims whose voices have been silenced. In the name of justice, I ask you to impose the only punishment that fits these crimes—the punishment he deserves. The death penalty may be the most you can do. But it's also the least."

Attorney Randolph K. Driggs delivered the closing argument for the defense. He advised the jury that "this [petrifying] decision will pale only perhaps if you were in the military and had to kill someone.

"I am the second least popular person in this room, because you have found my client guilty of murder, including [that of] his daughter. I am looking down the barrel of a loaded gun."

Quoting Ecclesiastes, Driggs counseled the jury that, "A grief-stricken heart undermines your strength. Be not faint-hearted when you sit in judgment." He admonished them that "passion is anathema to a decision-making body."

Driggs told the jury, "Your choice is not whether [Bill Suff] will die in prison, but when. He must fear others who will want to kill him in prison for being a child-murderer. And now for these [murders as well]. Mr. Suff will be living on the edge of the seat for the rest of his life. He will worry about his next step, his next move, and who's behind him.

"I don't see life without the possibility of parole as merciful. It is a just, horrendous punishment.

". . . Evaluate the life he lived, the person he is, the [harmless, productive] life he can live in prison. Life without parole is the appropriate punishment for Mr. Suff.

"Understand human nature—choose for your reasons, not for any tears Mr. Zellerbach or others shed. Life without the possibility of parole will be a horrendous punishment for Bill Suff. And appropriate."


The jury was sent to deliberate with less than an hour left in the court day, so most spectators and family members went home, assuming no decision would be reached until the next day. The jury almost immediately sent notification to the judge that a decision had been reached—deciding Bill Suff's fate in less than ten minutes. The judge instructed the jurors to hold their decision and deliver it in the morning, so that those who left would have a chance to return and hear it.

The next morning, August 18, 1995, the courtroom and the anteroom before it were packed to overflowing levels with those who wanted to witness the finish of the biggest trial in county history. Crowds of law-enforcement officers showed up to spectate at the reading of the sentence. A television monitor was set up in the jammed hallway out-side the courtroom so those who couldn't get seating could watch the proceedings. About a dozen television camera crews again stood at the ready outside the courtroom doors, and almost as many print-media representatives packed the front two rows of the spectator section inside. As before, at the reading of the verdicts, several of the female relatives of the victims again dressed in red, hoping the display of Suff's hated color would be a further torture to him.

Everyone waited anxiously, with greatly elevated moods, for the jury to return. Word had already circulated that the jury had reached its decision in just five to ten minutes.

The decision was, to many, very sweet. In all twelve counts of which he had been convicted of first-degree murder, the jury set the sentence at death for William Lester Suff.

Some jurors later revealed that, despite their certainty he was the murderer of at least twelve women, they suffered severe anxiety at the prospect of recommending death for Bill Suff—until the photograph of Dijanet Suff was presented. Several jurors stated that the moment they heard of the murder of the two-month-old baby, they no longer had any qualms or doubts about deciding on the death penalty for Bill Suff. To some, it was the fact that he killed his own baby. To others, it was the fact that he had already served prison time for murder and been given a chance to reform.

The jury foreman stated that Suff's near-fatal abuse of his second daughter, Bridgette, also hit him especially hard because, ironically, the courtroom testimony revealed she was born on the same day as his own daughter. He said a shock ran through him when he heard that date in court. He said Zellerbach's strongest argument in the penalty phase seemed for many to be his question, "If Bill Suff did not deserve the death penalty, who did?"

Several of the law-enforcement officers who had participated in the task force or traffic stop were present in the hall. They expressed a consensus of "great satisfaction" at the convictions and death-penalty sentence.

To Chris Keers, it was the end of a long nightmare and the fulfillment of a promise she had made to herself and the victims and their families. She asked no credit—and was accorded none as others from both law-enforcement agencies scrambled to claim responsibility for the arrest of the notorious Riverside prostitute killer. One newspaper even ran a two-part article all about how RSO investigator Bob Creed caught the serial killer. This was a curious contention, considering Creed wasn't even in the state at the time.

Chris found it all amusing, caring little about any of it. Only one fact mattered to her: William Lester Suff was going to die for the brutal murders he had committed.

The official sentencing did not occur until October 26, 1995, at which time both Bill Suff and the relatives of the victims were allowed to read statements, if they so desired.

Kim Lyttle's father regretted, "Unfortunately, Mr. Suff won't die as cruelly and violently [as did his victims]." One relative kept her statement brutally short, telling Suff, "May you burn in Hell where you belong!" Another ended her diatribe with the chant, "Snuff the Suff!"

For his part, Suff delivered a long, rambling lament about his innocence and unfortunate situation. He sneered that if the authorities were determined to see him executed, they should at least grant him the privilege of donating his organs for use in medical transplants, so the death of an innocent man would not be in vain: "In this manner, my death will serve mankind, rather than being just another corpse in a graveyard." The brother of one victim stormed out at that—slamming the heavy security door against the wall on his way, a door an average man moved in inches.

Near the end of his speech, Suff insisted to the court and the world that he was "not a cold-blooded, heartless monster." He said the only thing he was truly guilty of was being a hopeless romantic.